BITE THE HAND
THAT
FEEDS
YOU

BITE THE HAND THAT FEEDS YOU

JP TruDoc

ARCHWAY
PUBLISHING

Archway Publishing books may be ordered through booksellers or by contacting:

Archway Publishing
1663 Liberty Drive
Bloomington, IN 47403
www.archwaypublishing.com
1 (888) 242-5904

ISBN: 978-1-4808-7782-5 (sc)
ISBN: 978-1-4808-7783-2 (hc)
ISBN: 978-1-4808-7784-9 (e)

Library of Congress Control Number: 2019908435

Printed in the United States of America

Archway Publishing rev. date: 10/2/2019

To:
My Sunny Sally
My Life
My Inspiration
and
My Friend

THE NATIONAL PICTURE

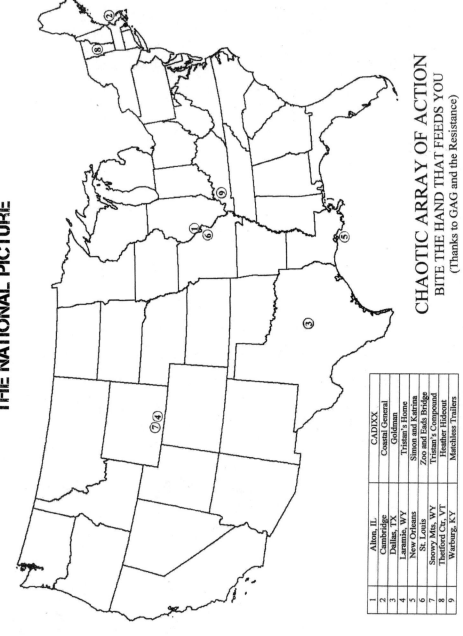

CHAOTIC ARRAY OF ACTION
BITE THE HAND THAT FEEDS YOU
(Thanks to GAG and the Resistance)

1	Alton, IL		CADIXX
2	Cambridge		Coastal General
3	Dallas, TX		Goldman
4	Laramie, WY		Tristan's Home
5	New Orleans		Simon and Katrina
6	St. Louis		Zoo and Eads Bridge
7	Snowy Mts, WY		Tristan's Compound
8	Thetford Ctr, VT		Heather Hideout
9	Warburg, KY		Matchless Trailers

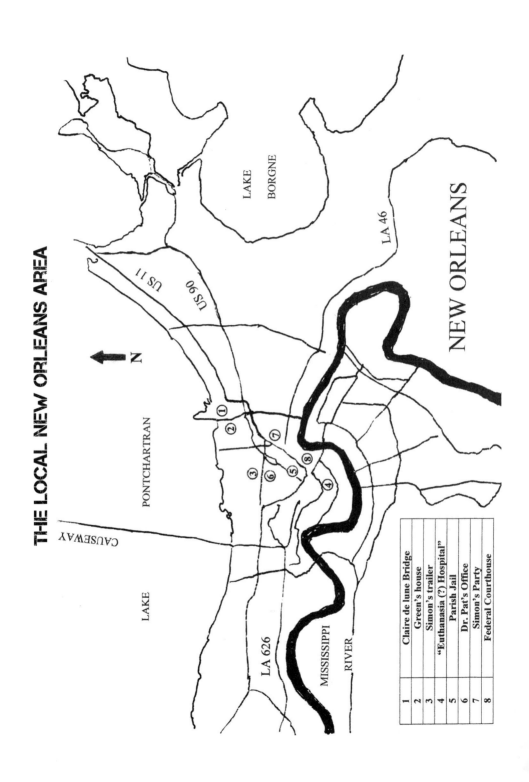

THE LOCAL NEW ORLEANS AREA

N

LAKE PONTCHARTRAN

CAUSEWAY

LAKE

US 11

US 90

LAKE BORGNE

LA 46

LA 626

MISSISSIPPI RIVER

NEW ORLEANS

1	Claire de lune Bridge
2	Green's house
3	Simon's trailer
4	"Euthanasia (?) Hospital"
5	Parish Jail
6	Dr. Pat's Office
7	Simon's Party
8	Federal Courthouse

CONTENTS

INTRODUCTION AND BACKGROUND

<u>Bite the Hand that Feeds You</u> is a novel, loosely based upon and inspired by events spanning roughly 2004 through 2010, including the landing of Hurricane Katrina along the Gulf Coast of Florida, Mississippi, Alabama, and especially, Louisiana at the end of August 2005. The primary setting for the story is the city of New Orleans and its metropolitan area. Dramatic, often shocking and disturbing events are described, related to the days immediately before, during and after the hurricane, as well as the ensuing months and years, when tens of thousand of citizens were living in RV travel trailers, supplied by FEMA (Federal Emergency Management Administration).

These trailers were known as "EHU's" (Emergency Housing Units [the term used in federal court proceedings]) or THU's, (Temporary Housing Units [the term used by others, referring to the same entity as the EHU]).

"Forming over the Bahamas on Tuesday, August 23, 2005, as Tropical Depression 12, the [weather] system was upgraded to a tropical storm and named "Katrina[1]" on the morning of August 24. The storm continued in the direction of Florida, becoming a hurricane (Category 1 = 74-95 mph) just two hours before hitting its Atlantic coast, north of Miami on the morning of August 25.

Katrina weakened over land, as it moved west toward the Gulf of Mexico; but regained hurricane strength just two hours after heading out to sea. It rapidly grew from a Category 3 (111-129 mph) to a Category 5 (greater than 157 mph) hurricane in about nine hours.

On Saturday, August 27, the storm remitted to Category 3, although it doubled in size. On the morning of Sunday, August 28,

---

[1] http://en.wikipedia.org/wiki/Hurricane_Katrina (direct quotes and paraphrase regarding Hurricane Katrina).

Katrina advanced again to Category 5, reaching maximum sustained winds of 175 mph.

Later in the morning and throughout the day, on Monday, August 29, Katrina made two more landfalls as a Category 3 and hit New Orleans from the south. The storm caused over 53 levee breaches throughout New Orleans, causing 80% of the city to be flooded.

Figure 1. Hurricane Katrina Seen From Space

Probably as many as 1500-1800+ died from a variety of causes as a direct result of Katrina. The storm caused over $81 billion in damages, making it the costliest storm in US history. The storm surge (water protection) failures, including those attributed to the US Army Corps of Engineers were considered the worst civil engineering disasters in its history." On Saturday August 27, two days before the storm hit New Orleans, mandatory evacuation was ordered – hundreds of thousands complied and tens of thousands did not. Many were trapped, and against this apocalyptic backdrop people suffered and died.

Thousands were stuck in flooded homes. If they were able to escape, they became displaced persons. Looting, burglary, assault and rape were not uncommon. Many died from drowning, neglect, homicide, and murder. Some hospital patients allegedly fell victim to euthanasia (mercy killing) at the hands of their caregivers who had to triage the hopelessly ill under their care.

In the days and weeks following the storm, all kinds of people, including escaped prisoners, migrated away from New Orleans by any means possible. Some returned months later to live with friends or relatives. Others were housed in limited hotel spaces at government expense.

—   —   —

In one attempt to solve the housing crisis, through a hierarchy of sub-contractors, FEMA began to supply and install RV trailers (FEMA trailers) within weeks to months after the hurricane hit on August 29.

Many of these FEMA trailers were modified recreational vehicles that were never intended to be inhabited for weeks at a time, much less months and years. None of the trailers met HUD (Housing and Urban Development) housing standards. More importantly, many trailers with excessively high levels of formaldehyde emanating from trailer components were knowingly provided to FEMA for distribution to displaced persons. Formaldehyde was suspended as a gas in trailer air, at levels that often exceeded dozens of times permissible governmental safety recommendations.

Formaldehyde is a simple but extremely toxic hydrocarbon chemical that is a known chemical carcinogen (nasal passages) and mucous membrane irritant. It is the chemical used to embalm dead bodies by morticians. Given its adverse health effects, formaldehyde, even at very low concentrations, can cause skin itching and irritation, sinus congestion, irritation of the eyes and upper airways and aggravation of a myriad of medical problems, including asthma. Exposure also causes more non-specific problems such as headaches, nausea, vomiting, diarrhea and loss of appetite, just to name a few. The toxic effects of formaldehyde are especially significant following excessive exposure to infants and the elderly.

Figure 2. FEMA Trailer

The formaldehyde in FEMA trailers resulted from the use of plywood and pressed boards containing uncured urethane glues. The "uncured" plywood was used in the manufacturing of cabinets and vanities installed in the trailer. Formaldehyde was emitted into the trailer environment via the out-gassing of these glues from within the wood. Normally when plywood cabinets and vanities are manufactured, the glue in the wood is given some time to "set-up" and dry out before it is delivered to the end-user, including the buyer of the RV trailer. Some manufacturers actually "bake out" their trailers by heating them for short periods of time before delivery. This process tends to ensure that most, if not all, of the formaldehyde is released into the outside air and not into the lungs, eyes and nasal passages of the buyer.

In the aftermath of Katrina, FEMA placed emergency orders for thousands of trailers, exhausting the supply of cured plywood components. Some trailer manufacturers, basking in the millions of dollars of FEMA orders, allowed the use of plywood components containing uncured, formaldehyde emitting glues.

The use of uncured plywood adversely affected not only thousands of trailer inhabitants, but also large numbers of workers who assembled the trailers prior to delivery. Many of them filed worker compensations claims for all sorts of skin and respiratory injuries.

—   —   —

The trailer manufacturers knew about the formaldehyde problem before they delivered the trailers to FEMA. When certain manufacturers were sued by trailer occupants almost three years after the hurricane hit, the legal discovery process uncovered some manufacturer's own documentation of measurements of excessively high formaldehyde levels in newly manufactured trailers. This data were known to top management.

In other words – the trailer manufacturers knowingly and willfully sold formaldehyde contaminated trailers to FEMA who, in turn, allowed these trailers to be distributed to unsuspecting displaced victims of Hurricane Katrina. As recently as 2015, similar accusations have been made against a major flooring retailer that sold Chinese made, formaldehyde contaminated flooring to the public.

The FEMA trailer was provided to Katrina victims to ease their suffering by providing "temporary" shelter. Instead these FEMA "toxic tin cans," as the trailers were called by some or even "gas chambers" by others, compounded their suffering by adversely affecting the health of many and increasing the lifetime risk of cancer for many more.

Many homeless hurricane victims lived in contaminated trailer environments for years, even though FEMA stopped providing these trailers in the summer of 2007.

During the height of trailer occupancy in May of 2006, when our characters, Sethie, Reggie, Reggie, Jr. and Simon Williams, entered their trailer, they joined tens of thousands of other families in their saga of increased problems.

Eventually, months and years after Katrina, lawsuits flew everywhere; some were successful, some not.

This novel is set against the drama of the events described above.

Depicted in the novel are many notable events, populated by fictionalized characters from all walks of life – including hurricane victims, treating and consulting physicians, lawyers, paramedics, police officers, national guardsmen, federal employees, subcontractors, an engineer, a federal judge, a Native American cowboy, and even another surprise or two. All of the characters participated in the real-life saga of Hurricane Katrina and none of them came away unchanged.

James P. Kornberg, MD, ScD.
Snow Drift Ranch – 6/11/2019

ENTITIES AND CHARACTERS

Name	Gender	Age (in 2009)	Affiliation	Comments
Adamson, Posie	female	50	Zane Adamson's twin sister	Assistant bank manager living in Ashland, Kentucky
Adamson, Zane	male	50	Matchless Trailers	Line Foreman (born 1959)
Ashton, Troy, Cpl	male	21	National Guardsman	In civilian life - a bank teller
Attington, Michael, JD	male	67	Attington, Benjamin and Carr, LLC	Co - Lead Counsel for Matchless Trailer Defense, NYC
Baines, Dawson	male	6	Canine	Tristan, Heather and Tess' Siberian Husky
Baines, Heather	female	52	Wife of Tristan Baines	Laramie, Wyoming
Baines, Tess	female	16	Daughter of Heather and Tristan Baines	
Baines, Tristan P. (MD, PhD.)	male	52	Husband of Heather and father of Tess	Clinical physician, ultra-specialist, engineer; medical and forensic causation expert; rancher, sometime hermit, and avid survivalist - Laramie, Wyoming

Name	Gender	Age (in 2009)	Affiliation	Comments
Carr, Doris	female	54	Attington, Benjamin and Carr, LLC	Co - Lead Counsel for Matchless Trailer Defense, NYC
Cooper, Cyrus	male	39	FEMA	Engineer and subcontractor coordinator
Cupples, Morgan	male	62	Owner of Mountain Missions Helicopter Charter	Friend of Asher Goldman
Foster, Angie	female	29	Helicopter pilot	Replaced Somersville when copter returned to pick up Tristan Baines
Franklin, Mavis	female	28	Matchless Trailers	Formaldehyde injured worker
Fuller, Ray	male	53	EPA	Enforcement Division super-visor, Louisville, Kentucky
Gasher, Gordon Alten, RN	male	47	CADIXX	Alleged whistle blower, fiend and paid assassin
Goldman, Asher, JD	male	46	Goldman and McDonald, LLP	principal part-ner - Dallas, Texas - Co-Lead plaintiff's counsel against Matchless Trailers
Goldman, Saul A., JD	male	49	Unemployed lawyer	Older brother of Asher Goldman

Name	Gender	Age (in 2009)	Affiliation	Comments
Green, Momma	female	50	Citizen and trailer occupant	mother of Sethie Williams and Samuel Green; wife of Pappy
Green, Pappy	male	56	Citizen and trailer occupant	Father of Sethie Williams and Samuel Green; husband of Momma
Green, Samuel	male	deceased	Citizen	brother of Sethie (Green) Williams and husband of Shonda (Hodges) Green - born 1975; killed 9/2/05
Green (Hodges), Shonda	female	33	Citizen	wife of Samuel and sister-in-law of Sethie Williams
Greenberg, Byron, Ofc.	male	24	NOPD (New Orleans Police Dept.)	Police offi-cer - squad car RUSS114; brilliant rookie and EMT
Gruber, Lila, MD	female	66	Coastal General Hospital - Boston	Director, Occupational and Environmental Services
Hastings, Carla	female	52	Madison County Health Dept. (Alton, Illinois)	Epidemiologist
Hatfield, Melanie Sgt.	female	26	National Guardsman	In civilian life - a middle school sci-ence teacher
Janes, Stacy, CIH	female	47	Environmental Health Services, LLC	CIH (Certified Industrial Hygienist) located in Pasadena, Texas

Name	Gender	Age (in 2009)	Affiliation	Comments
Javier, Susan, Ofc.	female	38	NOPD (New Orleans Police Dept.)	Police officer - squad car RUSS114; capable partner of Byron Greenberg
Jones, Laurie	female	42	NOPD (New Orleans Police Dept.)	Dispatch operator
Loeb, Percy, JD	male	64	Marcus, Greene and Loeb, LLC	Local Defense Firm for Matchless Trailers - Lead Counsel-Louisville,KY
Lowe, David, MD - Capt.	male	37	National Guardsman	Unit medical officer - cardiologist in civilian life.
Maguire, James, Ofc.	male	29	NOPD (New Orleans Police Dept.)	Police officer - squad card MAX 126 - carries AR-15.
Malark, Missy	female	53	Matchless Trailers	Executive Secretary
Malone, Otis	male	35	ERC Ambulance	Paramedic
Manheim, Morris, JD	male	52	Manheim and Pierce, LLP	Principal partner, New Orleans, LA - Co-Lead Counsel with Asher Goldman
Manus, Eric	male	37	UIPC - FEMA Subcontractor	Repairman coordinator, plumber and carpenter
Markham, Doloris	female	58	Citizen	Neighbor of the Greens
Markham, Easman	male	68	Citizen	Neighbor of the Greens

Name	Gender	Age (in 2009)	Affiliation	Comments
Markham, Rodman (Slick)	male	30	Citizen	Neighbor of the Greens and criminal drug dealer
Marquet, Andrew, Ofc.	male	41	NOPD (New Orleans Police Dept.)	Police officer - squad car MAX 126
Masters, Reginald, Col.	male	47	National Guardsman	Unit commander - layer in civilian life
McDonald, Iris, JD	female	44	Goldman and McDonald, LLP	Principal partner - Dallas, Texas - Co-Lead Counsel
McGavin, Callie, MSCJ	female	36	FBI	Analyst - St. Louis Bureau
McKenna, Chris, MD	female	57	Coastal General Hospital - Boston	Staff Physician
Michaels, George	male	27	National Guardsman	Soldier - in civilian life - veterinarian assistant. - marries Melanie Hatfield
Morgenstern, Jay, JD	male	54	Attorney	Close friend of Tristan and Joseph Trueblood
Olson, Denise	female	45	Matchless Trailers	Jimmy Olson's wife of 23 years
Olson, Edward (Eddie)	male	49	Matchless Trailers	Vice President - Warburg, Kentucky
Olson, James (Jimmy)	male	45	Matchless Trailers	President
Olson, Monty	male	deceased	Matchless Trailers	Founder and father of Eddie and Jimmy; deceased '00

Name	Gender	Age (in 2009)	Affiliation	Comments
Osborne, Frank	male	49	FEMA	Local office director
Palmer, Brad	male	49	Heather and Tristan Baines' brother-in-law	Thetford Ctr., Vermont - Writer artist and part-time mechanic
Palmer, Sue	female	48	Heather Baines' sister	Thetford Ctr., Vermont - Elementary school teacher
Renaldi, Dino	male	32	UIPC - FEMA Subcontractor	electrician
Simms, Patricia, MD (Dr. Pat)	female	60	Pediatrician - private practice	Simon Williams' physician
Sommersville, Raymond	male	44	Mountain Missions Helicopter Charter	Helicopter pilot - employee of Morgan Cupples
Swain, Laura, JD	female	32	Goldman and McDonald, LLP	attorney associate
Thomas, Janet	female	60	UIPC - FEMA Subcontractor	Office Director
Trueblood, Daisy	female	31	Wife of Joseph	School cafeteria worker - Walden, Colorado
Trueblood, Joseph	male	32	Very close friend of Tristan Baines and family	Rancher, cowboy and avid survivalist

Name	Gender	Age (in 2009)	Affiliation	Comments
UPIC	na	na	United Partners for Industry and Commerce	FEMA subcontractors that installed and maintained all FEMA trailers; had primary interface with trailer occupants
Vatouce, Paul, Ofc.	male	34	NOPD (New Orleans Police Dept.)	Police officer - squad car MAX191
Vincent, Margaret, Ofc.	female	26	NOPD (New Orleans Police Dept.)	Police Officer - squad car MAX191
Walker, Timothy, Sgt	male	43	NOPD (New Orleans Police Dept.)	Police Officer - wife Mary and son Thomas (Tulane student, missing after Katrina)
Washington, Abel	male	deceased	Matchless Trailers	Killed on the job by plywood bundle
Watson, Lionel, Ph.D., MPH	male	63	Close friend, confidant, and colleague of Tristan Baines for over 25 years	Toxicologist, epidemiologist, ex-cop, cleric, and ethicist.
Weiss, Maddie	female	27	ERC Ambulance Service	Paramedic and driver
Wheaton, Jessie, SA	male	44	FBI	Agent - St. Louis Bureau
Whitmore, Henrietta F. Judge	female	63	US District Court	federal judge aka "Henny," "The Harpy" and other

Name	Gender	Age (in 2009)	Affiliation	Comments
Williams, Junior (Reggie, Jr.)	male	14	Trailer occupant	brother of Simon
Williams, Rambo ("Dumbo")	male	6	Canine	Simon's dog (Collie/Shepherd) lost after Katrina
Williams, Reggie	male	36	Trailer occupant	father of Simon
Williams, Sethie	female	32	Trailer occupant	mother of Simon
Williams, Simon	male	13	Trailer occupant	formaldehyde injured child

CHAPTER 1 - TORMENT AND TORTURE

DATE: 11:30 pm - Monday, July 24, 2006 – (Post Katrina – 11 months)
LOCATION: St. Louis, Missouri (dilapidated abandoned warehouse near the old Eads Bridge, Mississippi River waterfront)

— — —

Heather was shivering and could feel the blood, her blood, dripping slowly from her chin where she had been beaten. Her entire face felt like it had been run over by a truck. She couldn't see a thing; the blindfold was tight. Her hands behind her back were bound tightly with tape, as were her feet curled in front of her. She leaned against a wall, barely able to remain upright.

The shivering became violent, causing her teeth to chatter, loudly enough to interfere with her listening. She forced herself to quiet down, desperately, hoping to hear any sign of her daughter. Tess was just 13, and will be scarred forever, whatever they did to her. It was already too late. Heather was a strong, determined woman and mother; tough enough to spit in the face of her captor. She was rewarded with a solid blow to her face that knocked her nearly unconscious. She thought it may have come from an open fist; but it might as well have come from a dinner plate, right to the chin. And she bled.

She hoped Tess was close-by. Heather heard her boldly protest and scream at her captors. Then, like the snapping of a wet towel on flesh, she heard the "slap," combined with a crunching sound. Tess was silent; and a door slammed in what seemed to have been an adjacent room; she hoped. Time went by, maybe two or three hours. Heather nodded off, and was now getting very thirsty. She had already wet her pants; but didn't care. She needed to remain quiet and deal with it; the thugs who had taken her and Tess were no amateurs; they were ruthless, unfeeling and obviously calculating, low-life bastards.

Heather thought there were only four of them. The one with the rather high pitched, rat-like squeal seemed to be in charge, although she couldn't be certain. What a gaff – one of the rat's buddy's slipped up and called him;….it sounded like "Casher" or maybe, "Gasher….," probably the latter, but she couldn't be certain. The rat screamed and pushed the big mouth onto the floor for his stupidity. Heather could smell his fetid sweat, as he fell next to her. When Heather demanded to know why they were being taken, Gasher told her to shut up or be beaten again, this time, to death, if necessary. And then what about Tess?

—   —   —

How could this have happened? She couldn't understand why they wanted her and her daughter. A leisurely day at the famous St. Louis Zoo, enjoying a snow cone and some popcorn. Her husband, Tristan, a physician and engineer, was testifying as an expert in a case in Alton, Illinois, about an hour north of St. Louis. He was appearing on behalf of several hundred homeowners who had had to endure the toxic stench from a nearby incinerator, for over 15 years. Tristan had enemies; but this? Just that morning she spoke to him. Everything was going fine. He said nothing. She and Tess were supposed to meet him for dinner at one of their favorite spaghetti restaurants in University City, down in the old Loop, just west of town. It wasn't crowded in the main concession area at the zoo. They sat and enjoyed the spectacular surroundings. The St. Louis Zoo was still one of the finest in the world, built on the enduring legend of its former director, Marlin Perkins, famous zoologist and star of the decades long TV show, Mutual of Omaha's "Wild Kingdom," that ran from '63, amazingly through '88.

So she and Tess decided to spend the day in "Perkins' land," waiting for Tristan to knock another one out of the park. His lifetime batting average with this type of case was over .950; and he cost his opponents millions. Tristan liked to wear the "white hat" most of the time, standing up for those who had taken enough abuse from those with immense financial power. He wore the "black hat" too, on occasion, if the case had merit; but he confessed he wore it only briefly to spy on the enemy from the inside – and believe it or not, he joked, the "black hats," the ones with all of the money, were the stingiest. They often paid late and complained about his bill relentlessly, to the stinking penny. Tristan loved his work; because he won, virtually each and every time.

Snow cone and popcorn were rudely interrupted by two men supposedly with a message from Tristan, insisting she and Tess come to Alton immediately. It was urgent. He had sent these two "gentleman" to retrieve them and chauffer them to the hotel, where Tristan was waiting. No cell call; it was too risky they said. The entire Baines family was in danger and Tristan wanted his wife and daughter by his side, now.

How could she be so stupid, she thought? They had a note, in what appeared to be Tristan's handwriting. How did they find her, she wondered? She had her cell phone with her. GPS? Or did they just fan out and cover the zoo, knowing that some 49 year old woman was dragging around her 13 year old, looking for the monkey house or stopping for some refreshments. It didn't matter now. "Why did they want me and my daughter?" she asked herself. "They were no friends of Tristan, duh!" she lamented, "God help us both."

—   —   —

About four months before this mess developed, she and Tristan had talked about his concerns for the potential dangers of his work. Tristan had become more and more paranoid. The whole thing out in Wyoming. The getaway, the guns, the money spent on extensive medical supplies. "My husband really believes the shit will hit the fan, someday," she mused. "So he wants to protect us. His motto has always been – 'If you have it, you probably won't need it; but if you don't have it, you will need it and curse yourself for being so unprepared, when the suffering begins.'"

3

Tristan knew that his work as a medical and engineering expert would make him serious corporate enemies. First he was an annoyance, then a gadfly; then a major pain in the ass, finally, a serious threat to the bottom line. After thirty years of hard work, Tristan had arrived. Whether it was suing an oil company for a negligent refinery explosion that killed dozens of workers, or going after a pharmaceutical company making millions off a drug that caused hideous birth defects, he was there on the big cases, front and center; but now in the cross hairs.

He was the poster boy of economic earthquakes for those in his way, not to mention the PR havoc his victories wrought upon the losers. Along with a few other notorious "frauds," he had become hated, actually despised, by those defendants with billions on the line. But faster than losing a grip on a greased pig, Tristan had become the beloved darling of plaintiffs, just happy to win a few tens of millions from those with billions – a mere accounting hiccup. After all, the losers could simply pass their losses onto the consumer, where else? Privately, Tristan sometimes lamented his adherence to the "ethics" of his trade. It's just the way it goes. To remain objective, he worked by the hour and couldn't take a percentage of the harvest he reaped for his clients. On one occasion, a mere $20,000 in consulting fees and six hours of testimony led to a $30 million verdict for "the firm." His client invited Tristan to Burger King for a victory dance. Not everyone can be a lawyer, he joked.

—   —   —

The bleeding had stopped but her jaw ached, badly. Her thirst was searing; her lips were dry and she felt faint. "Please, please bring me some water! Help! I need some water now. Where is my daughter?" she screamed, louder than before." Nothing. Nothing at all. At least 30 minutes passed. She screamed again. When she did, she kicked her legs forward and knocked something over, a lamp maybe or possibly some heavy cartons; she couldn't tell. But it did make a loud racket, certain to attract attention. A minute later, she heard the door open and heard footsteps move toward her. She was wearing down. Someone stuck a heavy plastic straw into her mouth.

"Drink! Now! You won't have another chance anytime soon," said the rat, in a venomous squeal. "Don't worry, it won't kill you. I have other plans. We could have taken your husband, Tristan; but why bother. You and Tess are a far superior catch. It was easy. After this, we expect that things will change. Too bad we can't fight back the way I want to – then your arrogant, piece of shit for a husband would join a few of his esteemed colleagues in perpetuity, resting peacefully in one of our landfills. But orders are orders, aren't they Miss Heather? Now drink. All of this will be over sooner than you can stuff a Thanksgiving turkey."

"Where is Tess, you bastard?" blurted Heather, as she greedily sipped what tasted like some electrolyte drink, maybe Gatorade." She felt her strength coming back. "Where is she, please!" she shouted again, immediately regretting the "please."

"Don't worry, she is safe and unmolested, just smacked around somewhat to keep her quiet. It must run in the Baines family – the little bitch bit one of my associates. I hope she has had her rabies vaccination. Clinically, the wound was not too severe; but you know, human bites are worse than those of dogs. I will see to it my friend gets a tetanus shot right away."

Heather's mind responded to the nourishment and rebooted. "This schmuck sounds like he's a medical man – maybe a doctor, nurse or vet. What's with the 'Miss Heather?' He must be a proper born and bred southerner, maybe from Mississippi, Louisiana or Alabama. If we get out of here alive, the police will want as much information as possible to track 'Gasher, the rat' down like a dog. Apologies to the dog."

But she felt herself starting to fold; she was worried to the point of indescribable gut wrenching pain. "Where is she? I demand to know. I am her mother. Have you no mercy?" cried Heather softly, instantly regretting her desperation, her weakness, expended reflexively, like any parent would whose child was in such danger.

"No mercy here, Heather;" spit Gasher, the rat, "no more than your husband shows when he espouses fraudulent theories on behalf of fraudulent claimants, who want nothing more than the green poultice placed in their greasy palms. 'Ah-h-h,' how they swoon, with the money. 'Now that feels good. Now I don't hurt no more; now I can breathe again. My lungs have healed. Just fork it over and I will be fine.' He helps these lying sons of bitches, most of whom have nothing to complain about. Yet, for his own payday, he backs their claims. And these common miscreants are angels, compared to the carrion crow of so-called trial lawyers who fund the farce. It has cost us hundreds of millions, even billions, for what – for nothing. Your proud, arrogant spouse will now suffer. Finally, we are organized and will turn back the tide of this job killing spree, led by so called experts; but really frauds, like Dr. Tristan P. Baines.

Don't fret, now, Miss Heather; it is really nothing more than just business. But I wouldn't say 'don't take it personally,' because it is personal. That's why I have you and little Tess here with me on this otherwise, lovely summer evening in the Gateway to the West."

Gasher couldn't resist spewing more, "It is personal, really personal; but I'll spare you the details for now.

OK, your brat is tied up like you in the next room. She's quiet now; because I told her I would kill you, if she continued to whine and scream. Don't worry, she is intact, just correctly scared shitless. To her credit, she's got some spunk; but believe me she will remember this outing for the rest of her life. That's the plan. Scarring old Tristan is one thing; scarring his family is better; far better."

Clearly insane, Gasher continued, "And wait 'til you see and feel the grand finale; believe me; you will have a front row seat." He had come within inches of Heather's face to validate his torment. Still blindfolded, she had felt the spray of his spittle on her face. Sickened by the intimacy, she stood fast, but was truly terrified. But as her maternal instincts were raging, she pledged "I will never forget this fiend. Before it's over, I will see his balls floating in a soup of my making!"

Reasons unknown, Gasher and his thugs left.

Quiet ensued, except for Heather's hearing the din of her own rapid breathing punctuated by an uncontrollable, staccato of sighs.

It was late; Heather could tell. She dozed; now feeling slight pangs of hunger; quickly eclipsed by anxiety and emerging fear. How long will they keep us here? Where is Tristan?

—   —   —

After about an hour of silence, Heather decided to snake her way along the floor toward the nearest wall. She guessed; then decided to move to her right. It took her over seven minutes, quietly. The floor was rough and it took some flesh off her elbows and hands, minor pain compared to the pain in her heart. They had taken her shoes but left her socks. Surprised, she hit a wall, with her head, no less; but fortunately, gently. Startled by the bump, she swallowed a cry, trying to keep quiet. She tapped on the wall with her bound feet, at first very gently, then more firmly. Nothing. She tried again. Nothing. On her third try, she kicked harder, risking detection and just a beating, if she was lucky. Nothing again. She lay there, trying to decide whether to journey to her far left and maybe, find another wall. She felt the tears welling up in her eyes. In the privacy of the moment, she thought she was going to fall to pieces. She lay there with tears dropping from her eyes to the floor, like quiet raindrops. Her nose ran and dripped the three or four inches into the puddle of tears. In a moment of disgust, she sat up, inhaled deeply, wiping her nose on her blouse. Just like a rancher, she mused, breaking the slightest smile at the indignity of her situation.

She dozed and was suddenly awakened by a banging, a loud banging coming through the wall against which she lay. Then a yelling, no doubt about it, "Mom, Mommy, are you there! Are you there?" It was Tess, yelling her head off.

The door in the adjacent room opened and then closed with a slam. She heard screaming, loud screaming and the blunted thud against the wall. It had to be bloody; it was just a matter of physics. Suddenly her door opened, and in a fanatical screech, he let loose.

7

"OK, you two pieces of human shit; I will move the timetable forward. You are lucky, Miss Heather, you and your stinking brat will escape with your lives; but you will leave me with a souvenir of this glorious occasion. Wanna know what?" belched the rat.

In the background, she could hear two others laughing, almost to the point of collapse.

Suddenly, taking some hair with it, he moved her blindfold off one eye. The light blinded her. After a moment, she stared into the face of her abductor, who seemed to care nothing to conceal his features. After all, he did look rat-like; with a sharp, pointed nose and small beady eyes. For all she knew, they could be red – but not so; they were light blue. His hair was sandy blond. He was tall and thin, almost Lincolnesque – maybe he was a Marfan's case like Honest Abe. He was wearing kakis and a blue sports shirt.

Heather could hear a scuffle, then to her simultaneous relief and terror, two brutes dragged in Tess, kicking and writhing, trying to get free. Impossible. Her hands and feet were bound and she was blind-folded too; but not for long. Gasher leaped at Tess, slapping her hard across the face, causing her upper lip to bleed. With the other hand, he then ripped off her blindfold, scratching her forehead with his nails. Tess saw her mother, with only one eye showing and began to weep uncontrollably. "Shut up, or else!" screamed Gasher.

"Let's get down to business, ladies," said the rat, quietly, with a maniacal calmness. "You must and will pay; but only a small fee for the transgressions of your fanatical, crusading husband and father. He bears a cross. He thinks himself a martyr for the poor, underprivileged and injured. Now he will think twice about his involvement in the bloody, unrelenting, litigation that has cost us all far too much."

The next three minutes were a blur. Mostly, Heather heard shrieks from Tess, screaming at the top of her lungs. But Tess was not the target; just the witness.

Heather's hands were unbound. She was slammed into a wooden chair with wide arms on each side. Her right arm was duct tapped to the chair in seconds with a rapid round and round motion by one of the rat's assistants. She could still hear the tape being ripped from the roll with its familiar, shearing vibrato. Next her left arm, same way. But no; this time something was placed under her left hand, maybe a large sock, elevating it above the chair. Why? She quickly found out why. Her palm was taped to the sock and the chair together, leaving her fingers and thumb dangling in midair. Her wedding ring, her treasure, was still on her ring finger.

She heard Gasher lapse into a psychotic rant. "Let the medical record reflect that the patient is in position and that the fourth finger of her left hand, that is, to the layman, her ring finger is hopelessly diseased. There is an annular, precious metal foreign body surrounding the proximal phalanx just distal to the MCP joint. Too bad. Let's put some betadine over the affected area. After all we don't want any infection, do we? Digital pain block? Nah, forget it. Why? This has got to be a memorable experience. Let's make it quick," vomited the rat with a smile on his face. "Scalpel, please. No wait. I have a better idea. Go out in my truck and retrieve my favorite tool…..for pruning my roses. It's right there on the dashboard."

Within 45 seconds, Gasher was handed a small, rusty pruning shears. The last thing Heather remembered was glimpsing the semi-lunar shape of one of the blades. For good measure, Gasher squeeze tested it several times, next to Heather's left ear. He knew she could hear the grinding of metal on metal. He was determined to impress his patient with what was coming next. Without repose, Heather suddenly felt the unrelenting pressure of the cold steel on her finger; or was it a delirium of terror? she wasn't sure which. "This asshole is serious," she thought. "Dear God. Tristan, you bastard, where are you?" she cried, as the room, the rat, and her finger disappeared.

—   —   —

When Heather came to, they were both lying in the rain, drenched and cold. Heather looked down at a dirty T-shirt, soaked with blood covering her left hand. They were literally lying in a ditch, filled with a foot of water. At least Tess was by her side. She remembered nothing after Tess's scream and the avalanche of excruciating pain, all against a background of psychotic laughter. How they found themselves within a few feet of the roadway, she had no clue. Tess could fill her in later. As the dawn started to break she could see the outline of a bridge about a half mile away. Then she saw the river. It had to be the Mississippi. The bridge had stone pillar supports. Only one fit the bill. It had to be the Eads Bridge, a St. Louis icon since 1874. Now she knew where they were. She had to get medical attention, fast. God knows how Tess was holding up.

Her brave daughter started jumping up and down in the light rain, moving into the path of the large truck, now two hundred yards away. It slowed; it seemed forever. The driver pulled alongside them; opened his window and looked down. "What the hell! Good God!" he exclaimed as he opened the driver's door, put on his emergency flashers and jumped to the pavement. Tess ran back toward her mother. Heather looked down at the bloody T-shirt, trying to feel her fingers under the fabric. The pain was so intense. Her delirium returned. It was surreal. The rain. The dawn. The driver running with Tess toward her. Heather was still on the ground. She squeezed the T-shirt again, this time over all her fingers and thumb.

Suddenly she flashed back to the rat, facing that malignant evil, witnessing his perverted glee as he calmly recited, as if to a child:

"This little piggy went to market; this little piggy stayed home; this little piggy had roast beef; this little piggy had none; and this little piggy cried 'Wee, wee, wee, all-l-l-l-l the way home!

Which piggy will it be, Miss Heather? You chose. If you won't then I'll just have to choose one for you. Cat's got your tongue? – Well then, here goes!"

Heather knew her thumb had "made it to the market." "But where was the piggy who 'had none?'" she asked herself as she collapsed, face forward, into the Mississippi mud.

CHAPTER 2 - MAY GOD HAVE MERCY - PART I

Many were stranded on the roofs of their houses when the flood waters rose and death surrounded them, cutting off their escape to safety. Some stayed, hoping for rescue; some left anyway they could - by a boat, if they were lucky. If they tried to swim to safety, they just became targets for injury from floating debris and a food source from native killers who felt right at home in those murky floodwaters gifted by Katrina.

DATE: 8:30 AM – Thursday, September 1, 2005 - Three days after Katrina
LOCATION: New Orleans, Louisiana - What used to be the corner of Lilly and Pagent, now under 15 feet of water - Samuel and Shonda Green stranded on the roof of their flooded home.

—   —   —

"Samuel, be careful where'n you aim that damned thing!" cried Shonda. "Whut in the hell are's you doin' anyway?"

"Listen, Shonda, I's got tuh signal somebody, we's been stuk here fo almost uh day," pleaded Samuel. "We'll die here; Those copters missed us even tho I's almost fell off the roof wavin' so; God, I's wish I had me sum paint!"

Samuel Green, 34, year old electrician's assistant, unemployed for eight months, stared at his wife of nine years. She was still beautiful in his eyes. Tall, slender, full-figured, not run down like so many of her friends – but what a mouth! Shonda never minced words; she was scared, hungry and embarrassed, having to crawl down the roof several times over the last two days to do her business and have to clean up with that filthy water. When the storm surge came in, like a few others who were prepared, Samuel and Shonda scooted up to the roof with some packaged freeze dried food, water, blankets and a flashlight all stuffed into a large blue zippered canvas bag that Samuel had wisely kept high on a shelf in the garage. Shonda kidded him about his stash; but silently thought that it was a good idea. But to Shonda's unease Samuel managed to sling his loaded hunting rifle and stuff a box of shells into the bag when he shimmied up the shingles that first day.

He got the gun in a trade for some electrical work that he performed for Old Man Thompson in '97. It was a beauty; about 1974 Winchester Model 70, chambered for the .270 cartridge, flattest shooting gun he had ever seen. The leather sling and cloth case were an additional bonus. In '99, he saved the $80 to buy a Bushnell 3-9 X 40 hunting scope that was on sale at Wal-Mart around Christmas. The sporting goods clerk at Wal-Mart helped him mount and sight in the scope at 100 yards, one day after work for just 10 bucks more.

Samuel had only used the rifle once in the past three years when he went out on a boat near Grand Bois with Shonda's cousin, Lenny. He was supposed to move down the coast to look for some whitetails. He had his in-state license; but, by God, he couldn't resist taking a shot at that 12 foot gator on the bank. Even though he had not practiced much at all, that Winchester and scope made the 60 yard shot easy. Illegal, yes; but what a thrill. The round was a bit much for the gator and took off most of its left front leg when it hit the chest cavity. The carcass was still in pretty good shape, and the $120 he got from Lenny's friend, who took care of such things, made the risk entirely worthwhile. No whitetail that day.

That first day, he and Shonda had cowered in the attic to weather the storm; protected, yes, but scared to death watching part of the roof blow away. They stayed there in the attic that first night - no lights, only rain and cold, to the bone. Samuel shined the flashlight beam at the eerily rhythmic surface of the floodwaters that were lapping up to the ceiling joists above the kitchen. The debris was mostly wood, fractured like broken Saltine crackers floating in onion soup.

Even in the soft case, Samuel had beat the tar out of that gun and scope as he dragged it up through the hole in the roof yesterday. Getting ready to shoot off a round into the air to attract some help, Samuel blurted, "Shonda, lookie there," as he pointed to a small fishing boat stuck in the boughs of some trees about 60 yards south. It was about a 12 footer, no motor and partially submerged. "I think I's kin swim to it and bring 'er back."

"Samuel, you's not uh good swimmer; you git yourself drowned; then whatta I'm gonna do then?" cried Shonda.

"Fo once, Shonda, shut up, woman!" returned Samuel, angered under the pressure of the situation and afraid that the boat would soon sink.

"I's sorry – Shonda; I didn't mean tuh say that – I's just think that I's kin make it; an if'n I do, I bring 'er back an' we's kin paddle our way east over to Old Bonhomme Road," said Samuel contritely.

"Then we's shud be able tuh make it onto the cloverleaf, walk up to Highway 90 then cross the canal over the Claire de lune Bridge north of I10; I's worked over there befo.

The District 7 police station is east of there; it's gotta tuh be abuv water line – we's kin make it; I's sure of it!"

"All right, then," mumbled Shonda, not wanting to plunge herself into widowhood; but badly wanting to get the hell off their roof.

A few minutes later, Samuel took off his shoes, socks, pants and shirt and handed them to Shonda. He knew that he was strong enough to swim 60 yards; but he had to go slowly. He had asthma as a kid – it ran in his family; but didn't bother him too much. Samuel was a big man, over 220 pounds and a lover of food, especially meat and potatoes. He slipped into the water and thought of his Momma, Pappy and baby sister, Sethie and her family. He had no idea exactly where they were or even if they were alive. He was a religious man, so he prayed as he moved into the water. Water, if you could call it that. There was crap floating everywhere and, God, did it smell.

As he moved to his right and began a sort of side stroke, he hit his head abruptly but lightly on a log floating next to his house. He tried as much as possible to keep the water out of his mouth and was successful at first. As he moved along, he picked up his strokes and splashed a little, once submerging his face into the filth and swallowed a little. It tasted like rust, oil and rotten grass, mixed with the smell of the dead rat he had found before the storm in his garage. It had been there for over a week and was swollen like a funny stuffed toy; except for the white maggots crawling from its mouth and belly. He didn't have any gloves; so he used a shovel to bury it in the yard; he didn't go too deep; now he wondered if it surfaced during the storm.

Samuel kept up his strokes with success; but he couldn't avoid swimming through the oil and plastic he saw on the surface. He turned to gauge his direction, then felt the bump. He couldn't see what hit him because it came from behind – just barely touching him. He rolled and gasped. Before him he first saw only a red plaid shirt – now, clearly attached to a bobbing torso – the torso of a man, floating face down; swollen 100 times more than the rat in the garage and making the rat smell like roses. A small yellowed swirl of God knows what trailed near the head. It was definitely a man – yes, he could tell by the clothes and his size. Samuel violently used both hands to shove it away with all of his might.

By God, he was strong, so strong that the body rolled, doing a 180 degree turn, so slowly, oh no, so slowly. Samuel did not believe in wicked things and had never been as close to death, especially decayed death like this. There was no face, not because the features were gone; but because the face was gone, torn from the skull. Samuel almost panicked as he kept stroking for the boat, now only 20 yards ahead. He suddenly realized that he was not alone in these flood waters. He wasn't superstitious; but he thought of the gator he shot – and especially that gator's kin and its extended family near Grand Bois.

Eight minutes later, Samuel reached the small dingy; it had a rope attached to the bough. He didn't dare try to get into it there, even though he thought of trying to climb one of the tree boughs. He just turned around, holding the rope in his teeth, and moved in the direction of Shonda and his roof. This was a bad arrangement, because he had to keep his mouth partially open. More filth, more spitting; and he struggled for over a half hour as he made his way home. It took him a few extra minutes because he had to stay clear of that gray, bloated mass marked by a plaid shirt. He finally reached the roof and Shonda who had maneuvered down to the water's edge to lend a hand. There was no way that Shonda could pull Samuel onto the roof. He just handed her the rope and because the water line was well onto the roof, he was able to shimmy onto the shingles by carefully grabbing onto a toilet vent pipe that penetrated the roof close by.

He made it. They had no paddle; but he figured that he and Shonda could lean over and use their hands, at least until he found something better floating on their way to Old Bonhomme and the Clair de lune Bridge. He threw everything into the boat; their blankets, water bottles and food; then Samuel held the boat while Shonda slipped in. Samuel then handed Shonda his hunting rifle.

"Be careful, it's loaded; but I's got the safety on," warned Samuel.

Shonda grabbed the sling and placed it over the seat. She then leaned over, grabbing the vent pipe, while Samuel made it into the boat. Away they went, trying to paddle in unison with their hands. It really didn't work well; but they made steady progress until Samuel spotted a three foot narrow piece of plywood, floating nearby. They moved toward it and Samuel pulled it from the water.

"Wait a minute, Samuel; there's another piece that I think 'll be better. I's think I's kin reach it," cried Shonda, trying to help."

"Be careful there; there's sum sharp metal attached tuh the side!" returned Samuel.

Before he could stop her, Shonda grabbed the floating debris. She felt the most peculiar sensation, no different from that time when your hand slips while trying to halve a bagel with a ceramic knife. The tissue parted so easily; then there was that sickening delay, just a few thousandths of a second before the pain set in. The metal was so sharp that there really wasn't much blood, at least at first. And then, like a baby's delayed onset scream, after she has fallen and just barely tapped her head on the edge of the coffee table, it hit Shonda like a ton of bricks – the pain was now excruciating.

Shonda had sustained a deep laceration over the palm of her right hand below her thumb. She could see the dark red, meaty, muscle and even part of the tendons that made her thumb move. While hurting like hell, the wound just oozed at first, an almost bluish-red, bloody seepage that steadily increased after a second or two. Suddenly, like the jet from a child's tiny squirt gun, something very red spurted from one corner of the wound, keeping perfect rhythm with her pounding heartbeat. She didn't know it at the time; but a tiny artery had let loose.

Samuel saw what had happened and by the time he could react, he pulled one blanket from the his bag and carefully leaned across the boat to grab his wife's hand. He wrapped it and pushed hard, watching the tears pour out of Shonda's already reddened eyes. Her face winced and he pushed even harder. Over 40 minutes went by and Shonda was slumped over her seat trying to get comfortable. She had held on and had not passed out, although she gagged at one point and threw up a little into the water. Samuel gave her some water and eventually coached her to press on the wound herself so that they could get underway.

"Kin you's hold on, Shon?" pleaded Samuel. "We gotta git sum help – you's need moh than jist stitches – an' you's need tuh prevent infection from that filthy water."

"I kin make it, OK – but I can't paddle none – kin you use that first board you found?" she asked.

"I's be fine; let's git going – I's hope there's sum way tuh see a doctor or git tuh the hospital; the world's insane an' upside down, Jesus, help us all," cried Samuel, now with moistness clouding his eyes.

Over the next few minutes, Samuel just watched his wife sitting there; loving her more now than ever, He watched her holding that blanket tightly around her palm and actually offering a tiny smile. He felt helpless, angry and determined all at the same time. Then, he thought, with a smile - the world was indeed upside down; Shonda sat there, indeed, not moving, just staring and quiet as a church mouse.

Samuel used the first piece of plywood instead of his hands – with great difficulty and Shonda sat quietly the whole way. It took him over four hours to make it the two miles to Old Bonhomme; they could tell that had made it by the street sign and the highways off to the south. Sure enough, the road was submerged; but the cloverleaf leading to Highway 90 gently rose from the water like the shoreline emerging from Lake Pontchartrain – or the way it used to be, anyway.

Samuel brought the bow of the boat to a grinding halt on the cloverleaf pavement. He carefully got out and was able to secure the tow rope to a nearby post on the roadway barrier. He steadied the hull, so that Shonda could put her good hand on his broad shoulder to pull herself onto the roadway next to him. They unloaded the canvas bag containing their emergency supplies and while Samuel was reaching for his rifle sling, they both heard the distant siren; they couldn't quite place it but it appeared to be heading west on 90 about 200 yards ahead. Samuel even shouldered his rifle to look through the scope to see if he could spot the emergency vehicle – but to no avail.

"Maybe, I's shud pop off uh warning sound to see if we can git them tuh stop. We gotta git you sum help, soon as possible," said Samuel, now in control.

"Samuel, that sounds like uh bad idea!" cried Shonda, "Those cops won't know whut to think, hearing a shot like that an' seeing the likes of you toting that big gun."

Samuel stuffed the soft firearm case into the bag, swung the rifle over his shoulder lifted the blue canvas bag and supported Shonda's left elbow, all the while helping her, as they walked up the clover leaf to highway 90 and the Clair de lune Bridge.

CHAPTER 3 -
SETHIE'S DREAM

DATE: - 7 am – Tuesday, July 25, 2006 -
(Post Katrina – 11 months)
LOCATION: New Orleans, Louisiana -
Corner of Margot and Uclair

—   —   —

Barely eight hours after Heather and Tess Baines were tortured in that dank warehouse near the St. Louis riverfront, Sethie Williams was ending a nightmare in her FEMA trailer in New Orleans.

—   —   —

"Reggie, we're gonna die up here – when are those FEMA guys coming?"

"Oh, hush your mouth, woman – you're really going to kill us all with your whining."

"I'm not whining, you bastard; I'm just worried about Simon. He's hungry, thirsty and wheezing again – this time it's really bad. Momma's sleepin' with one arm on each side of the roof an' is bleedin' bad from her elbow. Junior's got his legs wrapped around that chimney all night; the dog's swum off an' we're all hungry.

Pappy's stuck in that hospital over by the Superdome and is sick to death with his sugar problems. Dear God - I hope's alright. I'm sure he is - those doctors and nurses gotta care for him in the state he is. I need to see my Pappy again - I just gotta get there as soon as I can. When are those SOBs gonna rescue us? Reggie - I don't think your sign is large enough or ever will be seen. If you had painted just "Help!" instead of "Please Help," the damned sign woulda been twice as big!"

"It'll be seen alright – I'm just sorry I didn't have any yellow or red paint. Light blue kin be barely seen. What a minute, Sethie. Listen – hear that whippin' sound? It's getting' louder."

"Lookie Reggie, over by the sun – here she comes, that big black copter. Oh no, it's headin' past us and lookie it's droppin' somethin inta da water. It's a really big package, but itsa about six houses over, by the Markhams. Oh God, what'r we gonna do?"

"Hey, lookie, Sethie, I could maybe swim over an' git the 'tention of the Markhams. It looks like they're gonna win this lottery."

"Easman Markham issa terr'ble man an' don't share nuthin with nobody – don't waste yur time an' I don't want yur worthless self drownin' on me. Oh God, Reggie, Momma's waken' an' is rollin' down the side – quick Reggie, grab 'er, grab her, Please! Reggie, lookie! I'm not kiddin'; she's 'bout to go! Oh Jesus, Jesus, Jesus! REGGIE!"

—   —   —

Sethie Williams shook awake; she looked up at the ceiling in the dim light, barely focused. She was sweating again and had soaked her nightgown. Reggie and the two boys were sleeping and the sun was just coming up. There were small rivulets of water coming down the glass on the inside of the window. The rays of the morning sun, exploded when they hit the droplets, causing her to look away into the weakening darkness of her tiny bedroom. The AC was turned down as low as it would go, but the temperature in the trailer was still 75 and the humidity was awesome. Outside, at 7 AM, it was already over 80 with 95% humidity – typical for early July in New Orleans.

Sethie laid there – the trailer smelled of human sweat, mixed with the smell of fried fish, mold, urine, and something sweet.

She had noticed that faint sweet stench ever since they moved in three months ago. Junior (really Reggie, Junior) was sleeping soundly. He was softly snoring and letting an occasional fart, with a crescendo that would have embarrassed even him at age 14 had he been awake. Sethie knew their diet was terrible and all of the family was having constant bowel problems. Through the partially open door that separated her tiny bedroom with Reggie from the living and sitting area, Sethie could see Junior, tossing gently where he slept on the couch.

She could hear, Simon, her 10 year old wheezing loudly, with labored snoring and even honking every so often. He was sleeping on the narrow, upper bunk at the far end of the trailer, across from the bathroom, if you want to call it that. The short blue and white plaid curtains flapped lightly against the open window above Simon's head. He must have been craving some fresh air during the night.

Sethie counted because she heard him stir each time. The poor boy had awakened four times that night – not a bad night compared to some. Lucky she hadn't had to take Simon to the ER again for those terrible asthma attacks.

Sethie began to plan her day mentally. What a mess. Reggie was going off to his job loading trucks at Dymos. It was unbelievable he had any work at all. She had to get Simon to see Dr. Patricia Simms (Dr. Pat), his pediatrician to check on that wheezing and coughing that had gotten worse over the summer. Two ER visits since they had moved into the trailer. Maybe Dr. Simms could figure out what was going on. She also needed to pick up some more food vouchers at the FEMA office and had to be back to the trailer by about 5:00 pm to meet the UPIC[2] contractor to fix the toilet that had been backing up for the past two weeks, along with about five other things. Good luck she thought. She also worried because her car was running on fumes and the closest gas station was just taking cash.

Momma and Pappy's house, now hers, stood only 20 feet away – a mess on both floors right up to the attic. The UPIC guys told her that the house almost needed to be leveled because of the water damage and mold growth. There still was trash and flood debris all over the yard. She even saw more rats than usual slinking around the slab, especially near twilight. She seriously considered getting a cat, even picking up a stray, except it might make Simon's asthma worse.

—   —   —

---

[2] United Partners for Industry and Commerce

Sethie Williams just stared at the ceiling and could feel the small tear roll down her right cheek; soon two more, then she wiped them with her hand. How could this happen to me she thought; I had such high dreams. At least I've got my husband and kids; we're now only one of three intact families that she knew about in her neighborhood of 20 houses. Pappy used to tell what it was like when he grew up in the late '40s and early '50s – divorce was a sin and having kids when you weren't married….. "Well, jist forgit it he wud say." Now, I'm lying here, smelling like a farm animal, with no end in sight. Life was turned upside down by that bitch Katrina – too much grief for a heart to bear.

Sethie sighed briefly, then began to weep again - stricken by the havoc and pain Katrina caused in the last 10 months. Pappy was dead –probably murdered by those doctors and nurses who couldn't or wouldn't move him to safety when it all came down.

Then there were the fates of her poor brother and sister-in-law, Samuel and Shonda Green. She felt badly that she hadn't talked to Shonda for a few weeks. What a tragedy, God, what a horrible tragedy. It was a return to the jungle. No laws, just survival of the fittest or the ones with more firepower.

No one, no one will ever forget or forgive – worse yet, there will never be no justice for Samuel or Shonda, no comfort, no peace, not after that – Sethie had to call her sister-in-law tomorrow to see how she was doing.

And then there was Momma – now stuck up in Pine Bluff with her cousin. Momma called and told her that Arkansas didn't fare too badly. Momma also told her that after it was repaired or re-built, she and her family could live in their flooded house as long as they wanted. There was nothing there for her anymore. She said she couldn't live without Pappy. Oh, Pappy, where are you?

—   —   —

Sethie itched badly – especially her elbow and knees. She had never had skin problems before she moved into the trailer in May. She was the only one, except Reggie kept whining that his scalp itched all of the time. No one in the family wheezed like Simon, but the smells were awful and were noticeable to the entire family.

The odor almost knocked her out when she opened that trailer door for the first time. Reggie aired out the place but it only worked temporarily. Almost by magic, the place stunk again after she and the family had been out for just a few hours. Especially embarrassing, some visitors had commented on the odor – even the FEMA girl and two guys from UPIC. They probably thought that she was a poor housekeeper.

Sethie remembered the day that she and her family walked into that trailer, for the first time on May 22, 2006. Their hopes were high. It was going to be crowded, just barely enough room for the entire family –but it would be OK for a short spell. After all – it was a Matchless, the Cadillac of all trailers. It was brand spanking new and even had an air conditioner. 32 feet long and 8 feet wide – nothing like a house, even one as small as Momma and Pappy's – but it was new and it was dry and it was safe from some of the goings on at night in their flood ravaged neighborhood, what with the screaming, robberies and looting, and even occasional gunshots over the past eleven months since Katrina hit. And then there was Samuel, her big brother; she missed him; she missed him bad.

The white metal trailer was laid out for travelling in the lap of luxury as far as trailers go. It had a kitchenette, shower, toilet, dining cubicle, a small bedroom and sitting area, even a place for a TV and radio. The kitchenette had new, light brown, pressed wood cabinets, a small refrigerator, propane cook top stove and a stainless steel sink, but no oven or dishwasher. There were small storage areas under the padded seats in the dinette booth.

Sethie later found out that the manufacturer specifically said that their trailer was not meant to be anchored on a pad for permanent in-habitation. Who cares? - The FEMA and UPIC guys and gals fixed it up just right. They hooked up the water from Momma and Pappy's outdoor garden spigot and plumbed the trailer sewage right into the municipal sewer line in the yard. The trailer was set on 12 large cinder blocks, 6 on each side, right on Momma and Pappy's small driveway, near the curb. The electrical hook-up was identical to the meter poles used in trailer parks.

This trailer was going nowhere fast and the fix-up of her new home wasn't going much faster.

CHAPTER 4 - MAY GOD HAVE MERCY - PART II

The havoc and terror in the streets in some parts of New Orleans immediately after Katrina were beyond normal experience or even imagination. Communications were scanty or absent. There was no law and order in many places that could not be reached by the National Guard or the police and sheriffs departments. New and old scores were settled and unnamed bodies floated in the flood waters or lay dead behind dumpsters. Nerves were on edge and mistakes were made - some even deliberate resulting in death or injury to both civilians and police. It was not a place for children or any adult who called himself civilized.

Riots and lootings were a problem for law enforcement and national guardsmen in the days after Katrina. There were some reports that rogue police officers were even involved in the looting. What is known for certain is that several New Orleans Police Department (NOPD) officers were involved in the shooting and killing of two unarmed civilians on the Danziger Bridge over the Industrial Canal on September 4, 2005. Four officers were indicted on charges of first degree murder and several others on lesser charges for being involved in an attempted cover-up.

DATE: 12:15 PM – Thursday, September 1, 2005 - Three days after Katrina
LOCATION: New Orleans, Louisiana - District 7 Police dispatch center

—   —   —

"District 7, Police Dispatch, How can I help you?" said the Operator.

"I thinks ah herd some gunshots near here," said the agitated voice. "Peeple's broke into that TV place ans runnin' off wif stuff."

"What is your location, please?"

"I's near the Wendy's."

"Are you OK? What is your name, please?"

CLICK.

Laurie Jones paused for a second, then touched her forehead and brushed aside an auburn curl from her eyes. 16 years on the job; now 42 years old, divorced, single mom, exhausted - but appreciated. She had been on duty for over 14 hours because her replacement, June Plenkin, had not shown up for her shift. She could be dead or just stuck for all she knew. Laurie was past worrying for the moment. The dispatch center was on emergency power; but the ventilation was not working well. Too many bodies, now unwashed were crowded together and it was hot. It was like time travel or a visit to Europe; the natural smell of human sweat permeated the air and was starting to overpower the colognes, perfumes and deodorants. It was not stench….yet.

"Sergeant, this is Jones covering line 4. Some guy just called in saying he heard gunshots and there was some looting along 90 west, by the Wendy's, what's left of it. He thinks a TV store is being emptied."

"Thanks, Laurie," replied New Orleans Police Department (NOPD) Sergeant Timothy Walker; see who's closest; but also order Max126 and Max191 to head over there right away, if they're in the vicinity. Also notify EMS out of Montrose and fire."

"OK, will do," replied Jones.

Sergeant Timothy Walker, age 43, cop for 18 years, married, and three kids. One, Thomas, age 21 was enrolled at Tulane, majoring in business. The morning of the storm, based upon the best information from cell phone messages, Thomas and some friends decided to have a "hurricane party." He had called Saturday night and told them not to worry. They were just going to stay near the dorms. Tim and his wife, Mary, had tried to reach their son ever since Monday, when Katrina first hit. Cell service was out and the roads above water were all closed, except for emergency traffic. They just prayed and hoped that Thomas had the brains to have reached safety. Timothy was supposed to have been off duty until Saturday but was called in by his supervisor, because four other shift supervisors went missing and could not be contacted. Like Dawn, he had been on for over 14 hours with no end in sight.

Two squad cars responded immediately to the request from dispatch - sirens and all, including some of Walker's closest buddies in squad cars Max191 and Max126. Another, car Russ114 was several miles away and was called in for back-up. While moving up the cloverleaf, Samuel and Shonda missed hearing the first two responders and just heard the last one, Russ114, as it moved away along at only 25 mph, dodging debris, on the way to the call west of the cloverleaf. Max126 and Max191 sped by about 20 minutes earlier.

The response to looting and gunshots - two days after the known world had ended – totaled three squad cars, including six officers, three Remington 870, 12 gauge shotguns, and two AR-15 assault rifles chambered for .223 ammunition (the military favorite), along with each officer's standard Glock 22 chambered in .40 caliber, same as the FBI.

The ambulance and fire department had not been summoned for this call at this time – not yet, anyway. They were busy elsewhere.

Every department was short-handed; dozens of cops, firefighters and emergency medical personnel were AWOL, probably attending their own families…or maybe were dead or injured. Those that showed up, were brave, scared, bewildered, confused, focused and determined, all at the same time. They knew that civil order had mostly broken down; people had died and many who survived wished they had not. The young, the elderly, the sick and the strong had no where to go, nothing to eat and nothing clean to drink. Many men (and women) had become animals, jungle beasts, when their families and lives had been threatened and thanks to Katrina, mostly destroyed.

The National Weather Service said it best, the day before the hurricane hit – "The entire area will be uninhabitable for weeks, after the devastating damage to be caused by Katrina;" and so it was and more.

The first two cars, Max191 and Max126, cars made it to the Wendy's and adjacent strip mall at about 12:30 PM, while Russ114 lagged far behind. There must have been 140 people running amok. Trash, glass, debris, and fists were flying everywhere. All of the windows in the Wendy's were shattered and 10 or more people were looting the supplies. A jug of frying oil had spilled to the floor, causing several looters to slip around like they were competing in a TV game show. For reasons unknown, two men were pummeling an elderly woman who was lying on the ground next to the front door; her face was bleeding from a hideous scalp wound and her dress was half torn away.

About 30 yards from Wendy's, outside the entrance to the TV/Appliance store, a kid of about 14 was running away, after seeing the cops arrive; he was carrying a box containing a Samsung 36" LCD TV, too big for his arms; he tripped and fell and the box skidded into a trash dumpster in the alley next to the store entrance. With his pants torn and knee bleeding, the fugitive quickly looked back, eyes wide open with fear and scurried down the alley next to the dumpster. On the adjacent street corner, two gang-bangers in their early 20's decided to stick it out. One pulled a Charter Arms five shot .38 and let off a plus P round into the windshield of 191. Fortunately, both officers had exited the car when the round was fired. The driver, Ofc. Paul Vatouce, had grabbed his shotgun and positioned himself behind the trunk of the Crown Victoria squad car.

Vatouce's, partner, Ofc. Margaret Vincent, leaned over the hood of the car with a bull horn, calmly and firmly stating, "Attention, this is the New Orleans Police Department. You must disperse and go home immediately. We are all in the middle of a community disaster. Help is on the way. The mayor declared martial law yesterday. We will use force to disperse you unless you GO HOME NOW!" – then she turned to Vatouce and pleaded, "Paul, keep your head down – do not, I repeat, do not fire!"

Vincent's pleas were met by some people running west around the corner; others fleeing down 90 to the east; and a few others started

27

to taunt the officers; throwing trash and broken pieces of wood and metal. As a two foot piece of rebar skidded across the hood of Vincent's squad car, narrowly missing her head, one man shouted, "F-you; where's the help. We're out of food. We got no water. This is payback; we deserve this stuff."

At that moment Ofc. Andrew Marquet and his partner, Ofc. James Maguire, both having exited car 126, staying low, with one hand on the ground to keep their balance, scurried across the pavement and crouched next to Vincent, near the hood of the car. Maguire was holding his AR-15 and Marquet carried his shotgun. Maguire reached into his vest and removed a full 20 round magazine and locked it into the receiver. He left the safety on and the selector set to semi-auto. He then pulled back the charging handle and chambered a round. That smooth metallic ratcheting sound, confirming that the .223 cartridge had gone into the chamber, foreshadowed events to come. Officer Vincent looked over her left shoulder directly into Maguire's eyes without saying a word.

Maguire whispered, "We gotta do this, Margie – I'm not happy about it; but we have no choice – we've got our orders. Some of them want to kill us."

In the meantime, Marquet, trying to find a non-lethal solution, said: "I'm going to fire-off some rubber slugs, to drive them back." Marquet quickly loaded his Remington 12 gauge shotgun with five rubber slug rounds - the same ones sometimes used by park rangers to punish the Louisiana state symbol, a conniving, crafty, black bear that keeps pilfering a state park garbage can. Depending on the situation, Marquet knew that this round could be lethal to a human target.

Grabbing a quick glance, Marquet suddenly rose above the hood of the squad car and leveled his 12 gauge Remington at a 25 year old man, about 30 yards away, just getting ready to throw a brick in his direction. He fired, hitting the man square in the chest. His target went down with a howl and laid on the ground, desperately crawling away from the direction of fire. At this point, Marquet chambered and fired, chambered and fired, trying to pick his targets. He missed but with great effect.

The remaining crowd started to scatter in all directions, except for a dogged handful that had crouched down beside the dumpster and inside the door of the appliance store. Chambering his fifth round, he spotted another, older man, over 50, who stood and aimed what appeared to be a large caliber revolver at him. Marquet fired and ducked at the same time, just catching a slight puff of smoke emanating from the revolver. Before he heard any sound, he felt the .357 magnum round rip into his left shoulder. He bellowed to the heavens, "You son of a bitch! You shot me!" as he fell to the ground next to his fellow officers.

Margie immediately cradled Marquet's head, while Vatouce dropped his weapon and moved to the front of the car, putting immediate compression on Marquet's bleeding arm. While assisting Marquet, Vatouce called on his radio, "108, I repeat 108, Officer Down! Officer Down! - In need of assistance – Gunshot wound to the arm, need 24; send ambulance immediately." Still cradling his head, Margie softly ordered, "Andy, hang tight, I'm going to grab the first aid kit under the seat to see if I can stop this bleeding."

Exposing herself to the line of fire, Margie bravely reached inside the passenger door, reaching the field kit. Nervously, she opened it and first found the blood coagulant Celox-syringe which she opened and pushed into the wound to help stop the bleeding. Next she tightly applied the compression dressing, firmly tying it around Andy's arm. "I don't think we'll need the tourniquet, at this point; that Celox will help until we can get you evacuated to a hospital. I think the bastard missed the artery." But she wondered as the wound continued to soak the compression dressing like wet Kleenex.

Quietly watching his partner's treatment and waiting for the right moment to respond to the madness, Maguire belted, "That does it!" He waited a split second, as the rioter fired off another round, this one shattering the driver's window of the squad car. Instantly, right after that shot, Maguire, in one smooth, well trained maneuver, rotated the safety lever of his chambered AR-15, aimed and fired, hitting the shooter in the neck. The shooter fell to his left away from cover, laying on the ground. Before the attempted cop killer knew it, two more rounds spat from the AR-15, one missing and one hitting him in the left side of his chest, causing him to bleed out from a severed aorta, in a writhing, slippery mess. Those around the fallen looter looked on in horror. Most ran; but the remainder dropped what they were carrying; and almost as if at a Sunday prayer meeting, they all fell to their knees with their hands in the air.

Maguire, armed with his AR-15 and Vatouce with his shotgun very carefully surveyed everything that they could see. Vatouce grabbed the bullhorn and screamed at the 18 or so rioters, "Everyone –on the ground face down with your arms and legs spread. Do not move; you will be shot, if you try to get up!"

Everyone complied. The few onlookers, now more than 50 yards away, dispersed without incident. The two officers stood over the now prone group of 18, while anxiously awaiting back-up.

Standing there, Vatouce called back to Margie, "How's Andy doing?"

Margie responded, "He's holding on; but he's lost a lot of blood, and I don't want him to go into shock. I think I'm going to apply the tourniquet. So much for Celox and arteries. Have you heard back from dispatch?"

Vatouce answered, "No – I'm concerned that we didn't get through."

Suddenly, at that moment, around 12:50 PM, Russ114, pulled into view. Watching the crowd and barking, "Stay down, all of you!" Vatouce moved over to 114, occupied by veteran Ofc. Susan Javier and rookie, Ofc. Byron Greenberg. Vatouce knew them both, well.

Javier, a 38 year old capable, extremely attractive brunette, 10 years with NOPD, had made some history when she won her gender discrimination suit and the promotion that she had deserved for five years. The bastard who kept her on nights without mercy and other low level assignments got nothing more than a slap on the wrist and a few winks of approval from his kindred misogynist supervisors, who still littered the force.

Greenberg was as green as his name. 24, five foot nine, IQ of 147, graduate of a Jewish Seminary, qualified to be a rabbi, not interested in being a lawyer or a doctor, rejected by his Jewish parents when he became a cop (Jewish boys don't become policemen, tsuh!), compromised by becoming an EMT, noted by police academy instructors that he talked too much and asked too many questions (graduated 2nd out of 83).

Vatouce lamented, "Susan we've got a cluster-F here. Marquet's taken a round in the arm, and Maguire shot the perp and probably killed him. We're detaining about 18 looters. Did you hear our call-in for back-up and an ambulance?"

"Negative," responded Javier, but she continued "Hey, listen, Greenberg is an EMT – get over there Byron and see what you can do; I think that we should evacuate Andy now. We won't see any back-up or relief for an hour or more." I don't know how you got here as fast as you did."

Vatouce, grinning weakly, said "That's a damned good idea, Susan. Let's get Andy over to your vehicle and let Greenberg attend him while you head back. I think that you should take Maguire with you too, let him ride shotgun with his AR-15, just in case. Margie and I can hold down the fort until back-up arrives. That OK with you, Maguire? Vincent?"

Both officers gave the OK and they moved Marquet to the back of 114. Javier drove with Maguire next to her in front. He opened his passenger window and stuck the barrel of his AR-15 into the wind to make a statement. Greenberg sat in the rather uncomfortable back seat, cradling Marquet's head in his lap and started periodically releasing the tourniquet about every 10 minutes. But the blood loss was taking its toll. "Susan, we need to move – now!" erupted Greenberg.

Pulling away, at about 1:15 PM, Ofc. Susan Javier called dispatch, "This is Russ 114, repeat 114 departing 103R [riot] scene and 29 [death] at 90 and Desire Parkway with wounded officer Andrew Marquet on board en route to Marcus Med, north by way of Iris. Consider it too dangerous to head west. Can meet EMS on east side of Claire de lune…please copy, dispatch."

Ten seconds elapsed without a response and Javier repeated her message.

Another minute elapsed. "Dispatch, Dispatch, this is Russ 114, Badge 1442, Javier, calling. Do you read me?"

Garbled static only.

"The hell with it!" she blurted, with an exasperated shrug, while she leaned forward, pushing her speed up to 50 mph, carefully dodging roadway debris.

Javier looked in the rear-view mirror and asked, "Greenberg, you rookie SOB – how are you holding on? – keep up the pressure on that arm and don't let the tourniquet stay on for more than 10 minutes."

"Just fine, officer, Ma'am – remember who's the EMT in this vehicle. But this guy's really lost a lot of blood – he will need IV fluids in the ambulance and a blood transfusion as soon as he makes it to the hospital ER."

Javier continued, ignoring the baby cop, "Marquet, how are you doing?"

Still lying in Greenberg's lap, Marquet replied in a barely audible, falsetto gasp, "Doing OK, let's roll. I can't feel a thing."

While listening to his compatriots and not saying a word, Maguire stared out the windshield and both front windows like a cornered lion, eyes darting back and forth, at an exhausting pace. In the midst of this surveillance, he managed to calculate and remember - Sidearm - Glock 22 – one magazine of 15; three spares; no .40 cal in chamber; AR-15; three full clips of 20 left; weapon locked and loaded - 16 rounds left in magazine and one still in chamber; three rounds fired at dead perp – safety on – for the moment.

CHAPTER 5 - MAY GOD HAVE MERCY - PART III

DATE: 12:45 PM – Thursday, September 1, 2005 - Three days after Katrina
LOCATION: New Orleans, Louisiana - Westbound cloverleaf approach to Hwy 90 about 200 yards from the Clair de lune Bridge over the Industrial Canal.

— — —

Samuel and Shonda struggled the 160 yards up the westbound cloverleaf to I-90 where they were about 200 yards from the west side of the Claire de lune bridge.

"Samuel, I's gotta sit down, I's dizzy an' may have to puke," cried Shonda.

Samuel saw a small refrigerator turned on its side, among the debris on the north side of the highway and responded, "Come here, Shon; we's sit uh spell."

The two of them were exhausted, hungry and scared. Samuel realized that his wife's injury was very serious under the circumstances. Her open wound had been bathed in that filthy flood water. He knew that there was some medical center north of 90 on the east side of the bridge, probably about two miles away; he figured about one half mile east, then one and a half miles north. He had been taken there once for a shock to his left arm from some single phase, 220 on a commercial job over by Harbor Center, back in '03. Samuel was not a careless electrician, except that he was a perfectionist, sometimes to his detriment. If he had not tried to make his wires look so parallel in the panel that day, he would have spared himself a lot of pain, suffering and indigestion.

Samuel knew that he had probably missed that westbound siren by about five minutes – but figured that if something was going on in that direction, more help would certainly be coming their way. It was now 1:15 PM, by his cheap but very accurate Casio.

"Let's git goin' Shonda; I's figure we got 'bout an hour or moh walkin' to the hospital."

They both stood and headed west bound, closing the 200 yards to the Claire de lune Bridge. It took them 10 minutes to make in onto the bridge. No one was around. Samuel and Shonda walked onto the largest vertical lift bridge in the United States without any trumpets and fanfare; no ships in the canal; nobody they could see in control of this manmade phenomenon that had lived through Katrina. About a tenth of a mile across, it carried six lanes of traffic. They remained walking east in the far most northerly westbound lane, hoping to see any oncoming vehicle.

About midway onto the bridge, Samuel heard the increasing intensity "Wah, Wah, Wah" he thought was coming in his direction. A minute later, he saw the lights. Transfixed, by the sound and absorbing the beauty of the lights, he knew they were gonna be saved. He dropped his blue canvas bag, let go of Shonda's elbow and started waving his arms and jumping up and down. His rifle came off his shoulder and he barely caught it before it would have crashed to the pavement. He handed the gun to Shonda, who first drew back and then grudgingly accepted the weapon.

No more than 30 seconds later, he realized that this puppy was moving fast, no less than 60. The driver must have seen him and Shonda, because he moved over to the south lane to avoid hitting them. The ambulance was no more than 20 seconds or about 600 yards away, when Samuel was slapped with the reality that this guy was not going to stop.

In a split second, Samuel grabbed the rifle from Shonda, lifted it high in the air with his left hand, moved the three position safety fully forward and let off a round in midair, nearly missing the bridge support structure. He quickly brought the rifle butt to his waist, and pulled back and forward on the bolt re-chambering another round.

Otis Malone, the paramedic driver of ERC Services, yelled to his partner and fellow paramedic, Maddie Weiss, "Shit! Did you see that? Some idiot in the road just fired at us. There are two of them!" Without slowing at first, Malone couldn't decide whether to try to speed by or stop. Both were tired and irritable. This was the fifth run since 6 AM when their shift started. Every run was serious in the midst of living this science fiction apocalyptic nightmare. In a matter of hours, they found themselves traveling in a 21st century chariot through a 17th century Dutch landscape, after a flood. They were living the "but when," suffix of the "not, if," preamble.

"Maybe the guy's in trouble," said Maddie.

Malone growled, "Yeah, but we're supposed to meet that NOPD casualty coming our way. There's an officer with a gunshot wound that's depending on us."

Less than a second later, Samuel fired and reloaded yet again. This round was fired in the direction of the ambulance but deliberately wide to the right.

"We've got to stop," Maddie screamed, "The next one is going to hit us!"

Malone hit the brakes as hard as he could. ABS or not, the five ton vehicle, swerved, almost tipping and causing a horrendous screech with the predictable blue smoke and smell of burning rubber, while the tires painted the pavement with two wavy black tracks.

Malone did not try to steer; but ended up in the same lane as Samuel and Shonda about 30 feet west of them, cocked at a 30 degree angle to the north side of the bridge. Malone's driver's door was facing in Samuel's direction. He ducked and told Maddie to retreat to the rear of the vehicle. Malone's heart was racing and he remained silent; starting to carefully reach for his radio handset.

"Wait! Wait! Please wait suh! I's meant no harm – my wife's bin injured an we's need to git to uh hospital fast – Please, suh, I's sorrie foh firin' my gun. I's not intendin to hits you."

Malone slowly raised his head to the window and dropped the handset. "Maddie – come back up front; I think that we're OK; but we have to hurry, big time!" "Hey, buddy; come over here with your wife; we were on our way to meet a cop car transporting an injured officer coming in our direction. Wait, there it is! Maddie, I can see them. They'll be here in less than a minute or so."

Samuel swung around; looked west on the highway; spotted and then heard the police vehicle – the object of ERC's rendezvous. He stood still, not sure what to do next.

Officer Javier first spotted the ERC ambulance stopped on the bridge, cocked at an angle with its lights flashing. Maguire stiffened. He could not believe what he saw through the windshield. Only one ambulance occupant was visible with his head barely above the driver's window and his hands reaching over the opening – looking at a tall guy with two hands on a scoped hunting rifle - barrel aimed downward toward the pavement; but nevertheless in a shooters position.

Javier hit the brakes and skid stopped about 200 feet from the ambulance. Greenberg and his patient, Marquet both crashed into the hard back of the front seat. Tourniquet loose at the moment, Marquet's arm started to gush again. He was about to lose consciousness. In a millisecond, Maguire opened the door and was on the pavement on one knee with his AR poking through the open window. He took deadly aim.

He knew what he saw. But he thought about his bleeding comrade, now maybe dying, still in the car, just shot by a guy who looked just like the one in front of him

Maguire belted, "Nobody move! Everybody - hands up. But you, Mother F-ker! – put it down on the pavement NOW!"

Malone had no clue and opened the driver's door of the ambulance anyway, yelling "Hold on....wait. Listen this guy's...."

Shonda heard Maguire and started to raise her hands. In an adrenaline fog, Samuel stepped in front of the ambulance, still holding his gun, still in both hands. He pivoted and took a step toward his injured wife. The barrel swung in Maguire's direction.

In the last millisecond, Maguire thought he heard Andy's painful, now half conscious sigh. The sight picture was clear. There was no time. "I won't let them get another one of us today. Here goes number two........."

Samuel's blood and tissue followed the two bullets as they passed through his liver and heart on the way to the grill of the ambulance. He had nothing to say as he dropped his loaded weapon and collapsed at Shonda's feet.

CHAPTER 6 - THE SEARCH FOR TRISTAN BAINES - PART I

DATE: 6:15 am – Monday May 4, 2009 –
(Post Katrina – 3 years and 8 months)
LOCATION: - Helicopter in flight near
Colorado Wyoming border.

— — —

"If you don't mind me askin', do you really think we'll find him?" uttered Raymond Somersville through his headset to one of his passengers, the one sitting behind him, dressed like a guy who materialized out of the 19th century. No response - the man, with dark, ruddy, sun-damaged skin was transfixed, looking at the ground 3000 feet below. Great business, thought Raymond, being the pilot of a $1200/hr Bell (206B3) Jetranger helicopter. The longer he flew the more money he was going to make. This was an unusual situation for Raymond - flying a charter out of Fort Collins, Colorado, headed deep into the Rockies to hunt for a needle in a haystack, even if he knew the haystack's general address. He really needed to track his fuel and his time or it was going to be thumbs out to hitch home on some very remote road - if he was lucky.

Raymond tried again, "I know I'm the pilot; and I know where we're headed; thank God for GPS - but I'm told you know the guy like a book; do you think he's there? Will we find him? We filed our flight plan to head northwest into Wyoming, sweeping southwest of the Snowies; head east again and eventually land in Laramie, before returning to Ft. Collins. Good grief, we'll be covering some mighty remote, rough terrain - a place a man could hide in forever. We don't have unlimited fuel, you know."

Still no response, just the deafening noise of the rotor.

This trip reminded Somersville of some of the reconnaissance missions he flew in the first Desert Storm back in '91. At 44, Raymond was still in great shape and earning pretty good money, hauling the wealthy wherever they wanted to go. His yearly contract with Mountain Missions (MMs) was up June 30; but he reasoned if they gave him the 3% pay raise promised to him, he would go another round. Raymond loved Fort Collins. A great college town with plenty to do – about 80% of the benefits of Denver and only 30% of the indigestion, a pretty good formula for quality of life.

—   —   —

This early morning jaunt was prompted two nights before by a client that Raymond's boss, Morgan Cupples, owner of Mountain Missions, had worked for in the past. The client, his second passenger, was sitting directly next to him on his the left. This guy was also looking out the window, listening and not saying a word. He was a big shot lawyer out of Dallas, named Asher Goldman. Morgan told Raymond that Goldman was looking for somebody really important - at least to Goldman. Raymond was to do whatever Goldman wanted, as long as it was moral and legal. Asher had used Morgan's helicopter services before on several occasions when Morgan had his flying business in Fort Worth and had done a lot of work in the oil patch.

This mission was obviously not very cost sensitive. Goldman had told Morgan he really didn't care too much about the cost of the flight or paying for the help of the guy in the back seat, for that matter. The primary goal was to locate the man they were looking for and get him back to Dallas ASAP. The current situation was unusual for several reasons, the most important of which was Goldman's presence in the helicopter in the first place. Yesterday morning, Goldman had flown from Dallas to Ft. Collins in his law firm's Gulfstream to join the manhunt himself. Raymond wasn't sure yet whether having Goldman along for the ride was a good or bad thing. The guy behind him, supposedly the mission's blood hound, seemed utterly useless, at least for the moment.

So with barely a day's notice, the execution of mission fell on Raymond's back. Raymond wasn't completely in the dark - he had been briefed by Morgan and then, Asher before they were preparing to take off from Ft. Collins, in the pre-dawn darkness a few hours ago.

Raymond learned that the target of this manhunt was Dr. Tristan Philip Baines, a reclusive, brilliant, anti-social and, perhaps, a bit unbalanced, physician and engineer, wanted badly by Goldman; reason not yet disclosed. Trouble was, according to Goldman - this Doc Baines was probably not trying to be located or transported, anywhere.

Morgan had told Raymond not to assume this was going to be a milk run even if the rather strange and unusual doc was found. For all practical purposes, Baines was probably at his wilderness compound, out of contact with the outside world, except when he visited not very close, "nearby" towns for supplies - 30 miles and counting. No phone, no mail, no internet, no grid power and...no warning.

Doc Baines would have no clue anybody was looking for him, when and if they found him. They knew pretty much where they were headed because Goldman's legal colleague, Laura Swain, had the brains to check with the recorders in Albany and Carbon counties to see if anyone named Baines owned property west or south of the Snowies. She hit the jackpot. A cabin on 42 acres had been purchased by one Dr. Tristan P. Baines in 2007. There was no formal address - but Laura learned that the property was in an area east of Bennett Peak, off a primitive road, near a tiny tributary, of the North Platte River.

Checking his instruments, Raymond respectfully insisted, "Mr. Goldman, if you don't mind, can you tell me a little more about Dr. Baines and why you are searching for him? It may help, trying to locate him."

Before he seemed to finish, Asher interrupted, "Why don't you just call me Asher? Then I can call you, Raymond - we've got a long, intimate day ahead of us?"

Still looking down, Raymond replied, "No problem Asher; I was finished. Now, can you fill me in?"

Glancing at the man in the back seat to see if he was awake, Asher replied, "All in good time, Raymond. It's both a complicated and a simple matter that will take some time to explain - but here's a start. Once we find Dr. Baines, uh, Tristan, I need to persuade him to help me on a very important case down in New Orleans. My firm and I represent about 40,000 unfortunate, miserable, mostly poor, people who have suffered from chemical exposures inside the trailers given to them by FEMA after Hurricane Katrina.

I'll spare you too many other details about the exposures at this point; except to say that Tristan is a troubled genius who can help evaluate the exposures and correlate them with some of the multitude of medical problems with which my clients are afflicted. Regrettably, some of my people have asthma, skin rashes, cancer, miscarriages, you name it. Tristan is both an engineer and a medical doc - so he can figure out relationships of cause and effect for the courts.

He's like two experts rolled into one; and outside of the fact that he bills like a bandit, he is both an ass and an asset worth his weight in gold on this project." Asher continued, "Locating Tristan's place shouldn't be too hard; but finding him and then persuading him to help me with this case won't be easy. My most important weapon of persuasion is the guy sitting behind you. I hope that you two had time to talk a bit, while I kept you waiting this morning."

—   —   —

The man sitting behind Raymond in the cockpit fit perfectly into this wilderness mountain mission, seemingly, to nowhere. His name was Joseph True Blood, a full blooded Northern Arapahoe, one of Tristan's best friends, a man Asher had been lucky enough to find, much less convince to go on this trip on such short notice. Asher knew that money mattered, and he offered Joseph plenty- but more than money and less well known to Asher was Joseph's desire to re-connect with Tristan for a second time after the tragedy in St. Louis back in '06.

Joseph had arrived at 5AM at MMs' hanger at the Fort Collins-Loveland Jet Center about 10 miles southwest of Fort Collins. He had traveled most of the night. Joseph had been up north of Hayden, Colorado, west of Steamboat Springs, shooting varmints for two rancher brothers whose cattle were being menaced. He thought the predators were probably a pack of coyotes; but he didn't rule out gray wolves that may have migrated down from Yellowstone National Park, in Wyoming, where they had been reintroduced in 1995. The ranchers were both angry and worried – so they looked for the best tracker and marksman along the rugged and desolate Colorado – Wyoming border. They pondered four dead heifers and one steer, all born in mid-March, along with one mother cow that had to be put down. All that was left of the calves was hide and bones; whatever killed them even sucked the blood from the dirt because they were really hungry.

The ranchers knew more killing was coming. They had to do something, so they found Joseph at his double wide outside of Walden, Colorado by tracking down his wife, Daisy, over at the elementary school where she worked in the cafeteria. The offer looked pretty good to him; so with a nod from Daisy, off went Joseph in his '84 Dodge Power Ram.

Joseph had been in the backcountry for three days before one of the rancher's sons came to get him after riding over an hour on his ATV. Daisy had called with an important message from some man in Dallas who needed to find Tristan right away. Whoever he was, he appreciated the reality that if anybody knew where Tristan was, it would be Joseph.

Joseph had been camping on a small bluff when the boy found him in the mid-afternoon waiting for his next clear shot. His Remington 7mm magnum rifle mounted with his Nikon Buckmaster 3-9X40 sniper scope ensured a job well done. Joseph had already bagged four coyotes and had actually seen a pack of six wolves; but couldn't get a clear shot. After reluctantly delivering the message from Daisy, the boy knew right away that his family had lost their tracker. Any further pleas, on behalf of his father and uncle, for Joseph to stay with the hunt would simply disappear into that blue Colorado sky.

Well, reasoned, Joseph, the wolves, coyotes or whatever could wait. The ranchers' offer of $80/day and $50/pelt ($150 for a wolf, technically off limits) plus ammo compared quite poorly to the offer to skedaddle to Fort Collins and to be paid $500/day to take a helicopter ride to go looking for his old friend Tristan Baines. Besides, before heading back with the boy, Joseph reassured the dejected messenger that he knew where they could get another tracker for less money within a day or two.

Asher jousted Joseph's left knee - "Hey, True Blood – you'll need to start talking sometime. We're going to be in the area near Tristan's property in about 20 minutes. Do you want to get started?"

Tristan's buddy, smelled like a cross between a horse and a goat with a little chicken shit thrown in for good measure. He had obviously been in the backcountry or on the road for who knows how long. His John Deere hat was stained, and his smell permeated the cockpit. Asher couldn't hold Joseph's condition against him - he was the one who persuaded Joseph to come from the bush on this mission with only a few hours notice.

"What do you want me to say?" said Joseph, quietly, not removing his gaze from the window. "I'm thinkin'. I'm thinkin' about what I would do, if I were Tristan, under the circumstances. He's been out there for several months, maybe even over last winter. He knows these mountains better than I know my own, in northern Colorado. He may not even be on his property. I've been there before; but just once. If he wants to stay hid, we will have a hell of a time findin' him. I could keep you guys goin' for days, even with your fancy helicopter, reason bein' Tristan taught me a lot of what I know. Tristan's both a mountain lion and a pussy cat at the same time. If we do find him, we need to come up real slow - he won't know who we are. He may think we're comin' to get him. He won't think we're comin' to fetch him."

Raymond interrupted, "Hey, wait a minute - what are you talking about? Is this Doc Baines wanted by the law or something? Is he a fugitive?"

"No! No!" both Joseph and Asher responded nearly together. Joseph continued, "He's not a law-breaker or anything close to it. I doubt if he every lifted a pack of gum in his entire life. He's got some really bad baggage following him - being carried by some really bad assholes, who have already ruined his life once. I don't know all of the details myself - I just know that if and when we find him, we'd better make sure he knows right away that we are friend and not foe - or else, we may pay a big price with "double ought buck or even .223" written all over it. After four years as a medical officer with the army rangers, Tristan knows firearms as well as he knows the anatomy of the human body. If we scare him and he thinks those CADIXX thugs is comin', he will respond; and he's not the one who will get hurt."

Asher continued, "The assholes Joseph is talking about are the ones Tristan thinks are after him. CADIXX owns an incinerator facility in Alton, Illinois, up the Mississippi, just north of St. Louis. Tristan may be crazy and paranoid; but what is certain is that somebody kidnapped and really hurt Tristan's wife and daughter about three years ago on the same day Tristan testified against CADIXX in court. He proved that CADIXX was causing some people just outside the incinerator perimeter fence line to become sick with cancer after 10 years of sucking CADIXX fumes. The verdict was huge.

The cops never found out who kidnapped his family; but Tristan thinks it was CADIXX. As far as I know, he's got no proof - or if he does, he's not telling. His wife's thumbs were both broken and her left ring finger, wedding band and all, was cut off. His daughter, Tess, only 13 at the time was beaten to within an inch of her life and suffered a broken wrist and arm. They were found barely alive, along the Mississippi River, about a mile from the Eads Bridge, not far from the landmark St. Louis arch. Shit, they were enjoying the famous St.

Louis Zoo when they were taken. Again, it is a long story that we don't need to rehash at the moment."

Raymond suddenly realized that this trip was far more than he had bargained for. "Are you kidding me? What a horrible story!" he blurted. "I don't want to sneak up and surprise this guy - what a horrible story! You two just tell me what to do and where to go. If we find him, we may want to fly over and drop a note or something. I really do want to live to fly another day. Looking at my map and GPS, I suggest that we land at one of the larger ranches to ask some questions, before we start buzzing some guy who could take this copter down with a one second burst."

"Not to worry, boys; I brought a very loud Pyle megaphone just for the occasion," blurted Asher.

—   —   —

In the pre-flight briefing, Asher conjectured that Tristan was probably alone or maybe, only with his dog, if you want to call him that. His wife, Heather, and his daughter, Tess, were God knows where. The last time he had spoken with Tristan, just after the kidnapping, he had told him that both Heather and Tess were not safe living with him. Goldman had no real idea where Heather and Tess may have been living over the past three years; they may be back in Vermont staying with Heather's sister - and may have even assumed her last name - that's how bad matters really were.

Goldman agreed it was possible Tristan may be a target; but he still wasn't exactly sure why - he had not bought into Tristan's paranoia about CADIXX. The kidnapping and brutal outcome could have been just a coincidence, completely unrelated to his testimony in Alton on the same day his family first disappeared. For whatever reason, Goldman sensed that Tristan had not told him all of the details or what had actually happened. He just knew that Tristan was completely analytical and not usually emotional.

After talking with Joseph, Asher concluded that for the past three years, Tristan has been scared shitless, not so much for himself but, instead, for his family. There had to be a reason, a good one too. Tristan was too smart to ignore bad information - his bizarre behavior must have a logical underlying basis. Goldman knew, in due time, Joseph was going to be even more helpful in unraveling this mess, but finding Tristan would be the best way to clear up the CADIXX mystery - if he could get him to talk about it.

Goldman couldn't kid himself. He respected Tristan, especially since he had helped make him and his firm a notch short of $50 million, net, on eight cases since 1995. Matter at hand - he just cared that when he found him, Tristan's mental and physical state would not interfere with his usefulness in winning a case that could top $100 million.

Goldman smiled, recollecting that dinner in Dallas around 2002, right after a big win. Asher netted $2.6 million for his firm after distributing $2.1 million to 600 of his clients, only about $3500 each. Tristan's final invoice was little shy $150,000 for two years of work. Notwithstanding the win, Asher was razzing him about his bill, when Tristan launched a self-deprecating metaphor about his relationship with Goldman and his firm.

"You know, Asher, you generous prick, I am nothing but a race horse that you keep in your stable. You feed me oats, plenty of hay and keep me warm at night. You even tempt me with a beautiful filly, once in while. You come and mount me, usually without notice and expect me to ride like the wind. I usually do; and I almost always win. The problem is you never invite me to sit at your table up at the 'big house.' One day, I'm coming for dinner - you better have enough food on hand and just remember my turds will be way too big for your powder room toilet!"

"Good old Baines, I can't wait to see his sorry ass face again," thought Asher.

Asher turned again to the search - maybe it was true that Tristan was alone, with only his sled dog, Dawson, assuming the monster was still alive. If it was the same beast Goldman had met a few years ago, he was probably happier than Tristan to be in the mountains of southern Wyoming. Tristan had told Asher that Dawson was born in the wilds of Alaska and never did take to city life or to humans, in general, for that matter. Goldman recalled the time he tried to pet that wolf in dog's clothing. At first, Dawson was indifferent, then annoyed and then really pissed, causing him to withdraw his hand while he still had it.

— — —

The chatter in the helicopter was now on a roll. Joseph finally chimed in that he knew Tristan, Heather, Tess, and even, Dawson, like they were kin. Tristan was like a father figure to him and had known him ever since he was a kid. They first met when Tristan was doctoring, Joseph's Mom for pneumonia over at the local hospital in Laramie. It was back in '87, when Joseph was 10.

Tristan had both a general and specialty practice in Laramie at the time. Joseph's Mom had been misdiagnosed for about three days. One afternoon, her doctor mentioned the diagnostic challenges of the case to Tristan while having coffee with him in the hospital cafeteria. Tristan volunteered to go see Mrs. True Blood right away. Without culture specimens positive for potential bacteria, her doctor thought she had a viral pneumonia and was treating her supportively with IV fluids, some antiviral medicines and oxygen; but no antibiotics. Overtreatment with antibiotics was just becoming a major issue in the hospital - so for the moment none were ordered.

Tristan concluded that the cultures were falsely negative and that Joseph's mom was actually suffering from a rare bacterial infection. Within minutes, the IV antibiotics flowed and the encouraging results were seen within hours. Her fever broke within a day, and some color came back to her face. She even had an appetite again. Another day or two of struggling with the misdiagnosis of "virus" and she would have become a statistic.

Mrs. True Blood never saw a bill from Dr. Baines, another shock that almost killed her like the bacterial infection would have. After that scary time and miraculous outcome, Joseph idolized just about everything the good doctor Baines said and did. He wanted to be with Tristan every chance he could. Once, he even feigned a belly ache to get an appointment.

The feelings were mutual - Tristan and Heather had no child at the time - so they sort of adopted Joseph whenever they could. Joseph came from a family of seven - so his folks were grateful when Tristan and Heather spent time with their son. Joseph and Tristan learned together. They hunted, fished, camped and hiked - the more remote the better. Occasionally, Joseph's dad and older brother would come along. Heather came too, until Tess was born in '93, when Joseph was 16.

As Joseph grew through adolescence and early manhood, his time with Tristan became less - yet his bond with him became greater and stronger. They saw each other about four or five times a year, at least until '06 when the number dropped to near zero. In the earliest years of the decade, Joseph thought he was beginning to understand the man with whom he had spent countless hours and from whom he had learned so much. By 2006, before it all hit the fan in St. Louis, Joseph, then 29, conjectured that the almost 20 year difference between his and Tristan's ages didn't mean as much as it did in '87. Now it was the spring of '09, and he hadn't talked to Tristan for over a year. The last time was when he had joined him at his wilderness compound south of the Snowies in the early winter of '08, just after the first of the year.

But several months before his visit to the compound, Joseph talked to Tristan in the summer of '07, not long after Tristan had bought the wilderness tract for his "GOD" (Get Outta Dodge) option.

—   —   —

What a wreck he was. Tristan was in Laramie, at his home, then serving both as his clinic and office. Tristan had tracked down Joseph's latest phone number, by finding his older brother. He called Joseph and asked him to drive up from Walden for dinner. He was alone, except for Dawson - so dinner was pizza and beer.

Heather and Tess had been gone for over a year and a half and Tristan was a wreck. He came to the door, disheveled, sporting a two day old beard. The house, on the other hand, although a little cluttered, was as clean as a surgical suite. Where else could you find two computers, a small pharmacy, a slide rule, and three oxygen tanks, along with two generators, a defibrillator, and 12 different firearms, all in the same space - not to mention a two year supply of food and water surrounded by a 1000 book library and four or five hundred other gadgets, devices, and tools?

Joseph knew the scene by heart - he had seen it dozens of times before. Living with Tristan, Heather and Tess had managed in the midst of "preparedness gone wild" for years.

One of Tristan's mottos was "If you have it, you may not need it; but if you don't have it, you're screwed!"

Needless to say, Tristan had a hell of a lot of what he would need and too much of what he could do without, thinking he would need it just in case. Heather and Tess loved him anyway, even though he drove them crazy much of the time. They knew his heart was in the right place. Tristan couldn't say the same for Dawson, who really loved only winter, deep snow and the freedom to run in it.

"Good to see you again, Joseph. Thanks for coming by," exclaimed Tristan, "How is the family?"

Joseph soaked in the scene, bringing back mostly sweet memories. "Great, Tristan, thanks for asking," he responded, "Have you talked to Heather and Tess lately?" he asked.

"They're fine. I spoke to them two weeks ago. Nothing much has changed. You know I can't be specific - but they're with Heather's sister; but you already knew that," Tristan replied quietly.

Tristan smiled, "You may wonder why I asked you to come over tonight. It isn't just to let you beat me in chess again. Seriously, they still haven't caught the bastards who wrecked our lives in St. Louis, by the way, my hometown, in case you didn't know. Without burdening you with too many details, I have reason to believe that things could turn very ugly again, soon."

Now, Tristan painfully, lied to his friend, "Joseph, I have never really figured out all of the facts behind their motives; much less know exactly who was responsible. You know the CADIXX story - let the cops figure it out; I'll give them another two years to warm up. If I did know who committed this crime against my family, I would not take the law into my own hands. I am not a violent person by nature - hell, I am a physician. I do all I can to take care of people. As a doctor - I take lead out of people- I do not put it in," he lied again.

Joseph paused and looked at him funny. Tristan rolled his eyes and cleared his throat, "It's a joke, Joseph; get it?"

"I got it. I got it. It's not funny!" piped Joseph. "Don't tell me you wouldn't castrate those assholes without anesthesia, if you caught them."

"Quit getting me too excited, Joseph." Tristan replied. "Say, listen -have a piece of cold pizza and beer. I need to tell you something - but can't go into too much detail. I need you to check on my house in Laramie every few months. I'm getting out of Dodge for a while. Earlier this year, I bought some land in the Medicine Bow National Forest south of the Snowy Range, about 120 miles from here by road and 50 as the crow flies. It had a small cabin; and I have built onto it, alot, to say the least.

I'm going to live there for a while. I have made all of the arrangements. I have some friends who will be looking after the house too; but just wanted to have someone close like you to be in the loop, in case something goes wrong. My personal attorney, you know him; Jay Morgenstern, has a letter from me detailing how to get in touch with Heather and Tess, along with a bunch of other personal stuff. I want you to come visit me in the mountains, later when the time is right."

"Jesus, Tristan. Are you OK? You sound like you have lost your marbles!" pleaded Joseph. "You are telling me everything and yet, you are telling me nothing. How can I help you when you are just confusing me?"

"I'm sorry, Joseph, I can't be more specific. I can't rely on anyone but myself to get through the next several months. I can't stick around and try to deal with people who operate outside of the law, have no respect for the law and whom I have obviously pissed off."

"Tristan, what are you talking about? Who have you pissed off? You're not being clear at all. Listen, I will stick by your side whatever happens. I am here for you. I've got your back; you're like a second father to me. Just tell me what you're holding back, sooner rather than later; otherwise, I can't help you like you want me to."

"Not now, Joseph; Not now," whispered Tristan, as he rested his face in his hands. Please, just look after things while I'm gone. I'll probably take Dawson with me; but I not even sure I want to endanger him too."

At the time, Joseph never did find the exact location where Tristan was headed or whom Tristan had pissed off enough to want to do him harm. It bothered him; but he let it slide. He checked in with Morgenstern once in a while and moved on with his life, figuring he would see Tristan again in due time, hopefully under more sane circumstances.

— — —

Airborne now for over an hour, Raymond brought Joseph back to life, "You gonna answer my question, Joseph? Do you think he'll be there when we arrive? I gotta watch our fuel. We'll only have about an hour or so to look for him before we need to head to Laramie to refuel."

"Hang on there, a minute, Raymond, I'm still thinkin'," retorted Joseph as he looked out the window on the port side of the helicopter. "I just ain't sure."

Based on Laura Swain's research and Joseph's memory, they all knew they were looking for a small cabin, with an out building, since Tristan needed to have a workshop and place for his survival gear - but no one knew exactly what to expect. Since the weather was still cold and there was spring snow on the ground in the high country, Tristan would not have left his compound to sleep in a tent or under the stars even deeper in the wilderness.

Joseph knew the camping scenario was probably out of the question, anyway. Even though Tristan Baines liked to portray himself as the rugged survivalist, mountain man, he really liked to "rough it" with a warm soft bed and fireplace nearby. If there was diet soda available - all the better.

Joseph broke the silence, "He probably had to get supplies and building materials to expand the place. We should look for a cabin with some solar panels on the roof and maybe even a propane tank in the yard. Wouldn't surprise me if Tristan has built a new barn or garage to use as a workshop too. Oh - I almost forget to mention - Tristan always been worryin' about forest fires when we camped; so he has a large clearing around his cabin. It should make it a might easier to land."

"OK, Joseph, I think I got the picture," uttered Raymond, with a hint of relief in his voice, while he checked his fuel gauge. "I think I see Bennett Peak about six miles ahead by GPS. We'll skirt the south side and head down river staying about two to three miles east of its course. I'll drop down to about 1000 feet above the deck. Keep them gifted eyes of yours peeled. If you spot the cabin, I'll circle a couple of times, then we can drop him a note."

Raymond reached into the back seat and pulled up a one gallon plastic lunch pail in which he had packed two sandwiches, some chips, carrots and a diet soda. He reached next to the front seat and retrieved a plastic grocery bag. After he emptied the contents of the pail into the bag, he took a large black magic marker and wrote on the side of the pail:

"Joseph True Blood – Don't Shoot!"

Thinking as he hovered about 50 feet above the ground, he could drop the lunch pail; wait for Tristan to read the note; and then wave them in. It seemed like a good plan, enthusiastically approved by Joseph and Asher.

Too bad the plan was like sending a note to a cornered lion just before entering his cage to invite yourself for a burger and fries. Not a bad idea unless you want to become a burger; forget the fries.

CHAPTER 7 - TRISTAN, THE MAN

DATE: 8 pm - Saturday, 3/10/09 – (Post Katrina – 3 years and 6 months)
LOCATION: Baines home and medical office, outskirts of Laramie, Wyoming

—   —   —

Almost eight weeks before he became the target of Asher Goldman's search, Dr. Tristan P. Baines was in at his home in Laramie. It was business as usual, under the circumstances.

It was haunting and hollow to be alone without Heather and Tess. For a host of reasons, not to mention the uncertainty of GAG's unbridled freedom, the situation had become unbearable. Tristan had to have time to think, plan and execute - to stay alive and functional. He really did have to "Get Outta of Dodge" and get back to the compound for a while.

He hardly had any medical-legal cases, on purpose. His clinical activities were on hold. He knew his medical causation analysis was the best; and his clients would return; but he wasn't sure his patients would understand, even if they knew the truth. The truth about GAG, about the threats, about the total disruption of his private life and professional career.

His clients needed him and his expertise to win their battles, usually to put the screws to some very bad large, multi-national corporations, insurance entities, or just local, smaller companies, that didn't give a damn. Tristan knew that corporate bad behavior was usually defined by people, namely individuals, within organizations who had no accountability or sense of fair play, especially, when they messed up and hurt someone.

Unfortunately, when things went wrong, it was always selected individuals whose actions would crash-land the organization into a swamp of liability and disgrace. Rarely, when these individuals realized they screwed up, they would make an attempt to acknowledge the problem and to do something positive about it. More the rule, they would be too afraid to speak up for fear of losing their jobs.

Then there were the really dangerous ones, namely, those individuals who were forever clueless about any problems in the first place, much less the consequences of their reckless actions. Yes, those were the ones to dread the most.

Tristan had seen them all. He knew the way the game was played, and he played it better than anyone else. His skill set was based upon his realization that whatever happened in response to organizational bad behavior, the good, the bad or even the absent reactions of those responsible would be eclipsed and commandeered by, Tristan knew, ... the lawyers - those persons whose one and only goal was to protect the interests of the organization whom they represented. Their objective never was and never would be to do what was right for all parties.

As a defense expert, over decades of work, Tristan had served as the consulting medical and environmental advisor for dozens of corporations, governmental agencies, and smaller companies. He knew how mistakes occurred and how they were defended. He testified dozens of times on behalf of defendant companies, municipalities or other governmental agencies, including law enforcement and fire fighters. Tristan knew when and how they were going to "circle the wagons" to prepare to defend their interests at all costs.

On the other side, as a plaintiff's expert, Tristan was extremely adept at penetrating the defenses of the defense, because he had spent so much time on the inside of the circled wagons looking out. He had successfully masterminded the scientific, evidentiary strategy for the defense on countless occasions. Even when the foundation for a defense effort was viewed as meritless by his opponents, Tristan knew how to put his best foot forward, usually with positive effect.

So in the minds of his adversaries and friends alike, Tristan was notorious for being just as good at defending the indefensible as he was at destroying the invincible.

His primary deliverable was a coherent defensible, bullet-proof, medical and engineering analysis of cause and effect.

For example -

"To a reasonable degree of environmental engineering and environmental medical certainty, it is my expert opinion that breathing carbon monoxide at the measured and calculated levels caused brain damage in eight out of the sixty people exposed. Here are the people, and here are the details...."

When Tristan's testimony prevailed, as it usually did, his opinions could be worth millions of dollars or even more, a major chunk of it going to the lawyers.

After the proceedings, the happy winner would slap Tristan on the back and promise to pay his invoices. Maybe, if he was lucky, Tristan would be asked to dinner to celebrate.

On the other hand, the very unhappy and pissed-off loser, sometimes an insurance company would have to write a check. Then they would go over their notes, revealing how Baines had done it again. Many losers held grudges that did not go away.

To his friends, Tristan was known as that "Effectual, Analytical but Unmanageable Assassin," a label, Tristan considered to be somewhat embarrassing. Most wanted him on their team, as they should - because alongside his nearly 1000 successfully litigated and settled cases for both plaintiffs and defense, his number of losses could be counted on one hand.

To his enemies, Tristan was known as that "Obnoxious, Pig-Headed, Elitist, SOB," a label, he considered to be a compliment. Those who hated Tristan knew to depose him in the early morning, his time of weakest performance. Tristan was nocturnal, a man who preferred to testify at midnight, if he could arrange it. Of course, the judges and court reporters, much less the lawyers, would have none of it.

When Tristan worked for plaintiffs, or as he joked, when he wore "the white hat," he left minimally corrupt or merely misguided defendants for others to deal with. He only wanted the big fish; to catch them and to eat them, usually with a little butter and lemon over a raging campfire. Throwing them back was never an option.

At this stage of his career, Tristan worked only against those indescribably depraved corporate entities that had no souls. They were bankrupt, morally not monetarily. They had tons of money or other gratuities to bribe, threaten and destroy their adversaries to get their way. And they did get their way, nearly all the time. Real people ran these corporations - individuals who made the decisions that defined the choices, actions, and images of the entities for which they worked. But they were people just the same, often scared, calculating, defensive and dangerous. Tristan knew when soulless men and women were in charge, there would be no end to the damage they could inflict.

Tristan also never ignored those in government who could be as sociopathically destructive as their evil counterparts in the private sector. The ones on the public payroll, in fact, were often the worst of all.

Many had defected from their roll as supposedly trusted public servants. When they did, they were even more dangerous than their private sector counterparts. They often commanded budgets that were ten to one hundred times those in the private sector. It was easy to throw money around for this study and that. They could engineer outcome, in accordance with the political flavor of the month. Tristan knew some individuals were corrupted and bought - not in a flamboyant way, mind you; but more subtly, often with gifts, women, wine or a great post-retirement job offer, or maybe all of the above.

With success came a host of problems. Tristan Baines had stepped on a lot of toes, broken some ribs and fatally crushed some heads in his professional career. His case against CADIXX in 2006 was definitely one too many. Tristan knew it. He suffered for this success; it became a problem of prosperity; and it nearly cost him the lives of his wife, Heather, and his daughter, Tess.

— — —

During those early spring evenings in Laramie, Tristan pondered the situation in agony, without respite. It caused him paralytic pause, as he tried over and over again to figure out how and why things had gone so awry three years ago. That damned testimony in Alton, Illinois and the malignant follow-up events in St. Louis would not leave him.

The last straw was the dead, eviscerated rabbit he found on the center of his bed in Laramie, just a few days ago. He had left the house only briefly to run a few errands.

A note was attached to one of the rabbit's ears that read: "Sorry I missed you, Love, GAG, RN."

The alarm system in his home had not gone off. He had no idea how the intruders entered without triggering it. The lenses on all three of his security cameras were spray painted black. The hard drive revealed nothing except pictures of his leaving on his errands that morning after he armed his alarm system. There were no footprints in the snow. Nothing.

He immediately contacted Heather and Tess, back in Vermont where they were in hiding with Heather's sister and family. He told Heather. Their Laramie home was compromised. "GOD" was to be initiated. This plan, once commenced, involved a series of pre-planned, cascading events ranging from contacting his attorney and gathering important papers to closing down his house and mobilizing critical supplies.

— — —

Towing his snowmobile on a trailer, accompanied by his Alaskan-born, husky-wolf, Dawson, he left on Saturday, March 17, 2009, late in the afternoon. Because of the snow depth at that time of year, the trip took him four hours, instead of the normal two. He and Dawson made it to within a half a mile of his cabin, southeast of Bennett Peak, within the Medicine Bow National Forest, along a fork of the North Platte River, less than 50 miles south of the top of the Wyoming Snowy Mountain Range.

A better refuge could not have been found, if he had written it by prescription. The cabin complex included a barn/garage and main house, set on top of a 200 foot by 80 foot long natural geological bench against a 70 foot high cliff with running water nearby. Both buildings faced south and were situated within a one hundred and fifty foot firebreak clearing with only a few scattered ponderosa pines and aspens near the main cabin.

When Tristan and Dawson arrived, the snow was halfway up the door and up to the window sills, along the north side. His large covered wood pile was barely visible. It took eight round-trips on his snowmobile to carry his supplies from his truck to the cabin. The stuff left behind was expendable. He had to dig out the front door. Once inside, he found that the food he had left behind in the fall was largely intact, with the mice taking their fair share of some of the grains left out of plastic containers.

The cabin, made of seasoned 12" spruce logs, was forty eight by thirty six feet on the ground floor, built over a five foot high crawl space. Above the main floor was a loft area that added another 800 square feet. Every square inch of the cabin was accessible through the crawl space. Within the crawl space was a four foot emergency evacuation tunnel, made from corrugated steel culvert, that exited from the base of the rock bench about forty feet from the entrance to the cabin. The exit was camouflaged and made weatherproof by insulation and a plastic covering. Once removed the exit was secured by a padlocked, cage door, made of welded 5/8" rebar that permitted a key holder to access the lock from either the inside or the outside.

Tristan had furnished the cabin comfortably with a large sofa and two recliners, along with a large butcher-block dining room table. The countertops were made of stone. There were two bathrooms, one with a shower. It was a cozy, roomy, rustic, far from maintenance free, spot in the middle of nowhere, with neighbors no closer than five miles, as the crow flies. If you count the mountainous terrain, it was more like eight.

When Tristan arrived, all of the water lines had been emptied; and the drains had been winterized by adding RV antifreeze or propylene glycol. Tristan had a 250 foot drilled water well, producing about 10 gallons per minute of crystal clear, great tasting water. He was very lucky; because wells not too far from him, sometimes contained sulfur and iron contamination. His deep-well pump lifted water directly into a 1500 gallon cistern. The submerged pump in the cistern pumped water into a pressure tank in the cabin, keeping pressure between about 50 and 70 psi, a little less than the water pressure at his home in Laramie. His water was so good that he only needed an in-line sand and sediment filter. He didn't need to chlorinate the cistern water on a regular basis, just once a year to kill anything green that may have gotten a foothold in the house plumbing. He provided hot water with a conventional propane fired 60 gallon hot water heater that required no electrical hook-up.

Tristan housed his propane powered generator in an outdoor shed next to the house. In the summer, he was able to bring in a truck to fill his 250 gallon propane tank, set on a concrete pad, about 20 feet from the generator. The cabin roof had a very steep pitch to keep the snow off his solar panels. Through a photovoltaic controller, his solar panels trickle charged his insulated 24 volt deep cycle battery bank, keeping them from freezing when it hit 30 below.

Tristan designed and implemented duplicate and sometimes triplicate back-up systems. His overall instrumentation consisted of a conventional; yet clever design, involving the integrated use of a generator that put out AC current; a 24 volt DC battery bank, an array of 24 volt DC solar panels, 24 volt DC lighting throughout the house and an AC in/DC out commercial battery charger to charge the battery bank. Here's how it worked:

Tristan's battery bank could be charged by either his commercial battery charger (run by his generator) or by his solar panels through a photovoltaic (PV) controller. DC output from his battery bank was inverted to AC by a six kilowatt inverter (that could surge to 10 kilowatts) to run his conventional 120/240 volt house panel. His AC generator could also bypass his commercial battery charger and run his submerged pumps or the house breaker panel directly, if the battery bank and inverter were being repaired. His battery bank also directly operated DC lighting and a few other DC appliances, including a refrigerator. Tristan also had another refrigerator that ran directly off propane, without any electrical requirements. He could fuel his generator with propane, gasoline or diesel. He joked he had not figured out a way to run it on urine....at least, yet.

This power system was used to run his conventional forced hot air furnace; or to save fuel, he could also heat the cabin with an efficient wood-burning stove. All factors in place, without resupply and rationing, he could live in, at least, cowboy comfort for about 18 months or through two winters.

Tristan took pride in knowing that his seemingly complicated and redundant power system only scratched the surface of what awaited one when they arrived at his compound.

In the barn there were tools of every imaginable description, usually, in triplicate, along with supplies and spare parts to repair virtually everything in the main house. Among the larger tools were an oxy-acetylene torch, drill press, small lathe, table saw, radial arm saw and grinder. Tristan could heat the barn with a ceiling-suspended, propane fired, fan driven heater or, to save propane, with an old-fashioned pot-belly wood burner.

The armory, ammo and large array of medical supplies were carried in with him, when he came from his home in Laramie. He did not leave them at his compound.

Tristan, Heather and Tess's compound was both delicate and resilient. It was the place you would want to be, if society hit the fan, or if you intended to defend yourself from forces that did not wish you well, CADIXX, included.

— — —

Now Tristan was in his element. He was alone, but happy and comfortably safe, in a daunting situation in the middle of March in his remote Wyoming mountains. His situation was anything but carefree.

He had to fire up all systems, carry wood, get the water running and then wait to fix whatever this or that went wrong, an inevitable consequence of wear and tear and the elements, especially moisture and temperature.

Tristan was hyper-vigilant and on edge, sleeping less that he should and keeping his eyes peeled at all times. Dawson, on the other hand, without a care in the world, was in paradise - his equivalent to being "at the beach." The endless snow in every direction, released him from his suburban bondage. He would not stop rolling, sniffing, and digging in the stuff. His frolicking helped to pack down the three foot powder a bit, making it easier for Tristan's snowshoes. Otherwise, Dawson was useless, especially when he buried himself in the snow, so typical of his breed. He was not a good watch dog. Some say there are those poor watch dogs that will find a flashlight for a burglar. Dawson would not only find it for the burglar, he would also hold it for him. Case rested - effective vigilance fell to Tristan.

After settling in, Tristan lived in modest comfort for almost the next seven weeks. Then his life was turned upside down, again. During that time, most of the snow melted and he was able to bring his truck and trailer up to the cabin. During those 55 days, until May 4, he had plenty of time to think. His mind was littered with questions. He wondered if he had overreacted when he headed to the mountains. He could have called the police about the gutted rabbit on his bed; but he was absolutely certain those who had defiled his home would never be caught. Their criminal cunning rendered them immune from apprehension, much less prosecution. They had already escaped any comeuppance for their crimes against his family for the past three years.

—   —   —

Tristan fell into deep, disturbing thought. That lying bastard. The one who called Tristan at his hotel the night before Tristan was scheduled to testify in the CADIXX matter back in Alton, Illinois in July of '06.

The snake claimed he was the CADIXX plant nurse, who had new information that would alter Tristan's testimony against CADIXX. He wanted to see Tristan before he went on the stand to provide his expert opinions. Tristan was prepared to testify late the next morning about the 15 year history of how the CADIXX incinerator devastated the health of families living in hundreds of homes downwind and not far from the CADIXX fence line.

He had been working on the case for three years. It was a very big case - so big, in fact that the law firm that hired Tristan, permitted him to fly his wife, Heather, and his daughter, Tess, from Laramie to be with him while he was in court. Tristan took the firm up on their offer. Originally from St. Louis, Tristan, had Heather and Tess stay with his cousin, Penelope and her husband, Reginald, at their estate in the suburbs, on the day Tristan was scheduled to testify.

This charlatan "nurse" begged Tristan to have coffee with him at 7 am on the morning of his testimony, so he could give him documentation of fraud that would set the record straight. He told Tristan not to contact his lawyers right away, since there would be plenty of time before he went on the stand to notify them of the change in his opinion. He gave Tristan his cell phone number. Tristan began to spout a litany of questions and the whistle-blower hung up.

Tristan planned to notify his client; but the next morning, at 5 am, two hours ahead of schedule, he was awakened by the "nurse" who now identified himself as Gordon A. Gasher. It was the perfect last name, for such a bastard, Tristan thought, as he sat in his cabin and stared out the window at the snow covered trees. "Nurse Gasher," as Tristan sarcastically called him or "GAG," for short, said he was in the lobby and would wait for him. Tristan recalled how he had spoken with Heather the night before. She and Tess were heading to the St. Louis zoo for an early lunch and planned to meet up with him for dinner after he had testified.

Tristan was transfixed; the memories flew at him like bats fleeing a cave. He remembered how he quickly showered and dressed, meeting GAG in the restaurant of the hotel. Tristan was immediately suspicious. Gasher was very nervous, with the Mississippi Valley summer sweat beading on his upper lip and forehead. "Let's go out to my car," blurted Gasher. "I've got the documentation there. I didn't dare bring it in."

Tristan stared at this tall, skinny, pasty looking character with rat's eyes, set close together on a sharply defined face. The man's low set ears stuck out, finishing off his rodent-like appearance. His morning breath was horribly foul. Tristan concluded that un-nurse-like GAG probably feasted on something rancid for breakfast. "There was certainly no toothbrush to be found in this guy's bathroom," he thought.

Tristan replied, "I don't think so. What earthshaking information do you have for me? I don't have a lot of time. It is already 8:15, and I have to leave here at 10. I go on the stand at 11 and will also probably testify after lunch - so please give me the background. I can look at the documentation afterward."

"Suit yourself, doc," spit Gasher. Tristan became even more concerned at Gasher's demeanor and choice of words. "Look, doc; I have absolute proof that this bitch, Carla Hastings, the epidemiologist, over at the Madison County Health Department has got it in for my, employer, CADIXX. It's not to say that CADIXX has been perfect or anything; but the old crow has had a grudge against this incinerator facility for over a decade. Truth be known, our old plant manager jilted the old crone. He was married, and the two of them had an affair. He wanted to call it off and she didn't. He finally told her to get lost. Within a month or so, back in September, '91, the complaints to the EPA and the state started up, just about the time of the first data, she gave to you."

Tristan didn't move. He looked Gasher in the eye and said, "Tell me, Mr. er - Nurse Gasher; how do you know when I started my research and what data I evaluated? Have you read my report submitted to the court last fall?"

"We, uh, I know all about you, doc," said Gasher, now with a hint of a snarl on his lips. "I know how smart you are and about all about your successes. You have quite a reputation. You cost people not thousands, but millions. You probably help some people when you are right; but in this case you are wrong. Miss Hastings works for the county health department in which CADIXX is located. The incinerator and the town of Alton are both in Carla's county. Hell, you grew up in St. Louis, just 15 miles south of here, didn't you doc.? You were a big track star at Ladue high school, weren't you doc. The good old blue and white Rams, huh, doc?

Well, this bitch, Hastings, fudged data for years. She seeded the ore with fool's gold, showing the concentration of hydrocarbons, arsenic and lead that were supposedly coming from the CADIXX incinerator, were way above what the EPA and the state of Illinois allows. Well, doc; I've got the real data in my car; piles of it. Hastings worked with a corrupt laboratory, whose owners also had some grudge against CADIXX. They sent back data that was four or five times higher than what the environmental samples actually showed. We've suspected this problem; but could only prove it about two weeks ago. Now, it comes to you, doc. Will you look at the stuff I have?" finished Gasher.

Then Gasher lied, "One of my colleagues in the medical department at the plant is talking to your law firm, as we speak. We're assuming you will tell them you will change your testimony; or, at least, ask for some more time. Our lawyers think that when the judge meets with both law firms in her chambers, she will agree to a continuance. Otherwise, mistrial it will be."

Tristan was becoming very, very uncomfortable. The circumstances he faced were unprecedented. His instincts told him to wring this prick's neck and leave ASAP. On the other hand, what if he was telling the truth? Fudged data was not impossible; but Tristan knew this man had to be lying on all counts. But Tristan listened and listened, growing more uncomfortable by the minute.

Finally, he calmly asserted, "Mr. Gasher; I don't really think I should even discuss my testimony with you. If you have read my report, obviously given to you by CADIXX's lawyers, you should know my opinions on the adverse health effects on the hundreds of individuals, including many children, living around your incinerator, is not only based upon the data Miss Hastings supposedly adulterated. You are forgetting that we found very high levels of arsenic and lead in the attics of these houses. These metals came from your incinerator and built up over years. We analyzed the air filters in the heating systems, the carpets, even the dust from the vacuum cleaners. We knew that certain isotopes of lead, specific to your incinerator ash were found in these people's houses.

Finally, without snowing you with too many more details, I measured elevated lead and arsenic levels in 60% of these homeowners. It is CADIXX's present to its neighbors. So, respectfully, Mr. Gasher, or whatever your name is, you are full of shit and wasting my time. My next call is going to be the court to have you charged with witness tampering."

Now, Gasher became very calm and almost whispered, "Say doc, what time is it?"

Tristan, actually a bit startled by the question, reflexively looked at his watch and replied, "It's 10:00 am. Look, I have to go. I'll deal with you later."

Gasher, now looking like he had won the lottery, retorted, "I hope Heather and Tess are having fun at the zoo, doc. They spent a restful night at your cousin's place and had a nice breakfast."

Tristan, taken aback by the remark, uttered, "What are you talking about? How did you know.....?" Like a ton of bricks, it hit him in the gut. Restrained only by the hotel surroundings from grabbing Gasher by the neck, Tristan blurted, "I see where this is going. What is this, blackmail?" Suddenly, in a volcanic tone, he continued, pointing his finger within an inch of Gasher's left eye, "If you threaten to harm my family, you will die, more slowly and more painfully than you have ever dreamed. I will make the Taliban look like Mother Teresa - understand?"

Quietly, Gasher, replied, finally wiping his brow with a napkin from the table, "Oh, is that so" Doc. Why don't you call Heather and see how she is doing?"

As he spoke, Tristan speed-dialed Heather's number. She answered after two rings. "Hi, honey, what's up? Aren't you supposed to be heading to court about now? Did you eat some breakfast? You know you will bumble like an idiot, if you don't eat. I hope you got enough to eat.'..."

Tristan cut her off, "Look, Heather, I am fine. I just wanted to see if you had a good time at Penelope's. How's her eccentric husband? Still collecting Chinese opium pipes? What a weird hobby. Where are you now? Is Tess OK?"

"We're at the zoo, Tristan, on schedule - lucky you're not here or we'd still be at Penelope's."

"Very funny, Heather. Are you OK?" said Tristan as he glared at Gasher.

Heather responded, almost irritated, "You just asked that - look Tristan we're fine. I think you have the pre-trial jitters or something. Sorry I wasn't there last night to tuck you in."

"Look, Heather, I know this sounds stupid; but look around you - do you see anyone who looks suspicious or who has been following you? Please don't worry - I'm just under a lot of pressure here and this group I'm testifying against can be rough."

"OK, Tristan. No. Nobody is following us. We are fine. Oh yeah, there are two guys sitting about 20 feet from us. They're drinking some iced tea, it looks like. They look completely harmless and a little funny. We saw them about 20 minutes ago when we were looking at the elephants. They're in business suits. It's already in the 80's and hot. I assume they were cutting work to have some fun in the monkey house or something. They are harmless looking - hell, maybe they're a couple. Maybe, they're FBI or KGB or CIA, or........even Mossad! Satisfied, Tristan?"

"Heather, quietly put your arm around Tess and slowly walk away from those men in the opposite direction and head to the nearest security person. "Now!" said Tristan, nearly shouting at this point.

"Tristan, please - these men are engaged in conversation. There are about eight other people nearby, having an early lunch or snacks. I am not going to upset Tess. We are fine. Just go to court and knock it out of the park. I will call you around 4 pm. Talk to you later, honey - I've got to go - I mean I really do have to go....to the ladies' room, Bye!" and she hung up.

— — —

Tristan regained the dial pad and started to dial 911 - but stopped. Gasher said, "Dr. Baines, nobody is going to threaten anybody - I just wanted to let you know we are on top of this situation. My employer is simply trying to achieve justice. The stakes are high. We have done nothing wrong and can prove it. If you testify based upon erroneous, fudged data, you will be harming the 320 people who work for CADIXX and whose livelihoods depend on CADIXX's ability to function profitably. Your lawyers want 250 million dollars in damages for a non-problem.

Listen, Dr. Baines, I know I'm not a doctor; but I am a trained registered nurse. I know a thing or two about how my employer operates and about the health effects of the things that go up our chimney. I have just been asked to approach you to see if you can play fair and wait. I am sorry about my remarks about your family. I really am. Nobody is going to hurt them. In fact, I have no idea who those men are, sitting nearby Heather and Tess."

"Why you, bastard!" spit Tristan. "How do you know anybody was sitting near my wife and daughter? You couldn't hear my conversation." He entered 911 on the keypad and was just about to hit "send."

"OK, doc - I just wouldn't do that about now. Why don't you take a deep breath. You had better hurry - you're gonna be late. I'll catch you later this afternoon."

Tristan struggled to gather his composure. It was now 10:15. He had to leave at least 30 minutes to drive to the courthouse and park. He had to be in the gallery at least 15 minutes before he was to be called. There was a chance he could be called early.

He stopped, considering the easiest way to decapitate this bastard.

But he knew he was over a barrel. Heather and Tess were probably OK - it may be a bluff, but he could not take any chances. He had to disarm Gasher; he had no choice. Tristan said calmly, "I'll think about looking at your data. I'll mention it to our side. Understand? I'll see if they will meet with your lawyers. I will agree to take a week to re-evaluate the information you have in your car. Let's go outside and get it, so I can take it along. Since your lawyers have already spoken to our side, I am assuming they are going through the paperwork as we speak."

With a thin smile and somewhat widened eyes, Gasher said, "Thanks, doc. I'm happy you see it our way. You're a fair man. Don't worry; your lawyers have all of the information. As I said, I'll talk to you around 5:30 after you have testified. Thanks for being open minded."

With those remarks, Gasher stood up and left. Tristan looked at his watch again. He quickly went up to his room, picked up his brief-case, straightened his tie and went down to get his rental car. He made it to the courthouse with five minutes to spare. He was called at 11:05.

—   —   —

Tristan continued to stare out the window over the snowy landscape, thinking about what happened next. He had tears in his eyes - so much so, that he grabbed a tissue to wipe them and then blow his nose. He thought about his arrival at the courthouse, his 30 seconds with his plaintiff's counsel. He had time to mumble something about the possibility of new data that could influence his opinions. They looked at him like he was crazy; they did not know what he was talking about. He was called. He went to the witness stand. His attorney began to question him, on direct examination.

Tristan was gripped by the unreality of the situation. He knew his report inside out and upside down. He knew the data perfectly. He lost track of the morning's events - he worried, but then ratio-nalized that this asshole, Gasher, was bluffing. He could not depart from his report; he could not sell out these 110 families, all of those mothers and kids many of whom were really ill from choking on the poison CADIXX showered onto their bodies. Plaintiff's counsel was finishing:

"So doctor, please state your opinion to this court and the jury."

Absolute silence. All eyes in the courtroom were laser fixed on Tristan's lips. Absolute silence. Tristan let go a tiny cough. The judge's face frowned a bit. Tristan thought - "OK, already, let it go; let it go; bring the 'Sword of Damocles' down on CADIXX as they deserve." Now the "pregnant pause" was going on too long.

"Dr. Baines; we don't have all day, Sir," said the judge as he glanced toward the jury; then the court reporter, who was enjoying the brief intermission, looking at her nails.

Tristan straightened and finally said:

"Yes, of course, Your Honor."

"To a reasonable degree of environmental medical and environmental engineering probability, CADIXX has overexposed said persons with toxicologically significant amounts of carcinogenic hydrocarbons, arsenic and lead. This overexposure has caused the array of adverse medical outcomes listed in my report. As a result of this overexposure, all affected persons should be afforded lifetime medical monitoring.

These persons should also be provided with treatment for all acute, subacute and chronic problems, related to the CADIXX overexposure, as opined within my report," asserted Tristan, staring almost dream-like at the courtroom ceiling.

Tristan felt a burst of cold air, a draft in his cabin. He jumped, jolted out of his recollection. Dawson had pushed open the door and gone outside. He continued to feel the tears; now they flowed and flowed, big time.

When the defense concluded its cross-examination, the lawyer, said, "Dr. Baines, are you aware of any information provided to you in the last 24 hours that would have any impact on your opinions, in this case?"

Plaintiff's attorney, like a lightening bolt, erupted, "I object you honor. We have no idea what counsel is talking about."

"Please approach the bench, both of you," said the judge, to both attorneys. Along with two other lawyers, one more from each side, four lawyers went forward.

Tristan watched them intently. They withdrew and sat down. The judge turned to Tristan and glanced at the plaintiff's lawyer and said, "Objection, overruled - please answer the question Dr. Baines."

Tristan, stopped, for more than a few seconds. He heard the judge, much less politely this time say, "Dr. Baines, once again, sir, I insist that you answer the question."

Tristan halted, yet again. He bought some time. He said, "Will you please read back the question?"

The judge looked down at the court reporter who had been glancing again at her $50 manicure and instructed, "Please read the witness the question; he seems to have forgotten it."

The question was re-read.

Tristan, gathering his composure, exclaimed, surprising himself with the strength of his response "No, I am unaware of any new information that will have any effect upon my opinions in this case."

The defense attorney belted, "I have no more questions, Your Honor."

"Next witness," exclaimed the judge, "You are excused, Dr. Baines."

Tristan left the stand and hurried out of the courtroom to call Heather. He rushed outside, went to a corner of the court house steps and tapped in Heather's cell number. It went immediately to a recording. He became sick to his stomach, as he rushed to his car to drive to St. Louis...to his family, at once.

CHAPTER 8 - THE SEARCH FOR TRISTAN BAINES - PART II

DATE: 7:30 am - Monday 5/4/09 (Post Katrina – 3 years and 8 months)
LOCATION: Baines Wilderness Compound, Snowy Mountains, Wyoming

— — —

He was alone, detached, at his safe and unreachable compound, his sanctuary, – or so he thought and hoped.

The memories kept flying like bats, hitting him in his face, his brain and everywhere else. They hurt, and they were rabid.

Tristan dozed, as if in a trance, his head on a pillow, still pointed out the window at the unspeakable beauty and solitude that he couldn't see, at the moment.

He was again, back in St. Louis in the malevolent autumn of '06. Where did he go wrong? Heather and Tess disappeared for three days. They were found by a trucker next to a road, three miles south of the Eads Bridge. Bloody but alive. There was no evidence of any sexual assault in either of them, just abuse and trauma. Heather's left hand was wrapped in a bloody hand towel. They called for an ambulance. Tristan was notified. He and his cousins rushed to the hospital. Penelope and Reginald went to the waiting area. It was just after 3 am.

Tristan entered Tess' room. She was asleep. The nurse said she was malnourished; traumatized, had multiple contusions and a fractured wrist; but was otherwise alright. She lied. She failed to mention that Tess's mind was bludgeoned too and full recovery did not seem to be an option.

Tristan then went to see Heather. He approached the bed. She was awake. She smiled; her eyes bright. "I'm OK, honey," she cried, tears rolling down her cheeks. In the dim light of the hospital room, he looked down at Heather's form. A sheet covered her. An IV in her right arm. Her left arm rested by her side. He saw a Kerlix bandage covered her left hand. Even without much light, he could see that something was wrong. Tristan stood; went to the other side of the bed and sat down, barely lifting Heather's hand. She winced and let out a whimpered cry. Tristan looked again. Disbelief. He looked a second time.

She beat him to it. "It's gone, Tristan," she said with exasperation. She sat up in the bed, crying harder.

Then she unloaded, evolving into rage. "They said you would know why. Well, why, Tristan? They even took my wedding ring with it. They made me watch. Why? If I ever get my hands on that bastard, I will cut off something else and what goes with it. In fact, I won't need a knife!" she hissed.

Tristan looked at his wife's hand and the bloody spot on the bandage where it should have been. He tried to see if it was flexed and just hiding. No, it was not flexed; it couldn't be, because it was gone, cut off at the knuckle. Heather's ring finger was not there.

"Why, Tristan, why dammit, why?"

He tried to put his arm around her. To comfort her, to hold her, to say he was sorry. Bandage and all, she pushed his arm away.

— — —

Tristan was jolted back to his Wyoming reality by a large "Whoof" and howl - Dawson had decided to talk, as usual. His antics spared Tristan more pain, more sadness; but his mind could not stop ruminating about the tragedy he had brought upon his family and himself. The same thoughts rocketed through his mind, almost instantaneously, as they had on many occasions before.

The cops were still looking for the bastards who kidnapped and abused Heather and Tess. Tristan knew Gordon A. Gasher (GAG); but not the others. Tristan had met him when GAG had tried to force him to change his testimony. Unbelievably, after the ravage abuse of Heather and Tess, GAG travelled nowhere. He was easy to find. With arrogance and contempt for those tried to link him to the crime, he never even missed a day of work. Yes, the law knew where to find him. They brought him in for questioning; but he had alibis. Tristan identified him without any problem and told the police what he claimed GAG had done.

GAG denied everything. He told the cops; yes, he had met Tristan and yes, he had given him new environmental information about the lawsuit against CADIXX; but Tristan chose to ignore it and he never made any threats of any kind. GAG said poor Tristan, afflicted with intractable grief, was probably delusional, in the face of the horrific treatment of his family. GAG even offered condolences and prayer.

The cops brought in others suspects too; most were human debris, river rats from the gutters of St. Louis; the perfect potential accomplices to a man like GAG. In the end, they could charge no one. The cops said only that GAG may have been Heather's attacker. Yes, he met Tristan's description; but they could not be absolutely certain; at least certain enough to arrest him.

Almost unbelievably, both Heather and Tess missed GAG in the line-up. It was astonishing because they both had seen him close-up, albeit briefly and in poor lighting. This hurt a lot, especially because Tristan was not allowed to coach his wife and daughter during the line-up or beforehand. How could they have failed to recognize him? How was this possible? The cops had seen it before, on many occasions. Maybe traumatic amnesia they said.

There were no mug shots of this fiend; GAG had no record of prior offenses. They couldn't hold him for anything. So GAG went back to work, back to his supposed duties in the medical department at CADIXX, for all the world to see.

Tristan knew he and his family were on the GAG's list...at best, just for future harassment. And, at worst, for..., yes, he had to acknowledge the possibility, at worst, for…painful, tortuous, annihilation. One thing was for sure; GAG was not finished.

After all, thanks to Tristan's testimony, CADIXX was tapped out for $60 million in direct and another $70 million in punitive damages. The judge dropped the 70 to 40, so the tab was only $100 million total. Tristan was paid over $210,000 for his three years of work.

GAG had his marching orders; even GAG had handlers, or so they thought. GAG knew better. And it had become personal with Baines. Anybody else would have been dispatched to hell years ago. Somehow, even though he wasn't entirely off limits, Tristan and his family were not yet the subjects of the wildly popular "death warrant." But they told GAG - Tristan P. Baines had better not cost CADIXX or anyone else another dime, or else GAG will ante up next time, maybe with his own life.

While in horror of captivity, GAG had warned Tess to tell her Daddy to retire, now, not later, or else. "After all, between the two of you," GAG purred, "you and your Mommy still have 19 fingers left. But don't worry sweetie, one is all I need for the moment, until I get hungry again."

She told her Daddy. Tristan listened, carefully; but made no promises. He would and could not allow himself to be intimidated. He was determined to work to help others who needed him. Yes, the money was not bad; but he also needed to save himself, from those feelings of uselessness and irrelevance, he had feared all of his life. He would figure out a way to protect his family. He was committed to self-reliance and would not be blind-sided again, ever.

Tristan analyzed all of these things logically without even a hiccup of doubt. But one unmanageable demon arose. It had the power to destroy all civilized logic and everything in its way. And it had Tristan by the throat, more than he cared to admit. The demon of….revenge. This demon had become Tristan's partner and would not leave him until the matter was settled.

The fantasies were there, and Tristan was not sure he could avoid transforming them into action if the opportunity arose.

"Yes, when I fondle GAG's finger before I remove it," he thought, "not to mention the other parts I have in mind, I just may be inclined to rely upon my knowledge of nerve function and blood flow to ensure GAG's suffering both during and after the procedures.

Keeping GAG awake to enjoy his 'lessening' will become my chief goal. Amputation will be the easy part."

—　　—　　—

Tristan reviled the justice system. After he fantasized a schemed revenge, he pocketed his demon briefly and came to his senses. He thought only of Heather and Tess. How to protect them became his only concern. The path was obvious. He had to make them disappear. He had to hide them. It was the only way. As a family, they decided Heather and Tess were to live with Heather's sister, Sue, and her husband, Brad, in rural, upstate Vermont. Tristan insisted that both Heather and Tess use her sister's married name, Palmer.

With Heather and Tess away, Tristan decided to finish a few cases after CADIXX; but turned down most, but not all new ones that came his way. He won again, twice in court. The other cases settled successfully. The CADIXX crowd knew his whereabouts; but not that of his family, he hoped. Once, in December of 2007, shortly after another publicized victory in which his name appeared, Tristan came home to his house in Laramie and found a folder left on his kitchen counter. It was covered in blood. A raw piece of beef liver was lying on the counter next to it. Inside the folder was a copy of the final jury decision in the CADIXX case from 2006. He called the police. They came over and investigated; even contacted the police in Alton, again. Nothing came of it. Nothing at all. It drove him crazy at times; but he persevered. He had to. After that episode, he installed a $10K alarm system, cameras and all.

So now he was in the middle of nowhere, in the Wyoming wilderness; safe for the time being. He was not worried about Heather and Tess. He spoke to them about twice a month. He was careful, or so he thought; and he was very, very angry and very, very paranoid, a combination not fit for civilized behavior. And then there was that demon. It would not leave him alone.

Tristan had his mail forwarded from Laramie to the post office in the small hamlet of Snowshoe, about 20 miles away. It was now the first week of May. He was alone. It was OK; but lonesome. There was nothing he could do about it.

On that rare occasion two weeks prior when he had picked up his mail, there were three letters, one from a private individual and two others, each from different law firms. Nothing more.

Within the past year, before CADIXX, Tristan had worked with the private party, the source of the missive. He was a home owner whose house and yard had been contaminated with overspray from a crop duster. It was a case of outrageous conduct by the pilot, his employer and the insurance company. Through negligent disregard for wind speed and direction, flight path, time of day, and a host of other factors, the pilot might as well have directly sprayed the man's entire house and yard. Unfortunately, the chemical in the belly tank was illegal Malathion, an organophosphate pesticide, related to military nerve agents. At high enough dose, it could kill people, just like insects. If it didn't kill you, it could give you cancer and cause birth defects in the womb. Although complicated, the case was a good one for the exposed homeowner and his family, at least, in theory. Fortunately for Tristan, the case was on hold. The man was still looking for an attorney.

Enclosed in the letter was a check to Tristan from the homeowner. $50 to be applied against Tristan's $6238.15 balance. Tristan smiled. He liked the man. He knew he would be working for free again, at least for the next decade, at this rate of payment. If the man found a lawyer, he or she would take the case on contingency; maybe as much as 30-40% to be paid after a verdict, judgment or settlement. The percentage would be based on the gross award. Only then, would expenses be deducted, slated for payment, including Tristan's invoices, if he was lucky.

His next letter was from one of Tristan's stable of client law firms;

this one was in El Paso, Texas. They represented some border patrol officers that were knocked down by fumes from a leaking ammonia truck at a border crossing. The principal law partner asked Tristan's whereabouts and why he had not answered their calls at his home and on his cell phone.

Then there was the next letter. This one was from yet another law firm. Postmarked, Dallas Texas.

It contained a check for $200,000.

Somebody was desperate.

The letter and check were from an old friend and colleague, named Asher Goldman. Asher described a monumental case. Tristan had read about it the papers several times over the past three years. There were about 40,000 people living in temporary housing units (THUs), basically, stripped down travel trailers supplied by FEMA after Hurricane Katrina.

Asher explained that these people were exposed to a toxic chemical called formaldehyde that was released into the trailer's air from uncured glue in the plywood used to construct the cabinets, paneling, floors and some other items inside the trailers. The chemical was even used in the manufacturing of pink fiberglass insulation found throughout the trailer's walls, floor and ceiling, adding to the contamination in the air. Formaldehyde, as Tristan obviously knew, is the same stuff morticians use to embalm corpses. It pickles everything it touches. It also does a great job on living tissues, especially the nasal passages, eyes, lungs and bare skin - as an added bonus, it causes nasal and maybe even lung cancer.

Asher pleaded that many of the trailer inhabitants, especially the very old and very young, were ill with respiratory and skin problems, along with a host of other maladies. He confided he had relied upon another expert to help him on the case for the past two months. Asher claimed Tristan would have been his first choice; but he hadn't responded to e-mails or phone messages; so he went with someone else. He said he had regretted the move. In addition to a mediocre analysis, Asher explained, that this expert had failed to reveal he had been nabbed for three DUIs over the past three years. Oh, Asher knew the jury would love to hear all the details, if the defense could get them into the record.

Asher fired Dr. DUI on the spot; but he was still out the $25,000 retainer he had advanced the man. Strange – just two days after he was fired, Dr. DUI was killed on a rural road outside of Fort Worth in a suspicious single car accident. Pitiful – the poor bastard was probably drunk again. The accident was still under investigation

Asher needed help pronto. His latest hope was to send a letter and three representative, plaintiff medical briefs to Tristan, along with an invitation unlikely to be refused. Tristan liked Asher. They had worked closely together on at least 10 cases. Tristan had helped Asher make millions, and he had been well compensated for his efforts. Tristan read Asher's letter, offer and plea. He understood it; sympathized, and then tore the check in half, throwing it into the only wastebasket in the kitchen. Then Tristan went to lie down.

—   —   —

He slept for about an hour; but was awakened by the very loud sound of a copter rotor. Dawson didn't even move. Next, he heard a thud on the roof and the sound of something sliding down the metal with a scratching sound as it fell to his deck. Tristan rolled over and reached under the bed. He pulled out a 12 gauge Mossberg 500 pump shotgun, loaded with two magnum slugs alternated with three double ought buck. He chambered his first round, slid the safety forward to the off position and crawled to the area under the window by his back door. By the time he carefully raised his head to look out the window, the rotor noises lessened, as the chopper pulled away.

He saw a cracked object lying on his porch. Dawson got up and walked over to it, quite interested. He sniffed it all over. Then he licked the side of it. It looked like it could be one of those rigid plastic lunch boxes. There was some kind of writing on the top of it.

Tristan read the clearly marked message: "Joseph True Blood – Don't Shoot!"

Tristan moved the safety back to the on position. He left the double ought buck in the chamber and carefully leaned the shotgun against the side of the cabin, keeping it within reach. This could be Joseph or it could be a trick. He had not seen Joseph since early '08, when he invited Joseph to the compound for a few days. Ever since the Alton/St. Louis disaster, Joseph had been a pillar of strength for Tristan, especially in the early summer '07 when Tristan had asked Joseph to check on his and Heather's Laramie home every so often and to coordinate with Tristan's family lawyer, Jay Morgenstern.

Thinking about Joseph and Jay, Tristan had another unstoppable flashback, while he squatted with his back against the cabin wall and tried to listen for the copter's return.

The last time he had seen Jay was just before he left for his compound, after he had discovered the disemboweled rabbit on his bed at home.

—   —   —

"Tristan, god, you are a stubborn SOB; you don't have to handle it this way!" shouted Morgenstern, as Tristan turned to leave his lawyer's office. There are so many ways to ensure your protection, if you stick around. God pity anyone who would corner you in Laramie, anyway; I'd rather stick my bare hand into a fire ant hill than piss you off in the first place. I don't doubt the true reasons for your paranoia; but why not stay paranoid here in Laramie, rather than at the end of the world, alone? Please - don't leave!"

Tristan stopped, turned around and sat down out of respect for his old friend, "I'll repeat it for the third time, Jay, I've got to get away and figure out what I need to do next. I have kept a low profile; but I still need to earn some sort of living. Something I said or did, since '06 must have stirred up the hornet's nest. I've only had about eight or nine new cases over the past three years. None of them, except one was in eight digits. Hell, we won that one. It was against the Missouri Pinehurst and Acadia Railroad (NPAR). A very big deal up in North

Dakota, where they contaminated the water table under Mandan with diesel. My fee was in the mid-sixes."

"Shit, Tristan; I would think mid-sixes was enough to make you quit," fired Jay; "No wonder they hate you! You're costing them too much."

Jay wanted to inhale the last insensitive remark, as it was exiting his lips. Tristan just glared at him with his dark green eyes; a visage of the swamp in which he planned to drown his friend at his earliest convenience.

"I know, Jay. Yes, I am hated; but I have a hunch I have plenty of company. Others like me who cost defendants big bucks. Back in '06, I think my family and I may have been unfortunate targets of opportunity, simply the catch of the day. Yes, CADIXX wanted my hide, specifically, after that verdict against them. But CADIXX was not acting alone, when they came after Heather, Tess and me as a family.

I haven't quite figured it out yet. But there appears to be some interdependent network of criminal corporations, of which CADIXX is but one. These scumbags have paid dearly in court, through fines, or public humiliation for their various trespasses over the years. Their law-abiding veneer is about as thin as a one hour old wound scab; it can be scratched easily and once gone, it hurts like hell and bleeds easily. They probably keep an enemies list and act upon it when circumstances suit their needs.

I had no idea before '06, at the CADIXX trial, that this network even existed, and even now I am not 100% certain. But I have done the research. I have talked to others and have a working hypothesis, as of right now. Back then in '06, when they tried to intimidate me into changing my testimony, they began with words and, then, threats. Failing, they turned to a hideous, but measured degree of violence; I have no doubt that, next time, namely now, just three years later, when violent intimidation fails, they will turn to murder.

My family is safe, for now. I want these criminals to think I am behaving, for the most part. But it's me they really want. And I intend to spoil their fun. I have my plans, too. I will succeed, not only in protecting my family; but I will bring these bastards down hard. It will take time, mainly because I think they are protected by powerful, equally corrupt individuals."

Tristan paused and continued, "These goons must be backed by some extremely wealthy individuals who operate under almost invisible conditions. I don't think they are necessarily right or left wing by political persuasion; they're just greedy, depraved and powerful, a lethal triumvirate against good. In fact, it wouldn't surprise me if they are more left wing than right. Extremes of either ilk stink. Remember both the extremely far left and far right meet for dinner in the same restaurant once a week."

"Cute, Tristan," muffled Jay, still angry his friend was headed to his doom where they wouldn't find his body for months, if ever.

As if Jay weren't even there, Tristan continued on his roll, "What worries me is that I have shared my suspicions about CADIXX, GAG and this illegal network with the police in St. Louis and up north in Alton. They politely told me I was cracking under the stress of Heather's and Tess' ordeal and injuries.

I have a friend at the FBI, who at least didn't have me taken out in a straight jacket. She's looking into it now, as a formal complaint, since two states, Missouri and Illinois may be involved. I have even more friends at the EPA; they want to wait and see if the FBI comes up with anything, and then they may want to weigh in."

"Nice of you to let me know!" quipped Jay, sarcastically. "I didn't realize you had taken it that far; of course, I'm only your local family lawyer and hopefully, your friend."

Tristan spouted, "Gimme a break, Jay; where's your self-esteem? Hey, look; I gotta go; I have a ton of stuff I have to do.

You know where to find me. Be sure to treat Joseph well. I may need him sooner rather than later. If ever there was someone with the nose and hearing of a bloodhound and the eyes and talons of an eagle, it's Joseph. He's also a better shot than I am with everything but a .45."

"Great - hey, look Tristan, no gunplay this time, OK?" pleaded Morgenstern, "This isn't Cheyenne; and you aren't 35 anymore; even though it was self-defense"

Tristan stopped on a dime and stared past his lawyer like he was a pane of glass.

"Yo, Tristan, OK?" repeated Jay.

"OK, OK......I'll do my best," whispered Tristan, not wanting to unroll that memory any further.

—   —   —

Tristan lay on his side and read the message again. "Joseph True Blood – Don't Shoot!" What in the hell could that mean? Before he finished that thought, a deafening roar came from the back of the cabin. It was accompanied by a shower of decaying Aspen leaves, made airborne by the turbulence. Overhead, he saw the bottom of the fuselage of the Jetranger helicopter. He could not see any passengers.

As Tristan reached for his shotgun, he instinctively dove back into the house and pushed the safety back forward to the firing position. He also ran into the bedroom, donned some body armor and within 10 seconds put on his black ballistic nylon belt that held the holster for his Desert Eagle .45 and three spare fully loaded clips, each with fifteen man-stopping 230 grain ACP hollow points. He re-entered his living room and crouched down. As he secured the Velcro closure on his belt, he thought back to his conversation with Jay; but was immediately interrupted by an unrecognizable voice on an amplified megaphone.

"Dr. Baines - is that you Dr. Baines? Tristan, this is Asher Goldman, repeat Asher Goldman! Remember me? I am your friend from Dallas. I am here with Joseph True Blood, repeat, Joseph True Blood! We are here as friends, repeat as friends. No one is on board who will harm you in any way. May we land? Repeat, May we land? If so, please wave somehow and let us know."

Tristan sat on the floor with his back against the hearth of his fireplace. Thinking. Thinking - trying to get a grip. He couldn't see the occupants. He didn't recognize the voice on the megaphone. Tristan's demons were rising. His paranoid volcano was erupting like vomitus after food poisoning. He crawled in the opposite direction to his bedroom, again and went into a closet. He popped the trap door lid under the carpet and slid into the crawl space, turning on the lights as he jumped in. In the corner, he saw eight dead mice stuck in a glue trap and another one in the rocks, lying on its back with legs kicking and blood coming out of its nose. "Ha!, the D-Con and glue traps are working; but no plans to join them!" he laughed to himself, in a relapsing burst of his ADD, a worrisome de-focus under the circumstances.

Mentally focused again, he crawled over to the four foot entrance to his corrugated culvert escape tunnel. It led to an exit about 40 feet away from the cabin. Since he had arrived in late winter, he had kept the rebar barrier at the exit unlocked. He grabbed a headlamp from a hook in the crawl space and scurried through the culvert, with two feet and one arm for support, moving a bit like a chimp holding a shotgun. He swung the rebar barrier to one side on its hinges and slid out onto the rocks, facing the open firebreak field and his cabin well to his left. He heard the hovering, louder and louder and suddenly, he saw the copter starting to hover, with an obvious intention of landing.

—   —   —

Tristan felt genuine fear for the first time since his family's abduction. It was overpowering and incapacitating; it clouded his thinking. He burst from the culvert exit and fired one shotgun blast and then another into the trees, 90 degrees from the direction his next shot would take, if they didn't back off.

In the copter Raymond screamed over the internal radio to Joseph and Asher, "Did you hear that? I think the crazy mother is shooting at us. Mr. Goldman, shit, Asher, get your ass, back in here. Do not lean your head out again!"

In one smooth action, Raymond pulled away. At the last instant, Joseph lunged forward to the open side door where Asher had been crouching when he made his plea. He stuck his head into full view and started waving with one hand, literally leaning out of the door supported only by the grip of his other hand.

Tristan saw Joseph's face clearly. He screamed his name; but couldn't be heard over the din of the jet engine powering the copter. In a split second, Tristan burst forward toward the copter and in full view placed his shotgun on the ground, unbuckled his belt and placed it next to the shotgun. He raised one arm to the sky and started to wave.

His actions were clearly seen by Joseph. He yelled into the copter microphone headset. "Hold it! Hold it! He's dropped his weapons. He is disarmed and walking toward us."

"The hell with you," belted Raymond. "We're outta here, understand. I want to get home tonight alive and without bullet holes in this chopper. Can you imagine the insurance claim? Assuming he doesn't shoot us down, that maniac."

Raymond continued pulling away and gaining altitude. He was already a quarter mile south, when Asher, who had confirmed what Joseph had seen, screamed, "Listen, Raymond, it's OK. We have found him. We need to go back. He has laid his weapons on the ground. Turn around, now."

Without taking his eyes off his southerly course away from the cabin, Raymond persisted, "No way! No way! You can get someone else to pick him up. You know he's there. It just ain't gonna be me. I caught ground fire in Desert Storm and I ain't doin' it again."

Asher would have pushed Raymond out of the helicopter and taken over, had he known how to fly. He paused and calmly said. "OK, Raymond, it'll be a $5000 tip, if you turn around and pick up my passenger. You have ten seconds to think it over."

Raymond finally looked his way. "You are kidding aren't you, Mr. Goldman?"

"No, Raymond, I am not kidding; you have four seconds left," replied Goldman, seeing Raymond crumble a bit, in a manner as old as human history itself.

"Come on, you're kidding. You must be. In cash? Nothing to Morgan about this?" exclaimed Raymond, with some emerging evidence of a drooling grin on his lips.

"No, Raymond; nothing to Morgan - now will you turn this copter around and pick up my passenger or I will have you fired for breach of contract, and you will be making miniature windmills for the rest of your life."

"OK, OK, Asher; but just remember, in cash - hundreds, if you don't mind," bellowed Raymond, as if the last 10 minutes had never even happened. Feeling pretty good about it, Raymond turned the copter around and headed for Tristan's cabin.

— — —

Ten minutes later they landed. Joseph jumped out first and slowly walked over to his friend. They shook hands, hesitated and then hugged like two brothers. The moment his head was next to Tristan's ear, Joseph, whispered, "Tristan you are insane; but if we had been the bad guys, I have a feeling you should have used your M-16. Shotgun 'no good'um' range unless you want to get us from ambush on the ground."

Tristan smiled. "Joseph stop the 'good'um' range shit. A couple of .45's from my Desert Eagle into the tail rotor while you were hovering would have been just fine. How the hell are you?"

At that moment, Asher strode forward with an outstretched hand. "Tristan, it's been a while. Thanks for not killing us all. I have been looking forward to finding you so we can work together again."

"I tore up your check; and I am not interested; but nice to see you," responded Tristan, as he turned his attention to the tall, ruddy complexioned pilot, who walked forward with his sunglasses in one hand and his helmet in the other.

"Oh, Tristan, this is Raymond Somersville, our noble pilot, said Asher, as he thought about another five grand down the toilet.

"Nice to meet you Dr. Baines. Lucky you're such a bad shot," said Raymond as he thought of what he was going to do with five thousand under the table, out of Morgan's clutches.

Tristan did not like this guy at all. It was too early to tell why. He just knew. "Well, Mr. Somersville - no need to wet your pants. I fired 90 degrees away from my target into the trees over there. I would have changed direction had you tried to land, and I did not recognize you," Tristan retorted.

"What about the message on the lunch box?" said Raymond as he put his sunglasses back on.

"What about it?" said Tristan? It could've been anyone who knew I have a friend named Joseph True Blood. Anyway, I have never as-sociated the words "Don't Shoot" with Joseph in my life; especially when he was a kid and wanted to arm wrestle and kick-ass all the time. Probably still can't beat me. Let's go inside. I've got about 20 minutes.................just kidding," as he winked at Joseph.

From that moment on for the next half hour, all went fine, until Asher started to pressure Tristan about his Katrina/formaldehyde case. He explained he was in a terrible bind, and Tristan was the only human on earth who could turn the tide in favor of his 40,000 clients. He was working with four other law firms; but he was the chairman of their legal consortium and had all the authority to hire him. He wanted Tristan to name his price and come on board ASAP.

"Listen, Asher; I appreciate your flattery and offer; but I have more on my plate than I can handle. You know some of the back-ground; but not all of it. If I take on a case like yours at this time, I have no idea what will happen," he exclaimed, as he eyed Somersville at the counter drinking from a plastic water bottle. Joseph leaned back on the couch and stared at all three men.

"Tristan, you can not believe what these people have been through. They endured death of family, friends, missing relatives, loss of home and property and were traumatized forever. FEMA was supposed to be a helping hand, a hand that offered food and sustenance. A hand that fed you wholesome food; not rancid poison. These temporary housing units flew off the shelf so fast the manufacturers couldn't keep up with their cash registers.

We know that the two brother owners of one of the big trailer manufacturers, Matchless Enterprises, out of Kentucky, pocketed about two million each just in bonuses from this federal gravy train. That would have been fine, if the trailers they supplied FEMA hadn't been gas chambers. To boot, these slime molds, also wrecked the health of their workers to meet federal quotas. Finally, one of my associates, Laura Swain, the attorney who located you, is gathering evidence to show the bastards knew about the problem when they delivered the trailers for occupancy. Everybody who mattered knew about this problem - except the poor people who moved in and their health care providers. Tristan, this has been a major cluster-....you know what I mean. God, these people...we need your help"

Tristan had heard it before and look where it landed him. He knew that a high profile case like this would be like stepping on a land mine; and he might be taking Heather and Tess with him, again. He paid close attention to every word that came out of Asher's mouth; but out of the corner of his eye watched Somersville, who was now sitting on the couch, next to an end table illuminated by a small lamp. Somersville began fingering through a medical journal on the table top. Funny, as Tristan looked up, he saw him close the small drawer in the end table. Somersville saw Tristan looking at him and said, "Sorry, just looking for a coaster for my water glass."

Tristan looked down and didn't say a word. Frankly, he was speechless. He turned his attention to Asher again, noting that Joseph's head was bobbing backward, as he started to snore while looking up at the ceiling.

—   —   —

The pleading went on for over an hour. There was no bantering back and forth, only "Please" from Asher and "No thanks" from Tristan. In the second hour, Tristan could feel himself wanting to accept just to get Asher to shut up. He had heard these pleas countless times. This was a very compelling case. Maybe its high profile nature could be used to protect him, instead of putting his family and him at risk. He could use the money; especially since he and Heather had recently talked about Tess' educational aspirations. At last count she wanted to be a trucker or a brain surgeon; she couldn't decide which.

He was becoming delusional again - just like before CADIXX. A thought crossed his mind. Since leverage was the one and only weapon he had under the circumstances, he thought he could, at least, maneuver Asher in a way to test the limits of his comfort level. Those limits had been, were at the moment and always would be determined by one and only one thing - money. Not money for Tristan; there would be plenty of that - but money, for once, for the people who deserved it most; duh, those who suffered and were injured.

Two and a half hours into the visit, Tristan said, "Here's a possible offer - you get 20% net after expenses and you send 80% of your share to the legal consortium kitty that pays your clients?"

"Is that an IQ test or a question?" blurted Asher, "Are you crazy? Tristan, I have a staff to pay; I have overhead; I have to."

Tristan cut him off. "Asher, you have a Gulfstream to fuel; you have your home in the Bahamas and your cabin in Alaska, along with your 640 acres over by Lake Ray Hubbard. Oh, I forgot that you only wear your socks one time and then throw them away; Tut Tut. What will you do, if you had to wear a pair of washed socks?

I know you can't speak for the other thieves in your legal consortium; but you call the shots in your firm. The last case we worked on, your firm pulled in two million; I netted $45,000 and you took me to Burger King with an apology that you owed me dinner. By my calculations, each of your clients made $12,500!"

"It was $15,500, Tristan - come on you're not being fair. I am taking all the financial risk and am simply paid well when we win. If we lose, my colleagues and I get nothing," pleaded Asher, defending himself.

"Yes, Asher; but have you and I ever lost a case, including favorable settlements?" countered Tristan, as he again caught Somersville, this time looking in the cabinet above his sink.

"No, No, No, OK - I get it," whined Asher, who turned his head and looked at True Blood still asleep and honking louder than ever.

"I'll think about it - but I have to get at least 28%, not a penny less; and I expect you to cut your fee too."

"Asher, you're full of shit. I intend to charge you 28% more! And I would have agreed, if you had gone to 33% for your share; too late now!" exclaimed Tristan, now smiling a bit.

—   —   —

It went on for a total of almost four hours. Tristan said he would go only if they gave him two days to pack and prepare for departure. Joseph supposedly slept through most of the pleadings and negotiations. He later told Tristan he had watched Somersville almost continuously (a physiological fact that Tristan seriously doubted). There was a lot to do. Joseph stayed with Tristan and helped him pack. They cleaned and oiled every firearm and cached some of the less important ones after wrapping them in oil cloth and placing them, along with ammo in screw-capped 10" diameter PVC pipe. Each cylinder contained bags of silica gel to absorb moisture. They buried them, where even Tristan worried they would forget.

Tristan and Joseph bonded reflexively. Their mutual friendship and common purpose re-conformed like a rubber band that had been stretched and then let go. Tristan knew Joseph would have his back and vice versa, literally, in any situation, even one of life and death. Joseph didn't say much when Tristan asked him his opinion about his decision to take this case. Joseph wasn't a talker; Tristan was. Joseph seemed to appreciate the risks better than Tristan. His assignment to look after his second father would be more challenging and complex than ever.

After two days of fairly pressured preparation, Joseph took Dawson and Tristan's loaded truck back to Laramie, leaving Tristan at the cabin. The next day, on schedule, Asher reappeared by helicopter; but this time with a new pilot, an ex-air force type, name Angie Foster.

"On time, Asher; not always like I remember," exclaimed Tristan when they showed up at noon. "Who's your new chauffeur?"

"I'd like to introduce you to Captain Angie Foster, former USAF, now working for Morgan's flying circus," kidded Asher.

Tristan was polite, but now focused, "Where's Somersville? Is he sick or something? The circle of know it alls is enlarging more than I prefer. Asher, do we have a deal, at least with respect to your firm's involvement?"

Ms. Foster, who really looked great in her flight suit and knew it, said, "To answer your first of three questions, Dr. Baines, Raymond decided to take a few weeks off, suddenly. I think he took his wife to Hawaii; so here I am, sorry."

"No need to be sorry, uh, Angie," said Tristan, looking a little embarrassed at his impetuous tone. Defaulting back to being obnoxious, he continued, "Asher, do we have a deal? I can always hitch a ride back to Laramie," - another stupid remark, since he knew he would have to walk 80% of the way.

"Yes, Tristan, we have a deal. 30% net after expenses and your surcharge will be only 20%. That's a hell of a lot better than our typical arrangements. The rest of the consortium is getting 40% and beating their experts to take a 20% cut in their regular hourly fees, since the scope of work is so large."

Having crossed the Rubicon, Tristan shook on it. He went through his compound once more, locked the tunnel entrance, the barn and the cabin and flew to Laramie where they picked up Joseph. Morgenstern was given the pleasure of parenting Dawson for the next several weeks.

Joseph had never flown in a Gulf Stream before. He liked it a lot. He and Tristan even got separate rooms at the Ritz-Carlton in New Orleans. He wanted the same when Tristan sent him to Mississippi to look at some FEMA trailers, all Matchless made, still stinky inside, a full three years after Katrina.

Tristan hoped that Somersville and his wife were enjoying Waikiki about now.

CHAPTER 9 - THE NATIONAL GUARD

DATE: 9:30 am – Wednesday, August 31, 2005 (Post Katrina – two days)
LOCATION: New Orleans, Louisiana – near flooded intersection, not far from some houses under 14 feet of water.

— — —

26 year old Sgt. Melanie Hatfield was riding shotgun in the National Guard Humvee since midnight and was beginning to fade a bit, still with over two hours to go on her shift. She and her partner, Cpl. Troy Ashton, had been on patrol along the only dry pavement for blocks, looking for people in need. Both had been called up by the governor, from their homes in Baton Rouge before the storm hit, along with several thousand others. "Citizen Soldiers" – what a proud title she and Troy embraced and cherished. It looked like her training was paying off.

In real life, she was a slim but firmly built brunette and extremely bright middle school science teacher with the biggest brown eyes you have ever seen; at least that's what her Dad said. She was athletic and strong – perfect for the job at hand. Troy, on the other hand, was a bank clerk over at Cadwell Savings and had missed more of his monthly guard training, than he cared to admit. At age 21, he was already 20 lbs overweight, a burden difficult to hide on his five seven profile. He smoked off-duty and coughed on and off so much that it was really beginning to annoy Melanie, who politely offered him some Kleenex when it got too bad.

During this shift they had already taken some water to about 20 people and assisted 14 others as they waded to shore. They had also radioed in the location of six bodies floating in the floodwaters just off Mercer Avenue. During one hour of boredom, near dawn, Melanie teased – "Even though we're both tired, we guards can't let our guards down!" Troy wasn't amused. Their vehicle had made six passes back and forth over three miles, while both scanned in all four directions when they approached the flooded intersection at Chandlawn.

"Wait a second, Troy," Melanie shouted. "I think I see something on the ground over there on the right – can you see it?" The eyes of both guardsmen were transfixed. The black and gray figure was not moving – but it did not look like all the other debris they had encountered.

"I'll pull over – wait I see some movement Melanie," exclaimed Troy, as he brought the two and a half ton monster to a halt.

Melanie jumped, handed her M-16 to Troy and quickly exited her vehicle, closing quickly the 40 feet between her and the body lying partly in the water.

"Troy, Troy, it's not a child; it's a dog! It looks like a blue healer mix.' I think it's been injured," she called back to her partner, as she approached the poor thing.

"Melanie; pull back!" screamed Troy. "First, we do not have time for a damned dog and second; it may be sick or even rabid. Melanie you're going to get bit; stop!"

"Wait a second, Troy," Melanie cried. "This dog has a collar and it's bleeding from its right hind leg – it's got a linear gash that needs some stitches; I'm not going to let it suffer in agony here. It must have cut itself on something sharp; or wait a minute; this looks like this dog might have been shot!"

"Melanie, please! Let's go! We have to return to Jefferson after this reconnaissance; we can't get to Jackson – it's been flooded out. If we return with an injured dog, there will be hell to pay!" pleaded Troy. "Let me come see."

Troy jumped out of the vehicle and hurried over to join Melanie as she stood over the injured animal. "Melanie, this damned dog looks like it's done for; why not just put it out of it's misery?" he spouted, as he pulled his 92FS Berretta from his holster.

In one swift movement, Cpl. Ashton, pulled the slide assembly and let it fly forward, chambering a 9mm round. With his right thumb, he decocked the safety lever to the fire position and aimed at the head of the dog. Ashton hesitated for a millisecond glanced at his partner; then looked back to his target.

"Stop! You damned trigger happy cowboy – that's a direct order, soldier!!" screamed Melanie. "Remove that round from your chamber and reholster your weapon, NOW!"

"Why?" sputtered Ashton.

"Because, I said so," retorted Melanie. "We're not playing army now – we are on duty and you are no longer a bank clerk and I am not a school teacher – for the time being."

Glaring at Melanie, Cpl. Ashton complied. "OK - At least put on a pair of these gloves before you get near that thing. I'll get them from the back seat."

Donning the heavy leather work gloves, Melanie carefully approached the almost lifeless figure. The dog was lying on its left side revealing the three inch full thickness gash over its right back leg, mostly clotted over, but oozing a small amount of blood from the middle. He was a black/gray mixed breed, obviously unneutered male weighing about 60 lbs. He had huge, black floppy ears inherited from some forbearer in the hound category. What struck Melanie more than anything else was the large white diamond of fur that started on his forehead and extended onto his nose. That white diamond patch would make this dog stand out in any pack of mutts. His tongue hung from his partially opened mouth. He was panting heavily. The moment Melanie touched his ribs the dog winced in pain and lifted his head. He suddenly reared to the right grabbing Melanie's glove with his teeth, held on for a second; let go and then fell back.

"Good God; he must be in pain," said Melanie, as she decided to pet him gently on the head with her right hand. The dog only rolled his eyes this time and let her comfort him. Holding his head with her right hand, using her left hand, Melanie carefully rotated the dogs brown collar around to see the single tag attached to the leash ring.

"Hey, Troy!" Melanie continued, "His name is......wait, the tag is so worn, I can't really tell; the first three letters are so worn and almost gone; I can't read them; but the last two look like 'B' and 'O.' What do you think?"

"Hell, I don't know, and I don't care, Sir...uh Ma'am," responded Troy, now finally defeated.

"Well, I do care – Jesus, haven't you ever had a dog? What kind of childhood did you have?" belted Melanie. "I think I'll call him....God, look at the size of those ears...that's it; he must be 'Dumbo.' I'll name him after Disney's flying elephant. 'Dumbo' it is, at least for now."

Taking the next three minutes to calm Dumbo, Melanie then convinced Troy to help her pick up the injured dog and put him in the back seat. She sat with him, stroking behind his ears. As they commenced driving, after the 30 minute ordeal, Troy radioed ahead, "This is Badger 26, calling to report status, over."

"Roger, Badger 26; what is your position and ETA? Over," replied HQ.

"We are about 1.5 miles out, east of you, along Mercer Avenue, near its intersection with Chandlawn. We are bringing in a canine casualty; repeat, canine casualty, over," reported Troy, as he looked in the review mirror to make eye contact with Melanie.

"Would you repeat that, over?" questioned HQ.

"I said we are bringing in a wounded canine. Based upon her best available intel, Sgt. Hatfield has christened the pooch, 'Dumbo,' because he has big ears, go figure! Over!"

"Enough, Ashton!" blasted Melanie. "Ask them if George Michaels is around. I think that he works as a vet assistant for Best Pets near Baton Rouge. He's a corporal like you, poor schmuck. If he's there, put him on."

"Sgt Hatfield wants to know whether there is there a Cpl. Michaels from Baton Rouge, there; he may be able to assist our wounded cargo? Over," complied Troy.

"Will check, over," responded HQ.

About three minutes elapsed, then a voice familiar to Melanie radioed "This is Cpl. Michaels; over."

"Hand me that handset, Ashton," ordered Melanie. "Cpl. Michaels, this is Sgt. Hatfield." Breaking protocol, under the circumstances, she continued, "George, Melanie Hatfield here; remember me? I teach at Lookout Middle School over in Prairieville. I know you from Best Pets. You took care of my dog, Sammy, last June. You did a great job curing his ear mites. Over"

"Yes ma'am, I'm a vet assistant there; I think I remember you, sorry, not sure – but I do remember Sammy – how's he doin', over," said Cpl. Michaels, clearly with some relief in his voice.

"Corporal, I'm bringing in a wounded dog we found beside the road. He may have been shot or cut real bad – he needs stitches and nourishment. Can you give a hand?" pleaded Melanie.

"Yes ma'am; I'll ask Captain Lowe for a suture kit, some sterile water and betadine scrub, over" responded Michaels, now excited to help. David is a good guy and should be willing to help.

"OK, then; we'll be there in about 5-10 minutes dodging all the debris on the road, over," concluded Melanie, as she handed the microphone back to Troy.

Arriving in six minutes, Troy and Melanie pulled up to the HQ tent. No fewer than 10 guardsmen, including Dr. Lowe and Cpl. Michaels came out to meet Dumbo. In the midst of their heroic assistance to hundreds of displaced persons, this National Guard platoon found time and compassion to aid a wounded dog. Along with other animals, they had seen plenty of dead pets floating in the flood waters – probably, some with their masters floating right next to them. Michaels, with the supportive oversight of Dr.(Captain) Lowe sewed up Dumbo's wound and gave him plenty of water. He confirmed that the dog had been shot – just grazed, lucky for him.

— — —

Over the next two days, Dumbo was able to stand and take small amounts of food. Tail wagging was a good sign. Three days out, keeping him "under the radar," and pleading that there was no where else to take him (not true), Melanie kept him in her tent, where he slept under her cot. Five days out, Dumbo was running pillar to post, everywhere in the command center, now having captured the entire unit. He quickly became a beloved fixture and mascot, even winning the heart of the big cheese, Colonel Reginald Masters - assuming the SOB had one.

Dumbo, however, was Melanie's to keep when it was all over. No formal adoption here; no papers, consent forms or fees. It was just the way it used to be – a human in need of some love, in the midst of an apocalyptic disaster, found some in a wounded stray dog.

US soldiers are famous for this kind of thing – in every war and conflict in US history. Melanie knew that this dog, whatever his name was, had a master before Katrina hit. Maybe Dumbo's family was dead or missing – she didn't know and had no way of knowing. She was now his master and she intended to stay that way. She knew that if she gave Dumbo up to any authority, under the circumstances, he could be euthanized within days.

In less than a week, she had fallen head over heals for this guy. But admitting a little shadow of doubt, while curling her lips into a smile, she thought – taking on this mutt will be a big responsibility and cause a doubling of my dog food budget, once I get back to Baton Rouge.

Doubt quickly cast aside, she rationalized that love was more important than money. While hugging Dumbo around his neck, she thought - what's one more? Ol' Sammy needs a bud! Little did Melanie realize at the time, she would not return to Baton Rouge for many weeks that would turn into months. Her folks could handle her dog, Sammy, while she was gone. In the meantime, she had Dumbo; and she intended to keep him so that she could stay happy and sane.

CHAPTER 10 - THE MATCHLESS BOYS

DATE: 10:15 am - Tuesday, February 22, 2005 (Pre-Katrina 6 months)
LOCATION: Warburg, Kentucky; Office of Jimmy Olson, president of Matchless Enterprises, Inc.

—   —   —

"Hey, Eddie!" said Jimmy Olson to his older brother; "Look - procurement just sent me this purchase order from Frank Osborne, FEMA director down in Louisiana, for 800 trailer units; they want them custom built according to the Rockport configuration – about 32 feet by 8; they want delivery no later than June 1. Are we set up for this? I need to call Zane and see if we need to change anything on the line. We should have plenty of time and this is a great shot in the arm during winter."

At age 45, Jimmy Olson and his older brother Eddie, four years his senior, were running the biggest show in the county and almost in the state. Their modular home and RV trailer company, Matchless Enterprises, was now employing 264 Kentuckians – proudly putting a turkey on every Thanksgiving plate and a ham in every Christmas stocking, not to mention free passes to the Holiday Drive Inn, over in Valley View. Matchless didn't do a lot more than that for their employees, except provide steady work, at least during the summers. They were non-union and also weren't known for paying the best of wages. Ever since their Dad died five years ago, leaving them the business, Jimmy and Eddie were as uncomfortably tight as over-shrunken Levis. The problem was their privates got in each other's way, and it hurt most of the time.

The brothers fought constantly, usually in one direction - Eddie verbally beat on Jimmy; sometimes non-stop. But other times, when Eddie sensed that he had demoralized his brother enough, he slowed down or even let up, just long enough to allow Jimmy to come up for air, so he could start beating on him again.

Now, one must understand the situation - Jimmy fought back, according to his own rules. He whined a lot. Using this unbearable weapon, his brother often relented, just to get him to shut up. In this and some other equally obnoxious ways, Jimmy often held his own, much to his brother's displeasure. On many occasions, Jimmy fought his brother because he sensed Eddie's lack of business morals and did what he could to counter his behavior, sometimes just to set the record straight or to right some wrong, especially when it came to the treatment of their employees. What Jimmy underestimated was that as far as Eddie was concerned, a lack of business morals was simply a superficial sign of the absence of morals altogether.

"Jimmy," answered Eddie, "I've already spoken with Zane and he said we have made the cut to be included in the ACPDP Program [Advanced Crisis Planning for Displaced Persons] that Homeland Security has finally funded. It looks like they will release over $300,000,000 and we will be part of the gravy train with six or seven other RV manufacturers."

"Nice of you to tell me about the order, Eddie! – What? – Were you going to surprise me? I'm the president of this company and you're the vice-president; you gotta keep me informed!" belted Jimmy.

"I wasn't going to tell you anything, Jimmy, before I knew it was a certainty." I don't give a shit if you are the president – you are the president because I agreed to it – not because you earned it. Daddy told me to keep an eye on you, and I do so because I have to and because you are my kid brother. I toil with you on my back, in my ear, in my face and up my ass, because you are blood and for no other reason – Actually, I don't even like you, Mr. President."

Deflated, as usual, by Eddie's "kind" words, Jimmy hoarsely responded, "Look, Eddie; what are we going to do? We need to manufacture and deliver 800 Rockport units by June 1. It is now February

22. We run two shifts with 120 workers on day shift and a 100 on swing shift, producing 30 trailers per week, along with our other RV products. We have about three months or 12 weeks to complete the order and need at least a week to reconfigure Line 1. Leaving 11 weeks, we can only produce 330 trailers by June 1, much less deliver them on time.

We could activate Line 2 and could double our output, if we had the manpower," calculated Jimmy.

"Jimmy, you are mathematically gifted; but otherwise a financial dumb shit," sighed Eddie – "We can meet the deadline by adding a third shift – bringing on about 110 more people as part-timers. That would increase our production by 50% - getting us up to about 500 trailers in 11 weeks.

If we speed up the line by 15% and get these lazy ass workers finally earning their wages, we could hit almost 600 trailers by June 1. That'll keep FEMA and Osborne happy – you let me worry about the other 200 trailers we will still owe them."

"We tried speeding up the line before," Jimmy, nearly cried; – "It didn't work well. Remember that FEMA order, post 9/11 in early 2002? We ended up with trailers with some big-time problems – some that we had to deal with under warranty at great expense. Zane had warned us about this. We have to allow the QC [quality control] team time to check structure, road-ability, roof, electrical, plumbing and bake-out.

I am especially worried about the bake-out. If we don't heat up those trailers before delivery, all of those damned fumes coming out of the plywood glues will smell up the interior when we deliver them. I don't want to deal with those stinking activists who think the fumes are harmful. Hell, I told Zane they smell kinda good, just like a new car."

Eddie found himself drifting off after Jimmy's last remark. He mused, looking at his brother like he was a circus freak, while Jimmy was blabbing away. What came out of that mouth never ceased to amaze. Jimmy was obese, out of shape and ugly. Eddie worried there might be some family resemblance. He could stand the uglies in his brother, what with the thick glasses, saucer black eyes and billiard ball smooth head; but he couldn't take the pizza sauce on his tie.

To make matters worse, as it is well known among all social classes in the sweaty Midwest, the need for underarm deodorant in Kentucky is a big deal, anytime of year. Well, Jimmy Olson hadn't found any, at least that he liked. Body odor is a matter of personal preference, but Jimmy's particular sour scent was universally unbearable and made bad business sense, especially when it was cooking for four or five days. In business meetings, especially during the summer months, Eddie had to make sure Jimmy was seated at least two chairs away from anyone who mattered. Eddie was willing to run olfactory interference and take the hit for the sake of the business.

Eddie was no Clark Gable himself. In fact, although he wouldn't admit it, he did look like his brother, absent the pizza sauce and 50 lbs. Eddie was much shorter than Jimmy, and not quite as bald. He combed his black hair, what was left of it, across the crown of his head so that it looked like six thin, black magic marker lines drawn across the top of an incandescent light bulb. He had to use gel to keep the hair streaks in alignment, leaving the rest of his ivory scalp looking like a polished billiard ball, just like his brother's.

Eddie had a "Napoleon complex," or as some call it the "short man syndrome." The label is an unfortunate and mostly unfair, politically incorrect stereotype given to some short people that brand them with expectations of overly-aggressive, obnoxious behavior thought to stem from their insecurity at having to stare up at everyone around them. Eddie fitted the stereotype perfectly. He made certain that his height was never a liability by substituting his insecurity with a domineering, oppressive personality that steamrolled over anybody who got in his way, including his brother.

Eddie was very smart. He had served two years in the army just after Vietnam. He went to school on the GI bill at the University of Kentucky, earning a double major in chemistry and business. As a chemistry major, Eddie knew all about those fumes that Jimmy had referenced - namely, those that would accumulate in Matchless Enterprises, unless they were "baked out" or heated and ventilated prior to delivery to customers.

Yes, Eddie knew all about formaldehyde, that simplest of aldehydes in organic chemistry. Just two hydrogen atoms, each, singly bonded to one carbon atom that, in turn, is doubly bonded to an oxygen atom. Simple as that - but what an irritating and toxic chemical, not to forget its ability to cause cancer.

In fact, Eddie had been exposed to formaldehyde during a sophomore organic chemistry lab in college. Stupidly taking off his safety glasses to read a handout, he had leaned over a heated test tube filled with the stuff, a test tube momentarily pulled out from a vent hood by an equally careless lab partner. The formaldehyde fumes burned his eyes and nose, forcing him to run to an eyewash station and later to the campus medical department. He remembered the nurse's lecture on the dangers of formaldehyde, the same stuff, she warned, the med students had to endure while they dissected pickled bodies.

Both Eddie and Jimmy knew well that the fumes in their trailers were primarily formaldehyde emanating from uncured urea-formaldehyde glues, used in making the plywood cabinets, eating benches, wall paneling and even the trailer insulation. They both knew about this problem since 2002.

Eddie wasn't a health expert; but he understood that the "stinking activists" about whom Jimmy remarked, were credentialed scientists and physicians, who preached that formaldehyde could make you sick at the very least and could kill you at the very most.

Eddie's personal experience confirmed that no one can escape the burning, tearing, and pain of a formaldehyde exposure to the skin, eyes, nose or lungs. His follow-up research after his own exposure revealed that within the general population, there are also those who are more unfortunate than others. Following formaldehyde exposure, these people will not only suffer direct irritant effects on delicate tissues, like anyone else; but they will also have to live with being allergic to the chemical, a substance found in more products than you want to know. If allergic, people can be exposed to extremely small levels, even less than you can smell, and still have many of the same irritant symptoms, typical of acute high exposure.

From the nurse's remarks at the infirmary, Eddie also learned that formaldehyde could cause nasal cancer if you were exposed long enough at high enough doses. Or maybe even lung cancer, according to some experts. This part of the nurse's lecture was blurred by his sophomorically raging hormones and the smell of the nurse's perfume. The final blow came later, when he learned there may have been traces of formaldehyde in that ethereal aroma, as she scooted close and stuck a speculum up his nose to check for any formaldehyde burns.

After the last recollection, Eddie stopped his musing and rebounded to the drone of Jimmy's five minute, uninterrupted monologue.

"Don't you remember that big order in '01 after 9/11?" Jimmy remarked. "We had some supply parts issues; especially that "one-of-kind" shower head, the heavy duty, winter proof power cord and the birch plywood that everybody liked so much. It's part of the Rockport configuration specs."

"Jimmy, quit worrying, I told you!" responded Eddie, utterly exasperated with his younger brother; but remembering the '02 fiasco quite well. "The only problem may be the shortage of plywood that could cause a delay in our cabinet shipments – especially the birch ones. I'll ask Zane to call the supplier to find out whether there will be any problem getting all of the cabinets and vanities – OK?"

"What about Cooper?" Jimmy continued with genuine apprehension.

"Well, what about good ol' Cyrus Coo-o-oper......our illustrious, subcontractor co-o-o-ordinator over in Osborne's shop at FEMA - the man who's supposed to keep us toeing the line?" responded Eddie in a theatrical, mocking tone, while leaning back in his chair and rolling his eyes to the ceiling. "I have known that nerd for 10 years; I know the brand of whiskey he drinks, his wedding anniversary, his shirt size, his daughter's birthday and where he likes to go fishing down in Tennessee. And by the way, to make sure this all goes smoothly, I'll make certain that Cyrus and his family have a great XMAS, as usual."

Making eye contact again, Eddie patiently continued, "His boss, Frank Osborne, is as honest as Mother Teresa and does take his FEMA job seriously. You know that guy went to Purdue, got his masters in mechanical engineering, and then ends up working for FEMA. He told me once that he likes the security of Uncle Sam's hand on his thigh all day long.

But as far as Coo-o-oper is concerned; hell, he's putty in our hands. He might ask some questions, I feed him, about our line speeds and QC program. Maybe, even his boys will come in to inspect our line before we retool and, again, around two weeks before delivery. That's about all.

Cyrus will tell Osborne anything I say; because his benefits are simply 'Maa-tchless;' get it?" paused Eddie, continuing his theatre and smiling at his idiotic joke. Jimmy didn't move a muscle; probably missing the remark altogether.

Eddie continued, leaning forward and pointing his finger at his brother, "Osborne wants these trailers real bad. We'll make sure he gets 'em on time, regardless. – Ol' Cyrus will make sure Frank gets his performance bonus at year end. I doubt if he suspects a thing."

Jimmy finally responded, wanting to erase all that he just heard, "You know, if we make this delivery on time, we will stay in the pool for more government business later."

"We'll be in the pool, regardless. Don't worry about that. Where do you think ten percent of our marketing budget goes little brother?

Don't forget to get with Zane, sooner rather than later. We are going to have to let the workers know that it's gonna be time, real soon to earn those turkeys and hams. I'll get back to you by Thursday - gotta run," ended Eddie, as he walked out of Jimmy's office leaving the door wide open.

—   —   —

Eddie left Jimmy sitting there, chair leaned back, legs and leather boots on the desk; both worried and exhilarated at the same time.

He fell into an uncomfortable daydream. He didn't like what Eddie had been doing ever since their Dad died. His Dad ran a straight business and had built it from nothing. Outside of giving customers some gift certificates to a local steakhouse at Christmas or a bottle of whiskey on their wedding anniversary, he never did anything as illegal as the literal bribing of a federal contract coordinator, like Cyrus Cooper, at FEMA.

Jimmy felt inferior to his brother. He felt inferior in general. He had barely made it through junior college with an associate's degree in business; not like the real business degree his brother had earned at U of K. He wanted to open a restaurant, any kind; it didn't matter. Then his Dad died. Eddie was the chosen one. But he said he wanted Jimmy's help - even made him president of Matchless Enterprises, in name only. Eddie said that he wanted Jimmy to be the face of the company, so he could run it from behind the curtain - just like the Wizard of Oz, he said.

Jimmy Olson took a lot of joking about his name ever since he was a kid. Sometimes, around town, he saw the morons that razzed him from elementary school right up to high school.

"Hey, Jimmy Olson – cub reporter; where is your buddy Superman?" they laughed.

No one was laughing now, at least to his face. Most of these fools were stuck in meaningless jobs, deep in debt, divorced or living with a broken family.

Although he wasn't really a bad guy, at all, Jimmy was just in over his head. He was a puppet, like Pinocchio, with his brother as Geppetto. He honestly worried that one day his nose was going to start to grow at the wrong time. He hated to lie about anything; but found recently that lying was the rule, not the exception, if he wanted to keep big money rolling in.

Unlike Eddie who had been married twice, was now divorced, without ever having any children, Jimmy had been married 23 years to his childhood sweetheart, Denise. They were still married but lived in separate worlds, only celebrating the vacuum between them, every year at their anniversary. It all melted down after they lost their only child, their daughter Susan, when she was five, 16 years ago.

After the accident, Jimmy stopped taking out boats on any body of water, ever. He knew his wife held him responsible; but still forgave him, according to her Christian beliefs. He thought the bumpy ride crossing the wake of the cabin cruiser would be fun for Susan. He just didn't expect her to get flipped out of their boat, while hitting her head on the side. By the time he stopped and dove in, it was too late. She went down like a rock after her life jacket slipped off. It took the Coast Guard four hours to find her in the murky river bottom.

He had never recovered. Eventually, after his Dad died and his brother took him into the business, he started to find the slightest bit of pleasure coming back into his life. He enjoyed his position and many of those in his employ. Thanks to Eddie the company had been profitable over the past four years. He liked the high five digit salary and the bonuses that came with it. He wanted more of everything to keep Denise happy and to feel like someone important in town, compared to those losers who mocked him as a kid.

Money became a green poultice for his grief. The more the better.

On the other hand, Denise didn't seem to care about such things. Since they lost Susan, she hid in her shell like a turtle, rarely sticking out her head and preventing anyone from coming in. She drank a lot at first; but then, luckily, she returned to the church and a few of her old friends, who kept her from over indulgence. Their intimacy vanished, the day Susan died. "No more kids," she said to protect her vulnerability.

Denise knew nothing of Jimmy and Eddie's business and wanted no part of any of it. Eddie's ex's were long gone; had been paid off and were not about to complicate matters.

As he came to from his daydream, Jimmy reminded himself that he had to call his mom later with the good news, about the FEMA trailer contract. He figured Eddie may have told her anyway. He looked at his watch. It was nearly 5.

"Oh shit," he croaked as he came back to earth, "I need to call Zane to see how we can get started on the line reconfiguration."

—   —   —

About 30 minutes later, on overtime, Zane made it to Jimmy's office. Just when Zane arrived, Jimmy exclaimed, "Hey, look; let's go down to your office in the plant. We've got a lot to talk about." Zane nodded and walked next to his boss through the hall on the way to the major production area. He watched Jimmy as they walked, without saying a word.

Jimmy and Eddie's lead foreman was a tall man, with a trim, muscular build and a perpetual smile on his face - really. It was uncanny; the guy was always smiling; it was infectious. When workers argued and Zane showed up, they saw that smile and stopped the bickering. One guy said that Zane had some secret "fairy dust" that he sprinkled on people to make them stop fighting, just like the Ghost of Christmas Present did in <u>A Christmas Carol</u>, in the 1930's black and white movie version of the Charles Dickens book.

Zane sincerely appreciated the workers he supervised at Matchless Enterprises and the feelings were mutual. He was more than a foreman. He was a one man HR department. He heard grievances all day long, ranging from belly aching about the temperature of the water in the water coolers to inadequate time off for maternity leave. He was the filter between non-union line workers, the rank and file, and management, namely Jimmy and Eddie. He kept the peace and after the old man died, was rarely and barely appreciated, never by Eddie and rarely by Jimmy. He barely knew Jimmy's Denise; but sensed she knew that without him, Matchless would be history.

Zane Adamson had been very close with Monty Olson, Jimmy and Eddie's old man. Monty had hired Zane when he spotted him loading freight cars at Montgomery Station in '84, when he was only 25 years old. Monty, thinly grayed, even then, went up to Zane and asked him his name, rank, and serial number, so to speak. He had never seen such a strong, unceasingly tireless worker. Zane had been working construction and been laid off – so to the railroad he went to keep bread on the table.

Monty hired him on the spot and doubled his wages to $10.00/ hour with Christmas, Thanksgiving, Fourth of July and Labor Day off. No sick leave or other vacation, yet. Some of that would come - 15 years later. Who could complain? Ol' Monty Olson offered Zane more than he did any of the other 10 people working for him out of his barn and garage, rebuilding engines for cars and motorcycles.

Olson told Zane he needed a man with construction and carpentry experience to head up a crew of three to go to the southern outskirts of Warburg, the "other side of the tracks" trailer parks, to perform repairs for the two park owners. Both had complained to Monty that their trailer trash renters kept wrecking everything from wooden steps and bedroom walls to roof penetrations and screen doors when they tried to hang their Christmas decorations.

Zane turned out to be perfect for the job. His repairs were almost flawless. He was on time, never complained and was a natural leader of men. He grew with the company and became an indispensable arrow in Monty's quiver. Over the next few years, Monty's business expanded and by the mid-90's, he was manufacturing RVs and travel trailers from stem to stern, with Zane holding down the front lines.

Zane was a very kind and honest man. He never married and was a confirmed bachelor. By the time he was 46, in 2005, he got stares and smirks; those close to him knew he was straight as an arrow – just couldn't get close to women, emotionally or otherwise. With his mother gone, the one exception was his lifelong sibling love for his unmarried twin sister, Posie, over in Ashland. Zane and Posie were twins, alright, not in looks, but in just about every aspect of their charming personalities. Posie and Zane saw each other about once or twice a month. They shared a deep enduring bond, one that led to mutual trust in all matters. Each was the other's confidant and friend. Their close relationship was to prove pivotal when it came to matters Matchless.

Now, 21 years after Monty spotted Zane in that railroad yard and five years since Monty's death in '00, Zane was still "workin' for the boys." The facts were simple; Zane felt sorry for Jimmy most of the time, liked him some of the time and even respected him on occasion. He disliked Eddie most of the time, hated him some of the time and respected him none of the time, with a footnote that he feared Eddie more often than he cared to admit.

So here walked Zane, with the son of his deceased friend and employer, in tow, technically on overtime for which he never expected to be paid. His career-long call to honor, duty and Monty kept him around as the lead production foreman. It certainly wasn't his salary and benefits.

In February of 2005, Zane ran the first shift at Matchless, about 120 workers divided up into twelve assembly stations and eight critical QC (Quality Control) inspection points. They built the best looking trailers on the market, among the most expensive; but by no means the most reliably put together. In addition to the problem of getting the right parts at the right time, Zane had recently complained to Matchless' director of procurement (his damned buyer, for short) that a lot of the imported materials were poorly made and designed. From faucets that leaked, electrical outlets that failed to tires that cracked, he had seen it all. Maybe they lived that way overseas; but not here in the good ol USA. At least the carpeting, wall paint, roofing materials, plastic coated, pressed board wall panels and prefabricated cabinets were all made in America.

In the late 90's, Zane had pushed successfully for Matchless to begin buying plywood and pressed board products in the USA. With the use of urea-formaldehyde glues to prevent delamination, these products were more water resistant, especially next to the kitchen sink and in the bathroom, where humidity was a chronic problem. Back then, Zane had also pushed his buyer to purchase exterior plywood for internal use because there was even more of this formaldehyde based, water-proof glue used in the manufacturing of the exterior product. Zane reasoned – the more water proof the plywood, the less rotting and thank, God, fewer annoying and costly warranty claims. Formaldehyde be damned. Open the stinking windows.

This heavy reliance upon water-proof glues in cabinets, plywood and wall paneling caused the "chickens to come home to roost" after Matchless rushed to meet that windfall order from FEMA for several hundred trailers post 9/11, in 2002. The trailers were supposed to be built for standby use, not for immediate occupancy. To meet delivery schedules, Matchless relied upon fresh exterior plywood, containing incompletely cured glues, for cabinets, floors and walls. They did not observe the "baking out" or heating process, along with ventilation, needed to remove the formaldehyde vapors from the trailer's interior. Matchless was burned then; their call back on those trailers was over 30%, especially after FEMA inspectors detected levels of formaldehyde in sealed trailers over 100 times the government health limit. Lucky for Matchless, nobody sued. Lucky indeed because they were all warned by FEMA that had they delivered those trailers for immediate occupancy, they could have expected asthma in children and heart attacks, especially in older men, directly attributable to excessive formaldehyde levels.

After that disaster, Zane became a changed man. Now, he decided to do the right thing when it came to both his workers and Matchless customers. Too bad he sensed certainly Eddie and maybe even Jimmy cared as much about FEMA's warnings, as Madonna cared about showing her cleavage in public. Zane worried not only about the customers; but also about the workers under his supervision, the ones who had to handle the poisonous plywood and fabricate it to build those top of the line Matchless trailers.

He remembered more about the post 9/11 debacle in '02. Those damned fumes caused several Matchless assembly line workers to file worker compensation claims, related to formaldehyde overexposure. And Matchless paid dearly with a 50% hike in their insurance premiums.

So in 2005, everyone in management and Zane, on the assembly line, knew about these problems. Nobody wanted it to happen again. They planned to take their time on the February order; to toe the line and deliver functional, well built trailers to FEMA with the least number of problems by June.

Since '02, they had spent almost half a million to construct a special "bake-out" building to heat plywood, prefabricated cabinets and any other formaldehyde containing material before it went into the trailer. Even after assembly, the new standard operating procedure (SOP) called for the interior of each trailer unit to be heated to about 90 degrees Fahrenheit for at least 24 hours. While baking the unit, they would ventilate the hell out of the interior for as long as it would take until the level of formaldehyde was less than half the minimum federal guidelines. The final test was to take place in the interior of a trailer, sealed for two days. If it passed, then it could be delivered to FEMA.

—   —   —

After their five minute walk, Jimmy Olson, came into Zane's office next to the assembly line near the frame welding operation. The office was brightly lit; but small – only room for two chairs, a desk and a couple of filing cabinets. Zane's lap top was off to one side of his desk. Behind him he had a small table on which he kept a picture of his mother and father together with him as a child – sitting on a pony. He also had a picture of him and his sister, Posie, together, as kids.

"Zane;" began Jimmy, "Eddie said he told you about this FEMA order? He wants to add about 110 workers and ...," "I know; I know," interrupted Zane, "Eddie and I have already discussed the whole thing." "Why am I always the last one to know?" whined Jimmy. "Because....oh, never mind," sighed Zane, "Let's not go into that now."

"Bottom line," exclaimed Zane," We need to get going fast and make certain that we make this deadline. We need this business. I can get all of the parts, and our buyer, Eric, said that we can procure the birch plywood cabinets. They have some of the old inventory left that has been sitting around for months. Lucky us – we won't have as serious a problem with the glue in the plywood this time, compared to '02. But we're still going to bake the hell out of the cabinets and the completed units before delivery. By the way, this will give us a chance to really test out the new 'bake out' building."

"God, I seem to remember that worker compensation mess a

few months after 9/11, especially that damned insurance rate hike," Jimmy remarked staring at the picture on the table behind Zane, "Refresh my memory – give me the details again; exactly what was the issue?"

"The last time we had a rush order like this was in 2002, about five months after 9/11. We had 12 worker comp claims," lamented Zane, scratching his arm, as he remembered the whole thing. He should have been claim number 13, for his skin rash; but he never filed. "10 had some eye, skin and throat irritation. One or two even had some breathing problems. These 10 got better after we finished that rush order. Two of them kept getting worse when they came back to work; and we had to send them home. At first, doc Lucy – your old family doctor said it was probably some chemicals at work – she figured that out only because so many workers showed up to her clinic over the two weeks we were hustling to get it done.

I thought some of them were faking; but even I had some itching on my face and arms when I went into the trailers to help with the final inspection.

It went on for weeks. We had no idea what was really wrong.

Worker comp sent the two sickest to some doc over in Louisville, some guy named Morris Strickland, a specialist in chemical problems. What a 'know-it-all!' We had to send him all of the Material Safety Data Sheets (MSDSs) that listed all the chemicals we used in the plant. He even wanted the MSDSs for the materials used in our prefabricated items like the cabinets, insulation, and appliances.

$3000 later (Boy, I was pissed), I get a report that told me his opinion. He thought the problems were, in his words (that lofty asshole) 'consistent' with exposure to wet, uncured glue in the plywood used in the cabinets. The trailer cabinets are everywhere – in the bedroom, bathroom, kitchen area and even in the sleeping bunks. He also thought we needed to look at the insulation. He didn't pinpoint the exact chemical but said that it could be formaldehyde or something in the urethane, something called MDI. Can you believe it? Three grand and he sits on a fence like a frickin' crow! What a waste;

because a few months later, we get a general bulletin from FEMA, no less, saying that formaldehyde from these glues can cause just the kind of problems we had.

After all this, we had to let two workers go because Doc Strickland said they were allergic, not just irritated – so even a very small amount of re-exposure would cause the problems to come back. I hate to say it – but I think he was right.

He said we probably wouldn't have a problem, if we were shipped some of the old inventory with plywood that had cured.

Remember, until we built our "bake-out" building in '03, we ran heaters and fans in those trailers for two days before we delivered them, even if we had cabinets and other materials made from old stock. Our supplier suggested doing that to heat the glue and drive off all those bad-ass chemicals.

Eddie used to randomly sample new trailers and measure the formaldehyde levels in the interior of units that had been sealed up for about two days. He was in charge of that QC (Quality Control) function. Rarely, he would ask us to bake out an offending unit a bit longer to get the formaldehyde levels into an acceptable range.

He seems to know what he is doing, especially running the controls for that monster sauna. Man, I'd hate to get stuck in there without a respirator. The installer said the formaldehyde would pickle your lungs before you could spell the chemical name, assuming you could in the first place.

OK. So far so good. We have to toe the line on this latest order. Look, Jimmy, back in '02, I had enough problems with our workers crying a river and going out on worker comp. I don't ever want some customer coming back at us after we deliver. I got enough problems with the leaking faucets."

"You know," retorted Jimmy, "Regardless of what you've said, Eddie is not going to go along with any delays, formaldehyde or no formaldehyde. Meeting the deadline is all that he cares about."

"You let me worry about Eddie," said Zane.

Jimmy left Zane's office both delighted and apprehensive; but was upbeat as a proud son, when he called his Mom with the news about the FEMA order. Then he went home to spend a quiet evening with Denise, who knew what the order meant. She had lived through the indigestion of the '02 problems that had disrupted their domestic tranquility. Jimmy said he thought things would be OK this time. They had weeks to deliver materials that were better than those available in '02. Besides, Eddie and Zane would help him make sure that when problems came up, they would all be solved. He told Denise he could expect to make at least another $75,000 take home off the deal. Denise smiled.

Zane called Posie and made arrangements to have lunch with her over the next weekend. Eddie went out with friends to celebrate and brag, like Jimmy did, about the money he was going to make.

—   —   —

Miraculously, Matchless Enterprises delivered all but 100 units to FEMA, on time, by June 1. None of the trailers had formaldehyde issues, because, they went the "full court press" on all the units, even those containing older plywood that had already been cured.

The entire process was uneventful, except as Zane had more or less foretold, one worker had a problem with his respirator in the bake-out building. Under the new SOP (Standard Operating Procedure), workers working in the "bake-out" building while it was in operation were required to use supplied air respirators and full protective clothing. The respirator was a full facemask with eye and head protection. The air to the mask was filtered and came through a hose from an air compressor. The filter in the airline was supposed to stop any contaminants, including oil mist that could come from the compressor. The workers also wore a protective Tyvek ("bunny") suit and special gloves.

It was all supposed to work just fine; but in the case of one unfortunate worker, some oil from the air compressor penetrated the filter and made it into the worker's airline. Five minutes of breathing air contaminated with compressor oil and other crap resulted in a chemical pneumonia, three weeks in the hospital and a quarter million in medical bills. The worker eventually became permanently disabled.

All of this was on Eddie's watch. He knew about the filter problem and could have purchased a new oil-less compressor for a few hundred dollars more than the one that nearly killed his employee - the one he got "used" at some auction.

As far as the other 100 trailers were concerned, Ol' Cyrus Cooper, at FEMA, filed for an authorized extension citing a variety of factors, most of which were untrue. Eddie promised an even bigger kickback in the fall, nothing in writing, of course. All was well that ended well - or so it seemed.

In June 2005, nobody knew Katrina was going to hit in late August and turn the world upside-down for millions of people. Nobody at Matchless knew that within days, tens of millions of dollars were going to be thrown in their direction for trailers needed immediately, not for standby and storage; but for housing real, displaced and demoralized persons. And this time, these people would be living in Matchless RV travel trailers for months, or even years, not for the few days or even a couple of weeks on a camping excursion, for which they were designed. These travel trailers were never meant for long term stationary use, as semi-permanent dwellings, put up on cinder blocks in the sweltering Louisiana heat. But, so what. When money like this came into play, all bets would be off. The illumination of lessons learned in 2002, applied successfully in June of 2005 would be extinguished like a match in a hurricane in September of 2005 when FEMA came calling again.

CHAPTER 11 - DR. PAT

DATE: 3 pm – Tuesday, July 25, 2006
(Post Katrina - 10 months)
LOCATION: Orleans, parish water bldg, near Cheval St.
off Pomme Drive – New Orleans – temporary medical
office of pediatrician, Dr. Patricia M. Simms (Dr. Pat)

—   —   —

It was later on the same day as Sethie's horrible dream, more like a nightmare, and Sethie worried more than ever about her son, Simon.

Placing her right hand lightly on her bowed forehead and releasing a wistful sigh, 55 year old, Dr. Patricia M. Simms tried to grasp the magnitude of the misery in the next room. Even accustomed to the uncertainties and challenges of an inner city New Orleans pediatric practice, she never planned for THIS.

Great granddaughter of a Houma Indian squaw and a former plantation slave, Dr. Simms had been the wild success story among her peers in every parish from New Orleans to Baton Rouge since 1980. No affirmative action here. She graduated third in her class at New Orleans' Benjamin Franklin High School in 1968, only 11 years after its founding and eight after its desegregation. "Ben Franklin" was created as a high school for gifted children and Patty was, indeed, gifted. Honor student in pre-med at Alabama A&M in Huntsville, graduating in 1972, Patty earned a full-ride scholarship to Emory University School of Medicine in Atlanta. After graduating medical school in 1976, she interned and did her pediatric residency at Washington University Hospitals in St. Louis. Missing the real humidity of New Orleans, she returned to hang her shingle eight blocks from where she was born near Interstate 10 in Orleans Parish. Just two weeks after her 55th birthday and five months before Katrina hit hardest on August 29, 2005, Patty was elected president of the Louisiana Medical Society.

"Dr. Pa-a-a-t, Dr. Pa-a-a-t, is you alright in there?" loudly whispered Maggie Parsons, carefully trying to project her voice through the doorway into the doctor's office/exam room and away from the 24 people sitting in front of her.

Many physicians, including Dr. Pat, lost their patients' medical records in the flood following Katrina. They also lost their offices and had to set up shop anywhere they could. Some were able to use relatively dry and undamaged public buildings or share an office with more fortunate colleagues. Dr. Pat had set up her office, ironically, in a nearby Parish water building that had been spared flooding during the storm.

It was already 3 PM and Dr. Pat had seen 45 patients without a break for lunch and only 15 minutes off to use the patient bathroom, down the hall. Even 11 months after Katrina, medical recordkeeping remained reverted to the old 3 by 5 card method, since more expensive charting materials were still unavailable. It really didn't matter; there was no time to write elaborate notes anyway. With 24 patients to go at about 10 minutes per patient, Dr. Pat and nurse Parsons would be having their respective dinners at about 8:30 pm that night.

Still loudly whispering, Maggie continued, "Oh, by the way, we have a walk-in too; do you remember little Simon Williams, the kid with asthma, you used to see? His mom is pretty upset; they're one of the trailer families; says his asthma is really flarin' up; wheezin' all the time; even snores at night like his dad; won't eat much and has lost some weight, over six pounds since April; Been to the ER twice. Can we work him in?"

"Who did you say it was, Maggie? Simon who?"

"I said Simon Williams! He's 10 now. I remember him from our old office. I don't think we've seen him for over two years. Like the others, all of his records are either gone or in soaking wet boxes in your garage, doc."

"Do you remember his meds, allergies and history? – it's frankly a bit of a blur at the moment; Oh, the heck with it, I'm sure his mom will know his vitals; yes, work him in after the Newsome kid, in about 30 minutes."

"OK, Dr. Pat."

—   —   —

A worrisome case of chronic diarrhea, a cat bite and two ear infections later, Simon and Sethie walked into Dr. Pat's makeshift office at the parish water office building; the only reasonably dry and mold free place within half a mile from Dr. Pat's old office. It was a dreary place though – walls were battleship gray, adorned with some children's posters; old charcoal linoleum tile on the floor and the brightest damned fluorescent flickering lights in every hallway. It was the kind of place where even in the best of times the water fountain water tasted like warm aluminum foil.

"Dr. Pat, I'm Sethie Williams an' this is my son, Simon whose you saw about two or three years ago. His asthma is real bad. In the last two months I's had to take 'm to the Emergency two times. Seems he starts wheezing and jist can't get his air right. Last time his lips turned blue and I's thought he might not make it. You should see it. I's scared, Dr. Pat that it might happen agin. He still got some of the inhaler left yous gave him; but none of those pills you prescribed. The ER nurse gave us some more medicine too. About a month an' a half ago, I run over to Wal-Mart and got some more asthma pills to replace yurs. He hasn't been need 'em until he got worse about'n middle of May. I only used a few until he got really worse in mid – June; that's when we's started up on the inhaler again and had to go to Emergency the first time. And we's also needed the ER just last week. I remembered to shake the inhaler before he uses it; jist like you said, Dr. Pat. I's also got some papers from the last ER visit they gave me before we left. They's said to bring 'em to Simon's baby doctor. So here they are."

Apologetically, Sethie continued, "Ida brought him sooner; but I couldn't find you. My friend, Nisha told me that yous set up here in the water building, since your office wuz lost. I didn't want to go nowhere else; but to see you. I hope you remember him, Dr. Pat."

Dr. Pat replied, "Of course, I remember Simon; not too may of my patients are so cute and none other is named Simon; doesn't he have an older brother too?"

Very pleased, Sethie responded, "That's right, Dr. Pat, you're thinkin' of Junior!"

Back to business, but still smiling, Dr. Pat said, "Here, bring him closer."

Looking up and forgetting herself for a moment, Dr. Pat bellowed, "Maggie! – does Simon have a fever and how much does he weigh?"

Like her boss, under their professionally impoverished circumstances and without much concern for HIPPA patient confidentiality guidelines, nurse parsons yelled for all to hear, "99.2 and 74 pounds, the warm, skinny thing!"

Dr. Pat lamented, "Thanks, Maggie – now that you've got me sued by sharing, please tell those waiting that I may need a little more time; I'm only running 45 minutes behind at the moment." She took a minute to glance at the Emergency Room intake and discharge report that Sethie had given her. Her smile disappeared.

Sethie, does Simon have any allergies, say to medicines or does he have hay fever or problems with specific foods? I seem to remember that he had asthma at a very young age."

"Yeah, it wuz really tuff when he wuz a baby. Dr. Pat, we do have or oops had uh dog; his name wuz Rambo; my husband's crazy idea. We lost'em in the flood. No, Simon eats everything, when he eats; but he ain't eatin' very much lately, especially since his asthma been worse. He's even coughed so bad at few times, he's vomited his dinner, what little there wuz. When he duz eat, he jist eats the same diet as usual."

"Did you bring his inhaler?"

"Yes, here it's in my purse; and I brung the Walmart pills too."

Grabbing her bifocals and even squinting a bit, Dr. Pat read aloud, "Albuterol inhaler and Bronkaid caplets –are they helping?"

"Yes, doctor; but he's still sufferin'. We got flooded out an' barely made it. We went up to Baton Rouge an' even to Reggie's cuzins in Little Rock for a spell in the fall. My Momma came with us cuz we wuz at her house when it all hit. We got stuck up on Momma's roof for three days before we's picked up by boat. Two days before Katina, my Pappy was took to the hospital, Morton General. He had sugar problem. Dr. Pat, he died there when the storm hit. We don't know why and no one ever told us. Momma stayed; but we came back to see how the FEMA people were gonna fix Momma and Pappy's house.

At night, we all sleep in that new trailer that the FEMA folk give us in May. It's parked on the driveway at Momma and Pappy's house. An' it's cramped with me, Reggie, Sr., Reggie, Jr. and Simon; we jist got a curtain between where me and Reggie sleeps an' the kids' beds in the big room with the kitchen. Reggie, Jr. prafurs the couch. Simon keeps us up most nights recently."

Noticing Simon's wincing at her last remark, Sethie added, "But we's worried 'bout him an' love him so."

Dr. Pat had a double take when Sethie told her about her father's death in the hospital. She knew that Katrina sent medical personnel, including at least two nurses and one doctor fleeing for their lives. Pat had heard the stories, the horror. Not all patients could be moved in the midst of the biblical disaster. She didn't want to go into the painful subject with Sethie at this time by asking more details. But everyone knew that some patients who were critically ill at Morton General were found dead after the storm. 50, in fact. The details of 12 of the deaths were suspicious. One physician and two nurses were actually charged with second degree murder for committing pre-meditated euthanasia, but no one was actually convicted in the matter. The charges were eventually dropped. Proper autopsies were never performed. The syringes full of insulin found in the ward where the deaths occurred told most of the story, at least in the minds of those who should know.

Gently, Dr. Pat smiled, "Come here Simon; let's talk to you; my oh my, despite the long time since I saw you last, I can tell that you have grown. Honey, tell me how you are feeling? Do you hurt anywhere? How is your breathing?"

"I'm alright, Dr. Pat – my Momma's jist worried 'bout me. Sometimes, I can't catch my breath so good an' I miss playin' with Rambo, Dr. Pat. Do you know where he is? He jist swum away one night when we wuz on the roof – that night that Pappy nearly fell off into the water."

"Simon, here, let me examine you, open wide."

Taking her time, Dr. Pat examined Simon's tongue, the inside of his cheeks and the back of his throat. Using her tongue depressor, during the requisite "Ah-h-h-h," she unexpectedly sustained some spittle impact right on her lips from a rather wet cough. Attempting to abolish even the minutest reaction, she, nevertheless, paused, lamenting that her reflexes were getting slow and she should have seen it coming, in the first place.

Undaunted, she next examined Simon's eyes with a penlight and his retina with her ophthalmoscope. Having checked his ears and continuing to cloak any visible reaction in front of Sethie and Simon, she changed the speculum on her otoscope. She looked into Simon's nose, catching some discolored greenish mucous on the speculum tip. She tapped lightly on Simon's facial bones and on his forehead over his sinuses. She next felt Simon's neck for swollen glands, checked his hair and scalp, especially looking for any skin problems. After a moment, she removed his shirt and shorts to better expose his chest and belly. With her stethoscope, she first carefully listened to his lungs and heart.

"Breathe like usual, Simon, just slow and easy. Now take a deep breath, Honey, and blow it out real fast. Let me listen to your back too. Do the same thing, Honey, breathe usual and then real hard and fast. OK, now I'm going to listen to your heart. OK, Simon, just take a real deep breathe and hold it, hold it, real quiet for a few seconds; great; thanks Simon. OK, next I want you to lie back and just stare at the ceiling while I listen to your tummy and just poke around a little bit – Gosh Simon - there's a band playing in there – when's the last time you ate?"

"I ain't too hungry lately, Dr. Pat."

"OK, Sethie, figure out anything to get some calories into this boy. I'd say some ice cream, although it might thicken his secretions some. Even a hamburger and French fries would do at this point.

Now Sethie, I have some more questions. Do any of you smoke in the house, eh, I mean in the trailer or around Simon at any time?"

Sethie responded, "Well, Reggie used to smoke up 'til 'bout three years ago. He quit not only cuz he's worried 'bout whut he herd 'bout the dangers to his health; but also cuz he couldn' affo'd them no more; so none of us smoke an' that goes fo Momma an' Pappy too, when they wuz around."

"You must know, Sethie, that smoking around the kids is not good for their health either."

"Yeah, we herd that too."

"What about cooking food in the trailer? Do you have a vent over the stove?" asked Dr. Pat.

"Yes, we gotta a vent. I's like to cook fish every Friday. Reggie loves his fried fish," said Sethie. "But the oil smoke's sucked out the vent."

"Well, Sethie, we have a problem. Simon has some redness in the whites of his eyes, and in his ears and nose that I think is being caused by some kind of infection or maybe, some allergy. His lungs are very wheezy; but luckily, his heart and belly are OK except his intestines sound empty, as I said a minute ago.

Are you sure that Simon doesn't have any allergies? I seem to remember ragweed. I lost my medical records in the flood and have no earlier documentation.

"I think maybe it wuz ragweed, Dr. Pat."

"Has Reggie been painting around Simon or have you been cleaning the oven when he is in the room?"

"No an' No."

"OK – I don't have any time to ask more questions; we'll have to go into some of these issues further during a future visit, Sethie.

We are going to need to work-up Simon further. I am going to refer him over to Ochsner for some more tests, like lab, a chest x-ray and a breathing test. In the meantime, we're going to give him some amoxicillin and a decongestant. I'll renew his prescription for the Albuterol inhaler that will open up his lungs when he starts wheezing. Have him use his inhaler, one puff, three to four times a day as needed, making sure he uses it once before bedtime and before he goes out to play. I may also perform some special blood tests later to check for allergies and may have him see a kid's allergy doctor.

Oh, in addition, make sure that stove vent works and is on when you cook, especially oily frying. Then you should also run a humidifier next to Simon's bed when he sleeps. I realize that it is already real humid; but if you use distilled water, the cool mist will help his breathing. I'll give you a prescription; take it to Walgreens and ask for Tisha; she'll honor it and give you a good one. You'll have to buy the distilled water yourself.

Finally - are you sure you don't have a cat or something – what about Rambo – did he every cause Simon to have problems?"

"No that boy slept with Rambo every night, since he was a pup an' never wheezed a bit. God, how he misses him. Really, we never saw'em drown, just never saw'em after he fell off'n the roof at night. It wuz terrible, Dr. Pat. When we's all stuck on Momma an' Pappy's roof the second day, we herd sum gunshots 'bout six houses away. We couldn't see too good; but it looked like some kid or his dad wuz takin' shots at some small critter swimmin' by their place. Maybe been uh dog or cat or maybe even uh gator; all sorts of animals wuz out there. I saw Simon hug Rambo harder than ever an' then the next morning, just hours befo' our rescue, poor Rambo wuz gone."

Simon interrupted, "Dr. Pat; what kin I do to find Rambo? I's miss him so. Itsa bin so long, I don't think I's ever goin' to see him agin. Have you ever seen Rambo - here wait, I's got a picture of him, I kin show you."

Simon reached into his pocket and pulled out a crumpled but clear picture of a black and gray mixed breed - probably with some of Blue Healer mixed in - but with the biggest, floppiest ears, ones that didn't fit his head very well. More remarkable, was an astonishing marking on his head and snout - a pure white diamond that stood out against that dark fur.

Dr. Pat commented, "Simon, what a beautiful dog. I can see why you love him so much. You know, there are still some dogs missing that are being brought back to their owners." Maybe he will still show up.

Leaning forward with tears in his eyes, Simon pleaded, "Here, Dr. Pat; please take this picture of Rambo to keep, just in case you sees him. I gotta another one. I's like you to have it."

With polite refusal on her lips, Dr. Pat hesitated, looked at Simon's tears and said, "Honey, I will keep it just in case I see a dog that looks like Rambo. Thank you very much." She slipped the photo under a paper clip on Simon's chart and set it on the exam table.

Sethie leaned to one side and placed her hand to her mouth to block her voice from Simon's ears. Remembering the gunfire she heard the night Rambo disappeared, Sethie whispered, "Dr. Pat, I hope that Rambo dun drowned instead of getting' shot like that. Those neighbor boys is cruel an' no good. It wuz lucky, it weren't uh man in those waters, by God!"

Her eyes a bit glazed at the thought, Dr. Pat said, "Don't forget the inhaler, the medicine and the humidifier Sethie; now I need to tell you something important. If Simon doesn't respond to medication after an hour or so, I want you to take him to the ER right away or call me. Based on this note from the emergency room doctor during your last visit, Simon appears to be at risk for an asthma attack that won't stop until you go to the hospital and get treated. I don't want to scare you, but Simon could become really sick without treatment and could end up in the hospital. Or Sethie, even worse."

She tried to make Sethie understand the potential gravity of the situation; but didn't want to frighten Simon.

"Dr. Pat, Whadda mean 'or worse?'" said Sethie, now with a terrified look on her face, turning away from Simon to cloak her emotion.

"Sethie, please...., said Pat, moving her eyes toward Simon, who appeared distracted by the poster of Sesame Street characters on the wall and oblivious to everything else. "I mean that you could lose your son, it you don't act quickly when his medicines haven't worked. You have to be the judge. No one else. I think, in most cases, unless he is very sick, I'd give the medicines about an hour or so. You can call me and we can talk about in more detail over the phone, How's that?"

"OK, Dr. Pat," said Sethie, looking at her son while she was struggling to talk, "I's got the picture, I think."

"Thanks, Sethie. Simon, it was good to see you again, son," completed Dr. Pat, "I'll see you and Simon in two weeks."

After Simon and Sethie left, Dr. Pat took another look at the ER record Sethie had given her. Discharge diagnosis - "At risk for Unstoppable Asthma (Status Asthmaticus)," simple as that....or not so. Pat knew what that meant. She had seen it before, in the ER and even in her office.

Intractable, unstoppable, persistent asthma unresponsive to inhalers and pills. Without effective treatment and sometimes even with it, status asthmaticus or unstoppable asthma, squeezes the life out of you. You wheeze and you wheeze and you wheeze some more. You become exhausted as you fight for air. You can't breathe in very well – but worse you can't breathe out. The carbon dioxide builds up in your blood, making you feel the excruciating pain of suffocation.

Your blood lacks oxygen. The low oxygen affects your heart and brain. Your heart may begin to beat ineffectively and irregularly. You can't think. You then lose consciousness, screaming for air, like you were stuck underwater.....just before you die.

The good news was that Simon never got to that point; but it was close. Sethie and Reggie managed to get Simon to the hospital in time, where they were able to give him intravenous medication and other supportive therapy. But the doctors understood how close he had come and warned Sethie and Reggie about their son's risk of a terrible death.

Big problem - nobody had a clue about what could have caused Simon to become so sick prior to his two ER visits. It could have been a lot of things. Patients often never know what triggers those disastrous events. Anything from stress, dust and foods to molds, colds and .....

and a hell of a lot more. Sometimes they die without knowing. Pat knew that allergy testing was critical for Simon, and needed to get him over to Ochsner Clinic to see an allergy specialist as soon as possible.

She also knew she would call Sethie again early tomorrow and make certain she understood how deadly those two words "Unstoppable Asthma" could be for her son.

CHAPTER 12 -
THE TRAILER

DATE: 5:15 pm – Tuesday, July 25, 2006
(Post Katrina – 10 months)
LOCATION: - New Orleans, Louisiana – Simon's
FEMA (Matchless) trailer parked in the drive-
way of Pappy and Momma Green's house
at Margot and Uclair Streets.

—   —   —

Sethie had returned with Simon from Dr. Pat's office around 5:00 PM and went inside the trailer to cook up some hotdogs, canned corn and green beans for her family. Dessert – some marshmallow chocolate cookies with milk.

Everyone was home on time. Junior came in early after, hopefully, playing some baseball with a friend. Simon was resting, watching his mother hum a soft tune while she mixed the vegetables in a pot on the propane stove. The steam was accumulating above the broken vent hood, so she opened the screen door and the window. Reggie was in the bedroom lying down with a magazine folded over his face, all ears, waiting for the dinner call. There was a conspicuous silence - no panting, no whining, no barking – all added up to - no dog – what everyone missed most was the sound of Rambo's tail hitting the edge of the couch, like a drummer's wire brushes tapping a snare drum.

Reggie was still having problems with his foreman at DYMOS. Miserable old man, Fletcher, had him and most of the others on the day shift over a barrel. Jobs were scarce and bodies abounded. He could treat them about anyway he wanted; EEOC, OSHA-Schmo-sha – Fletcher could care less. You file a worker comp claim – you's to blame – you walk, as simple as that.

Barely over 60 and looking over 80, Fletcher drank a quart of Jack Daniels, every weekend. The man was a physical wreck. He was mean, especially in the morning when he was "fighting the urge" – the one that would have to wait until he sent his servants to the docks to get them trucks loaded up and movin' out. The general manager knew about Fletcher's fancy for spirited beverages and so did everyone else – Reggie suspected that Fletcher possessed some secrets about DYMOS that made him tolerated and even indispensable.

This week Reggie was on Fletcher's radar, and he brought his frustration home with him.

The family sat around the tiny eat-in, breakfast booth, and Sethie sat on the couch a few feet away. Everyone picked at their food. Sethie cautiously remarked, "Ya know, Reg, we's got sum problems – the UPIC or FEMA, I don't know which folks is coming around tonight to fix them problems we's bin havin'. They should be here any minute, now."

"Do we's got to talk 'bout dat now, Sethie? I's tired and hot and I's not had da time to fix nuthin', Reggie exclaimed in an almost soprano tone. He could see the hurt in Sethie's face who was just trying to keep their ship afloat. In a lower and more compassionate tone he continued, "I's sorry Seth. I's just had such a bad day. Fletcher's on my case, again, frum da minute, I arrives to the minute he let's me loose. Are ya talkin' 'bout dat vent "bove the stove, Seth? Cuz, I's think da motor's dun broke. UP...whut ever they's called; they need to git us a new wun."

"Yes and what 'bout, the toilet 'n drains ever'where. They's still backed up. Take furever to go down," Sethie complained. "And daz no water pressure, most'a time."

"OK, OK, if'n they's cumin' soon, I'll show 'em evern' thing," replied Reggie, looking over at Reggie, Jr. who was watching and listening intently to his parents talk. "Is there sumthin' else, Sethie?"

"You 'no there is, Reggie," responded Sethie with her upper lip actually quivering and her eyes glistening over. "We still git that awful smell, when we git home and 'da trailer's bin locked up. We git it, even with 'da air condition' on. I need to mention it to Dr. Pat."

"Ya'no," Sethie, "we's not 'da only ones with this problem; but I betcha they'll tell us not to worry none, jist like they did last time." Two 'em boys over'n work have 'dat smell in thir trailers too; sometimes caus'in problems. It strong; they say cuz it new; jist open da windas and it be OK. I's mention it tah UPIC when they git here."

Reggie was very handy; but had almost no tools. They had all been lost when the floods wrecked his and Sethie's real home - located about a mile away from where their trailer was now parked on Momma and Pappy's driveway. The boys loved their grandparents' home. The memories of Christmas, the 4th and Labor Day were priceless. Pappy and Reggie had taken on all sorts of fix-up projects before Katrina wrecked everything. The boys pitched in, even Junior, mowing the lawn, building shelves in the garage, fixing doors – you name it. Now Reggie found himself living in this shoebox with barely a screwdriver, pliers and hammer. He felt guilty about not being able to do many repairs around the trailer and Sethie was, frankly, pretty good about the whole thing. Besides the UPIC installers were supposed to keep things running well, if you could ever get on their schedule and if they ever fixed it right the first time.

Reggie had already known that UPIC was coming, because he overheard Sethie making the appointment, or should one say, appointments, all four of them. After three postponements, maybe they were going to show up tonight with a smile on their face and a hammer in their hand – or maybe neither, just another cancelation.

— — —

Under a FEMA subcontract, UPIC had seen to the installation of Sethie and Reggie's Matchless Rockport trailer on Friday, May 19, 2006. UPIC was a very big corporation, and it had a sweetheart deal to oversee the installation and maintenance of thousands of trailers that had been procured by FEMA in response to Katrina. Because of the incredible demand, UPIC actually used a lawn maintenance company, Ground Swell, to help place the trailer on the driveway pad, next to Momma and Pappy Green's house.

Sethie and Reggie's own home was damaged beyond repair. What with Pappy gone now and Momma's being up in Arkansas, somebody had to look after her parent's home while it was being refurbished. Work on the house was very slow and frustrating. Just because they had available workers, Ground Swell was also hired to completely clean out and gut the house to get it ready for remodeling. There was no other way – the flood waters had destroyed all of the floor coverings, sheet rock walls and ceilings. Only the wall studs and ceiling joists were slowly drying out. Mold was everywhere and that means everywhere.

When the men from Ground Swell arrived that day in May less than two months ago, they had placed the trailer on concrete blocks to level it and left the tires on. In the mad rush just after Katrina, this Matador model had been manufactured by Matchless to FEMA's specifications, just for this application, namely housing displaced persons for uncertain periods of time. The tires made it look like it was set up for RVing – but this model was meant to stay in one place. It was kind of funny – FEMA decided to install a recreational vehicle for semi-permanent occupation – more or less an ND/RV or a "Nailed-Down Recreational Vehicle" that was hardly recreational.

This ND/RV had no holding tanks for the two kinds of waste water generated by its human occupants. The first - gray water is the stuff that goes down the sinks and showers; and the second, black water (maybe better called brown water) is the other stuff. There was also no fresh water tank to supply clean water to the trailer. This ND/RV also had no generator or storage batteries because it was supposed to be hooked into the grid.

UPIC and its surrogate, Ground Swell already knew the plan – place the trailer on the driveway; level it; then bring in the UPIC plumber and the electrician. The plumber's job was to hook up the trailer to the city sewer system for both gray and black water and to hook up the still functioning water spigot outside Momma's house to the trailer to provide fresh clean water. The water had been tested and was OK for drinking and domestic use. The electrician's job was to connect the trailer to the LP&L (Louisiana Power and Light). Later, and it was a big deal, it was learned that this trailer was not supposed to be used for this type of application. The advertising brochure may have said that it could "sleep seven or eight" (Only God knows how or where) – yeah – maybe for a day or two – but how about 19 months?

Eric Manus, plumber and carpenter tapped on the screen door briskly, startling Reggie who was standing with his back turned away from the door. Behind him stood electrician, Dino Renaldi. Not only one, but both had made it. Sethie told Junior and Simon to go play outside. Both of these men worked for Janet Thomas, who was UPIC's office manger – the lady who reported directly to her FEMA overlord, Frank Osborne, local office director.

After they had wrapped up most of the punch list, they promised to come back within a few days. Dino had to order, as Reggie predicted, a new vent hood. Eric cleared the drains and toilet but concluded there were problems in the clay pipes that led from the house to the main line at the street – maybe roots – a problem for another day.

Sethie offered both men some coffee. But it was getting late and Eric knew that his wife was holding a late dinner for him. After suggesting a rain check, Eric asked, "I think that just about does it for now, Mrs. Williams. Will there be anything else? Do you have any questions?"

Hesitating, trying to decide what to say next, Sethie, began, "Please, call me Sethie. Did my husband talk to you about this bad odor, we's had to put up with since we's moved in? I's not sure whut's causin' it; but it's wurse when the trailer's been shut for a while. The air condition' doesn't really help none. Sometimes, when it's heavy, yur eyes an' throat 'ill burn. Cause of the pollen an' mold outside, I ain't sure where maybe it's makin' my Simon's asthma worse."

"Mrs. Williams, eh, Sethie; I wouldn't worry about it none – this here's a brand new trailer, and it's just like a new car. Think of it like a new car smell (Sethie had never owned a new car and had ridden in one only twice). There's nothing to worry about; I am confident that it's not hurting your son's asthma. You're right, the pollen and molds have been wicked this summer. If the smell bothers you, just open the windows for a while until it becomes less or goes away. You might also try some air fresheners; you know like the kind that you can get at Walmart or the Dollar Store."

Sethie had briefly forgotten Eric's name and awkwardly proceeded, "Well, Suh, that makes me feel a bit better. I's thought that Simon might be wurse frum the smell – but I's guess I's wrong. I's still goin' to talk to Simon's doctor, Dr. Pat an' see whut she thinks."

"Well, good night Sethie," concluded Eric as a he waved Dino over to the door. "And, Sethie, I'll be back in a few days to replace that vent hood and hook it up."

Both men waved goodbye again and passed Reggie out front, quickly explaining to him the work that had been completed and the items that were deferred. To be consistent, Eric mentioned Sethie's concerns about the trailer odor and reassured Reggie with the same "new trailer smell, just open the windows, explanation." Reggie said that he wasn't concerned at all; but would try to keep a couple of windows open when they came home after the trailer had been shut closed all day. Leaving the windows open at night when the AC was running was not an option.

The UPIC men did not leave until 9:30 PM. Sethie did not fall asleep until 3:00 AM – thinking she may be able to outrun another nightmare.

CHAPTER 13 - SIMON - PART I - THE DOCTORS MEET

DATE: 9 pm, Monday 5/18/09 and 9 AM, Tuesday 5/19/09 (Post Katrina 3 years 8 and a half months)
LOCATION: New Orleans, Louisiana, Ritz Hotel

—   —   —

"Damn this is a great room," exclaimed Tristan, out loud, as he looked around. It was already almost 9 pm; and he was sorry he had already eaten dinner.

Tristan thought - The SOB gave me a suite. Look at this refrigerator, packed with all kinds of great stuff. This time I'm going to enjoy myself on Asher's tab. I can't believe I took this case. But, I must admit; I miss it. All of it. The challenge; the science, the medicine and making a difference. And, I can use the money. These people were really shafted and I'm going to find out how, why and to what degree.

Two weeks had elapsed since his discovery and harrowing retrieval from the Wyoming wilderness by Asher and Joseph. His thoughts drifted to Heather and Tess. He had talked to them for over an hour on SKYPE just before he left Laramie. He made certain that they were both OK. The stress of being apart was difficult; but he knew he was a magnet for danger and even disaster. He couldn't take the risk - at least, not yet. His plan for leveling the playing field and making it safe for him to live a normal life with his family was in the works. If he succeeded, it was not going to be pretty for those who hurt him and his loved ones not too long ago.

Tristan checked his cell phone to see if he had a signal. Once he saw two bars, he thought - not bad, for the fifth floor of the Ritz. He gave it a try.

"Joseph, how did it go, this morning?" he asked with some apprehension. "Did they meet you on time and did you see trailer #4268, the one the Williams occupied?"

"Yeah, Tris; they took me out to that 600 acre storage facility in Marion County, Mississippi, out near Purvis. God- there must be over 100,000 trailers there. They had a pretty decent map. It only took us an hour and a half to find the right trailer. Of course, the defense had its videographers filming the whole thing. I wonder if Asher is paying for part of that?

Our industrial hygienist, Stacy Janes was there. We met for breakfast this morning. You know, Tris, she's a certified IH (CIH)- well trained at the University of Texas. While I was making all the physical measurements of the trailer proper, she was sampling the air and grabbed a lot of physical material samples from the trailer itself, like insulation, paneling and cabinet plywood. Defense had its CIH there too. I forgot his name; but I got his card. He and Stacy agreed to split some of the samples so each of us can have our own lab run the tests. Sorry Laura Swain wasn't here. I hear she's brilliant, even if she is a lawyer."

Tristan pondered Joseph's un-Joseph-like succinct and lengthy reply to his question.

"You're right; and by the way, Laura will be here with me tomorrow. I am going to interview Simon and Sethie later in the morning. Today, I had a chance to meet with Dr. Patricia Simms - they call her Dr. Pat - a really great lady. She's Simon's pediatrician; has been for years. The poor doc lost most of her patient medical records in the flooding. She still has about 2000 records molding in her garage and couldn't locate Simon's although she remembers him well. She saw him for asthma problems in July, 2006 and had seen him before the storm, too. She's the doc who has been prescribing Simon's meds and following him like a mother hen."

Tristan paused when he heard silence at the other end. "Hey, Joseph, you there?"

"I'm here, Tristan." responded Joseph, "I'm just fading in and out; intermittent signal. I'm gonna bring the rental car in tonight straight to the hotel. How is it? Do I have to share a bed with you like usual?"

"Oh bullshit, Joseph; yeah, they booked you a room in the basement. You're not sleeping with me. I can remember too many times in a tent or even under the stars when you gassed or kicked me out," belted Tristan with a smile on his face.

"Shit - you cooked the beans," countered Joseph, "You were too cheap to buy us anything else."

"OK - you're going to love this place. Asher didn't cut corners this time," said Tristan, in a more serious tone. "Just go to the front desk and tell them that you are the guest of Mr. Asher Goldman; who, by the way, now has a small office here in New Orleans. Asher has been making so much money from previous cases; he teamed up with a lawyer named Morris Manheim, his local counsel on the FEMA case.

This arrangement is going to make things easier for all of us. By the way, in case you forgot, the child prodigy attorney who found me in the middle of nowhere in Wyoming is the very same Laura Swain. She's just a kid, only 32. No personal entanglements - just work, work and more work. And she doesn't laugh much. I told her she was too serious. What do you expect from a Yale Law School type?

"What time will you be in?"

"About 2 am, barring hitting any alligators crossing the road," belted Joseph, acting a little giddy already from fatigue. "I'll tell you Tris - I ain't no Seminole; I'm Northern Arapahoe - we never see those critters in the Rockies. Closest thing danger-wise is a puma or maybe a grizzly. At least, I know how to deal with them. I've seen too many movies of those reptiles, eating little kids and stuff."

"God, Joseph, you sound like a nut-case. Just be careful, will you. I need you to get a good night's sleep, because I have volunteered your billable hours to Miss Laura tomorrow to help her with some case organization and heavy lifting of boxes. She could probably work without you; but I can't let you sit idly by all day long. Laura doesn't seem to be the type who would fret over a broken nail. She's a runner and a tennis freak. She told me she grew up in rural Connecticut, where her mom and dad were both family docs. How she ended up a lawyer is beyond me.

Say, if you work hard, you, Laura and I will have some dinner, New Orleans style after I have interviewed Simon and his mom."

"OK, Tristan - I will enrich your bottom line tomorrow. I'll see you in the am. I'll call, if I have any problems," ended Joseph.

—   —   —

Tristan sat down at the desk in his room, opened his brief case and began to review the case file again, especially the medical records given to him by Simon's pediatrician, Dr. Pat. Tristan had visited her earlier in the day in her new office, infinitely better accommodations than the temporary quarters she had had to endure in the parish water building for almost two years after Katrina.

Tristan was surprised when he met her. She was a small, petite, powerhouse of a woman, exuding intellect, warmth and kindness. She was about 60, groomed neatly, with minimal make-up, wearing a dark blue classically styled dress. Below her left collar, resided a small gold pin, crafted to resemble Mickey Mouse. How appropriate thought Tristan, as he complimented her on her taste. He told Dr. Pat how he had tried to "break the ice" with kids when he worked in the emergency room years ago by wearing a bright red tie adorned with Warner Brothers characters, like Bugs Bunny, Elmer Fudd, Daffy Duck, and the Road Runner. His tie was chaos - Dr. Pat's pin was elegant and discreet, even though it was a Disney design. Tristan laughed as he thought about how much he loved Disney characters, especially Donald Duck.

"I remember Simon," began Dr. Pat in a gentle voice with perfect articulation and no accent, even though she was a native of New Orleans. "I still take care of him. He was a somewhat allergic child, as I recall. His mom, Sethie brought him to me on several occasions before the hurricane. The child has persistent asthma and is at risk for the worst, and you know what I mean. Unstoppable Asthma (Status Asthmaticus). It's right there in the emergency room records. I lost his original records in the ensuing flood; or it is possible they are still among those that are unreadable, still stored in my garage. What a mess it was.

As I told you on the phone when we first spoke, I had to store almost three thousand records in soaked cardboard boxes for months after August of '05. We salvaged some; but many fell apart like wet Kleenex.

Tristan, I think what you are doing for Simon and his family is a noble and wonderful thing. Tell me what I need to do."

Tristan replied, "Well, for one thing, Pat, just be yourself. I am so very grateful to have you helping me piece together Simon's case.

At some point, I may request you to write me a short note, indicating your opinion about whether the formaldehyde exposure in Simon's FEMA trailer played any role in his asthmatic decompensation, and his risk for unstoppable asthma. You first saw him after he started living in the trailer; I think it was, on Tuesday, July 25 of '06. I know you saw him several times after that but the July visit was key. He had already been in the trailer since, I recall, May 22, earlier that year. So you saw him about two months after he began his exposure. He had been to the ER twice between the time he entered the trailer and the date you saw him.

When it comes to trial, your opinion about causation, as his treating physician, should be very important. I realize that you are not a specialist in this area of toxicology; but I can provide you with abundant information on formaldehyde for you to review.

Once you have all of the facts in front of you, you will need to make up your own mind as a pediatric specialist. If you don't think you can make the causation link between the FEMA trailer conditions and his worsening asthma, coupled with the increased risk of sudden death from asthma, don't worry about it. Your clinical documentation of his condition and his treatment will be very important. I intend to use that information anyway when I perform my own causation analysis."

Dr. Pat sat back in her chair and looked Tristan straight in the eyes. "This is unbelievable; do you do this for a living?"

Tristan, a bit shocked at the question, wasn't sure how to respond. He didn't know what he was in for - a compliment or a rebuke. "What do you mean? I am a causation specialist. I am a clinical physician but also an environmental engineer - so I look at exposure and diagnosis and then decide if there is a scientifically probable relationship between the two. I'm often the expert who decides who pays the bills."

Dr. Pat interrupted, "I know that Tristan; what I meant was; is this a full time job? Most doctors I know have no knowledge and no time to ponder these questions."

Tristan, feeling more comfortable now, replied, "Yes, at this stage of my career, I do this for a living, as you say, about 95% or the time. I still see patients at my office in Wyoming infrequently, unless I need to examine them as part of one of my cases. Those patients whom I see for specific medical problems, I treat without cost. I became sick of dealing with insurance companies years ago."

Dr. Pat was transfixed. "Tristan; I get the picture. If you do your job well, your conclusions about causation can really benefit patients. You get them compensation for injury; and also help them from being injured further. Just remove the cause of the problem and hopefully, they will get better, even without extensive medical treatment.

I probably have 50 patients who could use your services - but that's for another time."

Tristan and Dr. Pat buckled down and went over Simon's case in excruciating detail. She gave him copies of all his medical records since she had seen him after Katrina, including his ER reports, two before his first visit in July 2006 and four more since then. All told the same story and emphasized the same risks. There weren't tons of records; but what there were, told an important story. Part of that story was what Dr. Pat had tentatively diagnosed as a variant of a post-traumatic stress disorder (PTSD). She indicated it was the collective nightmare experience that caused this problem, on top of the worsening of his asthma and his exposure to formaldehyde. In some ways, the PTSD was worse, far worse than that. The unpredictable nightmares and flashbacks.

Dr. Pat explained that Simon had lost his Uncle Samuel, Sethie's brother, when he was shot by police a few days after the storm hit. She related the entire story of how Samuel was gunned down by New Orleans police officers who were leaving a riot scene, while they were transporting a seriously wounded comrade to meet an ambulance.

Unfortunately, Samuel had just stopped that same ambulance by firing a shot from his deer rifle, in order to obtain help for his wife who had suffered a severely lacerated hand. The timing, circumstances and miscommunications could not have been worse. Samuel stood there rifle in hand when the squad car approached. He laid the gun on the pavement; but it was too late. He didn't stand a chance and never successfully explained himself before he died of multiple gunshot wounds.

Dr. Pat concluded that Simon's uncle's death was only part of the problem. His maternal grandfather, Sethie's Pappy, went missing and was later found dead in a nearby hospital, thought to have been overdosed with insulin. No one was sure whether it was accidental or a deliberate mercy killing.

Next, Dr. Pat described a problem that should not have mattered much compared to the loss of his kin; but paradoxically, it seemed to matter more. Simon's dog, Rambo had disappeared. Dr. Pat couldn't understand the importance of this problem; she admitted she had lost her perspective until she stopped trying to look at the event from an adult's point of view. Once she started to think like a 10 year old child, matters became much clearer.

The loss of a deeply loved and treasured pet would not go away. After almost four years, Simon was still grieving and delusional. He was convinced his Rambo was coming back. He was fragile when it came to this subject. It still caused him to have night terrors. She concluded that the loss of Rambo had become the ground rod for Simon's collective trauma. He would not allow his parents to get him any other pet. Dr. Pat told Tristan she initially thought the problem would burn out. Now she wasn't so sure.

Funny thing, she related to Tristan. At Simon's first visit a few weeks after his family moved into the FEMA trailer, she learned he was pitifully traumatized by the loss of his dog. In fact, he gave her a picture of Rambo, just in case; so she put it in his medical chart. The picture was striking because Rambo had an easily recognizable white diamond, against the black fur on his forehead and muzzle.

Dr. Pat indicated that a few days after the visit, the Louisiana SPCA set up a lost pet center in her building. She posted Rambo's picture on a bulletin board along with her and Sethie's phone numbers. No bites; but strangely enough, the picture and their phone numbers disappeared a few days after they were posted. She could never figure it out. And it had continued to bother her since then.

Tristan didn't minimize the factors underlying Simon's PTSD; but he had to stick to his causation assignment. He had to clinically separate the PTSD matter from the potential physical injury that Simon had sustained while living in the trailer. Tristan realized he needed to refer Simon to the best lung specialists he could find for further evaluation. He had to see if Simon had sustained any long-term injury to his lungs, eyes, nose or throat from his exposure in the trailer.

He knew just where to go - Boston, where he could contact his old colleague, Dr. Lila Gruber, chief of the Environmental Medicine Unit at Coastal General Hospital - the best on the planet, for this kind of work-up. Maybe he thought, Lila could hook Simon up with a good child psychiatrist while he was there.

After looking at Simon's records, Tristan dove into the FEMA, EPA and OSHA literature on the toxicology of formaldehyde, especially articles that dealt with the adverse effects on children. He knew the literature inside and out; he could have written much of it.

He began scribbling notes about Simon, the timing of Katrina events and federal communications on the formaldehyde issue. Oh,

God, he thought, I need to make a timeline, as usual, the first order of business.

Tristan grabbed a yellow lined tablet and began to write what he knew and when. He knew he would expand it as he went along in the case. He was the causation expert, so he had to record as many relevant events as possible, including both environmental exposure and medical issues too. Like a biblical aphorism, every expert knows that timelines are the prerequisite magic in figuring out probable cause and effect relationships.

He began:

8/29/05 - Katrina hits New Orleans

9/05 - 10/05 - FEMA begins to move people into rapidly manufactured trailers, contaminated with formaldehyde. Complaints begin almost at once.

3/1/06 - FEMA issues first warning to ventilate trailers (i.e. open windows and doors), if one has problems with smell and/or irritation of eyes, nose, mouth, skin and lungs. - just a flyer - idiotic suggestion, given heat, humidity and need for AC units. NOT widely distributed - so most people, including occupants do not see this warning.

5/22/06 - Simon Williams and family occupy trailer #4268.

7/25/06 - Simon first sees Dr. Pat for asthma problems. Medical record doesn't reveal cause of worsening asthma. Two intervening ER visits since family moved into trailer. ER record warns of risk of sudden death and unstoppable asthma (status asthmaticus). Trailer not mentioned at this time.

7/1/07 - FEMA issues second warning about trailers - this time formal color glossy brochure is circulated to trailer occupants, many of whom take it to their family doctors. Williams family very

140

concerned - tries to find other living arrangements. Sethie takes brochure to Dr. Pat who recommends that they leave trailer as soon as possible.

7/19/07 - Congressional hearings on FEMA trailers and health problems.

10/1/07 - Center for Disease Control (CDC) issues warnings about excessive formaldehyde exposure in FEMA trailers.

11/9/07 - Williams family finally moves into Sethie's parent's home (family name is Green), according to medical record entry in early 2008.

7/14/08 - Per Asher Goldman- lawsuit is filed against both FEMA and Matchless Enterprises, among five other manufacturers and other subcontractors.

OK, thinks Tristan to himself. So far so good. It looks like Simon was exposed for about 536 days or 76.6 weeks or 17.8 months from May 22, 2006 through November 9, 2007.

Of course, this is a very liberal estimate because Simon didn't spend all day every day in the trailers. Rounding off these numbers and assuming, again, conservatively, he spent about half the time in the trailer, including sleep time, Simon was exposed for about nine months. So we have an exposure duration of nine months.

Tristan acknowledged to himself that he didn't know the exposure levels at this point. Without those, he couldn't figure the total dose of formaldehyde sustained by Simon over that nine month period.

— — —

Tristan suddenly remembered, thinking about how he tried to explain this type of science to Heather and even Tess. He recalled trying to reveal the concept of dose to both of them one quiet snowy night during better times. The three of them were sitting in the living room in front of a roaring fire. He thought he had a better chance with Tess, even though she was just 10.

"Listen Tess, honey. Dose is simply the exposure level multiplied by the time or duration of exposure. It's simple - let's compare two doses in a really fun way!"

"Uh-huh," said Tess, looking at her father, like this wasn't the first time he sounded like some nerd on a sitcom.

First, say, you eat one Hershey kiss a day for 300 days - then how many Hershey kisses have you eaten?" continued Tristan.

Tess who was very smart for a fourth grader and was becoming more tolerant of this kind of questioning from her Dad, answered, "300, Daddy; now, can I have some?"

"Great, Tess - you're right. Your "dose" of Hershey kisses spread out over 300 days is 300 total chocolate kisses, "exclaimed Tristan with a smile of love at his precocious daughter.

He emphasized, "This dose won't hurt you a bit; but might wreck your teeth at this pace and make you a little pudgier than you want to be."

"Oh, Daddy, - fine with me," she purred, wondering where he was hiding the loot.

Tristan continued, "OK, smarty pants; now, let's say you eat 12 Hershey kisses a day for 700 days, then what's your 'dose' of chocolate?"

"Mo-m-m-m-m!" hollered Tess. "Daddy's being mean!"

Overhearing Tristan's torture of their daughter and looking first at Tristan and then at Tess, Heather interjected, "OK, you know what - I'll deal with you later." She couldn't count the number of times Tristan had pulled this home schooling stunt.

Showing off, she went to Tess's aid, "The big dose is 8400 Hershey kisses; too many for little girls or a mean old Daddy."

"Tess, honey, Daddy was just kidding with you. Now, it's bed-time; I'll try to find a bag of Hershey kisses for you tomorrow."

Sitting in the lonely hotel room, Tristan smiled and felt some moistness in his eyes. He faded back to his timeline, then smiled again, thinking, the Tess/Hershey Kisses Model might be a good one for the jury.

Now immersed in his classical analysis, he said to himself, "I don't have all of the modeling figures in or the data that Stacy will come up with. I'll have to wait to do the dose calculations. Once I do those, I can compare them to the scientific literature, especially on cancer risk to see how bad Simon's exposure was. I already know that this poor kid sustained formaldehyde exposure levels in his trailer that sent him to the doctor about every 4 to 6 weeks for his asthma flare-ups.

Dr. Pat, like most of the other treating physicians had no clue about the cause. There was so damned much mold, rot, mildew and pollen after the flood, no one was sure. Probably all of these factors were important - but with estimated formaldehyde levels over 10 to 100 times the government limit, there can be no doubt it played a role in some people's problems. I just have to figure out whether, it contributed to Simon's asthma issues."

—   —   —

Tristan, undressed, took a shower and climbed into bed, lying there reading, starting to nod off; now at about 1am, the hotel room phone rang; and it was really loud.

"Jesus, Joseph," blurted Tristan, "What the hell's going on? It's one in the morning. Did you hit an alligator or something?"

Silence. Tristan almost hung up.

Suddenly, a soft, tired very female voice replied, "You said you burned the midnight oil, didn't you? No I did not hit an alligator, and I am not Joseph; this is Laura Swain; just had a question."

Tristan, embarrassed, by his outburst and his rather stupid question about the alligator, replied, "Oh sorry, Miss Swain, uh, I mean, Laura. Yes, I am wide awake, just reading the file in preparation for meeting Simon in the morning. By the way, did you give his mom the medical questionnaire, I sent to Asher?"

"Dr. Baines, I thought I was the one with the question. And yes, Ms. Williams received the questionnaire and should have it filled out by the time you see Simon and her at 11. I just wanted to know if you could meet earlier, say around 8 for breakfast, so I could go over some developments in the case. Asher said I was to keep you up to date, even if some of the material was procedural."

"How about 9?" replied Tristan. "I don't eat breakfast and I'll probably won't fall asleep until 3 or even 4. And, please call me, Tristan."

"Really? You're worse than I thought.....Dr. ..., uh, Tristan. You're sure you don't mind my calling you Tristan? Don't you ever sleep?" she answered.

"It's OK; it's OK, really. I'll meet you in the M Bistro at 9. I'll just have some coffee," Tristan replied, ignoring her second question and impressed that Laura was living up to her reputation, as extolled by Asher. Working at 1am, he thought, I may get to like this young lady.

—   —   —

At 9:15 the next morning, Tristan walked into the restaurant and saw Laura over at a table by the window. A ray of sunlight illuminated her hair and the file folder spread out on the white table cloth. She had already had some toast and grapefruit.

"Since we're starting near noon," she kidded, "I had time to run this morning and work out for half an hour. Joseph's going to join us in a few minutes. I called him this morning. He said he rolled in at 4 am. Thanks for offering his help. I can use it."

Tristan was impressed by Laura's appearance. He had never met her before. He had spoken to her on the phone four or five times; but was not prepared for what he saw. Tristan was old school. This young lady was just too pretty to be so smart. Twenty years her senior, he tried to distance himself; but he was drawn in, gazing at her in a most uncomfortable way.

He first noticed her light brown hair and blue eyes, gracing full, reddish lips and somewhat olive-like skin. She wasn't overly thin or too full figured (if that were possible, he thought with a grimace of embarrassment); she seemed just right, clinically, of course, he thought, again. He was trying to place her ethnicity. Then he gazed at her slender fingers surrounding the handle of her leather briefcase. "Stop!" he told himself.

Awkwardly, Tristan continued, "This is a little early for me; I try to start my day at about 10, on good days; but I am sharp as a tack at about 2 am. I used to run an emergency room from 6 pm through 6 am - so I'm the kind of a doctor, you want to meet at 3 in the morning; but not 7." Tristan fumbled, realizing he used this ridiculous attempt at humor every time he tried to excuse his circadian dysrhythmia. Most people, he concluded, were probably getting tired of his pitiful excuses.

Ignoring his excuses, Laura focused. "No problem - say, we only have about an hour. I thought I would bring you up to speed on some procedural issues that could complicate and restrict your areas of testimony. One is particularly troublesome; because it may prevent our ability to bring FEMA into the lawsuit," Laura warned, moving her hair out of her eyes and sipping her coffee.

Tristan noticed she held her cup with her left hand.

Must be good in math, he thought, as he recollected that 28% of his fellow engineers at MIT were lefties. Still detached from the matter at hand, he drifted, thinking again, "How did this daughter of two doctors end up in law school? What a waste!"

Both of them looked up, as a very tired looking, Joseph True Blood, approached the table. As he sat down, he caught the attention of a nearby, perfectly dressed waiter, who was approaching with a menu for him and Tristan.

"No need for a menu for me, man," exclaimed Joseph, "I'll have a cheese omelet with home fries, a slab of ham, four pieces of toast, orange juice and coffee. My friend here only wants coffee - black," Joseph blurted his order about 10 decibels too loudly for such an elegant breakfast joint. He loved having some fun at Tristan's expense, knowing his mentor ate like a wee bird for most of the day and then turned into a vulture at dinner time.

After proper introductions, while Joseph was busy consuming no less than 3000 calories, Laura continued, occasionally beholding the gastronomical feat taking place in her midst, "As I was saying, there have been some potentially complicating developments, Tristan; at least one that may interfere with your areas of testimony."

"Go ahead, what are they?" responded Tristan, now grounded and not really worried. He had been through this sort of thing before.

"Well, the first one you already know about. We could not file a class action lawsuit. The judge ruled that individual plaintiffs had to bring individual lawsuits against a specific trailer manufacturer and other parties, as appropriate. So Sethie Williams' suit is against Matchless Enterprises because they manufactured her trailer. There are also additional suits against several other parties but I won't bore you with those details right now.

Next, Asher estimates that within about three months the judge - do you know who she is?" said Laura, interrupting herself.

Joseph didn't break stride, just hunched his shoulders a bit, not caring if it was Judge Judy.

Tristan replied, "I had her before. No one other than Her Honor, Judge Henrietta Fabiola Whitmore. Asher calls her the "Harpy." So do I. No one to mess with. She has oil and gasoline running through her veins; transfused by some very important people. She's very careful, as Lady Justice, when she blindfolds herself and balances the scales of evidence and fairness - she just peeks a bit."

"No comment," winked Laura. "Anyway, Judge Whitmore has already ruled on the class issue - that is, as I said a moment ago - no class action; only individual law suits.

Next, she has already ruled that we can not ask for any medical monitoring - as you know, this means we can't ask for money to periodically examine plaintiffs in the future to check for potential adverse effects of formaldehyde exposure that may occur from living in the trailer.

We <u>can</u> ask for medical expenses to treat their existing problems, now and in the future, if we can prove that they were related to exposure in the trailer. That's where you come in, Tristan."

Laura continued, "Next, consistent with no medical monitoring, we can not ask for funds to check for cancer in the future."

Tristan interrupted, "That is BS! The Harpy strikes again! I've been through this sort of thing before, too. I will, without doubt, comment, testify and report on any increased risk of cancer, specifically, nasal cancer in Simon, once we agree on probable exposure levels and duration of exposure."

Slightly taken aback but clearly not unhappy with his enthusiasm, Laura said, "That's an issue we should bounce off Asher; but I think you are right. We'll just have to wait and see what you come up with. What do you think the numbers might show?"

"Just assuming that the numbers for exposure level are anywhere from 500 to 600 times the EPA risk based standards, the really conservative ones, this young man could be looking at an increased lifetime risk of nasal cancer of about 20 times the so called acceptable level. Not the odds I would want for my kid. Remember, however, defense will say these standards can't be used for such an analysis of risk" exclaimed Tristan.

He continued, "These trailer manufacturers knew damn good and well the levels were off the wall. They also knew that kids and old folks would be living in these units. They are at highest risk, for suffering adverse effects. Even setting aside the cancer issue, formaldehyde levels were high enough to cause serious problems whenever the chemical touched the skin, the moist linings of the upper and lower airways and the eyes, of course."

Laura continued, "I get all that. Well, now that I have your attention, let's go for the big one. Judge Whitmore plans to rule on whether Sethie can sue FEMA and FEMA subcontractors. She may say that the subcontractors were agents of the federal government and can't be sued under the principle of sovereign immunity - just like you can't sue your local fire department; or, if you do, there are limits on how much you can collect.

Much worse than that, it is possible Judge Whitmore may rule that Sethie can not sue FEMA at all, because there is a two year statute of limitations on her ability to sue. The defense says..."

"Hold it Laura - I've put together a time line. Let me show it to you," interrupted Tristan. I know where you are going with this." Tristan placed his timeline on the table. Joseph was still going strong, finishing his omelet.

"Great," she said as she looked down at Tristan's time line and mentally did some quick calculations. "As I was saying, the defense argues that the statute of limitations clock started running when Sethie knew or was supposed to have known that formaldehyde in the trailer was injuring her son. She then had two years to bring a lawsuit against FEMA - this according to federal law.

Defense argues, absurdly, that Sethie should have known that formaldehyde in her FEMA trailer was the culprit the day she moved in on May 22, 2006 because FEMA sent out this warning flyer in March. Well, as we know, she never saw any flyer; and if she did, she didn't know her son was sick from anything related to the trailer. Hell, she didn't take Simon to the doctor until July and Dr. Pat just treated Simon; she had no more clue than Sethie about what might be causing the problem.

If defense has its way and the two year statute starts running on May 22, 2006, it would run out on May 22, 2008. Well, guess what - Sethie's lawsuit wasn't filed until July 14, 2008 - And the defense knows that. Forgive me - but we are screwed if Judge Whitmore rules that the clock began on May 22, '06."

"How in the hell was Sethie Williams supposed to have put two and two together on this cause and effect issue when there was still debate in FEMA about the significance of the problem? You gotta be kidding me!" shouted Tristan, turning a few heads at nearby tables and receiving a rather harsh glance from their waiter, ready to recommend an end to their conference.

Looking Tristan in the eyes, Laura continued, "I see by your timeline that the FEMA color glossy brochure went out on July 1,

2007. Interesting - because, Ms. Williams, uh, Sethie, said that she received this information personally when the UPIC guy came around to work on her air conditioning unit. These are the people who took care of the trailers for FEMA throughout the time she and her family lived there, beginning in May, 2006.

Sethie was very concerned about what she read in 2007 and talked it over with her husband Reggie and Dr. Pat. She answered in her first deposition that the family started to look around for alternative housing. They couldn't find any; so they stayed until November, 2007 when her parents' house was finished. All tolled, Sethie's trailer was parked right on the driveway in front of her parents' house for almost a year and a half.

In fairness, you can argue that the two year statute should have started on July 1, 2007 with the glossy handout and run until July 1, 2009, even past now. The date she sued, July 14, 2008, then, would have been well within that two year window.

I am worried about this judge. If she rules that the lawsuit was filed after the statute had run out, we can't sue FEMA. There are limits on what we can get from FEMA; but we want to sue them, so we can bring into evidence all of their confessions and acknowledgements about the dangers of formaldehyde in the trailers. And even more importantly, we want to find out it there were any shenanigans going on between FEMA and Matchless Enterprises.

If this judge rules that Matchless and other contractors like UPIC have sovereign immunity, this case goes up in smoke. We won't be able to sue anybody."

Tristan let out a formidable sigh, "Knowing this witch from a couple of previous cases, I have a very bad feeling about this. If FEMA is out of the suit, even if we can proceed against Matchless and other subcontractors, I think the case will be weakened. The jury may be underwhelmed and we may lose anyway. We need the government's own endorsement of their malfeasance. Where does Asher stand on all this?"

"It keeps him up at night and whitens his hair," commented Laura without a smile. "We just have to proceed and hope for the best. In the meantime, it's 10:45; you're meeting Sethie and Simon in 15 minutes. Where do you plan to interview them?"

Tristan answered, "I reserved a small meeting room, not far from the elevator. I'll take them there. If it's too noisy, I'll just interview them in my room. It's a suite and we can sit down on a couch and chairs. I don't plan to examine Simon at this time; although I will need to determine whether I want to run some medical tests or obtain a referral.

Do you, young lady and this good for nothing, wanna-be gentleman wish to have dinner later? I think I'll be through around 4 PM." Tristan smiled at Joseph, wondering how his friend could need to eat again by 4 PM. Or for that matter, any sooner than at least two days after his meal for three lumberjacks.

"We're good," responded Joseph. "I'll help Miss Laura over at her office and see you here at 4:30. Where do you want to go?"

Tristan was expressionless because he had no recommendations. Laura turned to their now overly attentive waiter and asked, "Where can you get a good meal around here - not in the hotel, for dinner?"

"Yes, ma'am - there are several places close by," responded the waiter. "You can arrange for a limo driver to take you round trip. Although we would love to keep you here as our guests, one of the best places is La Chateau, about 15 minutes away. They have the best in New Orleans dining. Their chicken gumbo is to die for."

"That OK with you guys?" asked Laura.

"Sounds good to me," proffered Joseph.

"Yeah, OK with me too," said Tristan as he looked at his watch. "Hey, True Blood, you look hungry already," quipped Tristan as he headed for the lobby where he planned to meet Sethie and Simon.

CHAPTER 14 - SIMON - PART II - THE INTERVIEW, THE PROMISE AND TRISTAN'S ORDEAL

DATE: 11 am Tuesday - 5/19/09 - about three years eight and one half months after Katrina
LOCATION: New Orleans, Louisiana, Ritz Hotel

—   —   —

There he was, a bright eyed young man, wearing a brown corduroy suit no less, even though it was a little small on him. It may have been too hot to wear for a day in mid-May, especially in New Orleans.

He appeared to be of average height; probably had not gone through his growth spurt yet. He had black curly hair, black eyes and was wearing an apprehensive smile when Tristan extended his hand for a handshake. Simon reciprocated and offered a firm grip for a 13 year old. His light brown tie was slightly askew on his perfectly white shirt; and it was clear he had buffed his shoes just for this occasion.

Next to him was his mother, Sethie, also well-dressed for this critical meeting. She was wearing a black skirt, along with a light weight, casual blue and green blouse, resembling some sort of floral pattern. She carried a black leather handbag, gripped in her right hand. Sethie was tall and slim, actually, looked a little underweight at first glance.

As she approached Tristan after he had greeted Simon, she surprised him when she said, "Yur jist like I s'pected, Dr. Baines. I kin see yous didn't go to Howard University Medical School."

Cautiously, Tristan replied, "Mrs. Williams, that is true, although I guess I could have. I hope you won't hold it against me."

"No. No. course not, Dr. Baines; I wuz jist hopin'," said Sethie in a soft, somewhat defeated tone. "Maybe sumday."

Tristan decided to set this issue aside ASAP. "Well, first, off; may I call you Sethie or Mrs. Williams; which would your prefer. I hope I can call Simon, Simon. You can call me Tristan."

He broke the ice. Sethie smiled and said, "I's prefer Sethie an' Simon ain't no Mr. Williams, at least yet. By the way, Dr. Baines, I filled out yur questionnaire as best I could. It wuz like a book. I left a lot of stuff blank. Some of it I didn't git. Here it is anyway."

Tristan leaned his hand forward. "I'm sure it's fine. I admit it is a chore to fill that thing out. If anything is missing, I'll ask you and Simon about it in a few minutes. Let's see if that small conference room is ready. Have you eaten yet; would you like something to drink?"

"No, it's OK. Thanks. Simon, you thirsty, boy?" she replied.

"No, Momma. I's fine," said Simon, speaking for the first time.

"We et an early lunch, Dr. Baines. I's got to get back to work by 2 an' we's took Simon outta school for this," she continued.

"OK, then; let's get started," replied Tristan. "Please come with me."

Fortunately, the small conference room was not too small and even more fortunately, there were white table cloths draped over two adjacent folding tables, leaving plenty of room to spread out and talk. The hotel had left a pitcher of ice water and some clean glasses on a round serving tray. Even in the hotel air conditioning, the water sweating off the pitcher's cool surface left a dark wet ring on the serving tray. There were six chairs scattered around the room. Tristan grabbed three and brought them to the table.

Initially the drapes were closed; so the room was flooded with a cacophony of harsh fluorescence that sterilized everything in sight. Tristan decided to open the silly things and turn off the lights. The transformation to natural sunlight was a relief, increasing the probability, by Tristan's calculations, that the interview would be one of gentle data gathering and successful reassurance rather than harsh interrogation. Tristan had been there, probably 10,000 times before, and knew the little things that mattered. Especially, how to make a patient relax and believe the doctor could still perform magic, if given the chance.

They all sat down to begin what turned out to be a three hour interview.

Tristan covered each of the 156 questions that delved into every aspect of Simon's health, from the time he was born until present. He was particularly interested in how his symptoms and medications changed after he had moved into his trailer, on 5/22/06. Since Simon had moved out of the trailer on 11/9/07, about 18 months before this current interview, Tristan also wanted to see if he had recovered medically.

All of these questions were designed to determine whether the natural course of Simon's pre-Katrina asthma problem had changed over time permanently, temporarily or not at all, as a result of his breathing formaldehyde in his FEMA trailer. Over time meant the equivalent of about nine months of exposure, while he slept, ate and just hung around inside the trailer with his family.

As the interview progressed, Sethie warmed considerably; and Simon seemed to be enjoying the attention Tristan was showering upon him. But, as Tristan mentally tallied the results of Simon's and Sethie's responses, he realized that Simon's day to day problems lingered. More significantly, it appeared that his risk for sudden death from a bout of unstoppable asthma had not abated.

When it came to discussing Simon's emotional health, Tristan knew what he was in for, especially after his talk with Dr. Pat the day before.

Sethie began to vent in the most suffering tone.

"Dr. Baines," Sethie began, "Not only's mah Simon still sick but mah brother Samuel wuz murdered by da police on da Claire de lune bridge, jist after the storm. Da whole family's bin grievin' since. They say it wuz a mistake and wuz self-defense. I's don't know. Mah Pappy went missin' too and was found dead in the hospital, who knows why. Simon seems OK 'bout this; but he's still pining away 'bout losin' his dog, Rambo. It's a little better; but he still got night terrors an' says Rambo's cumin' back any day. I's think he needs to be mov'in on."

"My God, Sethie. I am so sorry to hear about this. Go ahead; tell me about these problems," said Tristan, reflexively, in as compassionate a tone, as he could muster. "I can understand why Simon and you are both losing sleep."

Sethie unloaded even more. Simon just wasn't any better and didn't appear to be improving at all. In fact, he seemed to be getting worse. The hospital ER visits, the admonitions of emergency room doctors. None of these existed before entering that damned FEMA trailer. Those 18 months had taken a hideous toll.

And then she dropped the same bomb a second time. Close behind Sethie's concerns about Simon's physical health was the monster Tristan equated to be a neurotically overextended grief reaction. Sethie had to face facts. Simon's emotional swings, tears, and night terrors appeared to be caused more by the loss of his dog Rambo rather than by the somewhat abstracted departures of his uncle and grandfather. This was hard for Sethie to bear. She knew Simon's dog was important. But the losses of close, blood kin should have mattered more. But they didn't. It was crystal clear. The loss of his pet had hit Simon like a ton of bricks and there was nothing abstract about it.

Tristan didn't tell Sethie that Dr. Pat had discussed these subjects with him the day before. He didn't bring up the suspected overdose of insulin the doctors had given her father, just before they had abandoned a few of the extremely ill in the hospital during the height of the storm. They rescued as many patients as they could; but they had to triage those who could not be moved without killing them in the process. So the unproven but highly probable allegation was that hospital personnel had euthanized some of the sickest patients, rather than leave them to suffer without food, water, medication and medical attention. It would have been more than she could take. It was not for today, and especially this interview.

Tristan let Sethie talk and waited for some spontaneous remark from Simon. None came. Tristan respected their grief; but he had to stay focused. Formaldehyde and its effects on Simon were all that mattered at the moment.

Tristan thought, "No, it wasn't all that mattered." He knew he was in the pond, up to his neck, sinking deeper by the minute. Suddenly, he felt guilty about trying to pretend he didn't care. He did care. The story of Simon's lament had to include the disastrous weight of his emotional baggage, even if it was not related to formaldehyde oozing out of uncured glue.

So Tristan gently questioned Simon about his losses. He realized the worst. In the midst of his world coming apart, it was true. Simon's dog, Rambo, had taken on what many would consider to be an unhealthy significance to him. Tristan thought that the dog must be gone, for good, by now. He probably drowned or was rescued, euthanized or adopted, never to be seen again. But he looked into Simon's eyes; saw the tears and the trembling lip. A young boy trying to keep his composure and contain his embarrassment without much success. Tristan was on board with Simon. He understood why the grieving process wasn't over.

Suddenly, Simon blurted, "Rambo's cumin' back; yous wait an' see Dr Baines. Even Dr. Pat wuz lookin' for him."

Tristan now looked down at his notes, contemplating the explosive strength of this land mine. Suddenly Sethie came to the rescue. "Say, Dr. Baines; kin I's take you to the bridge where Samuel wuz shot to see it yous self. It's kinda famous now.

Tristan didn't skip a beat. "Sethie, I would be happy to come with you. When would you like to go?"

Hows 'bout two days from now, on Thursday after I'm off work. I's try to see if'n my husband Reggie kin come along. We's pick you up here an' take you round a bit. I's don't think we'll bring Simon; he's bin there enough," replied Sethie obviously grateful.

"That's fine; I'll make certain I'm available. Let's talk tomorrow to firm up an exact time," finished Tristan, feeling extremely upbeat.

He had established the bond of trust for which had had hoped. He knew, on the other hand, what was in store at that bridge. He had now read about the shooting. Some said it was cold-blooded murder; others self-defense by the police. Neither verdict was the point now. He was interviewing a lady and her son who had suffered badly.

Tristan thought hard about Heather and Tess and what this job of his had wrought upon them. For a moment, he felt like throwing in the towel and catching the next plane to Boston, then renting a car to drive to Vermont to be with them. Yet he was glued to this case. He couldn't help it. He suddenly felt a slight shiver go down his spine, along with a very disturbing premonition of hurt coming his way. Yet he was still enthralled with the challenge and the science and had to admit he liked it, regardless the outcome or risk.

About a quarter to one, Tristan acknowledged Sethie's time constraint. "Simon, looks like we need to wrap it up. Your mom needs to get back to work. If I need to ask additional questions, I can reach you by phone. And I'm looking forward to seeing your mom and maybe your dad in a couple of days."

Sethie looked at Simon, then Tristan and started to get up from her chair. "Tell us, Dr. Baines; what's you think we need to do next?"

Tristan responded, "If I can obtain approval, I want to refer Simon to the finest Environmental Medicine facility in the world for further evaluation. It's a place called Coastal General Hospital in Boston. I have a close colleague there who can perform some very precise tests to see if the formaldehyde has caused Simon any long term problems."

As soon as the last words left his lips, Tristan glanced at Simon to see if his remarks had caused him any consternation. He worried less about Sethie. Sethie was smart enough to realize that Simon's case represented the plight of thousands of others who were suing Matchless Enterprises for millions of dollars. And his case was based upon his and his parents' claim that he had sustained injury from breathing the air in a trailer they had manufactured and had supplied to FEMA for her family's use. Again, he turned his attention to Simon. No change in his expression. Just in case, Tristan continued, "By the way Simon, you'll really like Dr. Gruber - she just like a grandma."

"I's already gotta gramma, thanks, anyway, Dr. Baines," replied Simon.

The next remark took Tristan by surprise. "Dr. Baines, pleaz, suh; kin you help me to find my dog Rambo? I jist…"

"Simon, Simon, yous can't be botherin' Dr. Baines with such things," interrupted Sethie. "Yous already got Dr. Pat workin' on this. You know, honey, it's probably bin too long. Maybe it's time to git 'nother Rambo, uh, I mean a new puppy; then you kin name him Rambo, Jr. just like your brother Reggie, Jr. is named after yur Daddy."

Sethie tried to pull back the last few words; but couldn't. She felt like kicking herself for making such a comparison. As usual, she had no idea how to deal with her son's grief. Maybe the new puppy route would work this time.

Turning to Tristan, Sethie continued, "Sorry, Dr. Baines. The boy's possessed 'bout this dog. He still thinks he's alive somewhere out there. I's tried to explain that the dog probably drowned or wuz picked up by some stranger after the storm. He's probably got a good home by now. He won't listen. He sometimes still has night terrors over this. Dr. Pat knows all 'bout it."

Tristan quickly digested Simon and Sethie's remarks. At first, he was surprised by Simon's request for him to join the Rambo search. But given Simon's obsession, the request was not totally unexpected. Dr. Pat had given him the heads up and expressed her worry that Simon's chronic preoccupation with the loss of his dog could lead to some rather negative mental health outcomes. He needed closure, one way or the other. It seemed like the proper time to contact Dr. Pat to discuss the matter. But more importantly, he had to offer some supportive but not overly encouraging words to Simon.

"Simon," began Tristan with a warm smile on his face, "I promise that I will talk to Dr. Pat, and we will put our heads together to see if we can track down Rambo. But if we can't find him, I want to make you another promise. I'll bet anything that Rambo still loves you more than anyone else in the whole world; and will love you forever. I will do my best. I plan to get some help from my very close friend, Joseph."

"Joseph?" blurted Simon, with some tears now welling in his eyes. "Yous mean Joseph, like in the Bible, Joseph?"

"Yes, Simon," continued Tristan, reaching into his pocket, retrieving a clean handkerchief and handing it to Simon, who shyly wiped the tears from his eyes. "I mean Joseph, like in the Bible, Joseph, except for one thing. This Joseph is a real Native American Indian and he is the best dog tracker in the whole world. He will help us find Rambo."

Tristan suddenly realized he had done exactly what he was trying to avoid, probably overpromise and underperform. It was too late. The tears were gone from Simon's eyes, and his smile appeared broader than ever. Tristan immediately found himself trying to remember where he had placed Dr. Pat's phone number. He would be seeing Joseph soon.

Finding one dog in a million, almost four years after the largest natural catastrophe in modern US history shouldn't be too difficult, mused Tristan to himself. The dog was probably dead or adopted, simple as that. Tristan had faced worse odds in the past; he just couldn't remember when. But he found himself overcome with empathy. For a split second he remembered losing his own dog when he was Simon's age. It was a long story that he didn't want to rehash in his head. He could still feel the pain, after he lost his collie, Skippy. He looked at Simon and came forward to give him a hug.

"Listen, son," Tristan said softly, "I'll make you a third promise."

Looking over at Sethie, with Simon's head resting against his chest, Tristan continued, "One way or another, I promise I will do everything I can to make you happy."

—   —   —

"So how did it go, Tris?" exclaimed Joseph, "Laura and I had a good day, and I am starving."

Before he could answer, Tristan saw Laura come out of the elevator walking toward him. She stopped to look in the window of the hotel's boutique dress shop. Tristan took advantage of her delay and looked at Joseph with a smile on his face.

"Listen, Joseph," he began. "First, it went exceptionally well. I love the kid and his Mom. But, second, I made a pledge to Simon; hang on and don't laugh; to find the dog he lost almost four years ago. I've represented your skills as an expert doggie finder. So, I guess we are now obligated to an impossible task or risk breaking a little boy's heart."

"Oh, really?" said Joseph with a bit of a hiccup in his voice.

Smiling, realizing Tristan would take it as a joke, Joseph quipped, "Wadda mean 'we,' white man? It sounds like you are the one in the deep yogurt. Anyway, what makes you think I, or, I guess I should say, we can find some scraggly mutt four years after that insane disaster? Do we have any leads?"

"Not really. We need to check the various branches of the humane society. Right after Katrina, there was some type of community lost dog posting effort." Tristan answered, sounding a bit flustered.

Now gazing down the hallway, he saw Laura break away from the dark blue cocktail dress with white lace trim she was eyeing in the window. She was heading in their direction again. He didn't want to share his promise to Simon with her, at least, not yet.

"Look, Joseph," he continued speaking more quickly. "We need to check in with Dr. Simms, uh, Dr. Pat; you know, Simon's pediatrician. She told me that about 10 months after Katrina, she posted a picture of Simon's dog, named, Rambo, along with Sethie's and her phone numbers on a posting bill board near her temporary office. A few days after she put up the information, both the picture and the number disappeared. I think you know what that means. Anyway, later…"

"Hi, Tristan! Sorry to interrupt. I hope everything went well. I've got a limo waiting to take us to one of the best restaurants in the Big Easy, La Chateau!" she crowed.

"It went smooth as can be expected. A great family. And, so you want to follow the breakfast waiter's advice. It's OK by me. I like the limo idea. Will they pick us up after dinner?" asked Tristan.

"You bet, Doc; Let's go," she smiled.

The three went to the elegant hotel entrance and waited for a few minutes when a black Cadillac stretch limo appeared. What a classic; it shined like an ebony mirror. Complete privacy glass, front and back, including passenger and driver windows. Tristan felt like he was going to be picked up by the secret service or something.

What a pity, he thought; it was starting to rain, messing up that shine.

The perfectly dressed bellman opened the rear door, and they all three entered the regal, black leather, rear compartment. Waiting for a tip, the bellman told Tristan he had instructed the driver to take them to La Chateau and drive along Canal Street, so they could see some of the beautiful mansions near the French Quarter. He promised they would be dining at the best New Orleans had to offer within 30 minutes, and the bill for the round trip limo ride and dinner would be going on Mr. Asher Goldman's hotel tab.

Tristan began, "What a day. What a day. Matters are becoming a bit clearer. What trauma that boy and his family have endured."

As they pulled away from the curb, after about 10 seconds both rear doors locked, not unexpectedly. "Obviously for safety reasons," thought Tristan. Joseph and Laura also noticed the mechanical snap/ thud that sounded more like the closing of a jail cell door than a limo door lock.

Now it was raining more heavily and the humidity was oppressive. The AC came on full bore, and it felt great.

As he started to elaborate on his findings to Laura and Joseph from the earlier interview, Tristan noticed the slightly tinted Plexiglas barrier just above the seat that separated their rear compartment from the front. It must have been an inch thick and had a sliding door on metal glides that was shut. Tristan looked for a telephone handset to communicate with the driver. It was right in front of him, just below the barrier about centerline, on the rear part of the front seat.

Tristan had been last to get in and was sitting directly behind the driver. Laura had scooted to the far window and Joseph sat in the middle. Joseph saw Tristan's eye movements and said, "Hang on Tris, I'll get it." He leaned forward, lifted the handset and pushed a button on the handle. He then sat back and said, "Hello driver. How long do you think it will take us to get to the restaurant? And, if you know your way around here, would you mind playing tour guide on the way? We'll make it worth your while."

Silence.

Tristan took the handset from Joseph and pushed the button himself without letting up, thinking maybe one had to hold it down to communicate. "Yo, driver; can you hear me?" belted Tristan.

Silence. The limo appeared to pick up speed.

"Shit, it must be broken," exclaimed Joseph.

Laura sat back calmly enjoying the ride, looking out the foggy window, through the showering mist at the passing houses. "It's probably busted," she said. "Just knock on the damned window to get the driver's attention.

"Good idea," said Joseph, as he tapped loudly on the Plexiglas with the dysfunctional handset, while he raised his voice and shouted, "Hey, driver, open the window; we want to talk to you!"

Laura nervously interjected. "Hey, guys we are not going down Canal Street; and I don't see any mansions anymore; just some crack houses and bad looking dudes hanging on the corner."

Now, grabbing the handset herself and banging on the barrier, even harder, Laura exhibited some lungs developed from her passion as a runner. And she let loose a few Yankee superlatives, like a sailor on a Connecticut pier. "Hey, open up, you asshole. Enough is enough. I know you can hear me. Stop this damned car now!"

Silence.

Despite the evolving severity of the situation, Tristan feigned shock and smiled at this outburst from Laura; But as he did so, he took off his shoe and started banging hard on the barrier without any success This bastard was taking them where he wanted, and it wasn't out to eat.

While Tristan and Joseph looked at each other, Laura tried to open her door. The handle was disengaged, and she could not get her fingers on the lock spindle buried too far into the molding.

The AC suddenly went off, and it started getting stuffy and hot within seconds. The temperature of the situation was rising fast too, just a degree or two short of boiling. Joseph could see a blurry, faint image in the rearview mirror up front. He whispered something in Tristan's ear. Laura missed the remark.

Tristan tried his door, like Laura, failing to get a response from the handle; just frustrating mechanical disengagement. Tristan sized up the side and back windows and realized it would be nearly impossible to break or kick any of them out.

Laura was the only one with a cell phone. She took it out of her purse and wailed. "I can't believe it, no battery left. And you two didn't bring yours. This is un-fricking believable!"

They traveled on for another seven or eight minutes, in what was now becoming a downpour. Banging was useless. They looked out the window. They had crossed the overpass, had taken an exit that took them toward the bayou in an area south of 90. They weren't sure.

All bets were off now. They were still in civilization with streets and people; but were headed to a place none of them would call home.

Tristan turned to Joseph, "Where in the hell is my escape hammer when I need it?" referring to a widely available tool with a sharp metal point, used for breaking auto glass in an emergency just like the one they found themselves in at the moment. As Tristan gave it further thought, he concluded that the tool wouldn't put a scratch in this glass anyway.

Joseph leaned forward. He turned to Laura and said, "I was hoping to avoid this; but it looks like we have no choice." In the next breath, Joseph pulled a compact Berretta 9mm semi-automatic handgun from a waist holster under his coat. He took the barrel of the gun and tapped it firmly on the Plexiglas barrier. "Hey, asshole! Stop the limo now."

Silence.

They could see that civilization was rapidly thinning out, next to the rain soaked pavement.

Joseph looked around. He knew that his Berretta may not penetrate the Plexiglas and, if fired in the confines of the rear seat compartment, was going to nearly blow out their eardrums.

He waited.

Street lights were now gone.

"Shit!" cried Joseph, "Tristan, Laura, hit the deck now and hold your ears!" As Tristan leaned to his right and literally laid in Joseph's lap, Joseph fired at Tristan's window. The blast was deafening. The bullet did not penetrate the window. A fragment of something, ricocheted and grazed Tristan's left thigh, causing an immediate yelp, while blood started to ooze through the rent fabric.

Recovering from the shock, the singular voice heard above the residual ringing was female. "Shoot through the f'ing seat," Laura screamed, "Or, I will!!" as she prepared to grab the gun from Joseph, if she had to.

Joseph put the gun barrel to the middle of the back of the front seat and fired. He saw the immediate extinction of the LCD in the radio up front. Within a split second, while Tristan was thanking Laura for such quick thinking, Joseph, screamed, "The next one is in your back, you bastard."

Silence.

The limo braked suddenly, skidding and fish-tailing, throwing all three passengers forward, each sustaining varying contusions and sprains. They all three looked at each other and didn't say a word.

Silence.

The doors suddenly unlocked. Recovering quickly from the minor trauma of the stop, both Tristan and Laura opened their doors at the same time. They bolted out.

As they exited into the downpour, they glanced back inside. For the first time the driver in the front seat, turned his head offering a complete profile, easily visible to all three passengers. They stumbled away from the limo through two inch puddles and regrouped behind it as it sped away, with Laura's door still wide open with tires spinning gravel and mud in their faces,

The three of them looked at each other and hugged in the rain. Laura was shaking and Tristan held her for a moment, while his leg wound continued to blood stain his pants. He disengaged, took out a handkerchief, tied it over the wound and applied pressure with his hand. Laura offered to help. She smiled at him while she moved her dripping hair from her forehead.

Holding his gun under his shirt, Joseph popped his ammunition clip and took two rounds from his pocket to fill the magazine to capacity. While looking around 360 degrees, he then reloaded and chambered a round.

Through the rainy mess, they started walking toward the main road, slowly, giving Tristan some time to get his minor bleeding under control. The rain was fortunately letting up, at least for the moment.

Twenty yards from what appeared to be a bar on the main street, hopefully with a phone booth, they walked, listening to the swamp critters, and sweating profusely from humidity you could cut with a knife. In the aftermath of the downpour, the street lights were a beacon of life, already surrounded by moths, so thick you could barely see the pole.

They walked, shoes squishing, taking long deep breaths of relief.

Just before they reached a sidewalk, Tristan turned to Joseph, "I know that SOB; there can be no doubt."

Joseph looked back at Tristan with firm determination and anger, planning some serious, deadly payback, "Yeah, I do too."

With some exasperation, holding his handkerchief tightly against his thigh, Tristan grimaced, "We'll deal with him later. He's mine"

CHAPTER 15 - KATRINA - THAT BITCH

DATE: Wednesday, 7/12/06 - about
10½ months after Katrina
LOCATION: New Orleans, Louisiana

— — —

Apocalyptic madness, heavenly kindness and a lot in between ensued in New Orleans after Hurricane Katrina. Temporary housing was slow to become available for thousands of persons who had been flooded out, couldn't get out, or even wouldn't get out, leaving their family, friends, churches, or jobs, to the extent that any of these still existed. Tens of thousands were relocated hundreds or even thousands of miles away to cities throughout the country that would take the survivors. People went to live with family members for weeks that turned into months that turned into years. Many never came back.

For those left behind, the standard of living as they had known it pre-Katrina, even if they were poor, plummeted to a devastated, pre-industrial level in which danger lurked everywhere. While authorities had their hands full, crime was the rule - muggings, robbery, vandalism and petty theft were the most common. Their numbers seemed to skyrocket compared to pre-Katrina levels, although, in the final analysis, many doubted the statistics since reporting was not very reliable.

Then, there were the assaults, murders and rapes. Scores were settled with impunity, mostly, criminal on criminal, although cop on criminal and even cop on citizen, allegedly mistaken for criminal, were reported. Horrible, unspeakable stories of rape eventually were revealed by victims whose lives were ruined even further by beasts in the form of men who should have been shot on sight - but there was no one there to carry out the executions. The victim suffered, life spared; but mind and bodies were scarred forever. Gunshots were heard frequently, along with distant screams of fleeing madness. Fires burned unattended in the early days after Katrina, since many fire trucks could not make it to the inferno; and if they did arrive, the hydrants did not always have adequate pressure - so the brave souls who responded; just stared while the structure burned.

On the other hand, humanity and civilization also flourished post-Katrina. People in neighborhoods rallied around their families and churches to look for missing strangers and loved ones. Food was shared; the elderly were cared for and children were hugged. Some families clung together with faith and resolve to rebuild, while others patrolled their ravaged neighborhoods with bats, shotguns and rakes - whatever it took to keep the peace while law enforcement and soldiers were spread so thin. Many punks disappeared, never to spray paint or terrorize again.

The past ten and a half months had been a tough challenge for Sgt. Melanie Hatfield. She embraced her duties with a passion that stood out even among her dedicated National Guard soldiers. Thousands of citizen warriors had stopped everything in their lives to come help. During the early fall, Melanie faced some harrowing situations, ones that she would have rather avoided. Take the time, while on patrol, in early October, when she had to shove the barrel of her M-16 into the chest of a man whom she caught beating a woman standing next to him at a displaced persons' shelter. The woman was aggressively refusing her attacker another swig from the whiskey bottle cloaked in a paper bag that she held to her side. He screamed in her face, demanding the booze. When deprived of his liquor, he took a short swing and punched her with an open palm on the side of her head. Dazed, she fell to her knees and dropped the bottle to the ground, where it broke, spilling its liquid contents in an irregular wet spot on the pavement.

Melanie had been standing guard with several other soldiers, only 15 feet from the incident. She saw the melee and reacted immediately by moving past four other people toward the abuser. A second soldier rushed to aid the kneeling, disoriented woman, later identified as the man's wife.

As Melanie lunged in his direction, the booze seeker also dropped to the ground next to his wife and actually fondled the broken glass and whiskey soaked paper. He touched his finger to his lips, rose up and started to swing again. In a split second, Melanie yelled at him to stop or be shot on the spot. It was a bluff. In the crowded parking lot, where the relief tent had been erected and people were standing, sitting or just milling around, Melanie knew that she could not discharge her weapon. Instead, in three more, quick leaps she assaulted the man and nearly broke his breastbone with a quick thrust to his chest with the barrel of her gun. Now he screamed and fell to the ground next to his poor wife who knew the monster he would become if he drank some more.

Within two minutes, Melanie's commanding officer arrived and called over a New Orleans police officer. The officer, with back-up from her partner, cuffed the dazed husband and started to take him away. Typical of this type of situation, the beaten wife, at first struggled to get up; but when she saw her husband being led away by the police, she literally sprung like a puma onto the back of the arresting officer and started to beat her about the face. Within 30 seconds, she was in cuffs, too; and was taken away in a separate squad car to face incarceration in one of the parish prisons, still laden with mold from the flooding of jail cells since September.

Situations like this were as common as the flies on your food or the mosquitoes on the back of your neck, typical of Louisiana, but dramatically worsened in the hell that followed Katrina. Melanie coped. She had the support and admiration of her fellow soldiers and especially, Cpl. George Michaels, the vet assistant from their hometown, Baton Rouge, who had helped fix up her rescued pooch, Dumbo. What a circus she and George had faced in the chaos after the rescue. Michaels had persuaded the battalion army doctor, Capt. Lowe, to help in the recovery and concealment of Dumbo for months, following Melanie's rescue of the stray in the first few days after the hurricane hit. Melanie still had no idea who owned Dumbo; and at the time, there was really no way to find out.

Dumbo became a fixture around the camp. The soldiers loved to watch his bright eyes, begging for a treat and his rolling on his belly, patiently waiting for a good scratch. Dumbo was definitely a contraband companion to this group of lonely soldiers. The commanding officer, Col. Masters looked the other way, but made certain to pet their new mascot whenever he came around.

Once Melanie saw the old goat throw a tennis ball into a pond next to their camp and watch Dumbo fetch it like a bullet. He swam through the brackish, foul smelling water and brought the now greenish stained ball back to him and laid it at his feet. He started to throw it a second time; but stopped, realizing he was being watched by Melanie and two other soldiers, all of whom were admiring their commander's unexpected humane behavior. Looking down at Dumbo's wagging tongue and pleading eyes, Old Masters, suddenly dropped the ball, stood erect in traditional military posture and strode away onto another mission. His head turned, no one could see his thin lips break into the fragment of a smile, while under his breath; he uttered "Whoof!"

Melanie loved that dog from the minute she found him. After a couple of weeks, she loved him as much as her dog, Sammy, safe at home with her parents in Baton Rouge. She loved Dumbo ever more each day; given the backdrop of abandoned animals almost everywhere she looked. Many had drowned or were left behind on rooftops, eventually to die trying to swim to safety. Once in the water, many of these pets became tantalizing tidbits for those creatures higher on the food chain. She feared even more that "policies were policies," and "orders were orders," especially when it came to people's pets. Right after Katrina, FEMA, the police and even some of Melanie's fellow guardsman officially enforced draconian, heartless policies that separated children and adults from their pets, during rescue or relocation. Melanie heard stories that in one parish, rather than argue with a man who clung to his dog during rescue, a pilot pulled a gun and shot the poor pet when the man would not board the helicopter.

Other stories were almost as bad - police pulling small dogs out the hands of children on buses and leaving their precious pets outside to wander without food or shelter. Many people smuggled smaller pets onto buses and helicopters, even putting them in trash bags, pants or blouses. Melanie heard that during a press conference, the director of FEMA, when asked about federal provisions to assist citizens in keeping, locating or caring for displaced pets, he responded that such animals were not his concern. Melanie also heard that one of the commanding general's of the National Guard estimated that between 30 to 40 percent of the people who refused rescue did so to remain behind to take care of their pets.

In the midst of all of this trauma and despair, human life came first - but compassionate officials and soldiers like Melanie found ways to circumvent the rules. Melanie heard that Captain Lowe had shined like a supernova during one incident. Copter blades whirring, dust and debris flying, the soldier in the door of one rescue chopper struggled with a 75 year old woman who would not give up her small poodle that she had smuggled aboard before take-off. Dr. Lowe saw the entire scene unravel before him. In a split second the Captain stepped forward and ordered the Lieutenant to take his hands off the dog. The soldier recited the rule that no pets were allowed on board during the rescue. Lowe barked, "You idiot; that is not a dog, it is this woman's medication!" The Lieutenant looked Dr. Lowe in the eyes; smiled; shouted "Yes, Sir!" and handed the dog back to the grateful lady as the chopper lifted off.

When she heard the story, Melanie hugged and kissed Dr. Lowe, risking whatever reprimand he wanted to throw back at her. Lowe knew why he was targeted for affection and only threw back a smile, while telling her to keep her mangy mutt on a leash more often and out of the garbage. Overall, life was good for Melanie because she knew that she mattered. Dumbo's rescue, acceptance and well being added to her sense of self-worth. His constant companionship made her daily hardships more bearable.

After New Year's Day, 2006, overall conditions actually improved for Melanie and her cohorts. Civilization began to return. Thousands were moved into temporary housing, whether hotel, undamaged apartments or temporary housing units (THUs) provided by FEMA. Soldiers were assigned to bring life back to normal, whether it was assisting police in keeping the peace or clearing endless amounts of debris from areas where the floodwaters had receded.

Melanie was anxious to go home and get back to her job as a middle school science teacher in Baton Rouge before the school year started in late August. She missed her parents, her friends and her dog, Sammy. Fortunately, she had been home on leave about every six weeks over the past 10 months. She still had a lot of work to do. Technically, she had to attend a teacher enrichment program in late July; but knew that the need for her attendance would be waived, in light of her National Guard duties in New Orleans.

Melanie's work-load had lightened considerably. In early July 2006, she was assigned to distribute food rations to the needy at a depot located within the New Orleans parish water building, near Cheval Street, off Pomme Drive, a building that had been largely spared damage during the hurricane and subsequent flooding.

Several other temporary operations were also situated in this water building at that time, including the medical office of pediatrician, Dr. Patty M. Simms (Dr. Pat), who saw Sethie and Simon Green, on Tuesday, July 25. During that visit, Sethie confided to Dr. Pat that Simon's asthma had worsened after they had moved into their FEMA supplied THU in May. But, she pleaded; Simon also suffered from prolonged grief. True, Simon grieved the disappearance of his grandfather, Pappy Green - grief that was totally understandable. True, Simon grieved the murder of his Uncle Samuel, his mother's brother on the Claire de lune bridge by those bastards in uniform who shot first and asked questions later -grief that was also understandable. But - to some of those closest to Simon, another, perhaps, less understandable but even more incapacitating source of grief still afflicted him after 10 long months - the disappearance of his dog, Rambo, the day after the hurricane hit.

Simon could never forget that terrible night when Rambo slipped into the water, never to be seen again. Simon thought about Rambo every day. He prayed that he would return one afternoon - walk up to the door of their trailer, jump into his lap and lick his face, just like he did when he was a puppy. Rambo's large white fur diamond on his head and nose were burned into Simon's memory and were perfectly captured on the photograph of Rambo that Simon had given to Dr. Pat at the end of his and Sethie's visit on that Tuesday, July 25, 2006.

Ten months after Katrina, people were still searching in earnest for missing friends and family members who may have ended up in Houston, Atlanta, St. Louis or a hundred other welcoming cities and towns. Bulletin boards had been set up all over town right after the hurricane to post information and requests about missing persons. These bulletin boards were still overflowing in mid-July. And people were still looking for their missing pets too. Dogs, cats, guinea pigs and even a few displaced goats and iguanas were the subject of wide searches, even on bulletin boards. In fact, the Louisiana SPCA managed one such missing pet bulletin board in Dr. Pat's and Sgt. Melanie Hatfield's parish water building, right there in New Orleans parish. It was huge, over about 4 by 16 feet, almost full of pictures.

Passing the lost pet bulletin board set up by the SPCA, on Tuesday, the day after Sethie and Simon's visit, Dr. Pat decided to post Rambo's picture, just on the remotest chance that his white fur diamond would be recognized by some good Samaritan who knew Rambo's whereabouts. It wasn't technically impossible because some miraculous stories of boys and girls reuniting with their lost dogs or cats had already been reported in the newspapers and online. So up it went, along with the other 80 or so photos posted. Dr. Pat taped it to a piece of lined yellow paper and under it, wrote the telephone number at her office, her cell number and Sethie's home number. Out of her own pocket, she even offered a reward of $100 leading to the safe return of Rambo to Simon's arms.

Tuesday passed uneventfully. The next day, Wednesday, while Cpl. Michaels kept an eye on Dumbo, Melanie worked her job in the parish water building. It was to be a day that Melanie was destined to remember for the rest of her life.

Chances were that throughout Tuesday and early Wednesday morning, several dozen people, gave little thought or notice to Rambo's big white fur diamond or to Dr. Pat's reward offer. Things changed just before Wednesday at lunchtime, when Melanie Hatfield, dropped her cup of coffee on the floor and nearly fainted after she spotted Rambo's picture, as she was heading back to her food pantry.

Literally, dazed and feeling as if she had been punched in the stomach, Melanie walked about 10 feet past the bulletin board before she stopped. She quickly turned and ran for the women's' bathroom on the other side of the hallway. She went and stood over the sink a moment thinking she was going to be sick. The bathroom was damp and smelled like bleach. Remembering the coffee mess she made on the floor in front of the bulletin board, she grabbed a handful of paper towels, wetted them slightly and walked out the door. She was embarrassed. She bent down and started to clean up the coffee when one of her fellow guardsmen stopped and offered to help.

"Here wait a minute, Melanie; let me give you a hand. Did you stumble or something? Are you OK?" said Molly Sweetwater, an engineer with whom Melanie had served for the entire time since Katrina. Like Melanie, at this point, just a week or two before their release from duty, Molly was helping at the food bank with Melanie. She was no particular dog lover; she liked to build pontoon bridges and fix things, activities during which a dog would just get in the way. But Molly knew Dumbo - everybody knew Dumbo - but no one loved and played with Dumbo every day, except Melanie, Cpl. Michaels and Capt. Lowe.

"Oh, Hi Molly - thanks. No, I just tripped; I'm OK," responded Melanie, turning to face Molly and rotating her body so that eye contact meant Molly wasn't looking at the bulletin board behind both of them. Melanie knew that there were over 80 photos, mostly of dogs, but a few of cats and two or three other types of pets on that board, even including two small pigs, a goat, and several different kinds of parrots and birds. She had not had time to look again at the one that caught her eye. It was shoulder high in the left center part of the board. She thought it was a photo of Dumbo- but not entirely certain. She wanted to clean up the mess and move her conversation with Molly down the hall away from the board, as quickly as she could.

"Wow, would you look at that, "belted Molly, turning to look at the bulletin board, "this thing is almost filled up. I wonder how many pictures there are."

Melanie could see Molly scan her eyes across the board. She was certain she would see the picture of the dog that so closely resembled Dumbo. Molly moved from Melanie and commented, "What a sad situation - people from all over are desperate to reunite with their pets. I'll bet most of them are dead." Drifting to the far right side of the board, and feeling slightly guilty, Molly continued, "It's too bad we can't help these people more."

Melanie knew she had to go for it. When Molly had her head turned for the briefest moment, Melanie quickly but stealthily moved to the board, turned her back on Molly and in one instant relieved the bulletin board of the picture in question, tearing it from its thumbtack. The picture was mounted on a small sheet of paper with two names and phone numbers written on it. She shuffled the paper as she quickly put it in her shirt pocket; and at the same time, she accidently knocked another picture, this one of a cat, and its thumb tack on the floor. She was positive that Molly heard something and may have seen her movements. Molly turned.

Before she could say a word," Melanie blurted, "Oh, look, one of the pictures has been knocked off - what a klutz I am - I must have hit it." Molly looked at Melanie. In Melanie's mind, she had seen the whole thing; but truth be known, Molly was studying the engineering magic by which the SPCA had supported 64 square feet of bulletin board on the wall with some sort of concealed attachments. Melanie smiled and replaced the photo that had fallen on the floor and said, "God, I hope this kitty finds its owner." As she strode away, she carefully tucked the end of the paper and photo deeper into her pocket, right above her heart.

CHAPTER 16 - MCKENNA AND COASTAL GENERAL HOSPITAL

DATES: Wednesday, 5/20/09 (morning after kidnapping attempt); Friday, 5/22/09 (meeting in Asher's office) and Tuesday, 6/23/09 (Coastal General Hospital) - about three years and nine months after Katrina
LOCATIONS: New Orleans, Dallas and Cambridge, Massachusetts

— — —

Back at Ritz in New Orleans, Tristan lay on the immaculate white sheets, filthy and soaked to the bone, murder on his mind, thinking:

"Who the hell was that bastard?............Shit, this is serious.......... What did he want?..........Whom was he working for?..........Why? Dammit, Why?..........I am certain we would have all ended up alligator bait, if Joseph hadn't saved our asses...........God, I should have been packing..........Poor Laura; now she's mixed up in this..........I know she'll call Asher and maybe call the cops. But what for? That guy is gone. I've got to arrange some follow-up for Simon..........I can barely think..........God, how I miss Heather and Tess. I want to call them now; but it's too late, and I can't tell them about this..........I'll call Asher in the morning. He may have some answers. I am almost certain I know that guy; but I need to talk to Asher first..........I don't have time to go after the prick right now; but I will find him, if it's the last thing I do.......... God, they have gone too far..........I never thought they would."

He lay there for over an hour – it was 3am and he finally fell asleep, if you want to call it that.

At 9:30 am Tristan rose, showered, shaved, dressed and sat down on the bed. He was still rattled and, to be honest, scared shitless, over the events of last evening. He was on edge, like a deer sipping a drink at midnight, from a waterhole surrounded by hungry wolves.

He rose, went to the hotel room door, opened it with the metal security latch still in place and peeked outside. Nothing; but he heard the chattering of two house maids a few doors down. He carefully opened the door just enough to be able to reach down to pick up his daily morning coffee, already preordered and supplied in two over-sized insulated carafes with plenty of napkins. He noticed the copy of *USA Today* lying next to the tray. He ignored it and slammed the door. Next he picked up the silver tray, laden with its heavy liquid cargo, and walked across the room to his computer table and set it down. He then walked back to the door, and reopened it only enough to reach around to insert the "Do Not Disturb" placard into the door lock card reader. He then returned to the computer table and sat down in front of the silver tray. He was already exhausted. No elaborate breakfast today, just a gallon of coffee, as usual.

He gathered his strength and his focus. It was now about 10:50 AM in Boston. He picked up the hotel land line and dialed. He had her direct number.

He was surprised when she picked up after one ring, probably waiting for another call. "Lila! It's been a long time. How are you and your family?" effused Tristan to his old medical colleague, "Did you receive the medical records on this young man, Simon Williams? I had them delivered hard copy with all of the releases."

Initially, she skipped answering his question, genuinely happy to hear his voice. "Tristan, you're right. It's been too damned long. Where in the hell have you been? How are Heather and Tess?" replied the Chief of Occupational and Environmental Medicine at Coastal General Hospital, arguably the nation's leading, Hautair affiliated specialty hospital in north Cambridge.

She waited a split second. Tristan did not reply, so she went on. "I sent you an e-mail. Yes, I did receive all of young Simon's records. I read them all. There really weren't too many. Just some notes from a Dr. Patricia Simms, apparently, his pediatrician. It's a very interesting case."

Within a pregnant pause, Tristan deliberately and a bit guiltily skipped answering Lila's inquiry into his whereabouts, much less the status of his family. Then he managed to squeak out, "Thanks for asking. Heather and Tess are just fine," he lied.

He sensed she knew; but was too polite to ask any more. Warming the chill of his deception, Tristan glowed happily to have garnered Lila's attention about his patient referral. And he wasn't surprised that she had read what he had sent; and was prepared to discuss the case. It wasn't too often that one could partner up with a legend.

Without exaggeration, Dr. Lila Gruber was a legend, an academic survivor and leader within the emerald, Oyve League rat race, even though she trained at the University of Vermont. Just goes to show, there is always more to learn at any good medical school than one human being can absorb – a fact that levels the playing field. And from the student's perspective, where it really counts, tends to make all good medical schools, more or less, equal. At 60, Dr. Gruber was a tenured, full professor of Occupational and Environmental Medicine; an accolade achieved largely on the basis of her uncanny diagnostic and therapeutic acumen, seasoned with a pinch of good luck. More importantly, Hautair Hospital medicine had never witnessed a kinder, more compassionate and effective teacher on any service. In the 1990's, she won the coveted "Best of Clinical Faculty (BCF)" award six years in a row. Kind of like the Golden Globes, BCF was bestowed upon a member of the teaching staff by a vote of the senior medical clerks and graduate interns and residents who served on any of the 12 specialty services at Coastal General.

A recent *US News and World Report* survey ranked Coastal General Hospital as the finest respiratory and immunological disease hospital in the United States for the fourth year running – a fact that made Coastal General the best on planet earth and the only place Tristan would consider sending Simon for a work-up. It wasn't

Tristan's first referral there; it was his 19th. He knew Lila when she started in her department in 1989; when she was only one of three faculty members, pioneering the rise of her clinical Preventive Medicine specialty, a place where strong and brilliant women could shine and be appreciated. She had come from the faculty at the University of Vermont, at the time. Another emerald steal. Hautair made her an offer she couldn't refuse – more clam chowder than Vermont could manage to cook up.

Tristan cut to business. "Thanks for reviewing the file, Lila; so where do we go from here? When can you see him?" asked Tristan, uncharacteristically, apprehensive, awaiting her response.

Lila began slowly, "Tristan, I can't see your patient. I mean I can't for at least three months. I am heading down to South America, specifically, Peru, a couple of hundred miles outside of Lima. I am heading a team of respiratory, allergy, dermatology and occupational medicine docs who are going to help the government design and implement a medical monitoring program for the workers engaged in the open pit copper mines there. We're working on a grant from the Ministry of Energy and Mines. The Hautair School of Public Health is sending four industrial hygienists to figure out all of the exposures. It's straightforward stuff – just need to make certain that we don't miss any potential toxins in our inventory.

I am sorry," she concluded, then waited a second before she raised her voice affectionately,

"Look, Tristan, you know what the hell I am talking about – you practically wrote the book on how to do it. Wanna come along?"

"Not this time; but thanks for the invitation," pouted Tristan. "Lila, this work-up is really important. His medical record doesn't tell the whole story; mainly because his records pre-Katrina are either lost or rotting away in still sodden boxes in a previously flooded garage. Pat Simms had been treating Simon before Katrina, ever since he was an infant. The poor kid had infantile asthma and was on medication; but was doing much better even after the hurricane hit.

But about nine months after Simon and his family spent a couple of days on a rooftop, praying for rescue, they all moved into a brand spanking new travel trailer provided by FEMA in late May of 2006. There was Simon, his dad, Reggie, his mom, Sethie, and his older brother, Reggie, Jr. - a wonderfully intact family. Their trailer was manufactured by an outfit called Matchless Enterprises, up in Warburg, Kentucky. Matchless had an order for several thousand trailers placed by FEMA after Katrina. They were on a tight deadline and had to speed up the manufacturing process to make the rapid delivery demanded by the feds in the fall of 2005. Trouble is; Matchless cut major corners and used cabinet plywood laminated together with uncured glue that emitted formaldehyde.

The trailers reeked with the stuff. An enclosed unventilated trailer could reach formaldehyde concentrations that were about 560 times the federal minimum risk level. This poor kid endured 18 months of overexposure to formaldehyde until he moved out in November of 2007. I don't need to tell you what it did to his asthma, much less increase his lifetime risk of developing nasal cancer. My preliminary calculations show that his risk for squamous cell cancer of the nasal passages is about 20 times higher than it would be, absent his exposure."

Tristan took a deep breath, hoping for miracles and then went on, "Dr. Pat, as she is called by her patients, has been following Simon since the exposure; but she didn't see him until July 2006, after he had been in the trailer for about two months. Sethie, the mom, had been using up old inhalers and over the counter meds, not knowing what to do. She had no idea that there was formaldehyde in the trailer – sure it smelled a bit; but it smelled new, like a new car.

There was a little bit of eye burning if they kept the trailer closed up in the hot sun – but things settled down after they opened the windows and doors. At night, when they tried to use the air conditioning; they closed up all of the windows and had no fresh air make-up. Effectively, the family was enclosed in a formaldehyde gas chamber. The adults and Simon's older brother, all asthma free, experienced minimal problems because they were not as vulnerable as Simon.

Lila, I think you get the picture. I need to perform some careful testing on Simon to find out exactly what the formaldehyde did to him. Personally, I think, his asthma is worse, even though he has been out of exposure for a little over a year and a half. Dr. Pat agrees. She has suggested...

"Hold it, Tristan; before you go any further," exclaimed Dr Gruber, "I want to hear all of this; but as I told you, I can't see Simon for at least three months. What is your timeframe?"

"Sorry, Lila. I tend to get carried away; still hoping you could perform the work-up," replied Tristan, aching with the disappointment that his old friend and colleague could not see his patient. "Simon needs a work-up within the next 30-40 days."

In a flash, feeling even worse, Tristan recalled those dozen and a half times he and Lila had worked together on some exciting and complicated cases. He smiled when he recalled first meeting her at an after hour social during a medical conference in Houston, shortly after she had arrived in Cambridge. Eight years Tristan's senior, unescorted and with 10 oz of wine in her, Tristan learned that Lila had already been working for four months under a less than nice, viciously ambitious, woman who had been the first chair of the nascent department. Lila played her like a violin. Tristan also knew the numero uno bitch and stayed away from her. From then on, Lila became Tristan's principal contact at Coastal. Five years later, numero uno left and Lila took over the reigns, running the department with far greater kindness that led to greater accomplishment and acclaim. Among dozens of others and a handful of superstars, Tristan came to the halls of Oyve for the benefit of his patients. And whenever he could, Tristan spent a lot of personal time in Bean Town. After all, he had done his undergraduate and post graduate training at MIT and Hautair – so he liked coming back as often as possible.

"OK, I accept my fate, even though Simon needs you," quipped Tristan, trying to annoy Lila and still hoping she could work him in before she headed below the equator. "As I said, I need to have Simon seen within the next four to six weeks, just when you are basking in the middle of some open pit mine in Peru. So, Dr. Gruber, what do you suggest?"

"I am not entirely certain – but I think I can arrange for Simon to see one of our finest, relatively new, highly qualified assistant professors. She has been with us for about nine years. Her name is Dr. Chris McKenna. Chris is doubly boarded in allergy and environmental medicine. She's great with kids. She has brought a lot of grant money into our program at Coastal over the past five years. I am not sure about her schedule; but I'll ask. If she can see Simon, I'll give her the records. I'll call you back one way or the other and arrange for you and Chris to go over the new patient protocol."

"Dr. Chris McKenna, did you say?" asked Tristan. "That name sounds familiar. Look, Lila, I'll e-mail you what I want done as the referring doc; and you can include it with your protocol. Let me know, if Chris can see Simon relatively soon and I'll call her directly. Say, I hope you have a great time in Peru. Be careful. Let me know how it goes when you return. I am sure McKenna will do a great job.

By the way, she may have to testify. Is that going to be a problem?"

"I doubt it," replied Lila. "She has done quite a bit of medical-legal work over the past several years. I'm surprised your paths haven't crossed."

"I'll have to ask her if she has any conflicts, especially involving Matchless Enterprises," responded Tristan, still sifting McKenna's name through his mind, without success. "God, I am bad with names," he thought.

"Well, Dr. Baines, old friend, I have to go. Send in your testing requests and the questions you want answered, and I will forward them to Dr. McKenna. I am sure she will call you within a few days," said Lila in first a professional tone and then an affectionate tone. "You send my love and best wishes to Heather and Tess. I'm sure she has grown like a weed. How old is she now?"

"16. I will send Heather and Tess your regards. Take care Lila and thanks," said Tristan, deliberately ending the conversation before

Lila had a chance to ask any more questions – questions that Tristan didn't want to answer.

She hung up and Tristan looked at the phone, slowly putting it back in the cradle by the bed. "McKenna, McKenna," he thought. "All right then, it'll come to me later. I've had so many cases…."

CHAPTER 17 - SAUL AND THE RESISTANCE

DATE: Friday, 5/22/09 - about three years and nine months after Katrina
LOCATION: Dallas, Texas

— — —

After their near death experience with the limo driver, Tristan and Joseph decided to follow Laura back to Dallas, rather then head to Laramie. Tristan had plenty of questions for Asher, starting with the arrangements he had made with his pal, Morgan and Morgan's helicopter pilot, what's his name.

Tristan and Joseph sat quietly in the waiting area of Asher's palatial office.

"Man, I am in the wrong line of work," quipped Joseph, as he stared at the almost overbearing signs of opulence. The soft brown leather chairs and the matching sofa perfectly aligned on the scarlet $100/yard carpet first caught their eyes when they walked in just before noon. The wall décor and the statute on the end table took their breath away. There, in front of them were no less than four Frederic Sackrider Remington paintings, perfectly and tastefully, archivally framed and mounted. And before them both was a bronze limited edition statue of Remington's famous "Bronco Buster," a lean, tough cowboy, right arm extended in midair for balance, mounted on the back of a fiercely bucking horse that wanted so badly to throw that cow-poke's ass into a corral fence post. If original, it would be in seven digits.

Tristan carefully read the brass, flawlessly engraved plaques under each of the four masterpieces, arranged side by side on the wall above the couch. The ones on each end were mounted in a portrait or vertical configuration and the two in the middle were landscape or horizontal. Tristan knew how remarkable these creations were. The one on the far left was "The Outlier," a proud Indian warrior, stoically glaring at Tristan with a rising full moon in the background. To the immediate right was "The Buffalo Hunt," featuring two mounted warriors plunging lances into a huge buffalo, crashing onto a fallen horse half its size. The next to the right was "The Smoke Signal," an exceptional depiction of one mounted warrior, pensively watching two of his comrades releasing a smoke signal from a blanket over smoldering branches, probably alerting his brethren miles away to….God knows what.

And, finally, the one on the far right was the enemy of the six Indians before him, "The Trooper," a mounted soldier with right arm held high in the air, holding a revolver pointed to heaven above. Joseph watched Tristan seated on one of the chairs, without comment and without expression.

"Relatives of yours, Joseph?" quipped Tristan, with a slight smile on his lips.

"Yeah, sure, all but the guy on the far right," answered Joseph with a clear dose of sarcasm in his voice. "I could build my dream house, by auctioning off just one of those paintings on e-bay."

Both men were startled slightly by the familiar voice beckoning behind them. "I can see you have succumbed to the wonders of Asher's collection, his unabashed, deliberate and some say, gauche method of creating a first impression," said Laura Swain. "Don't worry; he has about four more Remingtons scattered throughout the office. I guess he calculates that this show of opulence will inspire confidence in clients, some of whose cases have paid for these masterpieces. Do either of you want any coffee or something else to drink?"

"No we're fine," answered Tristan. "Laura it's great to see you again. You look rested, alive and well."

"Speak for yourself, my friend," erupted Joseph. "Laura, you do look fine. I would like some coffee please, black, no milk, no sugar."

"Will do," said Laura, smiling at Tristan's miscalculation. "Come this way. Asher is just finishing up a phone call."

The three of them, now bonded by their near death experience in the New Orleans rain walked down a well-lighted hallway, passing three more of the Remingtons, as predicted by Laura. They entered Asher's corner office, or one should say his desk in a living room. The orthogonal set of windows looked out over the Dallas skyline. The sky was blue and the noonday sun was bright. Tristan thought briefly - the "blue" sky over Dallas fell four stirrups short of the unpolluted blue one to which he was accustomed over the Snowy Mountains of Wyoming.

"Come in, all of you. Please sit down," said Asher in a genuinely friendly tone. "I guess...."

Tristan interrupted, "Asher, we could have been killed. What the hell is going on? Do you know who that bastard was who tried to lead us to our doom?"

Not waiting for a reply, Tristan continued or one should say bellowed, "That limo driver was none other than the helicopter pilot you paid an extra five grand to pick me up a little over two weeks ago. I am happy I didn't go with him then. I disliked that guy the moment I met him. Does your buddy Morgan, his boss, the great helicopter owner and operator, know about his pilot's extracurricular activities?"

Before Asher could answer, Joseph chimed in, "He's right; it was the same guy who flew us in, Asher. His name is Ray Somerset, Somershit, or something like that," he finished, as he took the coffee Laura handed him.

"His name is Raymond Sommersville and if it was the same guy, it will be Somershit, by the time this is over." corrected Asher. "Laura told me all about your near tragedy. I doubt that Morgan had anything to do with this. I did give that guy $5000 extra in cash to land so we could see you. He behaved like a coward, I now think deliberately. I have a feeling he had planned it that way. Cold feet at the last minute, bullshit. He was like a call-girl demanding an extra fifty bucks from a worked up John, to finish the job at hand, ...Sorry, no offense Laura."

"That sounds like the voice of experience Asher. You should be ashamed," laughed Laura, getting even for Asher's impropriety. Asher just looked stupid, having no come back to her remark.

"Asher, what gives here?" belted Tristan in a deadly serious tone, extinguishing Laura's laughter.

"Tristan, if I knew, I would tell you," responded Asher. "Obviously, someone does not want us and specifically you to succeed."

"Succeed? Are you kidding me? You mean staying alive, Asher," cried Tristan I am telling you, had Joseph not fired that shot through the back seat into the dash board console, you would have never heard from us again."

Abruptly changing the subject, clearly relapsing into his ADD tendencies, Tristan continued, "By the way, I arranged for Simon to be seen at Coastal General Hospital in Boston. I couldn't get Dr. Lila Gruber. She's on her way to Peru. Instead, Simon will probably be seen by a lady physician named, Dr. Chris McKenna. I sent a detailed clinical protocol request to Lila to get the ball rolling. I should be hearing from McKenna soon."

"Great, Tristan. I thought we were talking about life and death matters," said Asher, with an authentic look of amazement on his face. He had worked with Tristan before and was accustomed to these non-sequiturs in his behavior.

"I am happy to hear about the referral; but let's get back on subject and think about Somersville. I will order a more detailed background check on him. I have friends who can find his shirt size when he turned 21. And, by the way, I will get his military records as well. I do not want to mention anything to Morgan, at least, quite yet."

Asher suddenly became quiet, thinking. He completely checked out of the setting and the conversation, almost like he was in a trance, staring into space.

He didn't like the intuitive epiphany that sent a chill down his spine.

Asher suddenly recalled the recent conversation he had with his older brother, Saul, an attorney living in New York City. For the moment, Saul was an unemployed lawyer, who was in the midst of a near mental breakdown. As opposed to Asher, who wore the euphemistically designated "white hat" of the plaintiff's bar, his loving senior brother, an otherwise carbon copy of himself, had worn the "black hat" of the defense bar for his entire career.

After law school, Saul worked his way up the ladder starting as a lowly grunt, junior lawyer glued at the hip to the in-house counsel for a large construction company in New York City. He learned the ropes, in this position in the legal weeds, watching his boss cut every corner, pushing the envelope time and time again in opposing the unions and snuffing out the inevitable liability claims that came from shoddy construction practices.

After six years, Saul was promoted to assistant general counsel where he learned to implement every dirty trick in the book to protect his employer. He was given more and more responsibility and became better and better at his craft.

Asher had not followed his brother's career very closely. Over the years they sometimes spoke on holidays and birthdays; but rarely on other occasions. Both of their parents had died. Saul lived alone, was divorced with two girls, both now in their early 20's, neither of whom was close to "Uncle Asher." When they occasionally spoke, Saul customarily and politely, asked about Asher's wife and three teenage boys. They were just not that close. One thing for certain, however, Asher knew that brother Saul was making a lot more money than he was on a consistent basis.

Over about the past nine months things started to change. Saul wasn't the slightly pompous, sarcastic older brother that he used to be. Saul began calling every week or so. At first, it was just small talk. He wanted to know how Asher's family was doing. He started to ask Asher about their family history and even started to reminisce about their childhood. Saul was three years Asher's senior, so they didn't pal around together too much in school; but the questions came anyway, even when he began to kid Asher about some of his early high school girlfriends.

The emotional content of their communications escalated to a crescendo one day when Saul recalled how much he missed their mother and broke down into tears on the phone. For a while, Asher thought

BITE THE HAND THAT FEEDS YOU

his brother had some terminal disease that he was hiding. Given what Asher soon learned, such news would have been almost welcome.

They talked and they talked. And then the horrific details causing Saul's functional and spiritual degeneration began to leak out, like honey slowly seeping from an overturned honey bear dispenser – slow but sure.

Asher first learned that Saul was unemployed. He had some money saved; but still had to make alimony payments to his former wife and her new husband (the one with whom she had an affair) who were making a combined income in the very high six figure range. He complained he was drowning in expenses. Now without any money coming in, he was going to go broke, certainly within the next couple of years. He told Asher that he planned to begin selling off many of his assets.

All of this made sense to Asher; but, the paranoia was much harder to explain. Saul said he was in hiding; and there were those who planned to hunt him down to punish him badly, maybe even kill him. He dared not call the police, because he was warned that his family would go first – in front of his eyes.

Asher knew that Saul <u>had</u> worn the "black hat;" but no more. He ran and was now hiding from his recently lofty status as an esteemed member of that group who were paid millions to defend those with billions…at all costs and without mercy.

When they last spoke, on the phone, Saul spent two hours beating around the bush, not quite succeeding in telling Asher why – why he was in the midst of a mental breakdown and why, in addition to his own peril, Asher, yes, his kid brother and those around him were also in grave danger. They were going to face an ominous threat that had already turned lethal.

"They've had enough, I tell you, Asher," cried Saul. "It's taken about 10 years and it's now out of control. I should have known. Exxon Valdez, Karen Silkwood, this or that pharmaceutical recall, you name it. Asher, you're costing them too much. They have had enough. You and your buddy, trial lawyers and your enablers, that arrogant hoard of experts, have become too successful."

Saul stopped to catch his breath, and then continued, "Millions, not just in legal fees; but in outlandish settlements and occasional jury verdicts for claims that never should have seen the light of day.

Especially, the bullshit of courtroom pseudoscience; enough of so-called experts who are nothing but the purveyors of flawed theories and outright lies; enough of non-injured plaintiffs pouring their hearts out in court, crying crocodile tears, while limping to the witness stand; enough of liberal judges and dumb shit juries who buy it all and award you outlandish sums of money for absolutely nothing. That's how they see it, Asher."

"So, how do you see it Saul? And what does it mean, anyway?" Asher had asked.

"I agree with them and still do for the most part," choked Saul, "But, their methods, their methods, have gone too far. They have lost their minds. I can't be a part of it anymore."

"Part of what – what are you talking about, Saul? God, you sound incoherent. Make some sense. You're scaring the shit out of me, dammit," Asher pleaded and chided at the same time.

"OK, about seven years ago, they formed "The Resistance (TR)", said Saul, quieter, now. "They funded TR with millions, surreptitiously and untraceably funneled into several sham entities. They used the money for special operations to slow down and debilitate the efforts of the plaintiff's bar. They eventually focused upon crippling the effectiveness of that unholy cadre of experts who had caused them the most damage."

"Saul, who are 'they,' dammit!" screamed Asher, now fearing the direction of the conversation.

Raising his voice in response to his brother, Saul retorted, "I can't tell you, Asher, at least not yet. It'll be your death warrant, if you know. I am already DOA. I can't mix you up in this any further. I have already said too much. Oh God, this is really bad news….Look, you're not on the primary hit list; but several of your experts witnesses are, even if they work both sides from time to time. It's the ones that consistently cost TR the most. Those are the ones they want.

Asher, at first TR just wanted them silenced. They decided to have them dishonored, marginalized, hell, even, bought off, if need be. It didn't work. Sure there were a few that came into sudden wealth and retired; but most of those idealistic SOBs kept at it. Look, you've heard the stories, already, haven't you?"

"Go on, Saul," said Asher, now without emotion.

Saul continued, "One sneaky method was for TR operatives to contact plaintiff's experts at the beginning of new cases, just after the suit was filed, pretending to want to hire them, even if the plaintiff's firm had called first. The defense representative would always offer to send a retainer and then go on to reveal some insignificant point of 'case strategy' with the expert. Many experts said 'goodbye' and defaulted to wearing the 'white hat.' When the expert was later designated by the plaintiff's side, defense would cry foul and say that the expert had an insurmountable conflict and possessed critical, confidential information revealed to him or her that would compromise defense's case. Sometimes the court would disqualify the expert. When this ploy worked, boy, did it piss off the expert, who had probably learned nothing more than where defense was holding its next Christmas party."

"I lost two or three experts to that tactic, Saul – but I didn't realize it was so deliberate. Now I know, thanks, you jerk," pelted Asher at his brother. "Is that what you have been doing for the past 10 years, cavorting with scum, figuring unethical ways to tip the scales in your favor?"

"I told you Asher," responded Saul, "Something had to be done and still has to be done; but TR has morphed way, way too far over the edge. Now it's any means to win, anything – physical, financial, psychological intimidation, hell, nothing is off the table. Who knows with these maniacs, even abduction, castration and termination? Look, Asher, I gotta go now. I don't feel well. I'll get back to you later with more details.

And, by the way you've already lost one; I'm so sorry. I've called to warn you – another one may be on the way."

Asher exploded, "What do you mean, Saul? What did I lose? What 'other one' is on the way?"

Saul hung up.

They talked again two days later.

Asher wanted to mentally rejoin his guests at the conference table but couldn't. Still preoccupied in front of Tristan, Joseph and Laura, Asher remembered that next conversation with his brother.

Amid bouts of near incoherence, Saul revealed even more shocking details. It was all unbelievable. Asher thought his brother needed immediate psychiatric intervention. Saul cried on the phone that violence and death were not their original intention – just intimidation, discreditation, and a little bit of corruption were all it was going to take to silence the "white hats."

After careful deliberation, Saul and his ilk decided to specifically neutralize those without whom, the trial lawyers or plaintiff's bar could not succeed – the stable of experts and especially the thoroughbreds, the ones who won the big races. Those were to be TR's targets to be disarmed, maybe even to be bribed into silence or even better into equivocation, the "maybe this" or "maybe that" uncertainty that will doom a plaintiff's case. But many of them could not be bribed. Shackled by their liberal hubris, they could also not be silenced. They liked the limelight too much; and they liked to win, to stick it in the ear or some other orifice of those with billions, to cut them down to size and embarrass them in the eyes of the public and worse yet their customers. Those were the ones who had to go. TR called them the disposable frauds.

It all started out nicely; just some well funded lawyers who more or less created a think tank, a resistance, pledged to level the playing field. It escalated over a period of years, from legitimate scientific research designed to disgrace TR's frauds, to overturn their "white hat" expert theories. It sometimes involved performing detailed background checks to dig up dirt or to orchestrate unethical or even illegal enticements, hoping the "frauds" would take the bait and get caught, then thrown out.

Although it worked for a few, with some startling successes, it did not work for the vast majority of others, who remained lofty, standing on their scientific and ethical soapboxes. Unfortunately for TR, those whom they could not silence were also the ones who cost those with billions the most millions. So a new strategy had to be developed to protect the big boys.

Saul saw it coming but was in denial. It started slowly, a minor accident here and a not so minor accident there, some strong arm tactics, even a busted knee cap or two. Even the sending of compromising photos to a spouse or significant other. It still didn't work, not for the most important "frauds." So suddenly, within TR, there appeared a list of those "frauds" who were slated for special treatment. A year or so ago, special treatment just meant larger bribes or more painful accidents; but by the time Saul decided to quit, it meant much more. It now meant elimination. Violence and death had now become part of the TR's mission creep. Saul had not bargained for this. So he left. And he also went into hiding.

Asher sat there wallowing in the misfortune of his realization. For the moment, he decided to keep it all to himself. But he now knew why someone had tried to kill Tristan. He now knew why, Heather and Tess had been abducted and mistreated. The amputation of Heather's ring finger was the extent of TR's punishments back in 2006. It would be considered child's play today and clearly inadequate to finish the job. Today, both she and Tess would have been raped and murdered as payback for Tristan's honesty and success. Now they wanted Tristan, the "fraud" of all "frauds." Joseph and Laura would have been collateral damage. Too bad.

Then Asher thought some more. It came like a tsunami of horror.

The medical expert before Tristan, whom he first hired for the Katrina/formaldehyde case had had a drinking problem. He fired "Dr. DUI" after he had learned that the poor sot had had three arrests for drunk driving within the past three years. Asher had been afraid that the man's testimony would be compromised when the defense revealed his expert's drinking problem to the jury.

He had Laura fire "Dr. DUI."

The man was killed in a suspicious single car accident two days later.

Asher thought "My God, as far as I know, no one knew about the firing – we kept it quiet to prevent embarrassing him. It would have come out, but not for several days. Defense thought that "Dr. DUI" was still my expert when he was killed…..or murdered." A wave of nausea overcame Asher.

Suddenly, Asher came back, as if he had fallen through thin ice into a Michigan lake in December. He saw the faces, remembered the meeting, Tristan, Joseph and Laura. He especially remembered Tristan's rage and fear; but especially rage directed against Raymond Somershit…uh, Sommersville.

Asher decided not to spill the beans, at least not yet. It was the wrong time. And he wanted to talk to Laura in private, about the death of "Dr. DUI." He hoped there had been an autopsy, and he wanted to see the police report. He had to think; put it all together; make sense of it; but he had better do it fast before he lost his second expert and friend.

"Tristan, please, we need to talk, but later, in private," pleaded Asher. "Please trust me. I am working on it. I have already spoken to the New Orleans police. They will want a statement from you and Joseph. Laura has already made hers.

Now, back to Simon. Please stick around for the next few days. We have a lot to go over. I hope you intend to go with him to Boston. I will pay for it. Obviously, I will also send his mother, Sethie to accompany him. Laura is welcome to go if she wishes. Now you and Joseph go back to the hotel and rest. Let's get together for dinner tomorrow night."

"It won't wait that long, Asher. I want to speak to you tonight at the latest," blurted Tristan, now angry at Asher's dismissiveness. "Joseph, let's go. Laura, I hope to see you again soon. I am grateful you are well." Then they left.

CHAPTER 18 - SIMON - PART III - THE WORK-UP

DATE: Tuesday, 6/23/09 - about three years and ten months after Katrina
LOCATION: Cambridge, Massachusetts

— — —

Tristan woke up in another hotel room, this time with a great view of the Charles River and the Harvard Bridge, not far from his undergraduate and graduate school alma mater, MIT. The Regency Hotel had been around for 30 years. It was first built just after Tristan completed grad school at the "Tute," as the Massachusetts Institute of Technology was fondly called. Tristan remembered his first week at orientation. The old faculty rhetoric at some schools, designed to scare freshmen who had gathered with hope and shaky confidence was, "look to your left; now look to your right – one of you will be gone at this time next year." What a lousy way to start your college career. At MIT, this hazing rhetoric went like this. "Look to your left; now look to your right – there is a 97 percent probability that both of your fellow students got perfect 800s on his or her Math SATs (at the time there were only a handful of "hers"). "Well, I may already be in the lower third of my class," thought Tristan as an 18 year old nerdy upstart – "I only got a 788; missed one problem, I guess. What a way to begin. Intimidating, yes. Demoralizing, no!"

The rest was history. Tristan remembered going on to win his department's highest engineering prize four years later; and then he ripped through his master's in one more year, full experimental thesis, coursework and oral examination. He thought "At MIT, my thinking was honed like an ultra sharp titanium blade. My Hautair engineering doctorate dulled it some. Then medical school – ugh. It was like taking the blade at right angles to a grind stone. More art than science as far as I was concerned – but I ended up loving it." He really missed Cambridge and Boston; but he mused that there were just too damn many people, no real mountains within 2000 miles and too many liberals. He had found his home in Wyoming, one sanctuary where the 2nd Amendment still meant something, at least for the time being.

He looked out the window for several more minutes, and then checked his cell phone for any messages. He still had not heard from Dr. McKenna, who was scheduled to begin Simon's work-up at 9 am this morning. It was 7:30 already. Tristan had faxed over his referring physician's orders three days ago, and expected that Dr. McKenna would add her testing recommendations to his requested evaluation. He had done it this way 15 previous times at Coastal General with Dr. Gruber and three times before that with the "uno numero bitch," who had run the department before her. It had all worked out just fine. But now Tristan was a bit concerned. He had expected a message from Dr. McKenna, confirming she would implement his instructions. In any case, Tristan intended to meet Simon and his mother, Sethie, at the hospital this morning. He could meet briefly with McKenna then.

Tristan waited and left his hotel at 8:30 am to take the 10 minute cab ride to the hospital. He arrived in the waiting room at 8:50. There sat Simon and Sethie, boxed in on both sides by other waiting patients. The waiting room was three quarters full, putting a slight damper on the reunion.

"Hello, Dr. Baines, I's happy you made it. Thank you," exclaimed Sethie in a warm and dignified manner.

"I'm excited to be here with you and to visit the place where I went to school so many years ago. So, how do you two travelers from the Big Easy like Bean Town?" replied Tristan, unable to resist trying to lighten things up a bit.

"Boston's sure a big place," said Simon. "I's read about their baseball team, the Red Sox. I sure wish we had a team like that in N'Orlens."

"I'll bet by the time you're about 25, there very well might be one, Simon. Anyway, you have the football Saints and I'll bet they're gonna wallop the Patriots next fall. Wanna bet?" continued Tristan, now trying to take Simon's mind off the imminent evaluation, some of which, he knew would involve everything from scary (and not un-painful) blood draws to breathing tests and x-rays. And only McKenna knew what else.

Wishing again to confirm receipt of his protocol, Tristan excused himself and stepped forward to speak with the receptionist who was seated on the other side of a partition and counter upon which was mounted the sliding glass doors, so typical of hospital and physician waiting rooms.

Catching the receptionist, just as he completed a phone call, Tristan began, "Good morning, I'm Dr. Tristan Baines. I am accompanying Simon and Sethie Williams who are scheduled to see Dr. McKenna this morning beginning at 9. Simon is the patient and I am the referring physician. I made the referral through Dr. Gruber who subsequently, put us under the excellent care of Dr. McKenna. I sent over my referral request a few days ago and just wanted to be certain that Dr. McKenna has had the opportunity to review my input; and, of course, I would like to sit in with my patient and his mother, while Dr. McKenna takes his medical history. I will have a few more questions of my own."

Tristan soaked up the details of the office behind the glass and the presentation of the twenty something receptionist with his brown hair and wire rim glasses giving him a classic "Cambridge" look. He suddenly realized he had probably given the receptionist more information than he needed. Heather had scolded him innumerable times about this type of yakking. "Keep it short and to the point, Tristan. For God's sake you talk too damn much," she would say. Given the situation and how much he missed her and Tess, such an obnoxious scolding would have been music to his ears.

While he was speaking and planning his next move, Tristan noticed that the receptionist was glancing down at a folder to which was paper clipped what he clearly saw was his fax. The receptionist lifted the fax and was reading a second sheet directly beneath his, obviously a set of hospital orders.

Facing someone from whom he needed something, Tristan decided to shift to manners befitting the situation, namely, a begging tone, accentuated with some "Pretty please, with a double dose of sugar on top." Nearly groveling while still retaining a feeble amount of residual authority, Tristan continued, "I see you have my fax, and it looks like Dr. McKenna's orders also attached. While we are waiting, I would appreciate seeing what she has planned for young Simon over there."

Since he was in Cambridge, Massachusetts, a place obviously not lacking some rather authoritative egg-heads, Tristan quickly fantasized that he probably would have been better off saying something more or less along the lines of:

"Young man, since I am the referring physician and have come a long way to accompany my patient AND since your office has not had the courtesy of getting back to me to ensure you have integrated my orders into those of Dr. McKenna (who, by the way, is my distant second choice to perform this evaluation), I insist that you immediately make a copy of McKenna's orders and let me review them before we commence this evaluation. Time's a' wasting, please make the copy now."

Fantasy remarks flooding his brain (not his mouth), Tristan felt better. All in all, he was happy he had tried honey instead of vinegar.

But the receptionist still looked up at him as if he had taken the vinegar route. Suddenly, he stood up, glared at Tristan and walked away without saying another word. Tristan mumbled, "This interaction is heading south...fast." Tristan stood there, flat-footed for the next seven minutes. After four minutes passed, he reached for a magazine and started to read it while standing. Finally the receptionist returned and sat down.

"Dr. Baines, you say, eh, Dr. Tristan Baines, is that correct?" inquired the receptionist, still appearing to be comparing Tristan's face to the wanted poster he had seen the day before. "I am afraid I have been instructed not to give you a copy of Dr. McKenna's orders and to inform you that you will not be able to join her when she interviews Mr. Williams and his mother."

Served this dish of uncooked organ meat, Tristan stood there, waiting for him at least to say, "I'm sorry." Nothing came over the counter but a cold stare.

Part of the surge of indigestion, rage and vertigo that flooded over Tristan was caused by the receptionist playing to the ears of half of the three quarters filled waiting room, especially to Sethie and Simon. Risking further abuse, Tristan, figured, "What the hell?" and continued with "May I ask why on both counts (namely "no orders" and "no interview"). Dead silence, then a repeat of the same ritual. Without speaking, the receptionist again rose; and while looking away from Tristan, disappeared down the hallway. This time only three minutes elapsed before he returned with a small piece of paper in hand, sat down and then looked up at Tristan. This time the receptionist (a well-educated Boston lad), obviously fearing the Greek mythological metaphor about "killing the messenger," was more polite. He looked down at the paper he had placed in front of him.

"Dr. Baines, I am sorry; but Dr. McKenna told me to inform you that she is quite busy, is on a very tight schedule and will be unable to meet. Further, since you are not on the faculty at this hospital, you will not be able to sit in on the interview or be present during any other part of the work-up. She has read your faxed recommendations and will consider all of them; but must reserve the clinical prerogative of excluding any element she thinks is extraneous or contraindicated. Those elements she decides to exclude you can perform elsewhere, perhaps, back in New Orleans or out in Nevada where you live, if they have the appropriate facilities."

Like he was swatting a Walden Pond mosquito, Tristan blurted, "I live in Wyoming, not Nevada; I say, again, Wyoming, not Nevada – they're about five "Massachusettses" away from each other!"

The receptionist now became visibly flushed. Still fearing his role as a doomed messenger, albeit now a scripted one, he stuttered "Sorry, OK, Wyoming, Wyoming."

He then continued.

"Finally, Dr. McKenna said to tell you that I can provide a copy of her orders to Simon's mother; and then she can give you a copy of them if she wishes. I'll even make the copy for you," finished the receptionist hoping his last act of generosity would not become a post-mortem bequest from him to Dr. Baines.

Tristan, at this point was too stunned to say anything. He was actually speechless, only for the second time in his life. Now and the moment before he was born.

Slowly, Sethie stood up and walked to the window. Without any hesitation or emotion, she said, "Please, suh, you make a copy of them orders for my Doctor Tristan, now."

CHAPTER 19 - SIMON - PART IV - NEAR DEATH BY FORMALDEHYDE

DATE: Tuesday, 6/23/09 - about three years and ten months after Katrina
LOCATION: Cambridge, Massachusetts

—   —   —

Forty five minutes later Sethie and Simon were called for their medical intake interview, Simon's blood draw and a screening pulmonary function (breathing) test. Tristan made a couple of cell phone calls, one to Joseph and another to Asher to let them know Simon's evaluation was underway. He didn't mention McKenna's snub. "Let's face it," he mused to himself, "I am pissed, embarrassed and hurt. But paraphrasing the iconic bad guy, Lee Van Cleef in the 1968 spaghetti western *Death Rides a Horse,* I must remember that 'revenge is a dish best served cold.'" The last thought kept him going for the moment. He had to keep his eye on the ball.

Tristan sat in the crowded waiting room, carefully reviewing McKenna's testing protocol, revealed as a set of orders with diagnostic and procedural codes. At first, it appeared that his protocol and McKenna's were identical. Perhaps, after all, McKenna had recommended a testing battery that was a composite of both his and her recommendations. He scanned the entire protocol quickly and noticed immediately that McKenna had not included a pediatric neuropsychiatric evaluation to see if Simon had any evidence for PTSD as a result of the mental trauma from his trailer exposure and the worsening of his asthma. Also missing was skin patch testing for formaldehyde sensitivity. Tristan decided to move on. He could set those up later, may at LSU.

Tristan was captured in thought, calculating how the proposed data harvest could be used not only to diagnose and, if necessary, treat Simon; but also to determine whether there was a biological thumb-print of formaldehyde exposure anywhere on his body. After using formaldehyde measurements taken in Simon's trailer, in combination with appropriate mathematical modeling, it would be Tristan's job and only Tristan's job to determine whether there was a cause and effect relationship present that would stand up in court.

Causation analysis was Tristan's responsibility, no one else's. When he sent in his protocol to Lila (then lateraled to McKenna), he clearly specified that he wanted the talent at Coastal General to do only two things; diagnose Simon's problem and offer treatment, if necessary.

Under orders from Asher, who was paying the bills, Tristan was the best qualified to tie Simon's trailer formaldehyde exposure to the genesis or aggravation of one or more of his current medical problems. Tristan knew he was already leaning toward the probable conclusions that not only had the formaldehyde in Simon's trailer caused his wheezing and sent him to the ER twice in the first two months of his occupancy; but also that it had put him at risk for a bout of unstoppable asthma and sudden death. Cautiously, however, Tristan wanted to review all of the data first before he committed his opinions to writing.

He repeated in his mind, one more time for good measure – "Only Tristan P. Baines is to perform causation analysis." He wanted McKenna to stay out of it – not to speculate about whether trailer formaldehyde was the culprit. Tristan worried, "Did Lila get the message to McKenna?" He knew if he and McKenna disagreed about causation, once McKenna wrote her report, it would be too late and could very well sink Simon's case against Matchless.

Tristan thought carefully about the value of each test that he and McKenna had agreed upon. The first on the list was screening spirometry:

Screening spirometry (same as pulmonary function or breathing test) – Tristan knew young Simon would need coaching to take in as deep a breath as possible and then blow out as hard and as fast as he could for at least 15 seconds into a mouthpiece and breathing tube. The computer in the spirometry unit would measure the volume and flow rate of the exhaled air and calculate an assortment of volume and flow rate ratios, comparing all of them against some predicted pediatric values.

The test would be performed with and without Simon using his inhaler. If there is obstruction of air flow that improved after using his inhaler, it would help determine whether Simon had asthma and how severe his condition was at that point in time.

Usually, these test results would be compared to Simon's performance at some earlier point in time (his baseline) to see if he fared better or worse on his current testing. Problem was – there was no baseline. Dr. Pat had never tested Simon before Katrina and his subsequent formaldehyde exposure. At the time he would have been too young to follow test instructions, and the results would have been unreliable anyway.

Dr. Pat made Simon's asthma diagnosis the old fashioned way, by obtaining a careful patient history, conducting a complete physical examination, looking at the ER medical records and applying some first rate diagnostic thinking backed by 30 plus years as a pediatrician.

"No problem here," Tristan mumbled aloud, gleaning the attention of an elderly woman sitting next to him, adorned with a nasal cannula and plastic tubing attached to her portable oxygen tank. Tristan looked at the old lady and forced a weak smile as he read on.

Blood and urine tests - Tristan knew the composition of the various blood and serum panels ordered by Dr. McKenna. Once analyzed, these laboratory measurements would rule in or rule out a wide assortment of conditions, related to Simon's serum electrolytes (e.g. sodium, potassium and chloride), his liver, gall bladder, kidney, and thyroid health and whether his bone marrow was producing enough red and white blood cells, as well as platelets – namely whether he was at risk for or had an ongoing infection, was anemic or had certain types of clotting problems. The urine test would reveal an array of information about Simon's bladder and kidneys, hopefully ruling out any problems with bleeding, infection or any condition putting him at risk for a kidney stone.

Hardly moving his mouth again, Tristan exhaled, "Great!" His waiting room cell mate looked at him again. This time, now glancing at the protocol, she joked, "Hey honey, can I have a look at that?"

Tristan was visibly embarrassed at his near breach of patient confidentiality. He managed to peep, "Uh, sorry to disturb you Ma'am," as he stood up and walked out of the waiting room, into the hallway, where he continued reading.

Next, he saw the familiar:

12 lead ECG (or EKG), the electrocardiogram - In combination with a good physical examination, this common test would help to make certain that Simon's heart was functioning properly and that all four chambers were beating in unison, without any electrical disturbance.

Tristan read through four more examination elements, all of which elicited silent nods of agreement, now that nobody was there to listen.

Now he was miffed and a bit disgusted. What was clearly missing from McKenna's protocol was Tristan's recommendation for skin patch testing to formaldehyde. This test involved taking a specially designed, "Band-Aid-like" dressing saturated with formaldehyde solution and placing it on Simon's back or inner arm for 72 hours to determine if there appeared a fiery, red allergic reaction on his skin. The interpretation of any adverse skin effect had to be made by an experienced clinician. Tristan had made it clear in his orders that the concentrations of formaldehyde put on the patch had to be very low, so that it did not induce an irritant reaction. He also knew that there were risks to this type of testing, like actually causing Simon to develop a "formaldehyde allergy." If the skin test was positive to formaldehyde, it would be another nail in Matchless Trailer's coffin.

Technically, Tristan knew there was really no such thing as a "formaldehyde allergy." Formaldehyde is a small molecule that can actually "pickle" tissue. Any mortician could tell you that.

What caused the adverse reaction, loosely called "formaldehyde allergy or sensitization" was the body's immune response to the large molecule of formaldehyde damaged tissue. It was that large alien molecule that would catch the attention of the body's immune system, causing the production of antibodies or killer cells that would attack the invader. Once the body would rev up the immune reaction, the battlefield of destruction could be manifested in many different ways, ranging from annoying to life-threatening. Really sensitized patients would predictably respond to low levels of formaldehyde just like someone who is allergic to bee venom could end up in the ICU after one bee sting.

"What the hell," he thought, "I can have the test performed in New Orleans' but I would rather have it completed now as part of the current work-up. Depending upon the chemical in question, Lila routinely ran this test on several of my earlier patients. I wonder why McKenna failed to include my test recommendation?"

Suddenly, Tristan noticed that additional orders were written on the backside of the paper he had just reviewed. There were more tests – but what were they? What else did McKenna plan for young Simon? Tristan hesitated for a second and then turned over the page.

He quickly noticed that the back-page orders included x-rays and two other tests.

First the x-rays.

Even though the x-rays involved radiation exposure to an adolescent, Tristan agreed that both procedures ordered by McKenna were justified.

First, she ordered a frontal and a lateral x-ray of Simon's chest. "Not a bad idea," Tristan thought. "We might find some air trapping, consistent with his asthma, and we will have a baseline examination against which to compare any future problems."

Next, Tristan saw that McKenna had ordered a CAT scan of Simon's sinuses. "Again, not a bad idea," he agreed. "The information from this procedure will be particularly helpful; and could reveal evidence of chronic sinus inflammation, like a thickened lining, that was caused or aggravated by formaldehyde exposure, while Simon lived in his trailer.

Tristan read on, now feeling some degree of comfort and confidence in McKenna's judgment.

Next, he saw that McKenna had ordered a fiber-optic examination of Simon's nasal passages and vocal cords. "Not too risky," he thought, "it just involves using a fiber-optic device inserted through the nose to examine and biopsy, Simon's nasal passages, especially the lining (mucosa) to see if there are any abnormalities. On the way from the nose to the throat and the vocal cords in the windpipe, McKenna can specifically look for any abnormalities, especially evidence, consistent with formaldehyde damage, given Simon's 18 months of exposure.

And since, according to my calculations, Simon has incurred an increased lifetime risk of nasal cancer, he might as well have another baseline examination that could be referenced in the future. Worst case will be some bleeding and a sore nose."

Tristan read on some more. The next test worried him. Now he understood why McKenna wanted to take a look at Simon's vocal cords. Tristan couldn't believe his eyes.

McKenna planned to perform some inhalation challenge tests on Simon to see if direct exposure to formaldehyde was going to cause his vocal cords to malfunction! "Didn't she see the ER note, indicating that he was at suspected risk for a potentially fatal bout of unstoppable asthma?" he thought. "It was right there in the medical records sent to Coastal for her review."

Tristan knew that McKenna planned to put Simon in a closed chamber, while he breathed in the very chemical to which he had been exposed while living in the trailer for a year and a half. The dangers of this testing could be very significant – like death, for instance.

For all intensive purposes, albeit at fairly low levels, McKenna planned to force Simon to re-inhale that same vile substance that had off-gassed from uncured glue, left in his trailer's cabinet plywood by the manufacturer. Those degenerates at Matchless, in turn, sold it to FEMA that, carelessly offered it to Simon and his family, like the poisoned apple given to Snow White by her wicked stepmother.

The real issues crossing Tristan's mind were Simon's young age and his possible sensitivity to formaldehyde, especially if he were to breathe it again in another formaldehyde gas chamber, this one engineered by the medical profession, no less!

Tristan reasoned that if Simon was actually sensitized or "allergic" to formaldehyde, he could respond quite poorly to an airborne dose, similar to the level that existed in his trailer. Responding quite poorly could range from suffering some upper airway irritation with nausea, diarrhea, chest tightness and palpitations, to the development of edema (fluid swelling) of the vocal cords, larynx (voice box) and a sudden closing of the airway with unstoppable asthma, just like the ER doc had worried. "Oh God," he thought. This could lead to a heart attack, including, a rhythm disturbance with interrupted outflow of blood from the heart to the brain. Bottom line possible shock and death.

Tristan recalled Coastal General's reputation for overly aggressive work-ups especially during the reign of the Numero Uno bitch, Lila's predecessor. Perhaps McKenna was picking up where Numero Uno left off. Tristan remembered hearing about one patient who suffered a collapsed lung during a fiber-optic bronchoscopy, performed by a second year resident while the numero uno was taking a phone call about a pending $5 million grant to fund a "bigger this" and a "bigger that" in her department. The poor patient survived; but was rewarded with a week in the hospital, struggling with a chest tube and some permanent lung scarring that shattered his aspirations of becoming a triathelete.

"After all, Coastal General is a teaching hospital," replied Numero Uno to the Medical Incident Investigating Committee, trying to justify her implementation of the medical school aphorism, "See one; Do one; Teach one!" This methodology could theoretically apply, perhaps, to taking a patient's temperature or retrieving him a ginger ale from the nurse's station, but not to sticking a fiber-optic instrument into a patient's lungs, a procedure that could easily tear some lung tissue, causing it to deflate like a balloon. Well, at least, Numero Uno got her grant and an increased budget for travel and shrimp cocktails. And the patient did survive.

Now it had come to chamber testing a kid to the very chemical he dreaded, just to see if he developed some breathing problems, even though he could die in the process.

Tristan knew the plan. First give Simon a breathing test before exposure. Next expose him to levels of formaldehyde similar to those he experienced in his trailer; then run the breathing test again. The final tests would start by having Simon use either his own asthma inhaler or one from the clinic and then run the tests again to see if the use of the medication improved his test results. Usually not a problem, unless the patient was really sensitive to the chemical used in the challenge or unless the patient was at risk for something like a catastrophic respiratory disaster, like unstoppable asthma.

Tristan thought how insane this formaldehyde challenge test was. What was McKenna thinking? It was no different from taking a patient quite possibly allergic to nuts and giving him a peanut butter sandwich or smacking a beehive while someone likely allergic to bee venom stood nearby. In both cases, the diagnosis could be confirmed, at autopsy, in the morgue.

Tristan palpably feared for Simon's well being. He was now feeling a volcanic sense of urgency to act to stop this insanity. By now an hour and a half had passed. He re-entered the office and walked up to the counter where the glass slider was still open. He caught the same receptionist glancing down at a Cambridge student rag, with a front page article lamenting how the state of Massachusetts could fail to see the wisdom of legalizing pot for recreational use.

"Excuse me," chortled Tristan, reading the headline again, "Can you be kind enough to tell me when Mrs. Williams and her son, Simon, will be coming out? She may need a break for lunch, although Simon may have to wait until dinner time to eat. And, by the way, here is an order of my own. Do not, I repeat, do not perform the challenge test on my patient. Tell that to Dr. McKenna, please." Tristan proceeded to write his order on a slip of paper. He then signed it and handed to the guy behind the glass.

Pushing the note aside; but now marginally sympathetic to the cowboy doctor from "Nevada," the receptionist said, "Hang on, Dr. Lames, I will find out when Mrs. Williams and her son will be coming out. I'll try to get the note to Dr. McKenna, if I can find her." Figuring that nothing was worth trying to straighten out the idiot behind the sliding glass door, Tristan gave up and waited.

Two minutes later, the receptionist returned. "It appears that the young lad and his mother were taken out a back hallway to the pulmonary function testing laboratory in the next building, about a five minute walk from here."

Tristan gasped, "Is that laboratory, the location of the inhalation challenge booth?"

"Uh, I have no idea; I do not know what kind of booth you're talking about; but I can ask," replied the receptionist, trying to remain helpful.

"Never mind," fired Tristan. "Can I get to this lab through the hallways outside of this office, right now?" The receptionist had to get up, yet again, disappearing this time for only two minutes. He returned and gave Tristan some confusing directions.

Tristan rushed out the door, slamming it, just as he heard the last two syllables rolling off the receptionist's tongue. An overwhelming sense of fear drove him down the corridor. He really had no idea where he was going. The hospital was a gigantic maze, filled with human ants, running this way and that. A full fifteen minutes later, after getting lost for half the time and asking directions from four different people, Tristan ran down the main hallway of an adjacent building, planning a right turn into the corridor, where he was told the challenge booth was located.

Suddenly, he saw and heard the commotion. The code blue had just come over the public address system. The crash cart was already there and had been moved inside the office outside the chamber. Two physicians barged past Tristan, one knocking him against the wall. Tristan heard the "Sorry!" as the same doctor slammed past two more people emerging onto the life and death scene. Tristan carefully moved forward toward the open door. By now, there must have been seven or eight people crowded into the doorway. One orderly had been knocked to the floor and was getting up with the help of a nurse, standing close by. Tristan asked a nurse standing next to him, if Dr. Chris McKenna was among the physicians crowding the scene. She responded, "Yes, I know her. Should she be here? But then again, I haven't seen her. Why do you ask? Tristan swallowed hard and moved closer.

He could see four people leaning over a figure on the floor. He expected to find Simon and Sethie in the office area outside the booth. It just wasn't conceivable that this chaos could involve Simon. It wasn't even lunch time. Simon wasn't scheduled to be challenged until mid afternoon. No way. Suddenly, another doctor, barged past Tristan while a figure was being raised onto a gurney, fitted with a cardiac backboard to allow for effective, continuing CPR. The doctor who had just entered was an anesthesiologist, who proceeded to intubate the figure, now on the gurney.

Two IVs were in; the patient was intubated and on a monitor. Tristan saw the monitor, a foot above, everyone's head. Fine ventricular fibrillation, barely. No effective heart beat - fatal within minutes unless reversed, despite continuing CPR. The drugs poured in. Sodium bicarbonate, lidocaine, and epinephrine, among others. Tristan could not see over the heads of the people in front of him.

He could not see the figure on the gurney; but, off to his right, he heard an almost inhuman, quiet wail, like the crying of an animal that had just been hit by a car and was lying in the road, waiting to die. Over to the side, sitting in a chair, head in her hands, clutching a light blue handkerchief, sat Sethie Williams, out of touch and inconsolable.

CHAPTER 20 - SIMON - PART V - CAUSATION, MCKENNA'S TREACHERY AND CADIXX

DATE: Monday, 7/20/09 - about three years
and eleven months after Katrina
LOCATION: Dallas, Texas

— — —

Tristan stared at the expert report, having read it for the fourth time. It was very comprehensive and included a detailed incident report about the cardiac event; but no mention that the entire disaster may have been precipitated by an episode of unstoppable asthma that occurred when Simon was re-exposed to formaldehyde in the chamber. No apology, just a copy of the consent form, signed by Sethie Williams on behalf of her son, Simon. Attached to the consent form was a letter to Asher, written on hospital letterhead, by one of Coastal General's in-house counsels with a copy sent to a fancy Boston "silk stocking" law firm that specialized in medical malpractice defense. The letter was dispassionate. It highlighted those areas of the consent form that clearly delineated the risks of the inhalation challenge testing, including catastrophic pulmonary and cardiac events, just like the one that befell poor Simon.

Tristan glanced up, annoyed by the flickering in the fluorescent light in Asher's office that was casting odd shadows on one of Asher' Remingtons, hanging on the far wall. Asher was on the phone and had been talking for the past 15 minutes about some refinery explosion that killed five workers down near Galveston.

209

Joseph sat silently, occasionally glancing at Tristan, eerily, listening, while studying every detail of his surroundings. Tristan didn't feel ignored. Quite the contrary. He and Asher had gone around and around for over three hours that morning about McKenna's expert report and the legal indigestion attached to the incident. In the conclusion of the incident report, McKenna had written, to Tristan's astonishment:

"The patient suffered a paradoxical adverse reaction to the bronchodilator in his inhaler, administered during the second part challenge test. This medication led to his having a seizure and cardiac arrest. He was resuscitated uneventfully and remained in the hospital for three days for observation, without further incident. The patient was discharged on his usual medications, without his inhaler (see attached) and will be followed up by his pediatrician in New Orleans. A report outlining the findings of the patient's work-up will be sent to the patient's mother and his attorney in Texas."

Tristan thought, "This conclusion was ridiculous. The formaldehyde challenge was to blame, not the bronchodilator medication in the inhaler. Even the propellant in the inhaler could not explain the problem. Simon had used that inhaler for months before he was seen at Coastal General, without any incident. In fact, after the Coastal debacle, Simon kept his inhaler and used it following his discharge from the hospital. He has been using the same inhaler medicine ever since and has had no problems. It's the formaldehyde stupid!"

For whatever it was worth, Tristan also noted there was also no mention of his role as the referring physician. Fortunately for Tristan, in the thick of the paperwork, the hospital's lawyer had included a copy of Tristan's originally recommended medical testing protocol he had sent to Dr. Gruber and had obviously passed under the nose of Dr. McKenna. Thank God, Tristan's protocol made no recommendation for inhalation challenge testing to formaldehyde but it did include a request for skin testing and a PTSD evaluation, neither of them performed by McKenna.

Waiting for Asher to get off the phone, Tristan recalled his first reading of what was collectively now called the "McKenna Report," legal crap and all.

In the core of the report, writing as if nothing had even gone wrong, appearing ever in control, with flawless precision, McKenna delineated the full results of Simon's evaluation.

All of Simon's laboratory findings were negative.

Before his near death experience in McKenna's chamber, Simon's chest x-rays, showed findings consistent with asthma including a small of amount of hyper-expansion and air trapping, a sign that Simon was having trouble emptying air out of his lungs, not getting air in. After the disaster, the x-rays were worse.

Sure enough Simon's CAT scan of his sinuses showed evidence of chronic infection and thickening of the lining of the frontal sinus, a finding that was consistent with his exposure to formaldehyde, although it was not diagnostic of the effects of that chemical. There could have been other causes, like environmental allergies that caused his chronic infection.

It really didn't matter to Tristan. Whether Simon's sinus inflammation was caused by an allergy to kitty cats, petunias or formaldehyde, his exposure to formaldehyde in the trailer probably aggravated his condition. As long as he had back-up exposure data, Tristan saw that he could apply the same basic causation logic that he had argued dozens of times before.

Namely, absent Simon's exposure to formaldehyde in the trailer, his chronic sinus problem would not have been as bad as it was documented in McKenna's report. In other words, the natural course of Simon's underlying asthma was substantively aggravated by formaldehyde exposure in the trailer. Simon had a new disease, one he would not have developed had he not been exposed to "trailer formaldehyde." During his exposure in the trailer, Simon's condition became worse at every point in time, spotted with the historical stench of this chemical on his body, thanks to Matchless Enterprises and Uncle Sam. With the hospital data in hand, Tristan knew that he make a compelling argument for formaldehyde aggravation of Simon's pre-existing childhood asthma, the development of chronic sinus problems and even an increased lifetime risk for developing cancer of the nasal passages.

As far as the PTSD issue went, Tristan knew that the formaldehyde exposure was only part of the problem. He knew Katrina that "nasty bitch" and all that came with her were the main culprits. Tristan wasn't even certain he would bring up the PTSD. It might confuse matters and distract judicial attention away from the formaldehyde issue. Medical opinion overreach can kill an expert's case. Tristan knew that. But if he decided to go ahead with a claim of PTSD, Tristan thought that both his and Dr. Pat's opinions on this matter would be enough to satisfy the court. Then again, maybe not.

Absent PTSD, it looked like it would be a turkey shoot for Tristan; but then he read McKenna's astonishing conclusions about the chamber testing.

"Notwithstanding exposure to the allegedly offending agent, gaseous formaldehyde vapor, it is my opinion, to a reasonable degree of environmental medical certainty that the patient's paradoxically adverse, yet reversible reaction to the challenge vapor was non-specific and did not represent a true sensitivity to formaldehyde. As noted earlier, his problem was initiated by the use of his asthma inhaler during the second part of the testing protocol."

McKenna continued:

"A careful analysis of the estimated vapor concentration at the time of the adverse event (approximately 500 parts per billion) revealed that the formaldehyde level in the chamber was high enough to have caused the same effect in any patient with or without formaldehyde sensitivity. I, therefore, must opine that I have found no causal relationship between the patient's alleged exposure to formaldehyde while living in the Matchless Trailer and his reaction to chamber testing, or for that matter, his documented findings of asthma and chronic sinusitis. Further, evaluation to clarify such a causal relationship, to the extent that it could or could not exist, would include skin patch testing to formaldehyde at low levels to avoid an irritation effect. Such testing, if performed properly could suggest the presence of formalde-hyde allergy or sensitization."

Tristan read it again, culling through every syllable, sickened, like sifting through kitty litter when your cat had diarrhea.

Tristan knew these conclusions were BS. Unless sensitized and at risk for something as bad as "Unstoppable Asthma," persons exposed to 500 parts per billion of formaldehyde would not hit the deck like Simon did, even though they could become sick in other less lethal ways. After all the level in the trailers was often 50 times the so called "safe level" for long term exposure.

Simon almost died because he was sensitive to formaldehyde; so he reacted much more severely at levels that just made others less horribly miserable. Many people exposed to about the same level of formaldehyde as Simon, reported eye burning, cough, ear infections, worsening allergies, sinus problems, skin rashes, diarrhea, depression, sleep disturbances, and dozens of other problems, affecting almost all bodily systems; and to top it off these trailer dwellers were also at increased risk for nasal cancer, maybe 10 to 25 years later.

Tristan thought, "God, how can those bastards, those greedy bastards, who sold those trailers and knew they were gas chambers think they will get away with it? I guess because they have bucket-loads of money and lawyers who know how to spend it."

"And what nerve!" Tristan continued, "McKenna has the chutz-pah to recommend the patch testing that I had recommended in my original protocol sent to her well in advance of Simon's visit - a test, moreover, that she had excluded from his work-up in the first place. Now she suggests patch testing in her report to refine Simon's diag-nosis, like it was part of some diagnostic brainstorm, on her part, to impress the court. Given that she practically killed her patient, it is probably better that the testing wasn't performed and didn't compli-cate matters. Under the circumstances, it would have been hard to interpret, anyway. The poor boy's PTSD, with accompanying flash-backs and perpetual mourning over his lost dog didn't seem to interest McKenna either. Not enough hard science, I guess."

The door to Asher's office opened. Staring at Tristan and entering with two cups of coffee, balanced, but clanking together in her right hand, was Laura Swain, wearing a sympathetic, bright smile that accented her beautifully tailored suit and the black pumps that increased her height by about an inch or so to five nine. In her left hand she was carrying a large, clear zip-lock bag with a square piece of three eighths inch plywood in it.

"I heard all about it, and I read the report," she said, as she leaned forward and placed the coffees in front of both Tristan and Joseph, then set the bag on her end of the table. "These cases are never simple," she quipped, barely shaking her head; then, aiming at Tristan. "What are you going to do about it?"

Skirting her last question, Tristan said softly, "You remembered the way Joseph likes his coffee. And as luck may have it, I do take mine black, no cream, and no sugar. Thanks." Joseph nodded his thanks; but continued his silence, just listening, absorbing, and gathering.

"Lucky guess….I-I guess," she said smiling again, but with a role of her eyes, wondering about Tristan's silly attempt at ice breaking.

Now, missing the look that could easily have followed Laura's patting him on his head while he was stuck drooling in some future nursing home, Tristan continued,

"The report, yeah, I have read it several times. It is going to be a problem for our case. McKenna's no light-weight, even if her conclusions are dead wrong. The problem is that she has never taken the time to perform the hard work of analyzing the exposure data in the case. Without that analysis, she really can't offer an opinion on causation. Exposure drives the analysis. And in this case, there was so much of it, in the trailers."

"In that regard, I have brought you a piece of the offending trailer cabinet plywood," quipped Laura pointing at the bag on the table. "Part of our split samples; smell it to your heart's content! But be careful, the level in this bag is probably 200 times the level in Simon's trailer. It's been sitting in the sun on my car dashboard. Just curious to create a 'worst-case scenario.'"

Ignoring the poisonous exhibit, Tristan continued, "In a kid with pre-exposure asthma, now with chronic sinus problems and a near death experience with chamber exposure to formaldehyde at a level, I would submit would evoke a sensitization and not, necessarily an irritation effect, at least a case for aggravation can be made.

According to McKenna, the child was exposed to about 500 parts per billion (ppb) in the challenge chamber, about 2/3 of the OSHA limit. But I wonder, if it wasn't higher. Anyway, I must emphasize that the 500 ppb level is probably above the olfactory (odor) threshold that ranges from about 100 to 800 ppb. So, as he did in the trailer, Simon could probably smell the formaldehyde. Because he is sensitive, this level initiated his asthma attack; and it almost killed him.

Simon's severe attack of unstoppable asthma led to hypoxia and his having a seizure that, in turn, led to cardiac arrest. Therefore, all this, following exposure to a level like the one in his trailer probably means that Simon was already sensitized to formaldehyde. McKenna's conclusion that Simon reacted to his inhaler and not the formaldehyde is simply wrong."

Asher entered the room and sat down, hearing the tail end of Tristan's remarks, a replay of what he had heard all morning.

Without acknowledging Asher, focused 100% on Tristan to make certain that he was paying attention, Laura began,

"You know, I've been studying this report too. And I try to analyze it like a lawyer, looking for all the moving parts that are greased, or I should say, greasy, some of which are there but out of sight.

Listen, Tristan. I tend to be on the paranoid side. While it may be true his inhaler was irrelevant, like you suggested, maybe Simon was exposed to a formaldehyde level high enough to have affected any person – just in this case was high enough to have crashed an elephant. Reading the literature and given what happened, I wonder if Simon's exposure might have actually been as much at 20,000 ppb, or 40 times higher than she reported and about 27 times the OSHA limit, a number that McKenna did not want to report. So she reported the lower number to cover her chamber exposure screw-up and blamed Simon's inhaler for the disaster. That conclusion, as crazy as it seems, was better than owning up to almost executing Simon like a rat.

By the way, I spoke to the hospital's attorney two days ago and asked him who prepared the formaldehyde exposure concentrations for Simon's test. It was some tech who had worked for the hospital for many years. He wouldn't give us his name.

When I told him that we would certainly want to take his deposition, he said,

'Well go ahead; you will find him in the Cambridge City Morgue. He was found a week ago with a bullet wound to the head, face down on the Cambridge side of the Charles River. He had been there for about three days and was hard to identify. Especially because his face had been partially devoured by that famous line of Boston river rats, not unlike some of their politicians, well known to observant kayakers, Duck Boat pilots, weekend sail boat captains and members of the MIT and Hautair crew teams who row at dusk. Best seen at night, these rats are well fed, diseased and spoiled. They had quite a time with the lab tech. The rats got to some other parts of his body too; not a subject of polite conversation.'

How poetic I thought. I told him I would be back in touch."

Joseph quickly sat higher in his chair and stared intently at Laura, trapping every word, even more tightly than before.

Tristan, remarked, winking at Joseph, "Laura, I think you have missed your calling. You should have gone FBI. Your exposure theory and what I have a hunch was your own description of the rat-eaten wretch were concise, insightful and disgusting - all tools that would serve you well in full time forensics.

On a more serious note, Asher, I think we are in a bad place. I know you haven't disclosed McKenna's report to the defense yet. It seems that we have to do it, because it contains other valuable medical data that I can use in my final report that will support causation. If she doesn't write a supplemental report with a change of opinion, I will simply have to be more persuasive in my testimony. I think I can manage."

Tristan continued, looking a bit exasperated, "You know, I still haven't met the good Dr. McKenna. Right after the incident, she was suddenly called out of town, supposedly, with a family emergency. Another doctor, covering for her, while Simon was in the hospital, said her mom had had a heart attack, somewhere down in New Jersey.

I called Lila in Peru. She said she had spoken with McKenna right after Simon's cardiac arrest and recovery. She confirmed McKenna's story. Lila plans to cut short her Peru project and return to Cambridge in about 10 days."

Asher looked at the two of them. Laura had just told him about the dead lab tech yesterday. He still had not revealed anything to either of them about his brother Saul and "The Resistance." He planned to – but still, not yet. Asher's head was swimming. He sat there in one of his vacant stare modes, looking past Tristan and Laura at the Dallas skyline, but thinking with deep intensity,

"One thing's for certain - now there was a dead lab tech who had worked for McKenna, lying on a very cold morgue slab with a bullet in his head and one fourth of a face left. Dead men tell no tales. Was he murdered or could it have been suicide? Laura didn't comment about the latter possibility. This tech could have deliberately exposed Simon to a life-threatening level of formaldehyde. Did McKenna know about it? Maybe McKenna engineered the overexposure, figured she could blame the very dead lab tech and then duck the liability bullet because she was shielded by the procedural consent form.

In any case, if it was not suicide, then who killed the lab tech? Who would have wanted dead, the man who may have tried to kill his client, the star witness against Matchless Enterprises and FEMA, too, had he been allowed by the court to sue Uncle Sam? Good God! This was supposed to have been a straight-forward civil action, like so many I have handled in the past. Now, so much was unraveling!

Saul is right; they had had enough – so they have turned to murder. Could this all hang together? First, Dr. DUI found wrapped around a tree; next the foiled, attempted abduction and elimination of

Tristan, Joseph and Laura; next what could have been the attempted murder of Simon and next the death and likely murder of McKenna's lab tech. And, don't forget, the earlier mutilation of Tristan's wife, Heather, and the brutalizing of his daughter, Tess.

Another certainty – no one knew, knows or will ever know the actual exposure level that knocked Simon down except McKenna or the lab tech.

Another certainty – McKenna's conclusion in her report is BS. She is hiding something. Given the dead lab tech, she is the only one left who knows what really happened to Simon, namely how much formaldehyde he was exposed to and why."

Asher suddenly broke down under the excruciating weight of the burden of information he had been accumulating for the past month. Information largely supplied by his brother, Saul, now accentuated by the murder of McKenna's lab tech.

"I have to tell them all, either the truth, or, at least the facts as I know them," asserted Asher to himself. "I could never live with myself, if something happened to any of them. They have a right to back out of the FEMA trailer litigation now even though it may already be too late. They have a right of self defense.

Asher opened the locked right lower drawer of his desk and under about two inches of miscellaneous papers; he pulled out a color copy of the PowerPoint slide. It was sent to him by Saul four days ago, just after their last conversation.

Here he was face to face with Laura, Tristan and Joseph, secure in his office. He had had enough – no more secrecy, no more carrying the weight and fear alone. He quickly slid two copies of The Resistance slide across the table, one to Laura and the other to Tristan.

Laura spoke first, "What is this? Where did you get it?"

In a fraction of a second, Tristan added, glancing at Joseph, "What is 'The Resistance?' Why is 'CADIXX' on this diagram?"

"All in due time. I promise," said Asher, sounding relieved he had taken the first step. He certainly needed their help. "This is what appears to be an organizational diagram or chart of an insidious group called 'The Resistance.' I just received this information a few days ago, from…from… I have a brother, named Saul. He sent it to me."

"From your brother? You have a brother? How did he get his hands on this information?" blurted Tristan. "Asher, what is going on here?"

Laura sat quietly, studying the diagram.

"According to Saul, 'The Resistance' may be some type of industry group gone rogue, or even worse, gone criminal. Tristan, CADIXX and….and…., even Saul, may be part of it."

"Thanks for telling me," gasped Tristan, glaring at Asher. "Are you sure you just learned about this so-called organization?"

"Let me clarify," pleaded Asher. "Saul told me about The Resistance some time ago; but I swear, Tristan, I just received this diagram and I knew nothing about any connection to CADIXX, assuming one even exists."

Asher looked directly at Tristan. Laura was dead quiet, her eyes locked onto the diagram.

"Please, look at the heading, pleaded Asher. "You can see it seems to be something like an organizational chart – for The Resistance. Saul sent it several days ago, on a memory stick with a total of ten files, all password protected. He told me the password for this PowerPoint file. I opened it and printed the slide. I have no passwords for the other nine protected files.

This is part of a critical data base, none of which I really understand and most of which I can not even access. I need your help – all of you.

The title of the slide doesn't help us much. At the moment, I have no idea what these elements mean or how the chart functions. Saul was supposed to call me last night to go over it. No call. So here I am, left just guessing, especially where Saul's place was, or maybe still is, in that hideous organization. I am worried to death about him."

Asher stared at both of them, his pain showing clearly on his face and now his eyes welling up with the early vestige of real tears. He looked like a man who had unburdened himself, risking embarrassment, anger and worse, disappointment. He waited, studying his three colleagues.

Laura rebounded in a split second. "Asher, don't worry; and I think I can speak for Tristan and Joseph; we're here to help and we will." While reassuring Asher, she glanced at Tristan and Joseph, dragging them into her world of forgiveness and mercy. It was harder than ever to read Joseph, still silent without obvious emotion, although she thought she could see some preparations for slaughter, attached to the barely visible smile on his face.

Taken aback; but, frankly, moved by the painful emotion and tears he had never seen before in Asher, Tristan responded, "I am not quite on the same page as Laura; but I will do what I can. Let's get started. Let's zero in on the known assholes on the diagram. CADIXX is number one."

Asher continued, "I agree. We don't have a lot of time now; but I, at least, want to get started...."

Suddenly, without knocking, Asher's secretary poked in her head and said, "Mr. Goldman. She has arrived. Shall I bring her in or would you like to escort her in yourself. She is in the waiting room."

"The slide - later," coughed Asher. Then, he managed "I'll come and get her myself," to his secretary as she withdrew her head from the doorway.

Tristan started to veto the interruption; but decided to wait. And under most circumstances, he would politely have ignored such office bantering that was none of his business. But his curiosity got the better of him. Still studying the slide before he placed it into his briefcase, he exclaimed, "If you don't mind my asking, who is here to join us in this moment of madness? I hope she can be of some help.

Laura, what is this all about? Who is here?"

Tristan glanced up in time to see Asher leave the room without answering him. So Tristan turned his inquisitor's stare at Laura. Joseph sat up again. Laura turned Asher's slide upside down and stuck it into a stack of papers, then stood mute and shrugged her shoulders like a school-girl who had just flushed a joint down the toilet, a moment before her mom and dad came home early, smelled the weed and started to search her room.

Tristan was beginning to feel marginalized and left out. He looked again at Laura who was staring at the door. She knew damned good and well who was about to enter the office. And, he wondered if she had known about The Resistance for days, if not weeks.

CHAPTER 21 - MCKENNA AND A GLIMPSE OF THE RESISTANCE

DATE: Monday, 7/20/09 - about three years and eleven months after Katrina
LOCATION: Dallas, Texas

—   —   —

Tristan's day was going poorly; but within the next hour he was going to experience a new meaning to the word "indigestion." He was still staring at Laura, when, with Asher in tow, entered a trim, late thirtyish female version of Marine Gunny Sergeant Hartman, played by R. Lee Ermey in *Full Metal Jacket*. She had the same "smile" too. Whoever she was, she looked like she was born pissed off, was raised pissed off and was still pissed off when she entered Asher's office. Then, when she saw Tristan, she became really pissed off. Tristan was almost knocked over by her look; but held his tongue, for the moment, trying to consider the spectrum of identities that he could pin on this visitor.

"Uh, I understand, you two have never met," said Asher, wishing he was somewhere else, having miscalculated the exothermic reaction that was about to melt down his office and maybe the entire building. He had hoped for the best; but realized he had no plans for the worst.

Tristan, on the other hand, studied Ms. "Gunny Sergeant" Ermey with a curious look as calm as the surface of a birdbath just before an eagle planned to visit.

"Tristan, I apologize for the surprise; but I now have the pleasure of introducing you to...."

Tristan interrupted, with a glare at Asher, then, nearly choking, managed a smile to the visitor, "You must be Chris McKenna! What a pleasure and pleasant surprise to fi-i-nally meet you! Thank you so much, Asher and Laura for arranging this joyous meeting."

"The pleasure is mine, Dr. Baines," said Dr. McKenna, looking like a motion sick airline passenger struggling to find an air sickness bag. "Although both highly inconvenient to my schedule and otherwise most irregular, Mr. Goldman insisted that I meet with you in person here in Dallas to discuss the work-up of the Williams boy, uh, Simon, I believe. I am not certain what there is to discuss – it's all there in my report."

She sat down at the head of the table three chairs to the right of Laura.

Tristan waited, giving Dr. McKenna a chance to show any evidence of humanity. Perhaps in the form of a single compassionate remark, much less a private apology, for nearly killing her patient while performing a challenge test that Tristan did not request and would not have approved under any circumstances. Perhaps her apology could be then followed by an attempt at professional reconciliation for marginalizing and ignoring the referring physician, namely, Tristan, the expert with whom she was supposed to be collaborating. Maybe in a wet dream.

No dice.

Silence.

Tristan thought about introducing Joseph; then cratered the idea. Anyway, Joseph sat there, as usual, remaining stoic, quiet and observant. Tristan thought (more likely, hoped) he had seen McKenna throw a glance Joseph's way, maybe even a slightly worried one.

For a split second, Tristan even contemplated asking how McKenna's mother was doing, after her supposed heart attack; McKenna's excuse for hauling out of Dodge while Simon was recovering. But Tristan took a disgusted pause. He really didn't care. His senses were heightened. He knew what to expect. McKenna was intractable; as refractory and rigid as the alloy in the leading edge of an F15 fighter wing. He found himself wondering whether this woman had a mother at all.

Tristan decided to fill the void. "Dr. McKenna, we disagree on the most fundamental issue of this case. Given what you have reported as the level of formaldehyde in the challenge chamber, namely 500 parts per billion, to which the patient was exposed at the time of his disastrous, near death reaction, how is it that you think….."

She interrupted, cutting him off at the knees, probably aiming about a foot higher. "Dr. Baines, you don't remember me, do you?" she said with vitriol drooling off the words "…do you?"

Tristan actually felt her razor stare, quite capable of guillotining whatever part of his anatomy she cared to lop off. This time she actually looked at Joseph and dismissed him as if he were a potted plant. Joseph stared back like he was watching a camp fire. Tristan waited, composing himself and working hard to search the Rolodex in his memory, under the heading of "crows."

He responded quietly, maintaining his professional composure, at least for the moment. "Dr. McKenna. I just love guessing games. I used to play them as a child. I am afraid you have me at a disadvantage. Under what lovely circumstances, pray tell, have our paths crossed, so that I should remember you?"

Unfazed by Tristan's sarcasm, Dr. McKenna, said simply "Higgins Middle School."

Tristan, pushing 1000 major cases, took a second to set aside his Rolodex and allow his internal hard drive to come up to speed. "Hm-m-m, Higgins Middle School, Higgins Middle School, uh…"

Before he could speak, McKenna popped up, "Remember your defense report, defending the indefensible, Dr. Baines? 1998? Just before, I was offered my current position at Coastal General.

Thanks to your rather inaccurate calculus, 'out of left field' modeling, dubious clinical conclusions and stable of, shall I say, highly paid defense 'dose reconstructionists,' 125 badly injured and forever scarred middle school children were deprived their just compensation. I was never called to testify; but I examined each and every one of them, documenting the disastrous effects of the classroom cleaning chemicals on their lungs and immune systems. Remember now, Dr. Baines?"

Tristan could do nothing but smile. And the smile widened and widened and widened until he thought he was going to split his lips. "Acha!" he thought "So, now I get it. It all makes sense; this whole episode, her contrarian report, the cold shoulder, the unanswered e-mails and phone calls were the logically illogical result of a grudge – Nothing but anger and professional jealously – the bellwether of insecurity."

Remembering his recent waiting room humiliation, Tristan unwisely decided to rub it in – just a little bit, so he thought. Others who had worked with Tristan over the years lamented on more than one occasion the sad reality that the otherwise wise Dr. Baines had never read, much less owned a copy of Dale Carnegie's *How to Win Friends and Influence People*.

"Dr. McKenna, I do recall the Higgins case. In balancing my expert activities, I worked, in that dispute, for the defendant school system. It went to trial. We won; you lost. Our science was better. The children were truly unharmed. Their teachers reacted hysterically to fugitive odors from a few unfilled sewer traps and a variety of cafeteria smells. The classroom cleaning chemicals were never a threat to anyone's health.

As I recall, the children's attorney wept in open court, while I was on the witness stand when she realized she couldn't unhinge my opinions in front of the jury. Even the judge was embarrassed by the whole scene. Too bad you weren't there to see it. It was really unprecedented in my experience as a testifying expert. And I regret to say, and please don't take this badly; but even though you mentioned it, I just can not seem to recall your role in the medical work-up of those kids.

Really, Dr. McKenna, the allegations were frivolous from the get-go. The case never should have been filed. And, by the way, the superintendent of schools and her successors have been sending me holiday fruitcakes every year since. Two years ago, I wrote her back, of course, thanking her and relating it was unnecessary to continue to send me this festive offering. I do not eat the stuff; so I usually give it to my neighbor. Perhaps, I will save some for you, if you wish. After a month, it can be stored in your trunk as a spare tire!"

Now Tristan felt better; as good as a man could, thinking he had righted the wrongs of his recent encounter with arrogant dismissiveness. Awash with naïveté, Tristan next thought he had just saved his precious jewels. What a surprise awaited him.

McKenna stared at Tristan, emotionless, like a mortician, leaning over an open coffin, powdering her client's nose. Tristan thought he saw her lip tremble a bit. Wishful thinking.

Silence.

Suddenly, Joseph rose from his chair, towering over McKenna. "Gotta go, excuse me; where is John?" For a second, Laura took him literally, thinking "John who?" But, all eyes were saucers, as Asher, pointed down the hall, squeaking, "That way!" Joseph hustled. It didn't break the ice; it only made McKenna madder.

Not really expert at this lethal jousting, especially when it required him to remain silent, Tristan piped up, "Dr. McKenna. Can we discuss your report now? Perhaps, we can find some common ground that will benefit Simon and his family."

More economical with her words, McKenna said, "I do not like you, Dr. Baines. You are an unskilled bumpkin, notwithstanding your parade of academic papers and sheepskins. Your opinions on the FEMA case are as incorrect as were those in the Higgins case years ago. It is simple. Simon Williams was largely unaffected by his formaldehyde exposure while living in his FEMA trailer."

The room was heating up. Laura and Asher looked like they were about to duck under the conference table to avoid the shrapnel they knew was coming.

Tristan looked at the physician facing him, 10 years his junior, not quite as well trained, wondering what to do next. She had him. He knew it. Any strenuous effort to convince her to reconsider the data to Simon's benefit would simply empower her further.

In the seemingly interminable pause, Laura and Asher now watched with fascination, waiting for the next shoe to drop, figuring they still had time to avoid becoming collateral damage.

Tristan took a deep breath, then said, "Dr. McKenna, given that

the patient reacted to your formaldehyde challenge at such a supposedly low level, wouldn't you agree that he was hypersensitive to formaldehyde, a probable consequence of his trailer exposure?"

"How dare you!" she screamed. "How dare you! How dare you
phrase your question like a cross-examination? The question is compound and formulated by an idiot for an idiot. And I am no idiot. It
was the boy's inhaler that caused his arrest, you moron!

I know all about you, Dr. Baines. I know about CADIXX and the
misfortune you brought on your wife and daughter. You are to blame,
Dr. Baines, for all of it. Your incompetent meddling in the FEMA
case should have been shunned by Mr. Goldman. You should have
stayed in the backwoods, mountains or wherever the hell you hide,
where you belong with your Indian pal, who is probably making a
mess at the moment. Your opinions about the Williams boy will be
destroyed in court. You are out of your league and washed up. How
does it feel to be a eunuch at such a young age?"

Asher blurted, "Now wait a minute, Dr. McKenna! That is
enough! I asked Dr. Baines to join our effort. I advised you on the
phone that the primary purpose of this meeting was to try to syn-
thesize some common opinions with Dr. Baines that will benefit my
client, your patient. I didn't pay your, should I say, substantial fee
to come to Dallas from Boston to behave in this manner. In fact, I
didn't expect this juvenile display from either of you. The data harvest
from your work-up of Simon at Coastal will be necessary to help Dr.
Baines write his report too. There is obvious disagreement in how to
interpret it.

By the way, and I say this with caution, are you absolutely certain
about the exposure level Simon sustained when he, well, when he
became ill?"

McKenna glared at Asher and was about to say something when
Tristan unloaded.

"Became ill, did you say? Asher," remarked Tristan. "What a
polite euphemism for a near death experience, one that could have
been avoided had Dr. McKenna read the ER record, supplied by

Dr. Simms. The boy has been at risk for Unstoppable Asthma for years. He should never have been challenge tested in McKenna's gas chamber!"

Looking directly at McKenna, Tristan continued, "And by the way, what happened to your poor lab tech, who prepared the formaldehyde concentration for the chamber test? I understand his head collided with a 9mm hollow point in a most mysterious way."

Ignoring both Asher and Tristan, McKenna said, "There is no use continuing this discussion. I have rescheduled my flight back to Boston. I have important projects ahead of me. Sorry, I won't be staying for dinner. Bottom line, live with it. The formaldehyde concentration in that trailer was insignificant. I would have lived there myself. Those persons displaced like Simon should be grateful to God that FEMA and Matchless gave them a roof over their head. Now, I want to call a cab. How do I get out of this office, Mr. Goldman? Say 'Goodbye to Tonto for me."

Laura suddenly interrupted. "Please, let me have the honor of escorting you to the curb, Dr. McKenna. But before you go, I have a surprise for you."

McKenna turned her back to Laura and was now facing the door. She hesitated a moment to pick up her purse and small briefcase.

Fast as lightning, Laura reached down and picked up the bagged, evidence on the table, probably containing enough formaldehyde to embalm a cat. She unzipped the bag, containing the large piece of FEMA trailer cabinet plywood. It was a beautiful specimen, reeking with formaldehyde vapors, evaporating from dripping uncured glue. Laura took the specimen in her left hand and took two steps to approach McKenna's back. Gently placing her right hand on McKenna's shoulder, Laura reached around and placed the plywood under McKenna's nose.

"Breath deep, Dr. McKenna, and enjoy the fragrance of death, endured by your patient for 18 months, night after night. It did wonders for his asthma and his permanently damaged sinuses," whispered Laura into McKenna's ear.

Choking and spitting, McKenna turned like a maniac and knocked the plywood out of Laura's hand. With her other hand she shoved Laura, squeezing her left breast, causing Laura to lose her balance and fall across the table.

"As they say, I'll see you in court. All of you!" McKenna screamed, rubbing her eyes, as she burst out of the office.

Uninjured, Laura regained her balance, and came up with a smile She looked at Tristan – "God, you were right. You were right.

OK Asher, Now, where can we find this bitch on that organization chart?"

CHAPTER 22 - THE RESISTANCE UNMASKED

DATE: Tuesday, 7/21/09 - about three years and eleven months after Katrina
LOCATION: Dallas, Texas

—   —   —

Tristan had had a very rough night, barely sleeping three hours. His encounter with Dr. McKenna was disturbing, to say the least. Her grievance, grudge, whatever you want to call it came unexpectedly and with the vengence of a scorned woman. The Higgins School Case had gone to trial over 11 years before, in 1998; and, at that time, he had already been on the case for about two years. So he could have crossed paths with McKenna as early as 1996. He just couldn't remember her clearly. Based upon what Dr. Lila Gruber (McKenna's boss) had told him, McKenna would have been only 29, just out of residency, post-graduate training. According to Lila, McKenna had started at Coastal sometime around 1999 or 2000.

Tristan thought hard. There had to be much more to this situation than met the eye. Exactly whom had he brought into this case, clearly inadvertently? After all, he had been the one who referred Simon to Coastal General. He had not always agreed with specialists to whom he had referred patients; but this level of hostility and adversity was unprecedented.

He recalled Lila telling him that over the past five years, namely, from 2004 through 2009, McKenna "...has brought a lot of grant money into our program at Coastal..." From what sources and how much, he wondered? McKenna's behavior was so off the wall, so callous, so spiteful, and so utterly inconsiderate of their mission.

It was possible that he and another expert simply had diametrically opposite causation opinions about the same medical and exposure information. It wouldn't be the first time such disagreement had occurred. But Tristan was also intrigued with Laura's suggestion that Simon had actually been poisoned with formaldehyde; and McKenna was reporting the lower exposure, trying to cover herself to prevent a malpractice claim. One thing was for certain, this woman was not entirely who she claimed to be. How did she know about CADIXX, Heather and Tess and even my friendship with Joseph? Her disrespect for Joseph with the "Tonto" remark was terrible. Lucky Joseph was in the John, when she made it. Otherwise, who knows? She certainly had a broad neck for the slicing and plenty of hair for the taking. McKenna seemed to know a lot about people close to Tristan, especially those whom he trusted... "Oh God," he thought, don't go there."

He met Laura at Asher's office at 10 am. McKenna's report was front and center. It was a beautiful morning and the sun filled the conference room.

The four carafes of coffee centered on the conference table beckoned Tristan. He calculated (from prior experience), four cups per carafe – so four carafes means sixteen cups were waiting to be consumed. He knew the math. But he intended to have it obey his equations. So there were four cups in carafe number one - one cup each for Asher, Laura, Joseph and Tristan. Next – given one refill each, four cups would disappear from carafe number two. That left two unclaimed carafes containing a total of eight cups, sitting on the table crying to be consumed and cooling (albeit slowly) while waiting. Too bad for the others; but Tristan knew he would claim dibs on the rest to maintain his 10 cup a morning habit. This was fair – take a lot, give a little. After all, he reasoned, "This distribution of morning caffeine is the prerequisite to my functioning at peak efficiency."

Looking toward Tristan, Asher began.

"So, if she doesn't change her report, what are we going to do?" asked Asher. "I can simply not produce it; but if I do, the entire Coastal General medical database will also be thrown out including some of the material you will need to formulate your opinion."

Laura watched the two men intensively. As yesterday, Joseph sat pensively, quietly watching all three. If necessary, he knew the location of the nearest Men's Room, just in case he had to depart the scene of moronic wrestling of presumptively intelligent minds. As he listened, he relished in the universal truth that his intelligence was just as good or maybe even better, especially when it was designed to keep one alive.

"It's simple – just produce everything," answered Tristan. "I have a much better handle than McKenna on Simon's real life exposure in the trailer that set him up to become sensitized over time. I will rely upon FEMA's own warnings to the public to ventilate the trailers in March of 2006, a couple of months before Simon and his family even entered theirs. The feds knew about the possibilities early on."

"We may have a problem with that approach, Tristan," quickly interjected Laura.

"Remember what I told you in New Orleans. At present, we can't sue the feds directly, thanks to the ruling of the federal judge for the District of Eastern Louisiana, who is going to hear our case. None other than the Honorable Henrietta Fabiola Whitmore.

Recall Her Honor ruled that the two year statute of limitations for suing FEMA started to run in May 2006 when Sethie, Simon and their family moved into their gas chamber. Asher didn't file Sethie's lawsuit against Matchless and some other subcontractors until July 2008. We weren't even certain before we filed that we wanted to sue FEMA, and we figured that such a suit would have been doomed at best. But we figured if we did sue the feds, or even if we didn't, we could cross examine one or two whistleblowers who would perk up the ears of the jury. We knew they could spill the beans about FEMA's knowledge of the formaldehyde problem for years, not just months, before Sethie's trailer was even manufactured.

Until earlier this year, we didn't learn that our filing was two months too late to sue the feds. Without making too many excuses, no one and I mean no one would have thought for a second that such an outrageous ruling would have been brought down.

Who would have predicted that Judge Whitmore would agree with the illogical argument that from the moment Sethie moved in, she should have known that formaldehyde from uncured trailer plywood glue was the cause of Simon's worsening asthma? Hell, she didn't know anything about formaldehyde, even how to spell it, much less know it was coming from the trailer and harming her son.

OK, Tristan, as you said, FEMA had issued warnings in March 2006 to ventilate the trailers, two months before she moved in; but Sethie had never received such warnings, from FEMA or anyone else. Go ahead, bring up FEMA's knowledge and delay in disseminating it to make your case for the severity of the problem; but just remember Matchless' lawyers have already used the same information to sink our ability to sue FEMA. That is the situation, again, mainly because they insist that the warnings were 'out there' and Sethie should have seen, read and understood them.

In a fair world, FEMA's confessed knowledge of the problem should have allowed us to sue their asses, not, not sue their asses! At least we can still go after Matchless and their contractors who manufactured, installed and maintained those gas chambers.

This isn't the first time this judge has pulled this type of BS. I have a very bad feeling about her. When we received the ruling, Asher had me do some research. I learned of the case...."

"Stop! Enough, at least for now," blurted Asher, with a painful look on his face. "Our hands may be tied, Tristan; but in our case against Matchless and other defendants, we can still bring in some of the incriminating FEMA material and your causation opinion about Simon. Let's hope the jury gets just as excited listening to you as they would listening to some FEMA whistle-blowing canary.

Anyway, we need to turn our attention to what we started yesterday when our afternoon was so pleasantly interrupted by the arrival of the good Dr. McKenna, indigestion costing no less than $10,000 – not including her possibly wrecking our entire case – only another $50 million."

"Before we begin," retorted Tristan, "I see where Laura is going here. We need to check out this judge. I want to review Laura's research later, in detail. This wouldn't be the first corrupt judge in whose court, I have testified. I have seen some mighty absurd rulings come down where there appeared to be a nod and a smile between the judge and the defense. Like the time in …"

Asher stopped him. "I told you guys, enough for now. I need to go over this with you. It is tearing me apart, really. I haven't heard from my brother, Saul, for over two days, now. Look, let's take a break and reconvene in 15 minutes. I feel terrible."

—   —   —

Thirty minutes later Asher finally rolled in where the others had been waiting. He did look terrible and sounded terrible too; but he had their undivided attention.

"Look; Saul is my older brother, three years my senior. He is a prominent defense attorney in New York City. He's in some kind of trouble. His career had skyrocketed until just a few months ago. He has been keeping in contact with me; but only intermittently. I think he got mixed up with this covert, underground organization, he calls, 'The Resistance.'"

Remember, that organizational chart, the object of our attention, before McKenna interrupted yesterday?"

Laura and Tristan nodded.

Breaking his silence for the first time that morning, Joseph quietly offered, "Uh-huh, no doubt."

Asher, startled by Joseph's remark, stopped, looked at Laura and Tristan and continued.

"Joseph, so you do have a voice," he said with a smile.

"Wait and see," retorted Joseph, "Some serious stuff ahead. I think I know."

Not knowing quite how to respond, Asher stepped back from the table and continued,

"Saul said that 'The Resistance' was formed about seven years ago; believe it or not, in reaction to what its founders claimed to be the escalating, unfair, and outrageous jury awards and even settlements 'extorted' from defendants in toxic tort litigation suits.

It was formed very quietly by some of the more daring and dedicated defense attorneys from the legal departments of major corporations whose initials and names are part of the American vocabulary. Officially, the corporations never approved the actions of their legal zealots; but somehow large amounts of money appeared to fund the activities of 'The Resistance.'

This group was bad news from the start. At first they targeted powerful plaintiffs' law firms, using every dirty trick in the book to disrupt their effectiveness. They funded efforts to bury these firms with unbearable expenses to drive them out of cases.

Exhaustive, over reaching interrogatories with dozens and dozens of questions, delving into every intrusive aspect of plaintiffs' lives and even loves. Psychiatric records, elementary school records, traffic violations, prescription histories, you name it, they wanted it. Most of the interrogatories were fishing expeditions about subjects that had nothing to do with the claims. But they had to be responded to and that cost money.

They hired the most expensive and convincing defense experts money could buy, and buy they did in the form of expert causation opinions. Over time, they found this approach was money wasted, because when it came down to the finale, in front of the jury, it was simply 'my Hautair plaintiff's expert' against 'your defense expert from Yale.'

The court was simply left with a scientific stand-off, placed in the hands of a lay jury, between eight and twelve men and women, some of whom, respectfully, were not certain whether the earth rotated around the sun or vice versa.

Now this is not to say that juries aren't wise. They are; but the burden of scientific complexities laid at their feet was often too much even to read, much less to digest and analyze, so they were left to rely upon their gut feelings and little else.

Also consider what happens when you have a poor injured child making a claim against a multi-billion dollar corporation for only a few hundred thousand or even a million or two. More often than not, before any verdict or trial, out comes the corporate check book. They settle; and it costs defendants money, sometimes a lot of it.

Even worse are the situations when, in the absence of pre or intra-trial settlement, jury verdicts may be handed out against defendants. Sometimes these are in eight or even nine digits. Many are appealed at the cost of seven digits and settled later for about the same. Think about it; my firm and I have deservedly ridden the coattails of this delirious trend. My clients have benefitted; but admittedly, look who has the $50,000 per month office. No wonder they want my ass too.

Anyway, some prodigy within The Resistance made the decision that the way to fix the bleed was not to focus on the law firms; but to disarm their scientific effectiveness by going after their experts - doctors, engineers, industrial hygienists, geologists, all of them.

At first, they tried to stir up dirt on as many of these plaintiff's experts as they could. Their operatives looked for resume' fraud, illicit affairs, drug and alcohol problems, again, you name it. It was a lot of work. Sometimes it was effective; but it turned out to be a lot of heat and no light.

Then some bright young member of the 'Enforcers' arm of The Resistance, realized that only about two percent of plaintiffs' experts were costing defense 95% of their losses. That's when things began to sour. The 'enforcement' ghoul would ask, 'Why not target these dangerous experts, 'The Horses For Slaughter,' who cost us so much money?'

At first, they just played fairly rough. They thought they could please their corporate masters by discrediting or even bribing some 'Horses' or somehow driving them out of business. It worked on some; but overall, the effort had limited return. On a couple of occasions, a Horse or two even stepped forward to the court and tried to have the defense charged with witness tampering, a serious crime. After those fiascoes, malignant mission creep set in. As they say, the gloves came off.

The 'Enforcers' division of The Resistance decided to eliminate the competition altogether. And I mean eliminate. So they established a list of 'Horses For Slaughter.' Members of The Resistance never had the final say so.

First, they had to select any given target from the herd of Horses, namely one of the most damaging ones. They did their homework, gathering all of the justification they could to kill or otherwise, completely neutralize any given Horse. Then they submitted their 'case for termination or neutralization' to the 'Jury' for deliberation. The decision of the 'Jury' was not entirely final. Subject to approval or disapproval by, probably some woman (or maybe, even, man) from hell, named, 'Momma,' the final life and death decision rested with the 'General.' Then 'The Enforcers' took it from there.

Saul and I were supposed to talk and go over the finer points. His sending me this file was a very courageous act. The rest of the password protected files have hundreds of pages of corroborative data, enough to turn over to the FBI, at some point. But who knows what will happen then? Has the 'Resistance' dug its tentacles in that deeply, even to corrupt the feds? You never know. The situation at present is what an Army Ranger would call a 'Cluster-F___' and you both know what I mean.

Tristan your brush with nurse Gordon Gasher, presumably linked to CADIXX occurred in 2006, before hardball turned into 'targeted killings.' Today, they would have killed Heather, Tess and even you, if they could. The last assignment, I wouldn't wish on anyone, on this planet, anyway; especially with Joseph in tow.

In 2006, mutilation was sufficient. And it did reduce your effectiveness for a couple of years, until now. I think that's why, they went after you in New Orleans. Laura and Joseph would have just been collateral damage, although I think Joseph now has a special target on his back, especially after he scared the shit out of Raymond Somershit or Somersville, our helicopter pilot turned chauffer/kidnapper.

When the killings started, Saul wanted out. No one and I mean no one has ever crossed The Resistance and lived to tell about it. Saul thinks there may have been one or two who tried before him, and they have vanished forever.

My brother is a marked man. Deciding that blood was thicker than water, he started to communicate with me, actually, at first, to warn me. Then when you, Tristan, appeared on the scene, he redoubled his efforts to warn all of us. Saul wants to drain the entire abscess, remove all the pus and make it clean again. A tall order. He may lose his life trying.

OK, so now you know about everything I do about this mess. With your help, the three of you, we may be able to see how our FEMA case is being targeted, how to keep you three safe, and how to turn these assholes upside down and make them pay. They should not be able to profit by putting, already displaced persons, into portable gas chambers, period.

Until two days ago, I had no idea how The Resistance may be organized; but thanks to the memory stick and files Saul has sent me, I have a starting point to try to understand how they tick."

Asher reached back into his desk drawer and brought out The Resistance diagram, organization chart or whatever the hell it was his brother had sent him. Tristan and Laura retrieved their copies. Joseph looked over Laura's shoulder. She moved it so he could have a better view. Then they all sat down. Now they had time; they needed it. Tristan poured coffee for everyone. He looked straight at Asher.

Then something strange happened. Tristan's face went white. It was as if Asher had never said a word or explained anything. Looking at the diagram, Tristan suddenly appeared to have a profound grief reaction. Laura looked at him sympathetically; but then could hardly believe her ears. Nothing said earlier about CADIXX had sunk in. Denial, denial. Volumes have been written about the phenomenon. Denial's grip on Tristan was a measure of his horrific grief and guilt.

"I see CADIXX on here. What gives, Asher?" began Tristan.

"If this is an organization chart, it looks like CADIXX is somehow linked to The Resistance, and maybe, pays its dues to the 'Accountant' whoever that is. Then up the chain you go."

Asher, too, looked at Tristan in disbelief. Had he just been on Mars or what?

"Then, CADIXX and this gutter organization might both be involved in what happened to Heather and Tess," Tristan continued. "And maybe one or both were connected to our near abduction in New Orleans."

"How long have you known about this, Asher, dammit?" he asked, now raising his voice and looking at Joseph. "This is far more serious than I thought."

"Look, Tristan, I swear, I just got this from my brother two days ago," pleaded Asher, seeing the anger rise in Tristan's face."

"Well, now, I need to talk to Saul too. Where is he?" fumed Tristan, now glaring at Asher.

"I don't know," replied Asher, looking toward Laura for support or maybe to call 911, if matters continued to escalate. "Tristan, I'll find him. I promise."

Laura was on board. She nodded to Asher and walked over to Tristan and put her hand on his shoulder, beginning, "Please, Tristan, see if you can make any sense of Saul's scribbling. What the hell are those numbers all about? The question marks probably are just that – question marks. But look at what's written under the 'Jury.' It says, 'Me (360, 0, 48) et. al.'"

Laura turned to Asher, "This was sent by Saul, right?" Swinging her gaze back at Tristan again, she smiled sympathetically, continuing to try to calm him down.

"Yeah, I told you I printed it from the only file I could open," said Asher, also glancing at Tristan, hoping he was unarmed. If not, he knew Joseph was; an even scarier thought.

"Well, look at 'Me,'" said Laura, excitedly, "Maybe those numbers in parentheses somehow represent your brother, Saul. But how? There are four letters in 'Saul' but only three numbers."

"The numbers may not correspond to the letters in 'Saul.' Think simple," said Tristan.

Suddenly, breaking the silence again, Joseph blurted, "Initials!"

"You're right! You're right, old friend!" exclaimed Tristan, smacking Joseph on the back, nearly spilling coffee all over the table. "Those must be initials. It makes it easier; so now I need to think about the link between the numbers and letters. They look like old friends. You can see their faces; just can't remember their names. Numbers gotta feel as good in the belly as in the brain. It's got to be simple; lawyers probably use this chart all of the time...to see who lives and who dies."

"OK," said Asher in a very rational tone. "So the numbers may or may not be related to any letters. Let's look at the bigger picture. It's now a given - this diagram, titled, 'The Resistance' is undoubtedly some kind of organizational flow chart.

Including the "Accountant," there are six major elements in the diagram above what appears to be a list of 'members.' Starting at the top, you have the 'General' Directly below is the 'Jury' with, for god sakes, 'Momma' whoever the hell that is, in between the two. Directly below 'Jury' you have 'Accountant' with 'Horses For Slaughter' and 'Enforcers' between the two. And below the 'Accountant' are maybe, some members, including CADIXX.

It may or may not be rational to conclude that the 'Me' with 360, 0 and 48 written in parentheses within 'The Jury' element even refers to my brother, Saul.

Laura chimed, turning to Asher, "OK, so we'll look at the bigger picture. Let's start at the bottom of the diagram. I propose that CADIXX is a member. If we assume that information and/or money flows north on this diagram, CADIXX first sends both to the 'Accountant.'"

"Fine, then what?" said Asher. "The next step, as you say, northward, is to the 'Jury' with the 'Horses For Slaughter' and the 'Enforcers' in the wings.

"It makes some sense," continued Laura, looking at Tristan, who was doodling some numbers on a yellow pad. "It seems logical. Maybe the fate of each 'Horse For Slaughter' will be carried out by "The Enforcers." And maybe, the severity of the sentence is determined by "The Jury," subject to deliberation about each Horse's 'crimes.' The 'Jury' obviously reports to the 'General,' with big 'Momma' having some role, maybe a veto or something."

"Laura, that's a good start. Let's not make this too complicated," interjected Asher. "I think Saul intended to keep matters simple. Tristan, what in the hell are you doing?"

"What do you think, Asher?" said Tristan, slightly less pissed, but still angry at Asher. But Tristan was definitely lightening up. "I'm playing with my pencil. Sorry, Laura. That came out wrong. Now, what did I do with my coffee?"

"How the hell do I know?" exclaimed, Asher, deciding to push back. "Laura and I will deal with structure and flow of information and, probably, money on this chart. Shit. We are lawyers.

You stick to the numbers. You had six semesters of calculus at MIT, so what is taking you so long? I may have to turn to Joseph to read the 'signs.' He's probably right about the numbers representing letters. He'll crack the numerical code in minutes."

Tristan didn't take the bait. No time for a full blown argument now.

This bantering went on for the next 15 minutes. It was nearing lunch time. Theory only theory. Nothing really to go on.

Suddenly, exclaimed Laura, "I would love to place, McKenna, somewhere on here. Maybe she's Momma?"

Ignoring her, Asher said, "I'm going to try to call Saul again. We're just guessing. We have no clue what we're doing."

"Speak for yourself, Asher," belted Tristan. "I think I've got it!

"'GAG,' GAG,' blurted Tristan, smiling for the first time all day.

"I think you need some food or something. What in the hell are you talking about?" Asher replied.

Laura looked at the two of them, now with more pity than respect.

Suddenly, Tristan jumped up, smiling. "Yes, it is trivial. It is 'IOCO!' he blurted again.

"Dr. Baines, please calm down," said Laura, now smiling,

knowing Tristan was probably really on to something. "First, what is 'IOCO?'"

"It is MIT-speak for 'Intuitively Obvious to the most Casual Observer' or only an idiot would miss it, said Tristan.

"So, I guess we're idiots," said Asher.

"No, Asher, only you; but we'll deal with that later," quipped Tristan with a smirk. "Joseph, my brother, you are 100% correct. The numbers are letters."

"What is your brother's middle initial, Asher?"

His middle name is Aaron, so it's 'A,' replied Asher.

"That does it. That does it. I think this will work, and it is trivial," continued Tristan. That CADIXX prick, Gasher's middle name probably begins with an 'A' too. His first name is 'Gordon.' Now we'll call him 'Gordon Asshole Gasher. His number code is (48, 0, 48).

Appropriately, his initials are 'GAG.'

He doesn't work for CADIXX. He works for 'The Resistance.' He is the Chief Enforcer. And something tells me I know his job description.

Your brother Saul Aaron Goldman was or is on the Jury. He is 'Me' on the diagram. His number code is (360, 0, 48). His initials are 'SAG,' probably no relation to 'GAG,' just a coincidental rhyming.

The numbers are initials! The initials are numbers, period!

Laura asked, "Well what about the numbers (399, 255, 3) under the 'Horses?' And, for that matter, (63, 35, 528) under 'Momma?'"

Feeling the now volcanic urge for mortal combat with the bastards who harmed his family, Tristan, nonchalantly said, "Oh, the (399, 255, 3); those stand for 'TPB.' Those are my initials. I am ready. Let them come. There will be pain, and it will not be mine."

"Momma, what about Momma?" asked Laura, hopefully looking at Asher. "It's got to be Chris McKenna, 'CM;' with a middle initial. I don't know her middle name. Right Tristan, Right?" she now pleaded.

"Don't take this personally, Laura," said Tristan, now feeling better by the minute, thinking revenge was no longer hypothetical. "Because Asher did delay and did not include me the minute he had this information, I intend to invoke a minor punishment. Unfortunately, since I think you were in on it, at least a little bit, you will be collateral damage in the punishment.

Your assignment for tomorrow is to figure out the letter initials associated with (63, 35, 528). Once you derive the initials, I think you should have no trouble in delighting in your discovery of the identity of 'Momma.' Let me tell you now, the news will be bad; so prepare yourself. I'll give you a hint, W=528. [3]

You know, I may even kiss Saul when I see him. If you and Asher trip over the math, I may feel forgiving and tease you into solving the puzzle."

Tristan winked at Joseph, realizing that his friend had already identified all of the three initial combinations on the chart. Tristan was not surprised. He had taught Joseph to read clues; he just never expected him to surpass his mentor in so many things, including helping him to solve riddles, pick out a Stetson and even stay alive.

"Laura, I think you could handle it, now; but I wouldn't want to put Asher's lawyerly brain into overload," finished Tristan, now overtly gloating and winking at Laura.

"Say, I need to take the rest of the afternoon off. Asher, are you OK with that?" asked Laura. "I think I'll go to the zoo or something."

Shocked and almost speechless by Tristan's remarks, and checking to see if it was raining, Asher answered, "Go. Go already! Don't forget you calculator to please Professor Baines over here."

Packed up, Laura walked toward the door. She looked back at Asher and Tristan facing each other across the conference table like two sub-critical atomic bomb components about to go at it and blow the building away.

She stopped. Her feminine concern for preserving life took over. "Dr. Baines, do you like monkeys? If so, they respectfully request your presence at the Dallas Zoo. Bring bananas! And Joseph to help you find the way."

---

[3] NUMBERS = THE SQUARE OF THE LETTER'S PLACE IN THE ALPHABET MINUS ONE. (E.G. "H" IS THE 8TH LETTER IN THE ALPHABET SO ITS NUMBER IS 63; DERIVED AT $(8 \times 8 - 1) = 63$.

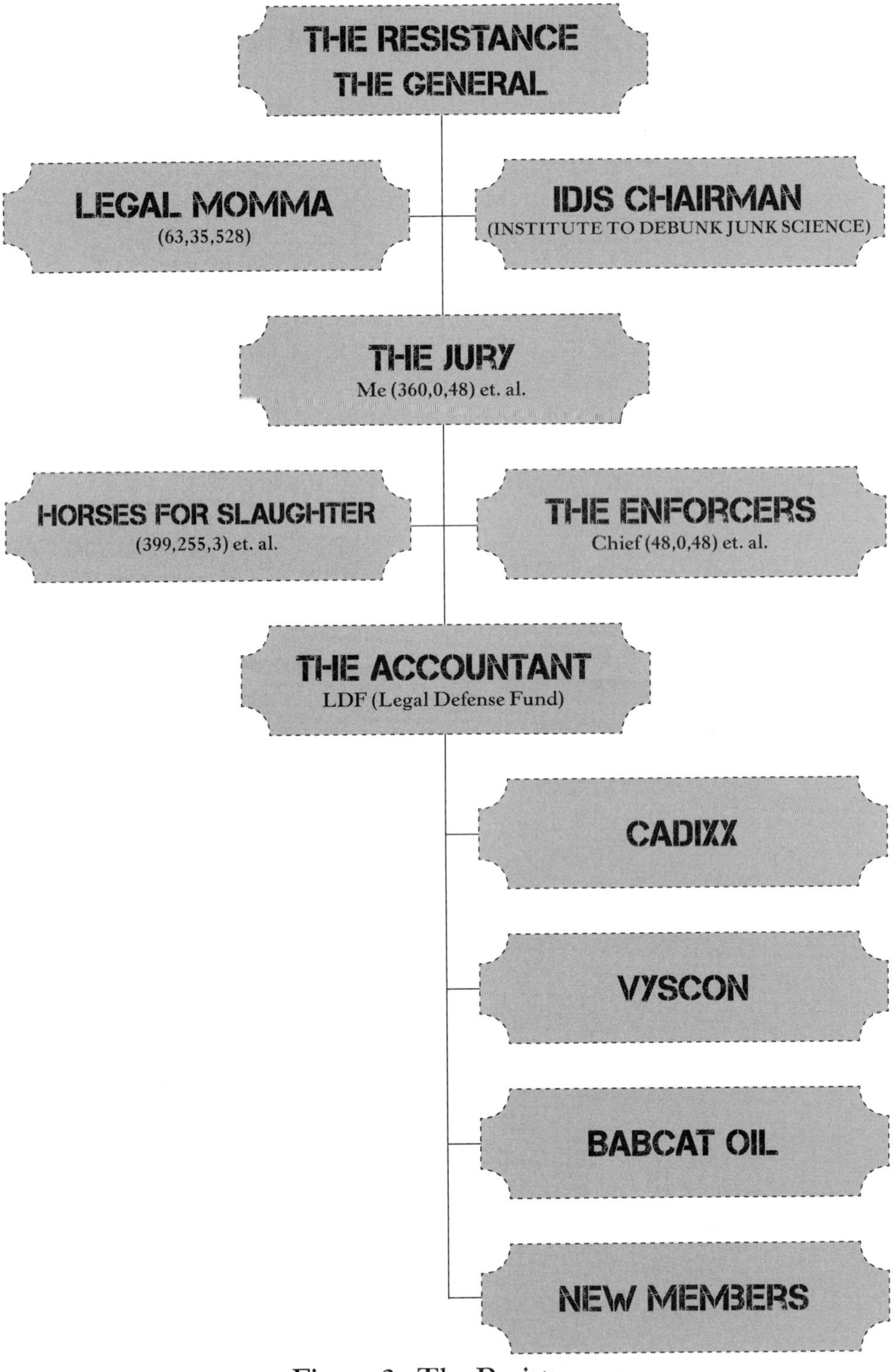

Figure 3 - The Resistance

CHAPTER 23 - A MATCHLESS OPPORTUNITY

DATE: Tuesday, 9/20/05 - About
three weeks after Katrina
LOCATION: Warburg, Kentucky;
Matchless Enterprises, Inc.

— — —

Katrina had hit only about three weeks ago. Millions had been trau-matized; Hundreds of thousands had been displaced. Thousands had died already or would shortly in the aftermath of this Biblical disaster. For some, however, in the business world, the horrifying hurricane wind just sounded like the clinking of gold coins, by the millions.

The government, with FEMA at the lead, stepped in to assist the needy in a multitude of dimensions. First, with the help of multiple law enforcement agencies and the National Guard, government was to establish law and order, a lofty goal, regrettably shattered by murder, rape, robbery, and mayhem. All the while trying to create law and or-der, FEMA and the Red Cross, turned their attention to the provision and distribution of food, water, medical care, and, eventually, shelter. No one dreamed that the latter provision, namely, shelter, would be destined, in tens of thousands of cases, to inflict a second wave of misery onto the victims of Katrina. It would have been no different had those in charge, distributed tainted food and water.

Nobody, not Eddie or Jimmy Olson, the owners of Matchless Enterprises or Zane Adamson, their foreman, right hand man and de-facto Human Resources director, could have foreseen their star-tling "problem of prosperity." It was September 20, 2005, and FEMA wanted four thousand trailers or THU's (temporary housing units) units by March 15, 2006, just six months away. They wanted the basically same design as those they delivered the previous summer. Then it was the Rockport RV travel trailer model, about 32 by 8 feet. It had one bedroom, bunk beds, a kitchen, eating area and just one bathroom. It was purported to be able to house six to eight people, if they wanted to become sardines.

This time, however, FEMA wanted modifications designed to allow the units to be hooked up to municipal water, sewer and electric. So they ordered the trailers stripped of some basic features that would ordinarily be used when traveling over the road. Since they were to be stationary, the new post Katrina FEMA models were delivered with minimal quality tires, just good enough to transport the unit to a location where the tires could be removed and the trailer could be put up on concrete blocks. The FEMA creations came without holding tanks for propane, sewage or fresh water. There were no solar panels, storage batteries and inverters. In the travel model, the inverter was usually used to convert 12 volts (direct current) delivered by the storage battery to 120 volts (alternating current), the standard household voltage expected from the "regular" plugs in the trailer.

FEMA reasoned; why spend the money? These trailers were going to get their juice from the local power company, were going to dump their sewage into the municipal sewer lines and obtain fresh water from the water company. The fresh water often came through a garden hose hooked up to a spigot on a house, close to the area where the post-Katrina FEMA unit was jacked up, sitting on blocks.

Even though these trailers were originally designed for relatively infrequent short term usage, under the plan hatched between FEMA and vendors, like Matchless, these babies were going to be used in one place for the long-haul, months or even years.

What a deal. Building and delivering the stripped down models to FEMA increased the profit margin for Matchless. And since the units were to become nearly permanent, there was also the need for long-term maintenance, provided at tax payer expense. So along came companies like UPIC (United Partners for Industry and Commerce) to complete all the hook-ups, trailer placement and installation. And, more importantly, to be on-call for repairs and other questions. That's where the money was.

It was a great plan except for a couple of major issues. Big ones - like FEMA and Matchless ignoring the reality that RV trailers like those delivered by Matchless were never intended for long term use under any circumstances. More importantly, if made into even semi-permanent housing, the mobile RV units were supposed to have met the myriad of requirements specified by another US government agency. None other than HUD (Housing and Urban Development). HUD would have nixed the project from the get-go. None of the "not supposed to be" permanent trailers would have met HUD codes regarding everything from occupant density to safety issues. But who cared? Certainly not Matchless and UPIC; they played "Catch me if you can" all the way to the bank, while FEMA cheered them on.

"We've got the man-power to boost production on Lines 1 and 2, on all three shifts, at least until Thanksgiving," shouted Zane Adamson, trying to be heard above the din in the background production activity outside his office.

"Not good enough, I told you!" yelled Eddie Olson, in return. "We have to increase line speed by at least 20%. If we do that, we will need more raw materials and prefabricated cabinets to feed the line at the beginning to keep up the pace and make our numbers.

It's no different than speeding up the process of manually making iced doughnuts. If the doughnuts are not there to be iced, the 'icer' will sit there waiting with his thumb up his ass!"

"Oh, God, what a thought" choked Zane, as he listened to Eddie's fourth rant of the day.

"This means we're going to have to either shorten the 'bake out' process in our new building or just use uncured material in the final assembly," continued Eddie, now really shouting. "We may just have to heat it later to get the formaldehyde levels to an acceptable range."

"Eddie, let's go into my office," responded Zane about one foot from Eddie's face. "We need to talk."

Both men looked at each other for a moment. Zane recalled Eddie when Monty Olson, Eddie's father was still alive. He was a good guy then. But now. Eddie had become a mean, immoral asshole and a big one at that. Zane didn't care why; he just had to figure a way to deal with it. Eddie was intoxicated with the success of the 4000 unit FEMA order and the $80 million it represented. He knew that Eddie cared about nothing but filling that order, at any cost, on time, whatever the casualties, whatever the suffering he inflicted on those who had the task of "making the numbers."

Zane knew that Matchless was never prepared to "make the numbers." They would have had a problem with manufacturing one or even two thousand units; but four? Never.

Then there was Zane's suspicion about how the deal came down in the first place. Two weeks after Katrina, he was outside the managerial suite, looking in, when Eddie and Jimmy spent over four hours with Cyrus Cooper, the federal government's sub-contractor liaison to Matchless from Frank Osborne's shop over at FEMA. He saw the "shit eating grin" on Cooper's face when he left. He overheard Eddie say "See ya tonight, Cyrus. Say 'Hi' to the Mrs. for me!" Zane was not stupid; that is for sure.

"Look, Eddie," belted Zane, "We went through this in '02, remember? We have to slow the line to give time for all of the material to bake out. That's why we spent half a million on your building to prepare the plywood and prefabs to go into assembly, essentially formaldehyde free. If we circumvent the process, we will litter the floor with sick employees again. And we run the risk of sending out contaminated trailers to our ultimate customers, those poor bastards left homeless by Katrina. We never should have taken on such a big order."

"Listen, you moron. You work for me." screamed Eddie, literally spraying spittle onto Zane's cheek. "My father took you in, a derelict bum, loading freight cars in '79. OK, you have helped the company and my old man over the years; but don't press your luck.

Hear me clearly. Never and I mean never question my authority or judgment. If I or my idiot brother thinks that we should have taken on a 4000 unit order from FEMA, then we are both right, by definition. You are nothing but a dispensable hired hand and your opinion on such matters is less than worthless.

Next, I do not care if I have to kill half my workforce and the poor slobs that end up inhabiting our trailers. We will make the numbers and hand over those trailers to FEMA and UPIC for delivery on a rolling basis, on time, over the next six months. Anyway, the workers and the Katrina survivors will manage. After all, I think this formaldehyde problem is overblown to begin with. I think the stuff makes the trailers smell like new cars, anyway."

Zane wasn't really surprised at the content of rant number five. He thought about his promise to Monty before he died; to keep an eye on things, including his two sons. Jimmy was easy. It was like monitoring the status of the end table next to your couch. Eddie was different. He was a rabid jackal, frothing at the mouth, ready to bite anyone or anything that got in his way. To injure and spread disease.

"OK, Eddie," said Zane softly, undeniably biting his tongue, "What are we going to do with the 400 tons of waste from this project, some of which will be contaminated with formaldehyde and other toxic materials? We're running about 200 pounds of the stuff per unit produced."

"I told you not to bring that up," frothed Eddie. "We'll deal with it; see?"

"I have to deal with it. The EPA will be on our necks, if we don't handle that stuff correctly," retorted Zane, realizing that he was starting to think of homicide. "Are you going to find a contractor to haul away that waste and dispose of it properly?"

"For the last time; you concentrate on keeping our faithful workforce's collective noses to the grindstone. Deal with the whiners who can't take the fumes and make the numbers." belted Eddie, now actually lowering his voice.

"And, OK, by the way, there is a company out of Alton, Illinois called CADIXX that will handle the waste. They have a big incinerator up there, along the Mississippi, said to be the fourth largest in the States. They have a fleet of modified ore carriers that will pick up the waste and take it for disposal somewhere in Alabama."

"Where in Alabama?" ventured Zane.

"Shit! I have no idea and frankly, I don't care!" returned Eddie, as he weighed his options with Zane after this major order was filled. He couldn't deal with nosey "do-gooders" running production at Matchless. He was not about to be accountable to anyone. He knew he would have to share the million plus year-end bonus with his brother, and he might even have to sprinkle a few bucks on the workers that had now swelled to over four hundred. He had to hire some "persons without papers" to make the numbers. In reality, he thought, they were the most productive. They ask not, want not, and bitch not, plus he could pay them in cash, as contractors, with no withholding, social security or any of that other bullshit.

Man, it was going to be a great Christmas!

—　　—　　—

DATE: Thursday, 11/17/05 - About
12 weeks after Katrina
LOCATION: Warburg, Kentucky;
Matchless Enterprises, Inc.

"Zane, what are we going to do?" exclaimed Missy Malark, raising her voice slightly to counter the assembly line noise just outside of Zane's office. "Over the past month, we've had as many sick days, worker compensation claims, OSHA recordables and just plain major bellyaching as we did all last year. We can't go on like this. We're hiring every warm body that comes through the door, without any serious background check, validation of work history or even social security number. And what's with the order from Eddie to pay some in cash? We can't do that. I talked to Jimmy about it, and he said absolutely not. I haven't told Eddie yet. He's going to blow his stack."

Zane stared at the executively dressed woman in her early 50's; light brown suit with a plain white blouse. Her hair, lightly streaked with gray had once been a beautiful auburn; but it still complemented her dark green eyes that now stared hard at Zane, directly above her reading glasses resting on the end of her nose. She was still a handsome lady. She knew her job as bookkeeper, payroll officer and all around executive secretary. Missy kept the OSHA 300 log of serious workplace illnesses and injuries and the summary OSHA 300A. It seemed like almost everything that had transpired in the process of ramping up to meet the FEMA trailer order had gone wrong.

Of course, Missy had help. She had hired three temps to plow through and fill out the mountains of paperwork associated with hiring over two hundred people over about an eight week period. "If they are breathing and can see lightning and hear thunder," said Eddie, "I want their sorry asses on the assembly line ASAP!"

The words echoed in Missy's ears. She had developed some sense of loyalty to "the boys" over the past 10 years; mainly because of her loyalty to their father, Monty, before he died in 2000.

Monty had spotted Missy working for a local bank, when he came in near closing time one Friday afternoon. He was waiting to get some papers notarized and ducked into her office to ask if she could help him out so he could get back to the office. She obliged with a smile. They conversed; and she confessed that she was up to her elbows in some sort of audit and had to work till midnight, on a Friday, no less. She told Monty she was "task oriented," and always finished her work, usually without looking at the clock. That did it. Two weeks later with a 50% raise over her bank salary, she was working for Monty as his executive secretary, really his old fashioned "Gal Friday. In many ways her story was similar to Zane's. Monty took them both into the fold and treated them with dignity and fatherly love.

After Monty died, Missy mourned. Then she sort of floated equally between helping Jimmy and Eddie; the task of a saint. But right after Katrina, when the big order for 4000 units came in, Eddie appropriated her services entirely.

Missy was unhappy and knew, like Zane, there was really no way for Matchless to meet FEMA's production deadlines. They couldn't even make it halfway without some major labor issues and injuries or even worse, as Missy feared to herself. Fortunately, FEMA had advanced adequate funds for Matchless to meet payroll, buy materials, pay insurance and a myriad of other bills associated with such a project, at least for the moment.

She already had two workers who had been admitted to the hospital for respiratory problems, one serious, requiring a one week stay. She had about fourteen others "out on worker comp," with no return in sight. The docs knew it was formaldehyde; and said so.

Eddie refused to hire a health and safety assistant, claiming he was more than capable of conducting periodic air monitoring for formaldehyde and a few other chemicals on the assembly line and in the "bake-out" building. Eddie also supervised the testing of trailers before they were ready for delivery and after they had remained sealed for two days. According to Eddie all measurements, including those on the assembly line were well below federally recommended standards.

"OK, then why the epidemic of complaints from the workforce?" Missy asked herself.

Zane saw the same series of events unfold before his very eyes and was worried sick about it. He and Missy both knew that Eddie was in a complete state of denial about the ability of Matchless to make the FEMA deadline. Previously, to meet the June 2005 order with about 330 workers, they could produce about 45 trailers per week. So with 440 workers, they should easily make about 60 units per week. But Eddie demanded more.

With overtime and heartless, not to mention overtly dangerous productivity demands, they were pushing 80 units/week. They had 24 weeks, so they could expect to manufacture only 1920 units, less than half of the 4000 promised to FEMA.

252

But there was also another problem. The production of every trailer generated about 200 pounds of "toxic waste" (about 1.8% of the trailer's total weight of 5.6 tons). Even producing only 1920 units, Zane realized they would still have to contend with 192 tons of waste that required special handling.

"But," he thought, "It would, at least, fall well short of the 400 tons they had calculated, if they were to fulfill the entire 4000 trailer order."

"Missy, has Eddie talked to you about making arrangements for toxic waste disposal with this group, I think it's called, CADex or something like that?" said Zane, admitting this other source of his indigestion over the past few weeks.

"I know about it. It's called CADIXX. Some big incinerator operation north of St. Louis in a town called Alton, Illinois, right along the Mississippi," responded Missy, sort of rolling her eyes and nodding her head, revealing her doubts about both the organization and any deal Eddie had struck with them.

"They claim to have a fleet of refurbished ore carriers that have been DOT and EPA approved to transport waste headed to a Class III dump site suitable for what the EPA calls 'Toxic (Non-Acute) Hazardous Wastes.'

Technically, our waste plywood, containing some residual form-aldehyde, is not a waste at all; but we have plenty more hazardous chemicals and other junk to contend with. In any case, Eddie said they dump all of it at one of their landfills somewhere in Alabama.

Say, listen Zane, I'm not too sure; but I think Eddie made a binding agreement with CADIXX. He promised to pay for their picking up, transporting and disposing of 400 tons of waste at their Alabama dump site.

If we don't make our FEMA quota, we won't have enough waste to hand over to them; but we'll still be on the hook to pay CADIXX to remove the entire amount. Maybe that's another issue that's eating at Eddie."

"Interesting thought," sighed Zane, "I've never considered this project as having a goal of producing a certain amount of waste and failing if we couldn't make it. Sort of like raising cattle and counting the tons of manure rather than number of cattle on the hoof. Uh - bad example, because the manure has value. Our waste has negative value. We have to pay to have it removed.

But, let's get back to our imminent failure to make the FEMA quota. We have our 440 people, at least for now; and are making about 80 units per week because we are now running seven days a week, with a lot of overtime, have shut down all other projects to concentrate on this one and are one whisker short of flogging the workers like dogs, a pace set by Eddie that I intend to cut back very soon.

Even so - I did some figuring. The news is bad. At this rate we will need nearly a year to produce the 4000 units. We only have 16 weeks left and we have only cranked out a few short of 650.

By the way, where's Jimmy on this?"

"Where do you think?" moaned Missy, letting herself go. "He's where he always is. His throat is under Eddie's boot; his mind is in the clouds or at the beach and his cahones, oh sorry, I slipped, forgive me....well, his cahones are, are, uh, gone, gone or maybe hanging over Eddie's fireplace mantle." She couldn't resist a knee jerk smile. She was so daring and so very proud of it. "God, listen to me, will you? I'm sorry Zane. I've just had it, and I sense doom in the air."

"Me too. By the way, has anyone told Cooper or his boss Osborne over at FEMA about our situation?"

"I know Eddie wants to wait until just after the New Year." answered Missy, still blushing at the daring remarks that made her laugh inside and feel so much better. "He thinks FEMA will forgive the pace and extend the contract date. One thing for sure; he won't give up on producing the full 4000 units. He told me he wants and needs that $80 million payday. Believe me; we'll need part of it to pay the increase in our worker comp premium next year. FEMA's advanced $20 million already. Thank God."

The crash and screams came without warning. They could hear it loud and clear, as if Zane's office walls, tempered window and solid core door didn't exist. Three men whom Zane knew well, rushed past the window, one carrying a large first aid kit and the other a Philips HeartStart cardiac life-pak. Zane and Missy both broke for the door together, exited and ran toward the commotion. Twenty five yards later, they both wished they were blind and deaf. They both saw it and heard it anyway.

The 50 sheets of plywood weighing over a ton were bound with metal straps into a single bundle on top of a wooden pallet. The bundle and pallet were on the floor of the receiving area; but the unit was tipped upward at a slight angle, as if something was blocking its resting flat on the concrete.

Zane saw the expressions on the dozen or so workers gathered around the scene. The fork lift operator, who had originally set the bundle down, had tried twice to set it flat. He had no idea what was obstructing his load. He now reinserted the forks into the pallet and was starting to lift the plywood off the floor. One worker had already called 911, the second he had seen the problem.

Coming around the plywood bundle, Zane saw another worker, tears streaming from her eyes like Niagara Falls. Her bare hands were dripping with gore. "I tried to pull him out;" she cried. "I tried to pull him out. My God, his head, his head. I can't look. I can't bear it."

Missy stepped forward, placing her arm around the worker, at the moment, too shocked to be hysterical. But that would come later.

Another worker had slipped in the mess. Zane saw him on the floor, both hands flat in a three foot puddle of a purplish, syrupy mixture of blood, sawdust and dirt. At the same moment, Zane saw pants covering two legs and a pelvis. The pants were stained, and there was the smell of a latrine in the air. The shirt covering the abdomen and chest was saturated with blood. The head; there was no head; just a pancake of blood, bone and brains. Looking at the shirt, Zane thought it was someone he knew; but wasn't sure. The fork lift operator wept openly. He turned to Zane, saying over and over again, "I'm sorry! I'm sorry! I didn't see him. This is the 20th bundle today. I normally move 12."

Suddenly, entering from the receiving dock, they all heard a shout. At first, they thought it was someone from the ambulance crew. "What the hell is going on here? Why has the line stopped? Why aren't you working? Zane, what goes here?" belched Eddie Olson, his face, crimson with anger, and his arm in the air.

Then he saw the blood and the man with no head, no face. "What happened here? Dear God, we're going to be down for a week. Has anyone called an ambulance? No wait, call the McGuiness Funeral Home. This is a tragedy; but we have to take this poor man's body out of here, now."

"What are you talking about Eddie?" shouted Zane. "I think this is...... is Abel Washington. We can't move the body at all. The ambulance is on the way. We need to call the police, OSHA, then Abel's family. The funeral home can wait."

The workers were paralyzed and shocked. They thought, "An argument? A stinking argument? Now? With their co-worker lying dead on the floor? What gives? Is this an insane asylum or the site of a fatal accident?"

"All of you, please, go back to your workstations. I am here now. It is all under control. Tell you what. We'll break 30 minutes early today. Please, go back to work now." ordered Eddie.

He turned to Zane, stepping over the worker who had slipped and was now being helped up by two of his friends. In the background, Eddie heard someone say, "The hell with you, I'm going home. Bobbie-Jo; are you coming?"

Eddie jolted, "Who said that? Who said that? I am ordering you back to work. Do you want to have a job tomorrow? I'll replace you in an instant?"

Eddie paused, noticing some blood on his right shoe. In the midst of this "tragic inconvenience," he was proud of his courage and felt an increase in momentum.

"Zane, you must come with me into your office, now," Eddie ordered.

A larger crowd was gathering. Zane did not move. Suddenly the ambulance crew arrived. They saw the scene. One EMT bent over the body; the other started back to their rig, probably looking for a body bag. The one who stayed took out his cell phone to take a picture, officially, of course.

"Zane, I said, to your office, this second!" repeated Eddie, raising his voice. Then, he made a decision, and it was a bad one. Standing behind Zane, Eddie used his right hand to push Zane's left arm, hard in the direction of Zane's office.

It came without warning. A full roundhouse; deliberately intended not to kill or maim, just to cause some serious hurt. Zane sucker-punched Eddie; and Eddie went down like a sack of potatoes. Suddenly, the cheers went up as if the University of Louisville had won the Final Four.

Eddie fell to a sitting position, stunned, for a moment; no, more like a full minute, a small amount of blood trickling from his nose.

Eddie came around and glared at Zane. Unpredictably, Zane suddenly tried to help him to his feet. A cacophony of boos filled the air.

Out of earshot of the crowd, like an evil therapist, Eddie whispered, "It's OK Zane; I understand. You've been under a lot of stress lately. You're simply out of control. I think we need to talk. You know, I could press charges; but I think we should let it go this time, don't you?"

"Eddie, listen........," Zane started, feeling absolutely no remorse for the punch; but suddenly thinking of his pledge to Monty, Eddie's father, to watch out for the boys, especially, Eddie, the problem child.

Eddie then glanced at the seven or eight workers staring at Zane and him. Surrounding a monumental tragedy, all of them were, nevertheless, mesmerized by the scene of two managers, awkwardly entangled, one holding the other from falling, one so loved, the other so very much hated.

Eddie continued, still watching the crowd out of the corner of his eye. But now Eddie was laser focused on a clearly emerging secret purpose of his own.

"Zane, I think I'm going to place you on an extended leave. You really do need a rest and maybe even some recreation too. Say, I'll even continue your pay and give you a couple of thousand..."

"Eddie, look, I'm sorry," effused Zane, Monty's visage practically standing before him.

You like to hunt, right?" continued Eddie, ignoring Zane's apology. "The second rifle season for deer is coming up next week down near Aniston in Alabama. Stay at the best hotel in town. We'll pay for the out of state license. Bring Jimmy and me some venison. Have a blast."

Zane rebounded to the disaster before him.

"Eddie, let's talk about it later," uttered Zane, now with complete exasperation, "We need to focus on Abel and this terrible accident? Now, where is Missy?

Eddie? Eddie? Where are you going?"

Zane watched Eddie Olson walk away from the scene expressionless, as if in a daze. He let him go. "What's the use of stopping him?" he thought. "He's poison."

Just as Zane looked back to the tragic scene, he heard the unmistakable noise of a warbling siren. The cops had arrived. Two squad cars and four officers, all looking for answers.

Including the arrival of the coroner, it took another seven hours before the authorities would let anyone leave. They decided to shut down the line, until further notice; and cordoned off the site of the death with yellow crime scene tape, just in case. Poor Abel's body was taken, after all, to the McGuiness Funeral Home, per the family's wishes, not Eddie's.

OSHA said they would be by in the morning... very early.

— — —

DATE: Monday, 11/21/05 - About 12 weeks after Katrina LOCATION: Warburg, Kentucky; Matchless Enterprises, Inc.

"Jimmy will see you now, Zane," said Missy Malark, a look of intractable sadness on her face. Like most others, she was still grieving over the accident that killed Abel Washington, especially in such a hideous manner.

"Come in Zane, please," said Jimmy Olson softly, with a touch of affection for his friend who was now in a most difficult and precarious position with his company, thanks to the Eddie Olson blow-up the week before at the scene of Abel's tragic death.

"Jimmy, I'm getting ready to check out for a while." said Zane bitterly.

"I know. I talked to Eddie," pouted Jimmy. "I hate to ask; but what's the status of the investigation?"

The disaster was only four days old. Jimmy had hid like a tortoise in his shell. Several media reporters tried to interview him on Friday, the day after; so Jimmy escaped out of the back of the building, with Missy covering his tracks. He was not to be found over the weekend and had finally come to work on Monday morning.

"It's only been four days, including the weekend," answered Zane, "But I've already been in touch with the OSHA regional administrator. She has been very professional; but we are in some deep shit over this situation. And it is spilling over onto the matter of our high level of other recordable injuries, presumably related to our line speed and the formaldehyde exposure. They've shut down line one indefinitely, until they figure out exactly what happened. I was with Missy in my office when we heard screams and a crash. We went directly to the scene; but neither of us saw the disaster actually happen.

I interviewed three workers who say they saw it all.

It was really quite simple.

Abel was using a ratchet and socket to tighten some steel framework. He was changing the socket to a larger size, when it fell and rolled across the floor under Marv's forklift. Marv had a full bunk of plywood about three and a half feet off the floor. He had stopped, preparing to lower the load. He hesitated, for reasons unknown at this time. Abel stupidly thought he could retrieve his socket so he scooted under the raised load to grab the socket, and at that precise moment Marv nearly dropped the load. He brought it down rather quickly.

Marv's a novice operator; but has been certified. We're not sure about the hydraulics on the fork-lift. They may be defective.

The first time the load was dropped, it was tilted slightly. Marv and everyone heard some screams. We think they came from witnesses, not Abel who was crushed instantly. Unbelievably, Marv raised the load and lowered it again to try to set it flat on the concrete. He didn't stop to see what was obstructing the load. It all happened so fast. There are dozens of questions and only a few answers at the moment."

"Dear God," gasped Jimmy. "That poor, poor man; can we do anything for his family?"

"Missy said she would try to think of something," said Zane. "She'll probably get back to you about it later in the week. I'll likely be gone. I have to meet with OSHA again later today.

Since Thursday night, between OSHA, the police, and the coroner's office, I've been grilled for over 30 hours. I came in for the Saturday shift on line 2, and one cop who was finishing up his report caught me there too."

Abruptly, as if coming out of another thought, Jimmy said, "Our lawyers have researched similar cases. We can expect a major citation; but we may get away with only having to pay a $10,000 fine."

A little disgusted, Zane ignored the remark and continued, "Also, the cat's out of the bag about our excessive line speed and the formaldehyde overexposure to our workers. We're just not baking out our raw materials long enough. Eddie has been having conniptions all week-end. We're so far behind, we'll never catch up. FEMA's got to be notified at some point."

"I know. I know," retorted Jimmy, sounding annoyed and overwhelmed, as usual."

Zane decided to press his own issue further, "You heard about my losing my temper and clocking Eddie last week at the scene of Abel's death?"

"Yeah, I heard. The whole company's heard," replied Jimmy. "Can't say, I'm sorry or pissed at you; but Eddie now views you as an enemy. I think he's made you an offer you can't refuse."

"I don't care." fired Zane. "I can't be a part of this any longer, anyway. I think I will take the leave so graciously offered by Eddie. I would enjoy some hunting and could visit my sister, Posie, over in Ashland, for a day or two."

"Well, before you go, you haven't heard the worst part yet," said Jimmy, now morphing into the ineffectual person Zane knew so well. "Eddie struck an agreement with CADIXX to remove 400 tons of toxic waste from this project at about $4000 per ton. We're on the hook for $1.6 million. Eddie is supposed to pay half by December 1 and the rest on April 1. Eddie told me last night he's not paying them a dime. He says we can't afford it. What waste we create will stay put. He says he has some other options, including storing it somewhere onsite.

Zane, I'm worried. I don't want the EPA on our back for this crap. I don't want to go to jail; but I also don't want to die, if we welch on the CADIXX deal. I hear they're a rough bunch. They don't deal, period."

"What can I say?" lamented Zane. "He's your brother. I've tried my hardest; but obviously have failed. Eddie sees me as his major obstacle to making 80 million FEMA dollars. After I talk to OSHA again, later today, I'm gone. You'll manage, Jimmy. I have all the faith in the world in you."

Zane extended his hand to Jimmy.

Nearly choked up, Jimmy said, "Zane, I'm sorry. I hope you'll come back soon. I can't make it without you; neither can Eddie and he knows that. It's just....it's just, he won't be stopped; and I'm not sure he can be stopped. Zane, please..."

"Jimmy, I have to go now," Zane interrupted. They shook and Zane leaned forward to offer Jimmy a brief hug. He knew Monty was smiling, as he left Jimmy's office.

CHAPTER 24 - THE TRIAL - PART I - DR. CHRIS MCKENNA

DATE: Tuesday AM, 9/29/09 - About four years and one month after Katrina
LOCATION: U.S. Federal Court, Eastern District of Louisiana, New Orleans, Judge Henrietta F. Whitmore presiding

— — —

Defense Cross Examination of Dr. Chris McKenna

"So, Dr. McKenna, is it true that Simon Williams, I believe, age 13, at the time, underwent a thorough examination at Coastal General Hospital, in Boston, on or about June 23, 2009, earlier this year?" asked Michael Attington, the 67 year old lead attorney for Matchless Enterprises.

"Yeah, uh, I mean, Yes," emoted Dr. Chris McKenna, with a look of boredom on her face.

McKenna stared past and to the right of Attington straight at the first row of the gallery behind the plaintiff's table where Asher Goldman and Laura Swain were sitting preparing for her re-direct examination. They had already asked her direct questions. After all, Dr. McKenna was an expert for their side. Her testimony was supposed to have helped Simon and his family.

Asher and Laura did not get what they had expected. It was bad, very bad; and they were scrawling and re-writing questions as fast as possible to try to repair her testimony; before she was handed back to them for more questioning. The face in the gallery behind them stared back; but his features were barely visible. Tristan Baines had not yet testified.

The trial had been going on for over a week, covering all aspects of property issues and background matters that documented the ordeal of Simon Williams, as a singular, pediatric plaintiff, but still the philosophical representative of 20,000 plus or minus 1000 other persons who had lived or were still living in Matchless-made FEMA trailers. To one extent or another, all had had the "pleasure" of inhaling formaldehyde along with several other toxins, including mold, for periods of a few weeks to well over two years.

It was not a class action; it was an individual lawsuit. Simon Williams, as represented by Sethie and Reggie Williams, Sr., was suing Matchless Enterprises, Inc. and several other parties, not including FEMA, in federal court, Eastern District of Louisiana for property damage and adverse health effects sustained while living in their contaminated trailer for about 18 months (from 5/06 through 11/07).

FEMA had ducked the bullet and was out of the suit, thanks to federal Judge Henrietta F. Whitmore. She had ruled one month before the current 9/09 trial that Sethie could not sue FEMA because she had waited too long to file her lawsuit. She said Sethie had from 5/06 until 5/08, two years, to sue FEMA. Sethie had filed her suit in 7/08, two months too late. The judge still allowed her to sue the trailer manufacturer, namely, in this case, Matchless, and certain other private parties; but not FEMA.

The whole thing was ridiculous; and smelled like a rat. The good judge started the two year statute of limitations clock the first day that high school educated, non-scientist, Sethie Williams first moved into the trailer, reasoning she should have known that formaldehyde in the trailer was the causative agent in wrecking her son's health.

But here was the problem. On the first day Sethie stepped into their trailer back in 5/06, she had no clue what formaldehyde was, much less that it was coming from the trailer plywood and insulation, and much less that it was harmful to Simon. How could Sethie have known? In 5/06, there was still a festering scientific cover-up within the industry and even, to some extent, within the government itself about the existence and dangers of "trailer formaldehyde." Even Simon's pediatrician, Dr. Patricia Simms, ("Dr. Pat,") was still over three years away from making the formaldehyde connection to Simon's worsening asthma. Once she made it, she knew why he had gone to the ER twice before she saw him in July, 2006.

Supposedly, there was no basis for Sethie to have been concerned; after all, they told her "Don't worry about the 'new car smell' in the trailer; so what if your eyes burn. Just open the windows and enjoy your windfall. Relax."

Judge Whitmore's decision to disallow a lawsuit against FEMA just two months before the trial in 9/09 made matters even worse. Too bad for the plaintiffs' lawyers – only a half a million was down the toilet, wasted in preparing for a suit against FEMA that never occurred. Add that to the good judge's 5/09 prohibition against plaintiffs forming a class action, left Asher and friends, at least theoretically, to file one case at a time. Nobody really expected 20,000 trials; but you never know; defendants had no reason to settle yet; even if it was in the best interests of its clients. They had not milked the case long enough to make it worthwhile. That's how law firms sporting over 400 lawyers operate.

Not being able to sue FEMA weakened Simon's case against Matchless; because it prevented the jury from hearing dozens of government witnesses and reviewing just as many exhibits that would have certified the formaldehyde connection as it was and when it was.

Among others at the trial there to testify on Simon's behalf, in addition to Dr. McKenna, were Dr. Pat and Dr. Tristan Baines, the latter, serving as Simon's medical causation expert.

"So, if you will, Dr. McKenna, please tell the jury and the court what you found during young Simon's examination. Oh, sorry, before that, to avoid a compound question, I forgot to ask, isn't Coastal General a Hautair affiliated teaching hospital?" asserted Attington, sounding like a rookie just out of law school.

"The answer to your first question is 'Yes,'" responded McKenna, not taking her eyes off Tristan's eerily indistinct visage in the gallery. "Now for your second question. As I testified earlier, just a few moments ago; and it is documented in my report, I found no probable evidence that Simon's exposure to formaldehyde in his trailer has caused any discernable adverse health effects.

In addition, his collapse at Coastal General was not a reaction to formaldehyde whatsoever. After his first exposure to formaldehyde in the chamber; but before his second, he was administered a bronchodilator to open his airways. He used his own inhaler. That is when and why he collapsed. Sometimes, patients, without explanation, out of the blue, develop a catastrophic heart arrhythmia after using their own inhaler, even if they had used it for years. Again the collapse was not related in any way to the formaldehyde challenge."

"Was the level of formaldehyde in your aerosol challenge chamber the same level as young Simon breathed while in the trailer?" asked Attington, glancing with some apprehension, over at Doris Carr, his 54 year old New York City law partner and 64 year old Percy Loeb, Matchless's legal representative in Louisville, not far from the manufacturing plant in Warburg, Kentucky.

Cost was not an issue for Matchless. No fewer than four attorneys, two paralegals and one research assistant were sucking the defense insurance carriers at a rate of about $800,000 per month. On Simon's side, there were only two lawyers and a secretary.

"To be honest, the level should have been the same or even lower; but Simon had a problem during the challenge, as I said; and the technician who prepared the formaldehyde dose, lost his life, not long after the examination. I can only assume, he prepared the challenge levels, as I ordered. My orders were to expose Simon at a level of about 500 ppb (part per billion); yes the same as what had been found in the trailer," responded McKenna finally taking her eyes off Tristan, glancing briefly at the death glare from Laura, then landing her septic brown eyes on Attington.

Sitting at the plaintiff's table, Laura nudged Asher, still staring back at McKenna.

"So, do you think she'll behave?" whispered Laura. "She sure made a mess of things, answering your questions."

"OK, OK, so she's a loose cannon; let's give her a chance," responded Asher, speaking loud enough for the court transcriptionist to briefly look his way, but not missing a syllable of the cross examination.

"OK, then; and what is an acceptable level for formaldehyde exposure in home dwelling?" asked Attington.

McKenna balked. She did not know the answer.

Laura whispered to Asher, "Tristan said the level should be less than 10 ppb."

"Don't guess doctor. If I said, around 10, would that seem about right?" asked Attington, possibly overhearing Laura's remark.

"Yeah, uh, yes, that sounds right," said McKenna, unfazed by her ignorance. Leave that information to the engineers, she thought.

"Dr. McKenna, you testified earlier that young Simon actually had a cardiac arrest during this testing and had to be revived outside the chamber. How long was he exposed before, he...uh, went down, uh....arrested, or whatever is the proper medical term for it?" fumbled Attington again, on the clock at $1000/hour.

It was clear he was out of practice. Asher noticed. He conjured Attington to be not unlike a millionaire third baseman for the Texas Rangers, who fumbled a slow roller down the third base line and threw it to a fan in the third row above the Ranger dugout.

"Look, I do not know exactly how long he was exposed before he arrested and was subsequently revived on the scene," said McKenna, now focused on Attington, looking at him like he were a chimp with a clown hat on.

She continued, "It does not matter; I examined him two days after the event and he was fine, except he was a bit hoarse. I could not tell whether this resulted from his cardiac collapse and subsequent breathing tube placement into his throat or from the formaldehyde to which he was exposed in the chamber. Under the circumstances, any adverse effects from trailer formaldehyde would not be discernable."

"Sounds very reasonable, doctor," said Attington, realizing the help that McKenna was providing to the defense. "It sounds like you agree with our experts. And so is it also your medical opinion that young Simon's collapse in the chamber can not be attributed to his formaldehyde exposure and that none of his 'so-called' worsening asthma problems can be traced to any theoretical formaldehyde exposure while he lived in his FEMA trailer manufactured by my client, Matchless Enterprises?"

Attington was stretching, he knew. But he had to drive home McKenna's opinion to the jury, knowing that Tristan Baines attributed the entire chamber tragedy to Simon's formaldehyde sensitivity, one that developed while he lived in his trailer. He had to establish that McKenna was undermining Tristan's opinions.

"That is correct," responded McKenna, virtually muted and expressionless.

Notwithstanding her help, Attington realized that McKenna was not his friend. She was still an expert for the plaintiffs. He decided to probe her part in nearly killing Simon by exposing him to formaldehyde in the test chamber. Attington's partner, Doris Carr was almost prepared to call for a recess before she watched Attington undo the progress he had just made. It was too late.

"Next," continued Attington, "do you think that Simon's collapse in the chamber was, in any regard, initiated by an asthma attack and by the way, were you there when Simon fell ill?"

Another compound question. The guy just couldn't help it.

Silence, 20, 25, 30, 35 seconds.

Judge Whitmore looked at McKenna. "Dr. please answer the question... uh questions, if you can."

"Will you please repeat the questions?" muffled McKenna, with a blistering look at Attington.

"Will the court reporter, please read back the question to the witness?" said Attington.

The reporter lifted her transcription tape and said, "Defense counsel asked, 'Next, do you think that Simon's collapse in the chamber was, in any regard, initiated by an asthma attack; and by the way, were you there when Simon fell ill?'"

"OK, Dr. McKenna," followed Attington, "Please answer the questions, one at a time."

McKenna hesitated again; this time for only ten seconds, then looked at Judge Whitmore and answered, I just testified, the patient had an adverse reaction to his bronchodilator from his own inhaler in the midst of the testing. A formaldehyde induced, acute asthma attack had nothing to do with Simon's collapse; and no. I was not there. I had other patient responsibilities to which to attend.

And even worse, doctor, you mean to tell this court that you planned an aerosol chamber challenge exposure for a patient who may have been sensitive to formaldehyde, and you weren't there for the test...because you had other patient responsibilities 'to which to attend?' Doctor, the boy almost died," exploded Attington.

Wondering if Attington had even asked a question, McKenna ventured, "Well, as regrettable as it was, he did not die. He was re-suscitated and lived, without any evidence of adverse sequelae to the event. And, I might add, these things happen. That's why the patient, in this case, his mother, signed a consent form. It says clearly in the form that the patient will not hold the hospital or me liable even if the patient dies during the test. They were warned. I am sorry it happened; but that's the way it goes sometimes."

Laura nudged Asher and whispered, "Who created this bitch, Asher? Out of what swamp did she crawl? I've heard of such arrogance; but never have seen such a full blown example. I hope the malpractice judgment leaves her in rags, scrubbing bedpans."

"You know, don't you," continued Attington, enjoying the kill, "Dr. Baines thinks the whole event and near death of young Simon began with an asthma attack, a problem you could have foreseen. And an event that you could have prevented had you read Simon's ER record and not planned a challenge test."

Suddenly, unable to contain herself, and ignoring that every word was recorded, McKenna spat, "Anyway, Dr. Baines' opinions are those of an unqualified beginner. I know what I say and what I say is true. Period."

This out of order remark made it past the judge; or maybe the judge just liked it too much to have it stricken from the record.

Notwithstanding her comment, McKenna was being cautious, extremely cautious. She had to be careful about what she said, because she knew that Sethie and her family had recently filed a lawsuit against her, Coastal General and the university for $25 million. The suit was in the discovery phase and would take months to take shape. McKenna had originally planned to pin the blame on the rogue technician for putting too much formaldehyde in the chamber. Instead, she came up with the asthma inhaler theory.

"Why not blame the kid for nearly killing himself? It might lessen her liability," she thought, although she really didn't care. She reasoned her personal liability was limited as an employee of the university, a theory, she would painfully learn was not true.

The hospital attorney was going to hide behind the consent form Sethie signed that excused everything up to and including a T. Rex invasion during the procedure.

In this case, Tristan had ducked the bullet even though he had referred Simon to Boston. He was saved because he was able to prove that he vehemently opposed the challenge testing; based upon a statement from the clerk at Coastal General who had heard his demand that the inhalation challenge testing be stopped. Miraculously, the unorthodox order Tristan had scrawled and signed on a scrap of paper had been saved. It eventually made it to Simon's chart on the third day of his recovery from near death in the challenge chamber. Lucky thing McKenna missed the note. Otherwise, it may have "accidently fallen from the chart."

Having showed, if not McKenna's negligence, then, at least, her incompetence for not directly supervising Simon's test, Attington decided to go in for the kill.

"Dr. McKenna, you have read Dr. Baines' report in which he stated, let me quote…"

"Oh shit, here we go," mumbled Asher, again loud enough to

catch the attention of the court reporter on the word 'shit.'" This time she frowned but kept going.

Attington didn't break stride, either, as he read fluently and loud enough for the entire courtroom to hear:

"Within the scope of the collective environmental engineering and medical data bases generated and reviewed, it is my opinion that Simon Williams' pre-existing medical problems, most specifically, childhood asthma, have been substantively aggravated by his 18 month exposure to toxicologically significant levels of formaldehyde in his FEMA trailer manufactured by Matchless. It is also my opinion that as a result of his formaldehyde exposure in his trailer, he is at lifetime increased risk of developing life-threatening status asthmaticus, or essentially, at times, unstoppable asthma.

Further, Simon's probable asthmatic attack that led to a seizure and cardiac collapse in the midst of the chamber challenge testing to formaldehyde also supports the preceding opinion."

My opinion is supported by the general causation scientific analysis of Dr. Lionel Watson, the medical report of Dr. Patricia Simms and the Coastal General medical findings reported by Dr. Chris McKenna.

On the environmental or exposure side of the case, I have relied upon several industrial hygiene environmental surveys of Matchless Trailers like those in which Simon Williams lived, and the numerous other governmental and private sector scientific reports that characterized, modeled and documented the dimensions of formaldehyde overexposure to inhabitants of these trailers."

"Can you tell the court whether you agree with this conclusion of Dr. Baines?"

Quickly searching the gallery again, so she could spit accurately into Tristan's face, McKenna turned to the judge and said just two words:

"It's rubbish!"

"Did you say, 'rubbish?'" Dr. McKenna, 'Rubbish?'" lighted Attington, suddenly standing more erect, and glancing at his table of defense cronies with a sly grin and raised eyebrows.

Laura turned to Asher. Forgetting herself she said, "Hey, look, I need to object!"

Asher responded knowing Laura was just expressing wishful thinking, "You can't object. Good God - she's our expert and our witness. We'll get her later on re-direct. I never should have let her testify. God, what a mess!"

Without answering Attington's "Yes or No" question, McKenna gushed, "In fact, I do not agree with Dr. Baines at all. He is completely wrong."

She leaned forward in her chair, aiming her gaze back into the gallery. Tristan was missing. McKenna's arrows were, thus, shot indiscriminately into the crowd.

Then she landed the big one, "Finally, he is not even qualified to draw such conclusions."

Both Laura and Asher suddenly looked at each other and slumped in their chairs at the same moment.

McKenna had now exacted payback for the Higgins case several years earlier in which Tristan had cleaned her clock.

She knew Tristan was qualified; but pride had forked her tongue.

In reality, McKenna had only the thinnest medical basis for avoiding scientific perjury.

Tristan had relied upon the formaldehyde challenge disaster to bolster his opinions on causation, true; but he had also relied even more upon the expert report of Simon's pediatrician, Dr. Patricia Simms. Although he did not hear her testify directly, he also knew that Dr. Pat had tried to "knock it out of the park," when she testified live the day before McKenna went on the stand.

Now hidden in the back of the courtroom, up to stretch his legs and to avoid McKenna's gloating stare, Tristan pleasantly recalled his second meeting with Dr. Pat the day before McKenna's treachery. Tristan had first met Pat at her office several weeks earlier, to go over

Simon's case in person. This time, Tristan had been entering, while she was exiting the courthouse just before lunch. She had just been dismissed from the stand. Tristan recognized her at once.

"Hello, Pat," exclaimed Tristan, "How was it?"

"Hey, yourself, Tristan Baines," smiled the trim, sophisticated, former president of the Louisiana Medical Society. "It went fine, I think." Independent of her stellar 30 year medical career, helping thousands of New Orleans' children, hundreds after Katrina, Dr. Pat had testified on only three previous occasions.

"I wish you had been there; you could tell me," she flattered.

"I would have loved to have been there; but I only arrived here from Denver last night," said Tristan. "I drove down from Laramie to catch the plane. God, it was beautiful at this time of year."

"You are forgiven," responded Pat, still sporting a genuine smile. She loved to talk to her colleague, one whom she had met only a few months ago, over the internet and on the phone and whom she had just met in person. "I am grateful for those articles you sent me. You know; I mentioned them in my final report."

"You can thank, Dr. Lionel Watson, my Durango, Colorado, toxicology colleague, epidemiologist, former cop and all around good guy," spouted Tristan with genuine enthusiasm. "I have been friends with Watson for over 20 years. He is a Ph.D. in Environmental Health and my smartest partner in crime. He pulled eight of ten of those articles. I contributed the other two."

"I remember him," said Pat, "Don't you recall? You mentioned him on the conference call, when we first got started."

"So, I did," covered Tristan. "I just get a kick out of having a friend named 'Dr. Watson,'" so I tend to perseverate. Last point; he's also an ordained minister, in case you have a Christening, marriage, or funeral to perform. I'll bet Watson would even do a Bar Mitzvah, if he had the opportunity. Anyway, so how was Attington?"

"I don't think he was very well prepared and was out of practice; but he still tried to discredit my credentials for drawing conclusions on cause and effect. He said he respected my clinical diagnostic skills;

but did not think I had the experience to conclude formaldehyde was a causative factor. The questions were to the point; it just seemed like he had his mind on other things….or people, like you and Dr. McKenna.

I'll tell you Tristan; watch out for that one. I mean McKenna, even though she's supposed to be on our team. Asher told me what happened in Dallas. She's got you in her cross hairs."

"I'll be OK, Pat," said Tristan, realizing she was correct. He could not underestimate how far McKenna would go to even the score for her Higgins defeat.

Still standing in the back of the courtroom, Tristan rejoined the present, long enough to witness the tail end of his Hautair "colleague's" screwing him to the wall. Ironically, he enjoyed the rise he had gotten out of McKenna. "Boy, that Higgins case, musta hurt!" he thought.

Asher would have his turn trying to morph the McKenna lemon into lemonade, or at least into inoffensive water; but then it would be Tristan's opportunity to make it all right. He was ready; but couldn't help noticing the massive blood spill on the courtroom floor; it was his blood; He should have seen McKenna's knife, fork and bib when she took the stand.

CHAPTER 25 - THE TRIAL - PART II - HENNY, GAG AND DR. TRISTAN BAINES ON DIRECT EXAMINATION

DATE: Tuesday pm 9/29/09 - About four years and one month after Katrina
PLACE: U.S. Federal Court, Eastern District of Louisiana, New Orleans, Judge Henrietta F. Whitmore presiding.

—   —   —

The night before his testimony on Tuesday, Tristan could barely function. After the mental trauma of encountering McKenna earlier in the summer and the far worse encounter with Saul Goldman's organizational chart of The Resistance, he found his focus was at risk. He was prepared for trial; that was not the issue; his potential decompensation was hinged to his learning that CADIXX and Gordon A. Gasher (GAG) were linked to this horrible organization. That degenerate sub-human was properly initialed "GAG." He terrorized and brutalized Tristan's child, Tess; and after the same, mutilated his wife, Heather, by removing her ring finger. God knows what he did with the ring? Now Tristan understood even more what sort of criminal monster he was up against.

Tristan had gone to the law in St. Louis after the first incident in 2006. Three years later, nothing. Until now, his family had stayed in hiding, and he had withdrawn. Actually, had he not taken on this

FEMA case and re-linked with Asher Goldman, he would have never seen the big picture that allowed him a better understanding of why Heather and Tess's assailants did what they did. But now he also realized how these bastards functioned as part of the nefarious activities of The Resistance. He didn't believe it; it was too shocking to swallow; there really existed an organization, obviously operating outside the law, determined to silence anyone who increased its members' liability and worse yet, put members at risk for financial or reputational loss. Their evolving MO was to kill and maim by any means, at any cost.

In the short term Tristan knew he had to focus as best he could. He had his testimony ahead of him the next day. The Resistance would have to wait until later.

— — —

On Tuesday morning, Asher decided not to re-call Dr. McKenna for further questioning, figuring he could rehabilitate his case with his star witness, Tristan Baines whom he would call next.

Judge Whitmore asked Asher how much time he needed. He said at least one and a half hours, so the judge called for a luncheon recess. It was 11:30 am.

"We will recess for lunch until 1 pm," declared Judge Whitmore, "Court adjourned."

Her black robe billowing in tow, Judge Henrietta Whitmore disappeared in an instant through a door that led to a short hallway outside her beautifully adorned wood-paneled chamber. The hallway was poorly lit. She stopped for a second and pulled the robe away from her petite neck where it had been chaffing all morning. She entered her office, moved across the front of her desk, went around it and sat down in her luxurious, dark brown leather, swivel chair, her feet barely touching the floor. She took a deep breath, happy to break from the boredom of the courtroom.

Behind her chair, next to pecan inlaid, wooden bookshelves, was a window, a portal to the small, but beautiful park across the street – a park where the judge liked to sit, incognito, whenever she could. She loved animals; and the park offered her the opportunity to feed some of the hundreds of sea birds that journeyed there across the Mississippi delta to seek shade from the blistering Louisiana sun.

She scooted forward to examine a couple of messages left on her green desk blotter.

Then she felt the pain.

Like the clamping of a lobster's claw, Whitmore felt a pinch where the right side of her neck met the muscles of her shoulder. It had been easy to grab her thin, 63 year old flesh and twist it like a warm piece of Turkish taffy. The pain blazed through her body with the hatred it conveyed.

She grimaced and tried to turn around. A sledge hammer of a hand pushed down on her left shoulder. She tried to reach for the emergency button under her desk, conveniently located, but never used except once when an insanely belligerent plaintiff's lawyer rose to invade her personal space eight years ago. Whitmore had her way with him. She destroyed his career and broke his spirit. After a year without parole in a Parish jail, he ended up working as a cook at a local fast food chain.

Tears filled her eyes. She watched the black gloved hand as it moved from her shoulder to her mouth to muffle her imminent scream. Now she was afraid that the lunatic in her chamber was really going to try to hurt her or worse. Skinning her shin, she kicked the underside of the center drawer of her desk, again trying to set off the silent alarm.

"Just sit still and I won't hurt you. You must know who I am," whined the almost feline, yet masculine, voice behind her. "I'm just checking in to make certain all is going smoothly, as planned."

In the chaos of the moment, she had no idea who was assaulting her in her own private office chamber, deep within the confines of the federal courthouse. "How, dear God, did he get in here? The window? Where are the security guards?" she thought.

The lunatic knew just where to squeeze. The brute had to be male. She could smell his fetid breath and body odor. He leaned closer. He let up on the squeeze.

"Come on Momma, you know who I am. I take orders, just like you," emoted the madman, whose breath now smelled a bit like vomit. He continued, "The General just asked me to check in and make sure everything is alright. For the moment he likes the way you are handling this case; but you know how it is; it's got to look right; we all know that.

But at the end of the day, this case better not cost our friends anything; and just as importantly, it had better punish our enemies 'to the full extent of the law.' And I don't mean man's law; I am talking about the 'natural law of the jungle,' Momma; remember those who are the strongest and show no mercy, eat better than all the others.

I'll move my hand, if you promise not to scream. If you do or if you push that button under your desk, your court will be adjourned indefinitely. So let's talk; but do not turn around, if you value life."

"OK, so what do you want?" Whitmore gasped. She still felt the iron palm on her shoulder, close enough to snap her neck.

"You know what I want, Henny, dear," responded her assailant, still smelling like cat urine. Whitmore jumped suddenly when her attacker used her family nickname, "Henny," short for Henrietta. Her parents and three sisters like to call her that "chicken" name, when she was a little girl. Now only her closest friends, who knew her intimately, risked using this sobriquet, and only with calculated risk. Of course, Henny, not surprisingly, alone in life, heard this name only on the rarest of occasions, inexplicably, like this one.

"I said - what the hell do you want? And how in the hell did you get in here?" Henny spat, feigning control and courage that, in reality, were totally absent.

"I said I was just checking up on the progress of the case. I am here to make an impression. I hope it didn't hurt too bad. But, you know, there is more, much more where that came from; and it will be much, much, worse, if you veer from your promised course of action. And you know it will be slow, very slow. So bad, you will beg to be water-boarded instead."

Henny sat there, almost wetting her pants. She was consumed

with fear. It was the voice, the vile, inspissated evil pouring from his lips. It was the voice of death and nothing less. Her mind sifted through memories of the tone, the delivery.

She thought she knew the invader. It was now coming back. She had only met him briefly twice before over the past seven years while things were getting organized, that is, when they were looking for the best people for the jobs at hand. Those were the days when they paid well. Now they didn't need to pay so well because they had the blackmail goods on everyone.

The fiend continued in a very business-like manner, "Since things are going reasonably well, I want to know if there is anything else we can do for you – anything within reason, of course. Maybe a new pump for your swimming pool; I noticed how cloudy the water has been lately, when I dropped by while you were at work. Or, maybe that new boat you have been looking at or even the little cottage outside Biloxi, along the beach, if you're a really good girl!

Have you prepared the jury instructions, yet? We will expect them."

Henny blurted, now with righteous indignation, "This whole thing is unnecessary. You, all of you, know where my loyalties lie. I should have the General shoot you for this," Henny continued. "One yell…"

"Oh yeah," interrupted the voice, "Before, one yell…, your neck will snap like a twig. I will disappear and you will be lying there like a fractured peppermint stick. Get used to it. After your performance in that last case against Zephyr Oil, you know the one, where those stinking tree-hugging hippies got four million. For what? It was on your watch."

"Sometimes the beggars have to win, you moron. Some have to win," belched Henny, now mobilizing her own internal evil strength. "Forget the cloak and dagger; I know it's you, Gasher." She suddenly mustered the courage to glance around. She saw his vicious grin."

"Good God, Gordon, you are pitiful, just pitiful," she said, now with tears of anger in her eyes.

"So you have me figured out. How nice…and how irrelevant," purred GAG. "OK, OK. I get it," GAG responded, looking at Henny, thinking he may have overplayed a little. After all he and Momma Henny were critical lieutenants in the Resistance. It didn't matter; he knew he wasn't finished with her because of the Zephyr ruling. More pain was on the way.

"I'll tell it to the General," continued GAG. Just like you say – sometimes the beggars have to win. But guess what? He doesn't understand any losses, ever. He has stakeholders, in very high places who hold him, accountable. After CADIXX, back in '06, it has become a life and death matter. So he definitely has to account for the likes of you"

"Gordon, you know you have nothing to worry about," offered Henny, trying to lower the temperature of their interaction. "This case is going as planned. There will be no losses and your 'buddy,' Tristan Baines will look like the fool that he is."

"Very good, Henny. That is just what the General and I want to hear," said GAG, suddenly calmer than before.

"Why don't you just kill him? No one except, maybe his deformed wife and teenage brat would shed a tear," blurted Henny. "Think how we would save. An accident would be the easiest way to go."

"You're above your pay grade, Henny," hissed GAG. "Leave matters like that to me. Yes, it would be simple, maybe. But he is no helpless quarry; and besides, you know the General has placed an asterisk by his name on our most wanted hit list. You know what that means, old gal."

"I forgot about that," sighed Henny. "I remember hearing the story some time ago. It is all rumor. Something about Baines having saved the General's infant daughter when he was working in some emergency room outside of Boston. Baines probably has no recollection of the event. The General and his daughter became nothing more than inconspicuous persons in the sea of faces Baines encountered day after day, month after month. Now it was years ago; but the General remembered. Against all protocol, he has asterisked Baines. Contain him; hurt him; hurt his family; but don't kill him, at least, not yet. He's debating about his Indian pal. The General may kill him just to make Baines mad."

"Well, Henny dear, I can read. I know the rules," said GAG, as he looked around, realizing he had to prepare for a rapid exit. "Baines is off limits; but accidents do happen anyway. I can face the General, if poor Baines accidentally runs into a knife or a .44 slug that happens his way. The General might be angry for a minute or two; but he will recover. After all, he could scratch one from the list, asterisk or not, who has caused so many in our organization embarrassment and financial disruption.

Now, Henny, I must leave you, so you will have to go to sleep for a couple of minutes. No ruckus now. I will help."

Like the sadistic expert he was, GAG suddenly repositioned his left hand over her mouth again and moved his first finger and thumb over both carotid arteries in her neck, on the left and right side of her windpipe. He pressed, just enough to rob her brain of blood and oxygen, just enough, but not too much.

"Go to sleep Momma. Go to sleep."

GAG held his grip for nearly 20 seconds, before he let go. He gently leaned Henny's head forward and placed it on her desk. He exited into the unoccupied courtroom and left.

After five minutes, she awakened with a sore neck, groggy, but with her tormentor's face in her mind. "He will die, slowly, someday," she thought. "I will make it happen. How can we have such a monster in our midst? I told the board that GAG, the sadist, is a loose canon; now I am certain. How dare he?"

But she quickly recalled the General's mantra, echoing in her mind. She heard him asserting the rules during their latest meeting just six months ago in the spring.

"Our clients and soul mates suffer every year at the hands of imposters of truth, the abortions of intellect, the entitlement mobsters who cost red blooded Americans billions a year. I will try even harder to stem the tide and God pity anyone who stands in my way."

"It didn't matter," Henny thought, "I will kill and replace GAG when the time is right. The General will stand with me on this one. How dare he so much as touch me, much less…much less."

—   —   —

Three minutes went by, and she relapsed briefly into the aftermath of her ordeal. "I am Judge Henrietta F. Whitmore. I AM Judge Henrietta Fabiola Whitmore," Momma told herself over and over again, rubbing her neck to relieve the pain. "That bastard GAG WILL die at the time and place AND by the slowest, most brutal method of MY choosing; I swear to God!"

She recovered slowly trying to ignore the reality of the moment. She did not look forward to the rest of the day. She knew that just after lunch, now only thirty minutes away, the worst of the worst was going to enter her courtroom, as an expert for the plaintiffs.

Here comes Dr. Tristan P. Baines. Here, in the flesh, was a man who had cost large, so called "misbehaving," American corporations nearly two billion dollars over the past few years. The fool thinks he wears the white hat and others wear the black. He is a legendary crusader for the "little guy;" but will work both sides of the street if he thinks the defense needs defending.

"I should have limited Baines' testimony or thrown him out altogether," she thought. "But the court needs to hear from him. After all, he performed one of his 'tap dancing' causation analyses on young Simon Williams. We will see how well he stands up to the daggers thrown by Dr. McKenna, supposedly his comrade in arms. Boy, did she put him down, maybe for the count. On the other hand, I admit that the good Dr. Baines is probably not the helplessly inept buffoon the defense would like to portray. I have heard the rumors, and I know the facts."

Again she relapsed, but this time fantasizing. "God, my neck and shoulder hurt; but I have a poultice. I will first make Gordon Gasher a eunuch; I will do it myself with a pair of pliers! Then I will kill him!"

Wearing a thin, evil smirk, she rubbed her neck one more time, tightened her robe and headed back to the courtroom.

— — —

Plaintiff Direct Examination of Dr. Tristan P. Baines

"Raise your right hand. Do you solemnly swear that the evidence you shall give will be the truth, the whole truth and nothing but the truth, so help you God?" launched the Clerk of the Court.

"I do," said Tristan Baines.

"Please state your full name and your occupation," said Asher Goldman.

"My name is Tristan Philip Baines. I am a physician and engineer," said Tristan, surveying the courtroom for familiar faces. He had been there about four score times before and felt quite at home.

"Please tell the court when you first became involved in this case, doctor," said Goldman.

"Well, I was first contacted by your firm around May 4, 2009, that is, this year," said Tristan, amusedly thinking about the definition of 'contacted,' that wild and wooly episode involving a helicopter search and his extraction from his compound in the Snowy Mountains of southern Wyoming.

"OK, what were you asked to do on this matter?" said Goldman.

"You mean my role as an expert?" asked Tristan.

"Yes, your role as an expert," clarified Goldman.

"Well, I was asked to provide a comprehensive evaluation of all medical and environmental information regarding the claims of Simon Williams. Specifically, the environmental information related to his exposure to formaldehyde in his Matchless trailer and the medical information related to his worsening pre-existing asthma and his adverse reaction to formaldehyde following deliberate, clinically planned, formaldehyde exposure, by another plaintiff's expert.

After completing my evaluation of the environmental and medical information, I was asked to perform a causation analysis to determine whether Simon's exposure to formaldehyde in his trailer was responsible, partly or altogether, for his worsening childhood asthma, and for that matter, his risk of developing a life-threatening condition known as Unstoppable Asthma. This is a condition in which the asthmatic attack continues and is usually resistant to outpatient medical treatment. Without prompt, aggressive care, in the hospital, the patient may die. Simon is at greater risk for this condition, as a result of his trailer formaldehyde exposure. It is a ticking time-bomb with which he will have to live for the rest of his life."

"Very good, doctor," said Goldman.

Asher Goldman continued with his planned set of questions covering all aspects of Tristan's involvement in the case, from his interview with Simon in New Orleans and Simon's evaluation at Coastal General, to his inspection of the trailer and everything in between. It went well. Tristan articulated his reasoning and factual basis for all of his opinions. Tristan's rendition of Simon's evaluation at Coastal General omitted the frightening details of Simon's near death experience, except to recruit the event to confirm that Simon was hypersensitive to formaldehyde, even though both Laura and Asher wondered whether he may actually have been poisoned.

"You heard the earlier testimony of Dr. McKenna, didn't you doctor?" asked Goldman.

"Yes, I did. I was in the courtroom," answered Tristan.

"OK, then - regarding young Simon's formaldehyde sensitivity, doctor, has this diagnosis been confirmed and is it persistent?" said Asher.

"'Yes' to both of your questions," replied Tristan, rubbing in Asher's predilection toward asking more than one question at a time. He was surprised there was no objection from the defense.

"OK, doctor, then, do you have an opinion about whether your diagnosis of formaldehyde sensitivity is causally related to his exposure to formaldehyde in his FEMA trailer manufactured by Matchless Enterprises, Inc.?"

"I do have an opinion," said Tristan.

"Doctor, please tell the court that opinion," said Goldman.

"My opinion to a reasonable degree of environmental medical certainty is that Simon's conditions, as stated earlier in my testimony, are probably linked to his exposure to formaldehyde in his FEMA trailer, manufactured by Matchless.

In addition it is my opinion that Simon's exposure to formaldehyde during testing at Coastal General led directly to a severe asthma event, consistent with, so-called Unstoppable Asthma. That event, inturn led to his probable seizure and cardiac arrest. The formaldehyde exposure during the testing and not his use of bronchodilator was the source of the problem. Finally, let the record reflect that I never ordered and, in fact, I opposed any type of formaldehyde inhalation challenge in this patient. The risk was clear. The test should never have taken place."

Tristan knew that his comments would help Simon's claim against Coastal General and McKenna for almost killing him that late June day, earlier in the year. Anyway "what's good for the gander is good for the goose," Tristan laughed to himself, reversing the order of the popular aphorism.

"OK, doctor, it sound's like you do not agree with Dr. McKenna's assessment on this matter. Is that the case?" asked Goldman.

"Yes, that's correct," began Tristan, "I do not agree with Dr. McKenna."

"So Dr. McKenna's rather assertive, negative remarks about your opinion on trailer formaldehyde exposure being the cause of Simon's problems are just one example of two experts having different opinions on the same subject? Isn't that true, doctor?" said Goldman, glancing around to meet the eyes of Michael Attington.

"I guess so," answered Tristan. Then venturing forward in the absence of another question from Goldman, he continued, "But it's more than just an honest disagreement."

"Objection, your Honor," blurted Attington. "The witness has not been asked a question and the last question is overly leading, and calls for speculation. Dr. McKenna has made her opinion quite clear. Dr. Baines is not qualified to render any of the opinions to which he has subjected this court this afternoon. I move to disqualify his testimony at once."

"Sustained," said Judge Whitmore, "Do you have a question, Mr. Goldman?"

"What?" blurted Goldman. "Mr. Attington could have voir diered Dr. Baines at the beginning of this trial, if he had been interested in disqualifying his testimony. He can't do this now!"

"There is precedent for this motion, your Honor," blurted Attington, even louder this time.

"Please explain, Mr. Attington?" said Whitmore, delighted at the interruption.

The court became a tomb of silence, awaiting Attington's reply.

"Yes, it was Evergreen v. ....Uh, your Honor, I will need some time to respond to the court on this matter. I would need a recess until tomorrow," said Attington.

Quiet laughter could be heard. Even one of the jurors coughed up a giggle.

Realizing she had to show at least a semblance of fairness and notwithstanding her wanting to support Attington, Whitmore continued, "Mr. Attington. I will not recess this court for you to go home and do the homework you should have brought to school in the first place. Now is there a question, Mr. Goldman?"

"Yes, your Honor," responded Goldman, wondering whether he could fix this mess. "Dr. Baines, why do you disagree with Dr. McKenna? Where has she gone wrong?"

Another compound question. Tristan couldn't believe it.

"To be blunt," said Tristan, "Why I disagree and where has she gone wrong can be summed up as one answer. Dr. McKenna has overlooked and/or ignored the abundant toxicology literature on formaldehyde sensitization and the confirmed industrial hygiene exposure information, related to the patient's trailer.

She did not analyze the exposure data in her report. This is a prerequisite to performing a causation analysis. She never did it. She is not an industrial hygienist or environmental engineer. I am both, in addition to being a medical doctor.

All of this information provides the scientifically probable foundation for my conclusions. Her conclusion that the patient's catastrophic response was secondary to his using his own bronchodilator inhaler during his testing is not probable.

This is the same inhaler that the patient has been using for over three years; before and after his visit to Coastal General. It is far more probable that the formaldehyde in the chamber caused the patient's problem rather than his inhaler.

In addition, as stated earlier in my testimony, it is my opinion that Simon's childhood asthma was substantively worsened by his approximately 18 month exposure to formaldehyde in his trailer. I base this opinion upon the report of Dr. Patricia Simms, Simon's pediatrician, my own analysis of the medical record, the research on general causation provided by Dr. Lionel Watson, my toxicology and epidemiology consultant, and my own medical and environmental engineering expertise."

"Thank you, doctor," said Goldman. "Now for absolute clarification, is it your understanding of Dr. McKenna's testimony that she can not associate any medical problem in Simon with his trailer formaldehyde exposure? If so, why?"

"That is correct and regarding the 'why has she gone wrong' question, you will have to ask Dr. McKenna," said Tristan.

"OK," said Goldman, wincing at the very thought of recalling McKenna for anything, much less to testify again. Her record of treachery would have to stand.

At this point, Asher thought that he had cleared the air for the jury, even if some jurors may have remained confused. "Actually, conflicting testimony between two plaintiffs' experts was not always such a bad thing," he thought. "It created the appearance of good science. Not everyone always agrees on everything."

"Of course, mused Asher, "it is not everyday that one expert calls another expert's opinions 'rubbish,' and claims he is unqualified."

In his heart, Asher hoped McKenna would lose big for nearly killing his client and smearing his principal expert. Next time he would lock her in her Oyve League tower and throw away the key.

One big question remained. What had really happened to McKenna's technician who had set up the exposure challenge? Of course his partially devoured and decaying body was found on the banks of the Charles River with a bullet in his head, but who put it there and why?

Shortly after the incident Asher had contacted his brother Saul, still in hiding and told him about the murder. Saul was clear on the matter.

"My best educated guess, Asher, is that the elimination of the poor slob bears the mark of the recently 'gone rogue' Resistance. The technician may have conducted an unsuccessful 'hit' on the poor lad. So you see what happens, when you fail to kill someone under contract. You die."

"Do you think McKenna knew anything about this?" asked Asher.

"Hard to tell," said Saul. "Probably not. I don't think she planned to kill her patient. It would have been too obvious; although her absence during the testing procedure certainly makes her look complicit. I'll do some more research on this gal and get back to you. Gotta go."

Asher worried about his brother and feared he may go the way of the murdered technician. "Time will tell," Asher thought. "He's just got to keep moving and keep his head low. The Resistance would not treat his treasonous behavior well, if they found out about it."

After several more questions, Asher was finished. He had established Tristan's opinions as clearly as possible and had done his best to counter the McKenna blitz.

He passed Tristan to Attington for cross-examination.

CHAPTER 26 - THE TRIAL - PART III - DR. TRISTAN BAINES ON CROSS EXAMINATION

DATE: Tuesday pm 9/29/09 - About four years and one month after Katrina
PLACE: U.S. Federal Court, Eastern District of Louisiana, New Orleans, Judge Henrietta F. Whitmore presiding.

— — —

Cross Examination of Dr. Tristan P. Baines

It was attempted murder on the stand; but Tristan was prepared. In fact he loved it.

"So, Doctor Baines, please tell the jury why you have changed your opinion right here in this courtroom?" hissed Attington, loving the "so when did you stop beating your wife" type of questions.

"I did not change my opinion at all," said Tristan calmly, enjoying his ring side view of the protruding of blood vessels in Attington's forehead. Tristan was the kind of man who liked to give an asshole like Attington hypertension, or maybe a seizure to boot.

"Is that so?" gulped Attington. "You stated in your report that the plaintiff's alleged exposure to formaldehyde in his trailer led to his worsening of childhood asthma and his lifelong, increased risk of Unstoppable Asthma. Isn't that true? Nowhere did you mention that his formaldehyde exposure at Coastal General led to his developing a seizure and cardiac collapse, did you?"

Tristan couldn't believe his ears. Even he was getting confused by this yo-yo. This idiot just read his opinion into the record when cross-examining McKenna and it clearly stated Tristan's opinion on the chamber debacle. What was he smoking?

Tristan looked over at Asher, waiting for an objection for mischaracterization of Tristan's testimony. Everything he said on direct was contained in his report, more or less, within a syllable or two. Asher was shuffling papers. Laura gave him the smile of "Off with his nuts; you can handle this one yourself."

Trying not to be condescending, Tristan said, "Mr. Attington, you are mischaracterizing my testimony. I am not changing any opinions. I stated them clearly in my report. Further, I am simply elaborating upon my opinions based upon questions posed by Mr. Goldman. As far as I know I am entitled to do that."

"Are you a lawyer, too?" Dr. Baines," yucked Attington, looking around to see if he could get a couple of laughs in the courtroom. He saw a tiny smile coming from Judge Whitmore and nothing else. Doris Carr looked like she had disappeared under the table.

"So, Dr. Baines, you don't know whether you can or can not offer opinions outside of those contained within your report. New opinions need to be cross-examined, you know."

"I don't have any new opinions. But if you say so - I guess that's why I am all yours," risked Tristan, completely out of order. He fought the urge to say more and won, at least for a couple of seconds.

"Oh," droned Attington, now looking down, carefully at Tristan's written report.

"Is that a question?" ventured Tristan, again losing the grip on his tongue and now stepping completely out of line.

"The witness will refrain from extraneous remarks and will wait for the next question. Is that clear, Dr. Baines?" belched Judge Whitmore, looking like the partially melted Wicked Witch of the West in the Wizard of Oz. Her other nickname of "The Harpy," known to the outside world was well earned. At her worst, she did resemble that mythical she-devil with a woman's face on a bird of prey.

Attington went for the jugular.

"Dr. Baines, is it true that your change in opinion was simply fabricated to counter the scathing comments made by Dr. McKenna?" said Attington, looking first at the Judge Whitmore then his partner, Doris Carr, who gazed back, expressionless, wondering where Attington was going with the extemporaneous line of questioning.

"Objection, your Honor," blurted Goldman. "Argumentative; the witness has clearly indicated that he did not change his opinion. He simply elaborated upon them during direct questioning. Mr. Attington can cross-examine the witness about every word he said."

"Overruled," smirked Judge Whitmore. "Doctor, you may answer the question."

"I did not change any opinions, as I have already explained," responded Tristan, keeping the civility of his answer as a high priority; and wondering, if he should enroll in an anger management class when all of this was over.

Attington decided to drop it and take a different tact.

"Doctor, why do you think Dr. McKenna commented that you were unqualified to render your opinion on causation in this case?" asked Attington. Then looking at the jury, he continued, "After all, she is affiliated with a prestigious Oyve League hospital and your official office is, I believe, somewhere in rural Wyoming."

"Objection! Objection!" blurted Goldman. "Your Honor; where is this going? Mr. Attington is simply badgering this witness. He is trying to confuse the jury by overstating the extent of honest disagreement between two of my expert witnesses."

Now Laura rolled her eyes and sank in her chair. "It is a good thing there were no dueling pistols available in the courtroom," she thought. Baines and McKenna would both pay big money to borrow them.

"Both of you, approach the bench, now" ordered Whitmore, who, already sunken into her robe, appeared to pop out like a "jack in the box" when she issued the order.

"What is going on here, Mr. Attington?" asked the Judge, now with a very calm even tone. "And Mr. Goldman, keep your pants on!" Out of the corner of her eye, she could see four of the jurors, engaged in two conversations and another one appear to wake up on the heels of the highly audible drama taking place before her.

"Your Honor, my line of questioning is intended to make the jury understand that Dr. McKenna's repudiation of Dr. Baines' opinions and credentials to offer those opinions disqualifies him as an expert," pleaded Attington, glancing at the jabbering jurors behind him.

"Your Honor, may I speak?" said Goldman.

"Go on, Mr. Goldman," said Whitmore, looking squarely into his eyes.

"This line of questioning is out of order," asserted Goldman, "The witness has made his opinions clear and has explained that his rendered opinions have not changed and are completely consistent with his report. Even though there are none, Mr. Attington can cross-examine Dr. Baines on any other so-called new opinions to his heart's content. And, with all due respect, Mr. Attington could have formally challenged Dr. Baines' credentials at the beginning by requesting a voir dire examination."

"Well, Mr. Goldman; you've made your point; but the bottom line is I like it. Objection overruled," smiled Whitmore, with her neck actually craned, bird-like, in a posture that made it easy to see how she earned her "Harpy" nickname.

Goldman was not only startled; but was visibly shaken by Judge Whitmore's remark. He and Attington withdrew to their respective tables. Laura looked at him and whispered, "This bitch has an agenda; big time. What the hell is going on here?"

Goldman whispered back, "Remember Saul's organization chart of The Resistance? Well, I think we may have Momma here in the courtroom, and she's a shrunken evil fetish in a black robe; And she's right in front of our noses."

"Following our conference, I would like the record to reflect that Mr. Goldman's latest objection is overruled," said Judge Whitmore.

"OK, Dr. Baines. Do you recall the question?" smirked Attington.

"No!" replied Tristan, clearly annoyed.

"Will the clerk please re-read the question for Dr. Baines," said Attington in an exasperated tone. Looking away from Tristan directly at the jury, Attington rolled his eyes. He then straightened his tie and scratched his nose while the clerk complied.

The clerk read back the last question, omitting the snide remark about Tristan's office address:

"Doctor, why do you think Dr. McKenna commented that you were unqualified to render your opinion on causation in this case?"

"Are we ready to go, Dr. Baines?" said Attington.

"Yes," offered Tristan. "I have no idea. You will have to ask Dr. McKenna."

Attington decided to change course.

"Doctor, please tell the court about the scientific methodology you applied to this case to derive your opinions about Simon Williams."

"I have already answered that question earlier in my testimony," said Tristan.

"Are you refusing to answer my question?" snarled Attington, his facial blood vessels showing again.

"Let me try to help you out, Mr. Attington," smiled Tristan, now on a trajectory that he calculated on the spur of the moment. "Let's begin by talking about Simon's exposure to formaldehyde while he lived in his Matchless trailer. Recall that this exposure was at least 50 times higher than acceptable standards.

We have several exhibits that were offered into evidence earlier in this trial. One of them is a piece of Matchless trailer cabinet plywood similar to that used in the Williams trailer. It came straight from the assembly line from a batch that was not baked out. With the court's permission, I think it was Exhibit #54, I would like to examine it to make a point."

"It is fine with me," said Attington. "Please bring Dr. Baines Exhibit #54."

The bailiff complied and handed Tristan a large polyethylene bag with a piece of bare 5/8" thick plywood about 16" by 24" in size. The bag had been left on the table for the past two days while the court-room had been secured overnight. The bag was slightly inflated but sealed by a zip-lock zipper.

Tristan took the bag in his hand. He reached into his pocket and pulled out a blue vinyl glove and put it on his right hand.

"Mr. Attington," said Tristan, "if you don't mind, I would like to hand you this exhibit and then explain my reasoning regarding the nature of young Simon's exposure."

The trap had been set. Tristan admired the stunt that Laura had pulled on McKenna in Asher's office a few months back. He figured it was bound to work.

Tristan held up the bag with his left hand about 20 inches above the witness desk. "Here, Mr. Attington, please take a look at this plywood. Its construction will be relevant to my opinions."

Attington hesitated. "No, Dr. Baines. I can see it from here."

Tristan sensed that Attington was wise to his intentions. He looked at the exhibit like it was a bagged rattlesnake.

"Well, then with the court's permission," continued Tristan, "to underscore my testimony, I would like to approach the jury and show the foreman, or should I say, forelady, this piece of plywood," Tristan knew he was bluffing. He didn't want to give it to anyone on the jury.

Attington hesitated again and glanced over at Judge Whitmore. "Your Honor, the defense has no objection; but we would like Dr. Baines to explain where he is going with his answer, before I agree."

Tristan replied, "It is really quite simple, I would like the jury to see a sample of the plywood that was in the Williams' trailer. I want them to keep in mind that this is only a little more than 2.5 square feet of plywood, whereas, there were several hundred feet of this material used in trailer in which the family lived. Again, perhaps, Mr. Attington, you would like to see it first?"

"No, as I said, Dr. Baines," gasped Attington," I can see it from here."

Loosing patience at this delay in the proceedings and obviously clueless about Tristan's intentions, Judge Whitmore interrupted, "Mr.

Attington, humor Dr. Baines, will you and take a look at the plywood in Exhibit #54, especially if it will move matters along."

"Your Honor, I would rather not," retorted Attington, now sounding like he was whining.

Sensing defiance, Judge Whitmore blurted, "Mr. Attington, step forward and look at the plywood; you are delaying these proceedings, Sir!"

Attington, glanced at Asher Goldman, then glared at Tristan, as he stepped forward. Laura was slumped in her chair with her hand over her mouth.

Tristan held out the plywood sample for Attington. As Attington reached forward to grab it, Tristan quickly unzipped the bag while less than a foot from Attington's face, exclaiming, "Here, perhaps you can get a better look, Mr. Attington."

The gas escaped with both a hiss and a "whoopee cushion" like flapping noise. The gas hit Attington right in the eyes and nose.

Attington got the whiff, but said nothing and used all the self control he could muster to avoid the horrifying grimace that wanted to come out, much less the scream of pain from his burning eyes.

"Oh, I am sorry, Mr. Attington," said Tristan, "There must have been some residual gas in that bag. I think it's been left in the heat for a while. Just bakes itself out. It smells just like a new car doesn't it?"

Attington quickly re-zipped the bag and dropped it on the floor. He picked it up while immediately, reaching into his inner suit pocket for a handkerchief. He turned from the jury and faced the gallery while he discretely mopped his brow and tears, then blew his nose. He turned back to Tristan and began to speak.

"Doc…er, ugh, ugh Bay, Bay, ugh," grunted Attington, who then began to cough violently. He suddenly turned and dashed toward his defense table and took several swigs of bottled water. He then poured some water into his open palm and splashed it in both eyes. He couldn't go on. He couldn't talk. His vocal cords were paralyzed for the moment. Doris Carr, his law partner stood up.

"Your Honor," said Ms. Carr, "If you have no objection, I will finish up with Dr. Baines. And given what has just happened, I would object to turning over this exhibit to the jury for direct handling.

"Doctor Baines," rebuked the judge, "please continue your answer, but without the theatrics."

Asher and Laura were so hysterical with laughter, they both thought they may have to leave the courtroom, one at a time. Attington sat in his chair for about three minutes then got up and left, headed to the bathroom to splash water into his eyes. He grabbed another bottle of water to drink on the way.

He regained his voice slowly over the next three days; but was useless in the courtroom until it came time for closing arguments. Several of the jurors also showed uncontrolled amusement but two others glared at Tristan who had kept a straight face throughout.

Judge Whitmore contemplated citing Tristan for contempt of court; but decided to let it go. Tristan had made Attington's exposure look like an accident; but it very well may have backfired. The jury saw it all. Some jurors probably didn't see any humor in Tristan's poisoning his inquisitor in real time.

Tristan addressed Carr's question and began with an apology and feigned concern that Attington would be alright. In reality, Tristan, would have been just as happy if Attington were never able to speak again. Blindness was another matter. Tristan went through the entire rigmarole again, identifying Simon's exposure, diagnosis and the relationship between the two. Carr let up and shortened the questions, concerned that Attington had not returned to the courtroom.

"Alright, Dr. Baines," said Carr. "I have no further questions."

Tristan remained silent, delighted that sometimes "show and tell" is a superior method to describing hypothetical concepts to the jury. Tristan went for broke with the formaldehyde reeking plywood. Letting loose on Attington, rather than the jury, was a wiser course of action and was much more fun. He hoped it hurt and hurt really good. He thought about Simon's intractable intermittent asthma and vocal paralysis when he opened that bag under Attington's face.

"Mr. Goldman, do you have any further questions for Dr. Baines?"

asked Judge Whitmore, making a mental note that Baines had now moved from number 12 to number 3 on The Resistance hit list.

"No, your Honor," said Asher, still trying not to break into hysteria.

"Dr. Baines, you are dismissed," ordered Whitmore, "But I want you to remain around for the next two days. Remember, you are still under oath and I do not want you talking about this case with anyone except Mr. Goldman and Ms. Swain. Do you understand?"

"Yes, your Honor," smiled Tristan as he gathered his notes and left the witness stand.

—   —   —

The remainder of the trial lasted eight more days and Tristan stuck around for two; but was not called.

He had dinner with Asher, Laura and Joseph, the night after his testimony. Tristan used this opportunity to talk at length about his concerns about Simon. He considered the lad both tough and fragile at the same time. This lost dog issue kept plaguing him. So he brought it up at dinner. Joseph was already in the loop; but Tristan assumed that he had made no progress, or he would have told him by now.

"I'm concerned about Simon," began Tristan, turning specifically toward Laura and Asher. God, Laura looks great, he thought.

Back in focus, he continued, "How is Simon going to manage, if we lose this case? And there's the matter of his mental perseveration, his obsession with finding his lost dog, Rambo."

"In answer to your first question, we will have to cross that bridge, if and when, we get there," answered Asher, "It's certainly a possibility when you consider how the cards are stacked. Now…"

"We know all about the dog," interrupted Laura. "Sethie filled us in. The great Tristan Baines and his trusty colleague, Joseph True Blood have given up man hunting for doggie dealing, uh, I mean, for a warm hearted, good spirited effort to make a little boy happy."

"Well, that's a nice thing to say," said Tristan, who found himself focusing more than he should have upon the pleasant shine in Laura's hair and the faint, but sensuous scent, of her perfume. "Part patchouli, for sure," he thought. He chalked it up to it having been a very long day. And he was lonely, very lonely, for his family.

"I'm working on it," added Joseph, turning to Tristan. "I talked to Dr. Pat right after you and I talked, weeks ago. My theory is that someone who found the dog saw the picture and the phone number and took both down from the bulletin board near Pat's temporary office. I've got a few good sources, who promised to look into the matter. And, Tris, I offered them $500 of your money for a lead. We'll just have to see."

"Nice, very nice," blurted Tristan. "Next time ask, ask, True Blood, before you offer a reward. Anyway, it'll be worth it. Hell, make it a thousand, and I'll split it with you!"

"Yeah, it will be worth it to make Simon happy; but don't add the 500 bucks, thousand, or whatever, to your bill, Baines," chirped Asher, winking at Laura.

"It's a small price to pay," said Laura, scanning Tristan and Asher. "But I seriously doubt anyone will claim the prize. I don't know how we can possibly find the dog."

"Not true," answered Joseph. "One source has already suggested the dog may have been taken by someone in an official capacity. Not many citizens would have been too anxious to bring home another pet in the aftermath of Katrina. That's assuming they even had a home. There were hundreds of strays everywhere. Some cops, fire fighters, or even the Guard may have had some strays following them. It appears maybe one just kept a mutt whose mug was posted, and didn't want to give it back. To many of the victims of that damned storm, losing their pets was just a twist of the knife.

When citizens were relocated, some heartbreaking things happened. One guy told me about a terrible scene on a relocation bus. A bus driver actually tore a dog from the arms of a man who had boarded the bus, telling him he couldn't take the dog with him to the relocation center. The poor guy went nuts. The dog was literally snatched from the man's embrace and set on the curb as the bus pulled away. Who knows what happened to his pet? Look, I'll have more to say in the next few weeks."

The dinner went well; but none of them cared to discuss what they could do for Simon, if his case was lost. Shudder the thought. In the aftermath of defeat, Simon would probably be stronger than all of them, Tristan thought.

The next day, both preparing to leave, Tristan and Joseph had breakfast with Laura and Asher. "I need to go home and see my family," said Tristan. "I will be gone for about a month, at least. I won't have a cell phone or a computer. I will call in to find out how things turn out. What about you, Joseph?"

"I'm heading back to Colorado. You know where to find me," smiled Joseph. "I hope you'll have some time to meet me in Laramie. We need to go back to the compound. I have special surprise for you when we get there."

"Really?" laughed Tristan.

"OK, both of you; get out of here," said Laura, slapping Joseph on the shoulder and squeezing Tristan's arm. Go to your families; but come back soon. Maybe we'll see you in Dallas."

Joseph and Tristan rose and headed for the door; but not before Joseph returned to the table and reached down, finished his orange juice and grabbed two pieces of toast and a napkin. Standing a couple of feet away, Tristan couldn't help himself.

"What's the surprise, True Blood?" pleaded Tristan.

"Uh, uh," joked Joseph, "Me no tell; you wait and see."

Laura turned to Asher, rolling her eyes.

"If I were you, I'd fire both their asses," she smiled, as she picked up her coffee cup.

"I don't need to," kidded Asher, "I never really hired either of them. Tristan's engagement agreement and latest bill have been molding on my desk for six weeks."

CHAPTER 27 - HOME AGAIN

DATE: Friday 10/09/09 - About four
years and five weeks after Katrina
LOCATION: Thetford Center, Vermont
and near Hayden, Colorado

— — —

Well, it was all over and both Tristan and Joseph needed a rest, away from anything related to the FEMA case. That included Asher and Laura. Tristan could now focus his attention on more important matters like reconnecting with his family and pulling in some of the IOUs in his search for GAG. Tristan was definitely ambivalent about what to do first. He knew Heather and Tess were safe and doing well. They had been living under Heather's sister's married name, staying with her and her husband in the wild Green Mountains of rural Vermont. But it wasn't too remote; not like his Wyoming retreat; at least they had power so they could have satellite internet and plenty of hot water. Tristan had been in touch on a regular basis. He had originally planned to go back east to be with his family, just as soon as he made certain his Wyoming compound was ready for winter. A better idea surfaced. The next time he talked to Heather, he was going to try to persuade her to bring Tess out to Laramie to go to school. The coast appeared clear or was it? He knew they were going to come for him at a time and place of their choosing, so they thought, he thought!

If the coast wasn't clear, one thing was for certain; this time, he would be prepared. God pity anyone who tried to hurt him or anyone he loved, ever again.

Torture comes in various flavors. He continued to bear the agony of guilt that flooded over him since St. Louis. He had tried to make it go away; but it stuck like the stench of skunk spray on your favorite dog. He fantasized and planned; then planned and fantasized.

He finally figured it out. The only poultice for his misery would be one saturated with the blood of the perps who had hurt his family. He would find them first and maybe even let the law do its job; but if not, then, all, repeat all options would remain on the table.

—   —   —

The season was peaking and the spectacular red, yellow, and orange leaves on the hardwoods exploded against the azure deep blue sky. As beautiful as the golden and sometimes reddish Aspens appeared in the Rockies, nothing could compare to kaleidoscope of colors of the Oak and Maple trees of New England in the fall. Tristan couldn't get there fast enough. He had been driving for over 22 hours over two days with only one stop, since he left New Orleans and had just crossed the Vermont/Massachusetts border. He was coming up US 91 and was just outside of Brattleboro. He had at least six hours of light left. He knew where they lived. It was remote by any standard. Heather's sister, Sue, and her husband, Brad, had been just as anxious to check out of civilization as had Tristan and Heather. Lucky for both families. Heather and Tess were safe and out of reach; or, at least, so it seemed.

It had been just over three years since Heather and Tess had sought refuge in her sister's farm, outside of Thetford Center, way back in the Vermont woods not far from the Ompompanoosuc River.

Four months before the exodus, back in St. Louis, the criminal amputation of Heather's ring finger had almost developed into a medical disaster. Notwithstanding prompt medical care and hospitalization within hours of her discovery by the highway, infection had still set in. It would have been far worse had she and Tess not been found in the rain by that good Samaritan truck driver. The infection was not surprising. Heather had laid in the filthy water filled ditch for several hours along a road on the St. Louis side of the Mississippi River just over a mile from the historical Eads Bridge and the St. Louis arch.

Only intensive IV antibiotics spared the rest of Heather's hand. Her two broken thumbs and Tess's broken arm and wrist seem only incidental to her tortuous mutilation. Tristan had gone out of his mind with worry during those first few days Heather and Tess had been missing. At the time, it was not immediately clear why all of this had happened.

The last thing Tristan could recall was the threat. Gordon A. Gasher (GAG), the alleged nurse medical director of CADIXX told Tristan that if he didn't change his testimony against CADIXX, he would be sorry. But Tristan knew he couldn't let down the several hundred households who had been sucking in the fumes from the CADIXX incinerator for the past ten years. Tristan didn't know what GAG meant, and he didn't take the threat seriously. He miscalculated, big time.

Who could have guessed that GAG would go after Heather and Tess? It seemed beyond the pale; but he did it, anyway. He just made certain they would never recognize him. The other goons who did the initial dirty work were dispensable and would never be seen again, anyway.

Somehow GAG knew that Tristan, Heather and Tess had been staying with one of Tristan's cousins at her beautiful home in St. Louis' most spectacular suburb. They had stayed there before on several occasions, in the lap of luxury. Tristan had very few relatives left in his hometown and his relationship with his three girl cousins was very special. He loved them all, like sisters. This time, like before, Tristan and family were welcomed. Tristan had work to do on this trip. Heather and Tess planned to have a great time shopping with Tristan's cousin and touring the town. What a change from Laramie.

While Tristan testified up in Alton, Illinois, just across the Clark Bridge from the Missouri side of the river, Heather and Tess planned a simple luncheon trip to the St. Louis Zoo. That's all it was supposed to be. A mother and daughter, together for the day. After Tristan finished up in Alton, the plan was for him to zip back to pick up Heather and Tess and join the rest of his family for one of their frequent visits to some special St. Louis restaurant, of which there were seemingly endless numbers from which to choose. So, over the years, they tried to visit them all. But this time, nothing, absolutely nothing worked out as planned.

Heather and Tess's kidnapping from the St. Louis Zoo must have been fairly easy. There weren't too many people around on that slightly chilly, early autumn afternoon. As Heather later told Tristan, when she was first confronted, one of the brutes warned her that any resistance on her part would result in Tristan's execution. So she went with them; the gun pointed at Tess under the bastard's shirt, greased the skids of their departure. Then the nightmare began. And it ended several days later when someone, probably, GAG, dumped Heather and Tess next to the river in a ditch, alive but only barely, much less a semblance of their former selves. Neither would ever fully recover. And that made GAG happy.

The trip up 91 took Tristan past White River Junction and Norwich on the Vermont side of the Connecticut River. The turn onto Vermont 113 was easy; and the ride over Thetford Hill and through Thetford Center was a comfort to Tristan's soul. He soaked up the solitude like a cactus hoards water. He had been there on two previous occasions, once while he was in medical school at Dartmouth. The second time was on a family visit to Heather's sister, in the late 90's, years before the really big problems began.

The remoteness and beauty of the area had great appeal; but it was still too heavily populated for Tristan's taste. At one point, Heather argued that to be closer to her family, Tristan could maintain his wilderness "fix" in the rolling hills of Vermont, instead of the absurdly remote areas of the Snowy Mountains of Wyoming. Tristan's response was clear. Comparing the Green Mountain foothills of Vermont to the Wyoming Rockies was like comparing a Seiko to a Rolex. He wanted no neighbors for miles, not hundreds of yards.

Tristan almost missed the turn onto Sawnee Bean Road, that dirt and gravel path up into the hills that would take him to Sue and Brad's small farm. He could not wait to see his family. It had been way too long. He had called ahead when he was outside of Norwich; but no one had answered Brad's cell phone. As Tristan pulled up the eighth of a mile driveway that led to the ten acre, flat clearing in the Vermont forest, he could see the modest but fairly good sized two story Cape ahead of him. It was painted a deep gray blue with white trim. Smoke was pouring out one of the two brick chimneys. It filled the crisp air with the wonderful smell of autumn memories, no different than his recollections of Wyoming.

He saw three figures come around the side of the large barn about 20 yards from the house as he drove up. No doubt the sound of his SUV's engine had caught their attention. To Tristan's immediate relief, he saw Heather, Tess and Sue. Brad was nowhere in sight.

"My God, oh, My God!" Tess screamed with joy. "It's Daddy; Mom, it's Daddy!" Before he could fully exit the car, Tristan found his daughter's arms around his neck, and she wouldn't let go. Heather stared. Then came a fleeting, slightest smile that quickly disappeared, leaving her almost without expression. Tristan knew why. She was not so quick to swamp Tristan with loving approbation. She loved him; but she was still being burned by all sorts of things, many heated by her husband.

"Heather, Tess, honey; my God, it is great to see both of you," effused Tristan with tears in his eyes that matched those in Tess'; but contrasted to Heather's unfazed stare. "And, of course, it is great to see you, Sue. I hope you are well. You all look so good. Where's Brad?"

"Oh, he's gone into Norwich to pick up a few groceries and to Dan and Whits for a repair kit for one of the bathroom faucets that's been leaking," said Sue, glancing over at Heather, who now shot her a thin lipped grimace that transformed into another forced smile as she turned back to Tristan. "He should be back in about an hour or so."

Not to mention Tess, Tristan knew he had caused pain to both women. Heather first and Sue second, the bystander casualty of Heather's suffering. Suffering it was, Tristan thought; I'm a husband and father gone, now hunted by GAG, that sociopathic lunatic, the chief enforcer in a rogue conspiratorial organization, The Resistance, that protected corrupt corporations who wanted to take it all and give nothing back. Tristan knew his latest "raison d'être" was to make certain they gave plenty back. So in the crosshairs, he remained. Why couldn't Heather understand? On the other hand, how could she, anyway? She knew nothing about The Resistance, because Tristan had not told her. He only learned about it a few months earlier. It would be too much, way too much to bear, at least, for now.

"So, Daddy; how was the trip?" said Tess, now hanging on Tristan's arm and pulling him toward the house. "Did you bring me anything from New Orleans?" Still only 16, Tess was a beauty, almost as tall as her mother's 5' 9" frame. Her long brown hair gleamed in the late afternoon sun, and her dark brown eyes would not leave her father.

"Oh, Tess; how you have grown," beamed Tristan, as he stared at his daughter's blue jean overalls and brown hiking boots with red shoe laces. "You are so tall and trim; are you still playing volleyball at school? And yes, of course, I brought presents for everyone, especially you!"

"Daddy, don't you remember? I switched to cross country running last spring semester because I aggravated my old wrist injury; you know, the one caused in St. Louis by you know who, you know when," said Tess, now with some disappointment in her voice at her father's apparent loss of memory or perhaps, his blocking of bad recollections.

Heather interjected, "Your father knows how you injured your left wrist, Tess, honey. He remembers the dislocation and the fracture of three bones including one in your arm from it being twisted like a pretzel, just three years ago. It is a miracle that it now seems alright. But you still have to be careful not to hit it too hard. Cross country running is much better suited to you than volleyball or any contact sport." With that remark, Heather gave Tristan a perfunctory peck on the cheek and continued, "Tristan, you must be hungry; come on inside; everything is waiting for you."

Tristan had expected Heather's reception; but it was a lot worse than he had feared. He knew the toll the last three years had taken on her. His wife and daughter had even taken on Brad and Sue's last name, Palmer. Overall, even though they were both safe, Tristan knew Heather was just treading water. Tess was holding up much better.

As they walked into the house, Tristan noticed that Heather still walked covering her left hand with her right and, at one point she ritualistically slipped her left hand under her jacket. He had seen her do this many times in the past. She was obviously very self-conscious about her missing finger deformity. At least both broken thumbs had healed without problems.

Tristan tried to reassure her that she looked just fine many times over the past three years but to no avail. She was a woman, and she cared about her appearance. Had she lost her finger in an accident or from some other unavoidable reason, it would have made a big difference to Heather. She told him that. But having it amputated with a pruning shears by an insane madman, who was now undoubtedly intent upon killing her entire family, if given the opportunity - that was a completely different story.

Tristan was starved. The aromas in the kitchen were intoxicating. "Should we wait until Brad comes home?" asked Tristan politely, directing his comments, primarily to Sue.

"No, go ahead," said Sue. "There's Vermont sharp cheddar and some crackers over there on the counter. Dig in. I have no idea exactly when Brad will come home. There'll be plenty left for him."

After a short while, during which Tristan filled up on his favorite cheese, the four of them sat down to dinner. Tristan's favorite. Tennis balls. Not the kind batted across a net; but perfectly cooked chicken breasts wrapped with breaded stuffing and shaped into a ball, covered with specially seasoned sour cream sauce. The balls were complimented with mashed potatoes, green beans and salad, along with home made sour dough, fan tan dinner rolls. Grade B maple syrup harvested from their own trees, drizzled over vanilla ice cream completed the culinary rapture. He felt like he had died and gone to gastronomical heaven.

When they finished, it was after seven. Brad was almost two hours late.

While Tess helped her aunt with the dishes, Tristan and Heather walked out onto the porch built in front and on one side of the house. They were alone as they rounded the corner away from the door. Tristan put his right arm around Heather. She resisted, then relaxed, conforming her body against his, as she knew it was meant to be.

Heather closed her eyes. Without opening them, she turned her head and buried her nose into his sleeve. She took a deep breath. No sense was stronger, more powerful and more instantaneous. Over thirty years flashed before her, landing on their time together as teenagers, before they knew much of anything. Yet, the smell of her man had not changed, the faintest aroma of clean sweat, mixed with his favorite after shave, still hanging around since the morning. Pheromones just don't lie.

She thought about forgiving; but felt it was not the time. Instead, she decided to enjoy the security of his familiar grip and the presence of his strong, still firm body against hers.

The leaves danced in the breeze, nearing sunset. Together, Heather and Tristan gazed at the nearby hill, as the trees split the beam of the setting sun, causing light to pepper the side of the house with eerie shades of dusk. He held her closer, wishing he had brought a sweater. Without any hesitation, Tristan turned and took Heather's left hand from her jacket. He brought the back of her hand to his lips and kissed it.

"I love you, and I am sorry," he said softly. "You know I do. I love you so much I have to make certain that you and Tess are safe. I will solve this problem; so we can get back together, soon, as a normal family. I know the next steps. I will take them lawfully; but if I am unsuccessful going by the book, I will eliminate the problem anyway."

Heather looked at him, right into his eyes for almost a minute. Her eyes were now completely filled with tears. She broke away from his gentle grip and slipped her left hand back into her jacket pocket, out of sight from the world.

She regained her composure. "Tristan, I've heard this before. For almost three years now. But you started up again. What, for the money, the fame, the excitement? You don't need any of it! We have to try again. The whole thing stinks; we know who did it. He's still there, working in the light of day at CADIXX, the bastard. So, I couldn't be sure; I couldn't recognize him; so they didn't arrest him, It's outrageous. What do they think? Some aliens abducted Tess and me and cut off my ring finger, broke both of my thumbs and then broke our daughter's wrist and arm? Thank God that's all that happened; oh, of course, except for the beatings by the two hooded vermin, and two days of starvation."

"I can't make this up to you, Heather; but I told you I am working on a solution, a final one that will bring this man down, for good. But it is complicated."

Tristan started to tell all and decided not to. Not yet. If Heather knew about The Resistance, she could become utterly dysfunctional. After all, he had just learned the big picture himself earlier in the summer, thanks to Asher's brother Saul. Heather still thought it was a local lunatic, a CADIXX thug who wrecked her, not the twisted representative of something as big and ominous as The Resistance.

It was better that way. Heather and Tess had nowhere else to go and for the time being, they were safe, or so it seemed.

Brad was now nearly three hours overdue.

—   —   —

"Joseph, keep that mud off my floor. Take your shoes off!" exclaimed Daisy True Blood to her husband.

"I love you, honey; but I'm going to kick your ass out the door, if you mess up my house," she said with a grin. She remembered the last two nights. It had been heaven to have her man back home. She missed him, and he missed her. They feverishly made up for lost time, and she had not slept better in months. She was warm, satisfied, and energized. Joseph, too, seemed to have an extra kick in his step, and Daisy claimed full credit for his smile.

Joseph went back to the door, took off his shoes and smiled that smile. It was great to be back home. He had called the rancher brothers he had left last spring. They were still losing livestock to predators. He gave some thought to going back over there, to give them a hand. Their ranch was the one Asher Goldman had plucked him from to go looking for Tris about five months before. It was beautiful, wild and rugged country. The way things used to be is the way they are now, even in the 21st century, north of Hayden, west of Steamboat Springs on the Colorado side of the Colorado-Wyoming border.

His and Daisy's double wide was east of the brother's ranch, off Colorado 125, just outside of Hayden. Everyone knew Joseph was the best human cattle guard for 100 miles around; but before he could resume that job, he first had to complete about 10 repair projects that had accumulated over the months since he left. Daisy would have none of his wanderings until she could reliably get hot water for the shower and make certain her electric blanket went on when it said "on." That wall plug needed replacement, and Joseph knew it.

"Cattle guard; Joseph thought. "Well now I have reputation as a "Cattle Guard. I get the joke." He smiled to himself, thinking again what he already knew. Namely, everyone knows out west, and probably in most rural areas across the country that a "Cattle Guard" is a heavy duty grate made of parallel tubular steel pipes that is placed in a roadway to prevent cattle from crossing a fence line. It's great, if you want to keep a gate open when cattle are inside, and you don't want them going outside. The parallel pipes are spaced just perfectly to dissuade the critters from getting their hooves caught.

The joke at Billy's Bar and Billiards in Hayden was that when "Billy" Clinton was elected president in '92, he was told there were 5000 too many "Cattle Guards" employed by the US Forest Service in Colorado alone. So according to local rumor, the new president asked his wife Hilary what she thought he should do. Again, according only to local rumor, since Colorado was a red state in those days, Hillary said, "Fire them all; Get their asses off the payroll and save the taxpayers some money." Well, again, only according to local rumor, President Billy tried to do just that. He even wrote an executive order. Look it up; they say!

And so that's what happens when you apply an Oyve League education to an Aggie problem. "Those blue-blood schools sure tore out those Arkansas roots!" one boy roared, one Saturday night against a background of Waylon Jennings, while he finished off his 8th Coors of the evening at Billie's.

Joseph smiled again. He knew the serious side of his "Cattle Guard" reputation had already erupted like wildfire across three counties in Colorado and two in Wyoming, especially since he was full blooded, Northern Arapahoe. Hell, he even thought he'd be famous as far south as Rand, that hamlet just west of the Never Summer Range. The lighter side of his reputation, he planned to take in stride, the cowboy and the Indian way. He looked forward to basking in the limelight a little. Why not? Many ranchers could use his services, and it paid pretty well to boot.

But the Snowy Mountains and Tristan's compound were also beckoning. But not without Tristan. These majestic beauties were just a hop, skip and a jump about 25 miles north of the Colorado - Wyoming border. He had to get back up there and meet Tristan to winterize the place, before severe weather came in.

In the six months he had been gone, Joseph had earned a year and a half's pay. Daisy couldn't complain; they really needed the money. She liked her job at the nearby elementary school cafeteria, the only one for fifty miles.

"Well, so how is Tristan?" asked Daisy, clearly expressing a mixture of sincerity and patronizing obligation. Daisy knew the history. How Tristan and Heather had nearly adopted her husband and made him a member of their family. For that she was eternally grateful. But. There was always a "but." Whenever Tristan called, Joseph responded. It didn't matter the time of day or night, the day of the month or the season of the year. When Tristan called, Joseph jumped. Daisy knew it was also true the other way around, although, she could count on one hand the number of times Joseph had called Tristan, first.

Like the time the sheriff of Routt County called the Colorado Division of Parks and Wildlife, asking them to send one of their game wardens over to interview Joseph. It seemed like he might know something about some elk poaching that had been going on near Pearl Lake north of Steamboat Springs.

"Should I tell them?" Joseph asked Tristan, with a frantic tenor in his voice. "It's not like they don't have a right. It was once our land; OK, a 150 years ago. I get it; but they don't see it that way. They're my cousins, Tris. They think the hunting is better in Colorado than up in the Wind River. Hell, if life were fair, they would be hunting in Chessman Park in downtown Denver."

"OK," responded Tristan, trying not to make the situation more serious than it already was. "You don't know which cousins, right?"

"Right," answered Joseph. "I don't know which ones. My uncle just said something."

"Fine, then you don't need to lie," relieved Tristan. "You must have 40 cousins up there and if you don't know which ones, just tell the warden, you only heard rumors about possible kinship. Just make certain they don't blame you. If they do, don't bother with a lawyer, call me. I'll get there right away."

Daisy was grateful and so was Joseph. The whole thing blew over, when the warden caught two hunters from California with five butchered animals in a large covered trailer 10 miles from the Colorado-Utah border. Apparently elk meat brought big money from the one percenters living near Silicon Valley. Six digit fines and prison time were the result. The two animals taken over two seasons by Joseph's Wyoming cousins fell under the radar.

Joseph enjoyed his time together with Daisy. Since the school year was in full swing, they only had nights and weekends together; but it didn't matter. He only managed seven of the 10 repair projects over the next three weeks. Then he got itchy feet again. Before the snow started falling heavy in late November, he had to meet Tristan again back at his compound SE of Bennett Peak in the Medicine Bow National Forest, just on the southern fringe of the Snowies. In the meantime; but not before volunteering some plumbing skills at Daisy's school for three days, Joseph decided to resume his cattle guarding for the boys over near Steamboat Springs. They were happy to have him back, even for a couple of weeks.

Joseph mused. One of the brothers mentioned for him to keep an eye out for rustlers, just in case. Joseph knew that in the current day, if he was to find one, he would have limited options with unlimited liability. He missed the day when a rustler caught in the act could be executed on the spot. It was better then; no messy trial, presenting of evidence, crippling expense. Just justice. You catch a man stealing another man's cow, and you die.

Now circumstantial evidence that is another matter, Joseph figured. Then, you had to give the guy a chance to prove himself innocent.

No, Joseph didn't want to hunt rustlers for someone else. There were game wardens for that. Coyotes were another matter. After all, he thought, he could accidentally shoot some kid and end up swinging at the end of a rope, just like, range detective, Tom Horn did, up in Cheyenne only 106 years earlier. Even back in 1903, the cards were stacked against justice. If Horn had hit his mark 30 years before that, in 1873, he would have been given a ticker tape parade in Denver. Hell, if Joseph wasted any two legged target in 2009, it would be lethal injection, just after winking goodbye to Daisy and Tristan on the other side of the prison's one way glass.

On Friday November 13, 2009, right on schedule, Joseph headed up Colorado 125 until it changed to Wyoming 230 at the border. Then on toward the area west, southeast of Bennett Peak, across the North Platte and onto a poorly maintained forest service road, nicknamed, "Cougar's Gotch Yur Neck" Road near Pot Belly Creek. From there, hell, he wasn't even sure he wouldn't get lost. But he knew Tristan knew the way, like the back of his hand.

As Joseph headed out in his '84 Dodge Power Ram, still running good, even knowing what he faced on the journey, he thought how the world had changed. A good or bad guy in a helicopter could be on his ass within 40 minutes coming out of Laramie.

— — —

"Heather, what do you think about my taking Tess with me back to Laramie and then out to the compound for a couple of weeks? I know I would have her for Thanksgiving vacation; but it would give me time to make up for some lost parenting. How about it?"

"You'll have to ask her, Tristan," said Heather, emoting a thin smile, actually impressed that her husband had shown the interest. "Come to think of it, I approve."

A bit shocked, Tristan responded, "Great! I'll ask her in the morning. I think she has already turned in. Wait, let me....."

"Oh my God," screamed Sue standing out on the porch, having a cigarette and looking over the driveway, just as the moon was rising above the trees. "Someone just pulled up in a car and stopped! Their headlights are in my eyes. I can't see. I'm going to go look."

"NO-O-O-O-O!!!" screamed Tristan, as he ran out the side door of the house to his car. "Come back into the house, Dammit!"

"Heather, cut the lights and take Tess into the bathroom. Lock the door and get on the floor," he bellowed as the screen door slammed. "Sue, stay down!"

Tristan dove on the ground on the passenger side of his SUV and carefully opened the door, cursing the dome light that went on immediately. Under the seat, he pulled out his IMI .45 caliber, "Baby Eagle," his favorite, among those Israeli weapons he owned. He had never shot anyone before, and had no intention now; but God pity anyone planning to harm his family. The only two words going through his mind as he pulled back the slide to chamber a round were "Home Invasion."

Locked and loaded, Tristan crept around to the front of the house. Still blinded by car headlights, Tristan thought he may need to take them both out. He loaded a 10 round magazine into the .45 and slipped two other freshly loaded mags into his back pocket.

Silence.

Tristan could hear a motor running, against the dead quiet of the surrounding forest. The moon had yet to rise above the trees.

"The perps must have gone around the side of the house where I exited. Oh, shit," he thought.

Tristan moved five paces forward, in a crouched position and took aim at the left headlight. Not knowing his target, he hesitated.

He saw movement by the side of the car. His finger pulled ever so slightly backward, within a millimeter of irretrievable and irreversible, deadly destruction.

Preparing for the blast, Tristan overheard, on the porch to his left, just out of sight.

"Hey, ya, honey; light one for me, will ya? I've had a hell of a night!"

Sue stepped back, almost knocked over by the smell of bourbon.

"Hey, ya, thanks, guys," called Brad to a silhouetted figure standing behind what was now a clearly opened car door. His driver companion inside stuck his hand out the window and waved.

"Sees ya, tomorrow," continued Brad. "That's if'n I live to see the dawn, Ha! Ha!"

"Don't be too hard on him, Mrs. Palmer. It's all our fault," floated a voice from the vehicle.

Sue walked to the side of the porch and looked down.

"Tristan, what the hell are you doing there with that gun?" peaked Sue. "You're scaring the shit out of me. Put that thing away."

"Hey's, Tristan here?" slurred Brad, now looking over the side of the porch at his brother-in-law. Then he saw him, ignoring the gun and the crouch.

"Hey, Tristan, boy; come on up here and have a snort with me before I turn in."

With that, Sue grabbed Brad by the arm and led him into the house. "I want to hear all about it, Brad....later," finalized Sue.

As the front screen door slammed, Heather stepped onto the porch and glanced down at Tristan, now faintly illuminated only by the front porch light. He was still standing there, but now with safety on.

"Tristan....Tristan." No words came.

Finally, she said, "I asked Tess, a minute ago. She hasn't seen you out here, thank God. Tristan.....I...I think you need to leave, maybe tomorrow or the next day. Wait...., I take that back. Tomorrow.

Tess stays.

Maybe next time."

Tristan looked up at his wife, with tears welling up in his eyes and only two words raging in his mind,

"Home Invasion."

Yes, it could have been a "Home Invasion."

Maybe next time.

Tristan left Sunday morning, the 11th of October for the long drive to his house in Laramie. He didn't want to leave; but was not given much choice. On this schedule, he would be about three weeks early for his rendezvous with Joseph at the compound in mid-November. He figured he could catch up on some rest at home in Laramie and figure out his next move to save his marriage, his career and maybe even his life and the lives of those who meant the most to him.

He hadn't bothered to tell Heather about his losing the case. He had planned to – but not under the circumstances. He wanted no sympathy. He just wanted relief from the threat hanging over his head. Tristan recalled that poignant remark, allegedly attributed to Sherlock Holmes, addressing Dr. Watson. To Tristan's best recollection Holmes, in a predicament, in which the police had let him down, turned to Watson and said (paraphrasing),

"Dear Watson. We are alone; but not helpless. When in this situation, we must act; within the law or outside of it. It does not matter. Survival is all that matters."

And to that, Tristan added, "Revenge, however, cold, tastes still, like the nectar of the Gods!"

Tristan loved the concepts; but kept them just that – concepts; not plans of action; at least not for the moment or until his back was against the wall and he had no other choices. Pre-planning the revenge part, well.....

CHAPTER 28 - COMPOUND VIOLATION

DATE: Friday, 11/13/09 - About four years
and seven months after Katrina
LOCATION: Baines Wilderness Compound, Snowy
Mountains, West of Laramie, Wyoming

— — —

Tristan leaned over to pet his Siberian Husky, Dawson. God, how he had missed him. It had been over six months. As usual, Dawson, just stared at Tristan with those glacial blue eyes, against his reddish brown and white fur. Not much else to expect, Tristan thought. No effusive licking or even noises. Just the stare of the wild, detached, but still barely connected. He tried for five years to figure the dog out. "This breed...," he would begin, then couldn't finish the sentence. Heather used to say, "If you want a slobbery lap dog that follows your every move, humps your leg all day long, and won't leave you alone, get a mutt......or a husband, she would joke." The joke aside, Tristan had always wanted a piece of Alaska, and now, with Dawson, he had one. After his last trip to Vermont, Heather could look for a mutt.

Dawson didn't do tricks. He just pulled and pulled, like his sled-dog ancestors. Tristan knew not to expect him to heel when he was walking. After all, Dawson pulled for a living, just like his dad, a two time Iditarod top ten finisher. Thank God for Jay Morgenstern, Tristan's friend and personal attorney in Laramie, who agreed to take Dawson when Tristan was suddenly called away for his FEMA case in May. Now, he was back with Dawson for the entire winter and maybe more.

Tristan had stopped by his home in Laramie and checked in with Jay at his office. Tristan's home was fine. Just needed a good cleaning.

No more dead, eviscerated rabbits on his bed, like last March, with a note pinned to one ear, saying "Sorry, I missed you. Love, GGRN" Gordon Gasher, RN no doubt about it. "Why the tormenting, without deadly effect?" Tristan kept wondering.

Tristan continued driving along Wyoming 130, keeping his mind on all that had happened over the past six months. Much of it was still up in the air, like the trial appeal; but mostly his deep, yet recently shallow relationship with Heather. He was on solid ground with Tess. He almost brought her back with him to Wyoming for a week or so. Although at first in favor of the plan, Heather balked and said "No." Right after that awkward moment outside of her sister Sue's home.

"You want to do something useful with your aggression," Tristan recalled Heather saying. "Then find GAG and have him arrested or dump him in a Wyoming mine shaft; I don't care which. If the mine shaft option, I demand that you cut off his balls first. If you won't, then, find me; I insist, because I will find a dull butter knife and do it myself."

At the time, Tristan thought Heather's rant was both funny and sad. On the one hand, she wanted Tristan to reek revenge on the maniac who had disfigured her and harmed Tess. On the other, she essentially kicked Tristan out for exhibiting protective "aggression" a behavior about which she was obviously ambivalent.

He had difficulty making Heather understand the now seemingly ridiculous scene at her sister's house. Tristan could see himself standing below the porch in a crouched position, with a loaded .45 pistol preparing to shoot out the headlights of an unknown car. Unbeknownst to Tristan that car had just delivered Sue's drunken husband, Brad to the front door, four hours late for dinner. There crouched Tristan, ready for mayhem, while Sue led Brad inside, stopping by the kitchen sink first in case he threw up.

In retrospect, according to Heather, his behavior at Sue's home looked like some neurotic overreaction, or worse. "Where was the threat?" she asked. But as silly as he appeared, Tristan knew he had reacted promptly and correctly. Had GAG and his cronies found and tracked him to Sue's and then decided to attack, he could have, at least, offered some protection for this family. But realistically he knew that his deadly .45 would have been feeble self-defense against what GAG probably had up his sleeve.

That led to another question. He wondered, again, why the worst had not yet already happened. In this day and age, it should be easy for GAG and The Resistance to track him, and maybe even to kill him... and his entire family. So why were they leaving him alone?

He set the question aside as he pulled up the gravel driveway to the entrance to his compound off French Creek Road at 2 PM in mid-November on that Friday the 13th. It was already getting very cold at night, down in the 20's and high teens and barely breaking 45 in the daytime. Today the sun was shining brightly in the waning afternoon. Tristan saw Joseph's Dodge Power Ram parked next to the far corner of the house. He had about three hours of daylight left and wanted to scout out the place. He had not been back there since Asher had pulled him out in May.

Standing in the living room, looking through the window, Joseph spotted Tristan coming up the path. He walked out onto the front porch, carrying the body of a dead something, about the size of a cat. It was dried and rotted, very little tissue left. You could see the eye sockets, filled with the slightest bit of inspissated gelatinous remains. Funny, it didn't smell too much. The mice had their fill and the maggots had already left. But unmistakably present was that dreaded, ghoulish, trademark, another note pinned to the creature's ear.

"Ring around the rosy, pocket full of posy, Heather and Tristan shall both fall down. Neither rain, nor snow nor heat of the day will obscure the mess that will soon be Tess. Dear doctor, fair heart, once and for all - lay off; retire; do not be bold .... for I know where maple syrup is boiled and sold."

"What else, dear God?" uttered Tristan, breathless, like someone had just punched him in the chest. "I need to get to a phone, now."

"First, Tris," calmed Joseph, "This note is probably three months old. He already knows about Heather and Tess's seclusion; but has not struck. We have time. It wouldn't surprise me if he tracked you there. Then again, maybe not. If he wanted to hurt you, Heather or Tess, he could have done it anytime. The real question is why hasn't he?"

"Just the question I have been asking myself," blurted Tristan. "I know where he is; the asshole is still working at CADIXX, as the incinerator complex medical director – Nurse Gordon A. Gasher. We've got very little on him, if anything right now. If I want my problem solved, I will have to take matters into my own hands. That would be easy. But what if I'm wrong? Now that's a question, Heather would ask."

"Look, Tris," said Joseph. "I haven't told you the rest. The cabin has been ransacked. We may have some video. They missed two of the cameras that were inverter powered off the third battery bank. I started to look for images on the hard drive they missed in the closet. It will be better with a full screen monitor. I found one left undamaged, in the shop."

"Let's go inside and see what we can see," said Tristan, in a nearly incoherent whisper. "I want to clean up tonight and haul out of here by noon tomorrow. I'm going back to Laramie; and as soon as I get into cell range, I'll call Heather and Tess. I want them with me in Laramie. I'll also ask Brad and Sue to come along, if they want to; but I doubt they'll leave Thetford Center. Hell, they should, the winters in Vermont are worse than Wyoming. Let's get started."

For the next four hours, Tristan and Joseph cleaned up the mess. Fortunately, many items were almost indestructible, like certain tools that remained intact. It did not look like pillage with the intent to steal much; but instead, it appeared the intruders simply wanted to send a message of destruction. Electronic equipment scattered and trampled; furniture broken and slashed; medical supplies thrown on the floor everywhere and four broken windows in the back. The perps missed the crawl space entrance to the escape tunnel. Nothing was broken or damaged that couldn't be replaced or repaired. Much of it would have to wait until next spring.

"Look, Jay; I've got a first class problem," expounded Tristan to his dear friend and personal attorney in Laramie.

Jay Morgenstern, 54 years old still had reddish hair, but now abundantly streaked with white. He kept it long and combed completely back. He was a tall man, topping six feet two inches, and his face bore the marks of more than a half century in the Wyoming wind and sun. Part of his right earlobe was missing. The price he paid in a scrape with a rather bold coyote, intent on eating Jay's cat for a midnight snack. He and Tristan went back 30 years when they struggled together as robust young men, sewing their wild oats and much more.

"Tristan, we've been through this before," answered Morgenstern, looking Tristan straight in the eye. "You knew this would happen, sooner or later. You took the job in Texas and Louisiana, OK. You resurfaced; I understand. But these assholes are smart. They operate like rats. You kill off a few; but they come back, sometimes in greater numbers. You have to find the nest and kill the females and ratlets, or whatever you want to call them. If you return to the compound and they show up again, you will just need to kill them and bury them there. Don't expect any help from the law. You have a Bobcat with a bucket. Just do it; but don't tell me or anyone else about it. I don't want to know."

"Jay, thanks for watching Dawson," offered Tristan, at best, only partially absorbing Morgenstern's remarks; more likely, ignoring them altogether.

"I've called Heather and Tess. They're going to arrive in Denver tomorrow evening. It was the earliest flight they could get from Boston. I went to the house, and it looks great. I slept there last night. Thanks again for keeping it in good shape. Joseph's going to stay over for a few days and give me a hand."

"I'll be here if you need me," continued Morgenstern. "Look, go home and get some sleep, Tristan. You look like shit! And keep a sharp eye. It is good Joseph's there. It may take two of you."

Joseph sat silently throughout the meeting. He operated with a different calculus, as he watched the interaction between the lawyer and his special client. Joseph and Morgenstern got along just fine; but didn't know each other very well. Joseph worshiped the notion made famous by President Reagan 25 years earlier, "Trust; but verify." Yes, he trusted Morgenstern, but at the most obscure level, not even one he cared to share with Tristan, he felt a hiccup of uncertainty; enough to prompt him to plan to verify. He had his ways and would do it soon.

Tristan and Joseph returned to the Baines' modest three bedroom log home about two miles from the center of Laramie. They were still within Laramie's greater urban area, if you could call it that. Laramie is just not urban by most standards. Anyone, especially someone from the Denver's suffocating sprawl would consider it virtually rural.

Later that evening, after some pizza and beer, Tristan and Joseph sat on the couch in the living room in front of a cozy fire.

"They know where I live, you know," said Tristan, almost choking on a whisper and looking at his friend through some very tired eyes.

"I know they know," responded, Joseph, fingering the barrel of the loaded pump shotgun, leaning against the arm of the couch next to him. "Just a 12 gauge Mossberg 500, not a Remington 870," Joseph thought in his professional capacity as a cattle guardsman. "It'll still do."

"What a way to live," mused Tristan aloud, smiling at Joseph's confidence that the Mossberg was on safety. With that, Tristan felt the light-weight .380 Sig P238 in his waistband. He also had his .45 Baby Eagle in the bedroom, the one he had brandished in Vermont, looking like such a damned fool. Now that Israeli masterpiece was the ultimate companion, but it was simply too big to haul around the house. "Shit, what a way to live. I'm not bringing Heather and Tess back here. I'll make other arrangements."

"Yeah, make other arrangements, yeah," sighed Joseph, feeling the effects of the beer. "I'm going to bed. It's all yours Tris. You're on first watch. Wake me at 3 am. Goodnight."

Tristan watched the exploding crackles of the Ponderosa logs, lamenting how short lived they were. As a botanical exercise, he had thrown a couple of hard rock maple logs into his trunk when he left

Vermont. He wished he had brought more. "Might as well thrown them in," he thought. "Let's show those Wyoming pine trees what a real log is like." They disappointed him. They didn't last much longer. The fire was too hot.

"Nothing lasts forever," he mused. "Just another shitty letdown."

CHAPTER 29 - RETURN TO DALLAS

DATE: Monday 8/30/10 Five years post Katrina and a little over two years after commencement of the law-suit against Matchless - about five years after Katrina.
LOCATION: Dallas, Texas

— — —

Against a tumultuous background of family squabbling with Heather, Tristan brought his family back together.

Heather had finally agreed to bring Tess and come back to live with Tristan in Laramie. Tristan thought the three of them would be safe so close to town. He had a lot of connections and plenty of friends to look after his ladies; but self-reliance was at the top of the list. Heather already knew how to handle firearms. She had qualified in several civilian combat shooting courses over the years, using a 9mm Beretta semi-auto. But she preferred a non-jamming revolver by the bedside drawer, specifically a five shot, Lady Smith .357 magnum in stainless steel. Tess went to the range as well; and had plinked a lot in the Vermont woods with her mom and aunt, while her uncle was soused. Heather had started Tess with Tristan's old, but reliable .22 Ruger Mark II. When Heather and Tess flew back to Denver, they had the handguns, speed loaders, and magazines sent as baggage. They left the ammo behind. There was plenty more to be found in the state of Wyoming.

When he returned to Texas, after the frantic, "Tristan come quick; I need you and will pay your rates," call from Asher Goldman, Tristan relented. But this time with Heather's firm support and back-ing. And based upon the temporary plan for Heather and Tess to live with Jay Morgenstern's sister. Tristan insisted. Living alone in the

Laramie log home was out of the question, given GAG's note left at the compound. The compound, of course, would only be sought as a final battleground, on Tristan's turf, if it came to that.

Before he found GAG's note, Tristan had gone about the matter of security according to the unwritten civilized rules that one might expect of a law-abiding, physician, just trying to keep his family safe.

Consider security at his compound, or "cabin" as he liked to call it in polite company. He talked to a friend who was a park ranger assigned to the Medicine Bow National Forest. And he spoke with the Sheriff in Carbon County, whom he knew very well. The Sheriff said he would give the "heads up" to the solo deputy patrolling in his area. That officer was one of six to ten, at any given time, responsible for a county of nearly 8000 square miles, or an area almost 18% greater than the areas of Connecticut and Rhode Island put together. Sure, no problem any call to the sheriff's dispatcher could put a deputy on the doorstep of Tristan's cabin, maybe within three or four hours, if he was lucky. Of course, there was no reliable phone service within 50 miles, so no 911 call could even be made. The feds could offer essentially a "Good Luck" and nothing more. For the time being, given the GAG note, the compound was completely off limits to the Baines' family, even if Joseph was with them.

The only way to decompress the festering uncertainty hanging over his family would be to neutralize the threat. He thought big; but Tristan wasn't sure he had the stomach for proactive mayhem that would probably be illegal, unless viewed as self-defense.

Then he realized what he already knew - the worst part. Real criminals always have the advantage. They have the element of surprise; they attack without mercy or remorse, at the time and place of their choosing. Then they fight to win to finish the job.

Tristan had motivation of revenge going for him; but he knew he was basically a decent human being; one who dealt out passion and mercy for a living. Even if all of the circumstances were just right, could he do it - take a human life or inflict pain and suffering on another living soul, regardless of justification?

Tristan assumed a weak smile. At least he had Joseph.

Joseph could do it as easily as swatting a fly with his bare hand, just to make certain it was squashed properly.

After Tristan and Joseph returned to Dallas to meet again with Asher and Laura, Tristan decided one last time to play by the rules and hope for the best. He had to. He had promised Heather to pull out the stops; but to let the law do its job. Otherwise there would be no relief, no shelter, no piece of mind. Only tears and bloodshed.

Once back in Texas, Tristan contacted the police department in Alton, Illinois to tell them about CADIXX. For what it was worth, an Alton detective lateraled this information to the St. Louis police department, since they had jurisdiction over the place where the crime had been committed against Heather and Tess. He even told the police about The Resistance. He told them about the four year old threats made by Gordon A. Gasher (GAG), the man, if you want to call him that, whom Tristan knew had committed the outrages on his family. But No proof. And threats were just that, threats. There was only so much they could do, until bad things happened, again.

The St. Louis police knew about Heather and Tess' abduction and injuries sustained back on 9/25/06. But that investigation went nowhere. Regardless, Tristan decided to tell them even more, thinking it would help prompt a widespread conspiratorial investigation or something like that. So he also spoke about his near abduction on 5/19/09 in New Orleans, the death of McKenna's lab tech about a month later and even the "accidental" death of Dr. DUI, Asher's first expert, whom Tristan replaced in the FEMA litigation.

They were polite even up to the point when they asked him if he was off his meds. One detective with whom he spoke could not have been nicer; she said to send everything in and the next time he was in St. Louis to stop by for a minute or two. In the meantime, if they thought the information he sent warranted follow-up, they would call him. They never said not to call again; but the medication remark made him decide to try a different tactic.

He called the FBI office in St. Louis. Believe it or not, he found what he thought was a sympathetic ear. After a complaint intake, he was assigned to Special Agent Jessie Wheaton. Wheaton presented as a no nonsense man in his mid-forties who immediately seemed to respect Tristan's concerns. Maybe Wheaton knew something. He asked him to send over all the information he could muster on CADIXX, this guy with the initials GAG and The Resistance; and he would look into the matter. He said he would talk to the St. Louis police to see if they would share their file.

Then Tristan heard nothing. He called twice over the summer; got Wheaton once and was politely told to be patient; they would get back to him. That was four months ago. At least they didn't ask if he had dropped his meds.

Thirteen months went by. Tristan had to admit it; he had come up with nothing, zilch. He felt it again, the need for revenge and the recurrent fear of becoming a victim. He must find GAG first. At the same time, he must certify the reality and danger of The Resistance, to willing ears. "Yeah, right," he thought.

The first case had not gone well, at all. It had been a long, costly and brutal battle for some justice for FEMA trailer occupants who had suffered for months or even years. Matchless had ducked the bullet, for the time being, with a jury verdict in their favor, against plaintiffs Sethie and Simon Williams, issued on October 8, 2009, about four years and five weeks after Katrina hit.

Shortly after the verdict, Goldman and McDonald, LLP, Asher Goldman's law firm, filed an appeal with the United States Fifth Circuit Court, also located in New Orleans. They hired a specialty firm in Atlanta to handle the conducting of legal research and the preparation of briefs. Plaintiffs objected to the statute of limitations ruling by Judge Whitmore and a lot more. They knew the appeal would take months and probably up to a year or even longer.

For one thing, in the first round, Matchless had been the beneficiary of federal Judge Henrietta Whitmore's ruling prohibiting Sethie from suing FEMA directly, because Sethie supposedly had waited too long to sue.

The ruling was outrageous; because it assumed that Sethie knew about the formaldehyde problem the moment she moved Simon into the trailer with the rest of her family. Even Dr. Pat, Simon's pediatrician, initially had no idea what was causing Simon's asthma to flare up - so how could Sethie? It didn't matter, Judge Whitmore said the two year statute of limitations clock started in May 2006, when Sethie and Simon first stepped foot into their trailer, and ended two years later in May 2008. Sethie sued in July 2008, two months too late.

There was also the matter of certain jury instructions issued by the Harpy at the last minute, just before the jury recessed to go into deliberation to try to come up with a verdict.

Even without the statute of limitation order, Asher knew that any such favorable lawsuit against FEMA directly would not have resulted in much of a monetary award from the government anyway, because the feds have limited financial liability. More importantly, being able to pursue such a lawsuit against FEMA would have provided the now-missed opportunity to present evidence and live testimony before the jury that would have probably sunk Matchless.

The jury would have seen and heard, first hand, FEMA officials testifying that they knew about the potential formaldehyde problems in their trailers, before the Katrina batches were manufactured and distributed...and so did their contractors, including Matchless. They knew about the problem; but did not oversee the safety of the trailers Matchless provided. The trailers were simply handed over to UPIC for installation, no questions asked.

Without Judge Whitmore's ruling, Matchless would have been justifiably sued out of existence. And, probably all tolled, FEMA trailer victims would have received at least $200 million. But, alas, it was not to be. The Matchless case was finally lost in the fall of 2009. The chances for a favorable reversal of Whitmore's ruling on appeal were very slim, but not, none. There were other matters cooking that could sway the opinions of the judges who sat on the U.S. Court of Appeals.

A few days before the October 2009 ruling, Tristan had returned to Vermont, and Joseph returned to Wyoming, hopeful. But then, after they heard about the depressing outcome, demoralization set in. Neither placed much hope in a reversal of the unfortunate verdict by the Court of Appeals.

One fact really made the unfavorable Matchless verdict into a festering sore. Tristan learned from Asher that he had polled the jury after the fact. Several jurors said they would have voted in favor of Simon and Sethie; but they were instructed by the Judge Whitmore to ignore the evidence presented by Tristan and others, not affiliated with FEMA. Critical evidence revealing the government's knowledge about the formaldehyde problem in FEMA trailers before Katrina. Absent this last minute very troubling and suspicious jury instruction, Asher told Tristan they would have won the verdict. But, alas, it was not to be.

Needless to say; this last minute jury instruction seemed as procedurally out of line as was the statute of limitations ruling. It was under careful scrutiny by Asher's consultants in Atlanta and would probably go into their brief before the U.S. Court of Appeals later in the year.

— — —

While awaiting the appeals process, new medical cases emerged, alleging more formaldehyde injuries, one by one in the spring of 2010. Given the results of the first trial, Tristan was surprised when he was called back in to help. Goldman reiterated his confidence in him, blaming the loss on the Whitmore's rulings and her interpretation of the law.

Tristan's new assignment was to evaluate three men who had sustained formaldehyde injury to their skin; not injury to their lungs, noses or eyes.

Tristan did his job, infected with his old zeal, and a desire for another temporary respite from everything else. Heather was incoherent when he agreed to return to the batter's box.

But this time his reports were even more devastating than before.

His causation conclusions vaporized the excuses of a substantial array of remaining defendants, including UPIC, the clowns who had set up the trailer gas chambers for FEMA. The prospect of trying cases for each of 364 more people, all with formaldehyde induced skin damage, was too much for the defendants; so they caved in...and settled for over $148 million. The federal court agreed and issued oversight orders for implementation of a settlement agreement.

There was a festive atmosphere in Asher Goldman's office on Monday morning, five years to the day after Katrina struck. Tristan and Joseph had been invited back to Dallas to help Asher and Laura finish up the settlement and to offer any assistance they could on Asher's appeal. Even given the magnitude of the settlement, the 10,000 FEMA trailer plaintiffs were to be awarded only a few thousand dollars each. Asher would recoup his expenses and make a million or two in the process; enough to put him in a festive mood, with a smile on his face. And Tristan would be paid, a lot.

Tristan watched Joseph as he assisted Laura while she boxed additional work product and research material from the failed first case against Matchless to send to their consultants in Atlanta to help them prepare their appeal. Their colleagues in Georgia had prepared the first draft of their brief; but wanted to look at some of the raw case material before completing their final for submission to the court by October 1.

Laura and Joseph had scoured seven filing cabinets in one closet, gathering most of the requested information. They were next preparing to open another closet, containing more filing cabinets in an effort to locate five more documents that may have been misfiled with other cases.

Joseph quipped, "Say, Laura; this door is locked. Do we need to go in here?"

"Probably not; but let me get the key from the front desk," she replied. Laura thought she had almost everything and was preparing to have eleven banker's boxes of information sent to Atlanta by UPS pick-up before five that evening.

A few minutes later, Laura returned with the key. She and Joseph opened the closet. Joseph felt around for the light switch, found it and flicked it up. No light.

"Oh, dammit, the bulb's out. We have a lot to do and only a few hours left before pick-up," blurted Laura. "If there's much here, it will have to wait until tomorrow before we send it along."

Joseph, feeling justified by his usual over preparation, smiled at Laura and reached into his left shirt pocket for a penlight that he carried with him everywhere. Actually, Tristan had given him the light and had told him he always carried a similar one to look in a patient's throat while he said; "say ah-h-h." Lately, Joseph had only used it for such mundane matters as locating dropped keys on his car floor, so he appreciated the opportunity to put it to better use.

"Great penlight!" said Laura. "I was just about to reach for mine too. Yeah, Tristan gave me one after our second meeting in New Orleans. Told me I should carry one in my purse. He tried to give me a second one; but I drew the line. OK, so where in the hell is the bulb?"

"Wait a minute;" laughed Joseph, no longer thinking himself special, while looking around the darkened closet. "It looks like there are five more filing cabinets in here; but what is that over on the floor? I think I see four more banker's boxes."

They replaced the overhead bulb, turned on the light and stowed their respective "Tristan-Lights."

Laura had correctly assumed that the filing cabinets were for other cases. It would take her at least an hour or more to look through them for potentially misfiled FEMA trailer documents. So just as she was about to postpone the search, Joseph, who had been studying the boxes on the floor, exclaimed, "Say, these boxes are unopened and were sent from Marcus, Green and Loeb, LLC, the defense firm for Matchless over in Louisville."

Asher suddenly entered the closet doorway. He had left Tristan seated in the conference room, around the corner, reading True West Magazine and looking for the article he had written on cholera in the Old West for the current issue.

"Let's bring them into the conference room, now," exclaimed Asher, a little surprised and admittedly peeved, as he looked at Laura. "Put them on the conference table." Joseph retreated, not wanting to be in the line of fire.

"Hey, look at the dates, Laura, said Asher. "This stuff came in almost a week after the verdict; but why were they pigeon-holed?"

"Respectfully, you might want to ask yourself that question, Asher," retorted Laura, as she spied Asher's initials on all four boxes. "It looks like you signed for them. Maybe you were up front when UPS delivered them?"

Thinking back; but blanked out and unable to side step the evidence, Asher replied, "Uh, I see the initials but have no recollection of signing these in. OK, sorry. I still don't know how they ended up unopened in the wrong closet. Forget it. Let's see what's inside all of them."

Laura listened, relieved but contemplating what would have transpired had the initials been "LS" instead of "AG."

Trying to lighten the mood and his embarrassment, Asher said, "Say, Joseph, why don't you pull out that big scalping knife of yours and let's open them up? Tristan, are you a 'go' on this?"

"Sure," quipped Tristan, as he put down True West and stood next to the conference table. Let's have a look. With your luck, Asher, you're going to find something that would have won you the case!"

"You know what you can do, Tristan," retorted Asher. "Joseph, we are all waiting."

Joseph reached into his back pocket and brought out a Gerber Gator, his large folding knife with its famous thermoplastic grip and serrated blade. He slit the tape on all four boxes before Asher had time to make another obnoxious comment about Joseph's heritage. Actually Joseph loved the attention. His ego was intact, and he basked in playing the stereotypes that accompanied his cultural roots. It was kind of fun to see that slight wisp of apprehension on Asher's face as he wielded his knife.

So, why not; Joseph finished and quipped, "Now lift scalps,

referring to the lids of the banker's boxes. They ready to come up; but be careful of blood!"

"OK, Joseph," smiled Tristan. "You win....or should have won, anyway."

"You damn right, paleface." laughed Joseph. "Now where were we?"

The four of them each took a box and emptied its contents onto the table, examining every document carefully. Laura pulled out a yellow legal pad and started to write out the inventory for each box separately.

"Most of this stuff is useless," Laura remarked, commenting on the contents of her box. "But here's some information on the pre-fab cabinet supplier and a few more Material Data Safety Sheets. I also see some e-mails. Wow, there must be forty pages. I am surprised they are here. Someone must have 'accidentally' sent them and here they are. How stupid! I can't wait to read a few."

"Hold on," interrupted Tristan, rummaging through the box assigned to him. Here is a large file labeled 'Zane Adamson.' Isn't he the guy who disappeared in the fall of '05? I asked about him when I sent Joseph to perform our trailer inspection last year. I thought he was still around, and I wanted Joseph to talk to him. He was the line manager when the big FEMA order came in."

"Yeah, I remember him too," echoed Joseph, as he looked into Tristan's eyes, virtually reading his mind. "The industrial hygienist hired by Matchless to shadow me when I looked at their trailers said he took a vacation late in the fall of '05 to go hunting or something and got lost, somewhere in rural Alabama. There was a huge search for him; but he was never found."

"Man, I could have used this file before trial," lamented Asher, while Laura nodded in agreement. "Let's see what is in here. Don't forget, we may find something that will help us in filing our appeal, especially if it shows there were errors or lies in the material facts presented to the court by Matchless. It doesn't just have to be a procedural mistake by Judge Whitmore."

Tristan began to scour the copies of originals in the Adamson file.

It had several hundred pages, all tucked in a manila file pouch. At the end there were about thirty pages of e-mails, all stapled together.

Tristan pulled the file out and placed it on the table. He removed the oversized black clip and stared at the first page. He fanned the first thirty or forty pages. The file appeared to be in perfect chronological order with the date of November 22, 2005 on top. There was a single line note that read:

"To file: Gone Hunting, with Eddie's best wishes. Should be back in one week."

Tristan decided to spread out the first few dozen pages for closer examination. When he made room on the table, he accidentally pushed the manila folder onto the floor. As he picked it up, he saw a small blue envelope next to his shoe. It evidently had been tucked into the folder and knocked loose when the folder hit the floor. Written on the envelope were the same words "Gone Hunting" obviously in original script, not a copy. Tristan placed the envelope on the table and rallied the attention of Laura, Joseph and Asher.

"What do you think this is?" said Tristan quietly. I found it inside the Adamson folder. It's sealed and may be part of this man's original file."

"Let me see that, please," said Asher, reaching over to pick it up.

"Be careful," said Tristan. It looks like some sort of personal note; it may not be part of the original file; but someone included it with the copies. I wonder why; but worry what's inside. Remember; this guy went hunting and disappeared. We may be handling evidence here."

"You may be right," blurted Asher, now glancing at Laura, "But exactly for whom should this note be preserved? It was sent to us as part of our discovery request. We've already handled it. There are probably five sets of prints on it? What do you want to do; look for some DNA on the envelope glue?"

"Yes, indeed, maybe so," defended Tristan.

"You're a lawyer Asher; I'll leave the task of evidentiary preservation and chain of custody up to you!" Tristan continued, whispering "Asshole!" under his breath.

"Enough, let's open it!" said Asher. "Joseph, gimme that knife of yours, please."

They opened the envelope. Inside was a handwritten note, easily legible. Laura read it aloud as follows:

I am going deer hunting in Alabama. Leaving 11/22/05. Should be back in about a week.

Why this note? If anything should happen to me, get in touch with my twin sister Posie Adamson in Ashland, Kentucky. She lives at 1222 Portland St. Her phone is 606-227-4407. She will tell you why.

Signed,
Zane L. Adamson
11/21/05

Laura finished reading the note. All eyes went toward Asher. "OK. OK. You're right. This may be evidence, after all," he said. "Tristan, what do you think?"

"What do I think?" started Tristan, "I think we should call the FBI first, since Adamson's disappearance occurred across state lines and then call Posie second. I wouldn't involve the local police at all at this point. God knows; they may have been in on Adamson's disappearance. I want to know what Posie knows. If she's alive, she may know something about her brother's disappearance and be in possession of information material to our first case and our appeal. Hopefully, old Zane will talk to us from the grave.

Laura, what do you think? Laura?"

Tristan glanced over and saw Laura, leafing through the stapled stack of e-mails at the end of the Adamson file.

"God, look at this. Look at this, will you," exclaimed Laura. "Material facts, hell; this is a bombshell! Do any of you know anyone named Lance Whitmore? It look's like he was in communication with Eddie Olson, one of the Matchless owners. I don't know how

Adamson got a hold of this e-mail; but here it is. It is dated 6/20/05 and reads:

'Eddie - Received fifth and final check for this round of services. Many thanks, Lance.'

No last name. But the e-mail address is <lwhitmore12@newnet. come>

Anybody know anybody else named Whitmore? Duh! Maybe Judge Henrietta Whitmore, is kin?"

Asher turned to Laura. His eyes looked like saucers. You could almost see the dollar signs. "Let's try to get a hold of Posie first. Then call my travel agent. I think the three of you need to spend some time along the south bank of the Ohio. I hear Ashland is a most beautiful place to be in late summer. The humidity and the temperature are usually the same. Any objections?"

CHAPTER 30 - POSIE AND ZANE

DATE: Thursday 9/10/10 - About
five years after Katrina
LOCATION: Ashland, Kentucky

— — —

Ashland is an interesting, fairly small town of around 20,000, located in northeastern Kentucky, along the Ohio River. Known especially for steel, good medical care, and The Judds, it was also the home of Posie Adamson, Zane's twin sister. It was not hard to find Posie. Posie and Zane were born in Ashland, and Posie had stayed there her entire life. When Tristan, Joseph and Laura arrived to visit her, she was still working at the same bank she had joined after her two years at the local community college in 1979. She had worked her way up to assistant branch manager and liked it just fine. She made only 15% less than the branch manager and had 75% less indigestion.

Neither Zane nor Posie had ever married. Both were as straight as the Cherokee and Shawnee arrows that flew around Ashland, long before they were born. The twins simply could not form close relationships, except with each other. They were close siblings from the beginning and became even closer after their parents died suddenly in a terrible winter auto accident when they were both 12, in 1971.

It was very tough going for the two of them after that tragedy. The twins' maternal grandparents raised them through high school and one year after, until their grandmother died suddenly of a stroke. Posie and Zane shared an apartment for two years, until Posie graduated community college; then they went their separate ways. They may have been apart physically; but mentally and emotionally, they were as close as they were in the womb. They wrote, talked and visited each other several times a year.

Posie got the job at the bank; but work was much harder to find for Zane, who never went to college. He bounced around with many different menial jobs. Without much training, he floundered; that is, until the day Monty Olson saw him working his rear end off, loading those railroad cars, near Montgomery in 1984, when Zane was 25. The rest is history. For the next 16 years until Monty's death in 2000, things went well for Zane. They even went fairly well for the next five, until Eddie Olson sent Zane on a hunting trip in the fall of 2005, right in the middle of Matchless Enterprise's monumental "ramp-up" to produce 4000 modified travel trailers for FEMA, after Hurricane Katrina.

Zane was the Line 1 foreman; but Eddie knew Zane was unhappy with the way production was being handled. Eddie knew Zane had cursed the "ramp-up" that had injured many and even killed one of the workforce. Eddie knew Zane was morphing into a bigger problem everyday. An obstacle to the millions Eddie knew he deserved; so Zane had to go.

What the hell - Zane needed some time off. He must have had a premonition of doom before he left. Only he knew why he went. But he left a note in one of his files at work. He took this file, along with several other critical ones and moved them into some boxes stored in Jimmy Olson's office. Then he took other files and put them out of order and out of reach in Missy Malark's old filing cabinet. Just in case.

In the note he had left behind, he instructed anyone who may find it to contact his sister, Posie, in Ashland. He knew if someone found his note, there was a great chance he was toast. Well, Zane went hunting and then went missing in the fall of 2005. The note in the misfiled file made it into some defense discovery documents sent to Asher Goldman's law office in Dallas. The note was found, and Zane's instructions were followed. Tristan called Posie and then, along with Joseph and Laura, came calling in 2009 almost four years after Zane's disappearance.

Before Zane went hunting in Alabama near Anniston for the second rifle season, he had gone to visit Posie for a couple of days. She recounted the story to the "Goldman Trio" in the living room of her modest two bedroom, two bathroom home on Portland Street where she had resided since 1990.

"Thank you for seeing us on such short notice, Miss Adamson," said Tristan, with a tone of genuine warmth in his voice. "As you know, your brother left a note, instructing us to contact you, if he didn't return to work. We just found the note four days ago; so here we are to help in anyway we can. We want to learn more about your brother too."

"Please, call me Posie," responded this tall and thin, like her brother, lady, now 50 years old. "I still can't believe he's gone. It's like I have been cut in half. I have not healed. The doctor says I'm in denial; but I will never give up my hopes that he will return someday. I told him not to hunt alone; it was not like him. He is such a good outdoorsman. He knows the woods, the critters and how they live. He just disappeared, like out of thin air. I can't bear it even though it has been almost five years since I last saw him here, right in this living room. He stayed with me for two nights. I made him his favorite ham and grits, with apple pie for dessert the night he left. God, I am carrying on again. I am sorry."

"Please, Miss Adamson, uh, Posie," interrupted Laura, "I can't imagine how difficult it has been for you. Please do go on. We want to hear the whole story. Did your brother mention anything about his work, while he was here? Did he have any enemies that you can think of?"

"Oh, the police in Anniston asked me all of those questions, years ago. They have closed the case, I think. The Calhoun County sheriff's office and even the Alabama Highway Patrol weighed in. They searched for over a month and couldn't find a thing. They knew, in general, where he was going hunting. It was rough terrain. Not a trace. Not a trace. It's like he left the earth. They found his Jeep; but that was it. Winter set in; there were animals. Oh God. I can't take it. He'll be back. I know he'll be back. He's probably just got hung up some-where. He always wanted to go to Alaska; so that's probably where he's gone. Maybe he's fishing for salmon. He's a God fearing man. He probably just broke and needed some time off for himself. I told him I would keep his letter and not open it, just give it back to him when he returned. No need to worry, God will protect Zane. You will see."

Tristan, Laura and Joseph all looked at each other. Tristan then focused on this poor lady clinically.

The words came out of his mouth as fast as a bee sting gets your at-tention. Laura's words came out, just as fast and they spoke in unison.

"What letter, Posie? What letter are you talking about?" said Tristan and Laura like they were singing in a choir.

"Oh, I have it put up on my closet shelf." replied Posie, now strained. "But I can't let you see it. I promised I'd give it back to Zane after he brought me some venison. He'll be mad if I showed it to you. He said to hold it until he got back. It's true he said to open it if he didn't return; but he'll be here any day now; any day now."

She was breaking. Tristan asked Joseph to go in the kitchen and get Posie a glass of water.

Tristan stood up from his chair and took the liberty of going over to the couch to sit next to Posie. He saw what was about to happen. He had seen it hundreds of times in his clinical practice. This woman needed some human touch to open the abscess of her grief. Tristan took the next liberty and took Posie's right hand and placed it between his. Then, like an avalanche, the tears came. She wept and wept. Laura joined Tristan on the couch and put her arm around Posie. Joseph offered water. Posie took a sip; then wept some more. The beautifully cathartic scene went on for twenty minutes. Posie nearly emptied a box of Kleenex. Then came the unnecessary shame of embarrassment.

"I know he's gone; but I just can't bear it." she cried. "I am so ashamed. He was my life. I know we didn't live together anymore; but I saw him so often. After our parents died, we really only had each other. Grandma and grandpa did their best; but it wasn't the same. When grandma died so sudden, it was like our poor parents died all over again. We both comforted grandpa; but without Zane, I don't know what I would have done. Dr. Baines, do you think he'll be back? You're a doctor. Am I crazy? Help me figure this out, please"

Tristan knew why he had come; now he felt some guilt about his intentions. He needed information to fortify Asher's appeal of the loss of the recent lawsuit against Matchless and the Olson boys, Zane's employer. But now he saw clearly that Posie was suffering from a delayed grief reaction and chronic situational depression that had erupted into an acute attack of near hysteria and delusional incoherence. His passion, sympathy and empathy as a physician kicked in, big time.

He was not about to treat her; just to understand and comfort her. But, she had spilled the beans. There was a letter? Maybe or maybe not. He wanted to know for sure. He nodded to Laura, thinking that she would be the best one to take it from here. Joseph sat quietly trying to figure out Anglo behavior. It really wasn't any different from what he had seen among his own people, but, despite the noise, Anglos seemed to grieve more quietly.

"Posie," said Laura, now having removed her arm from Posie's shoulder. "Can I get you anything?"

"No, thank you," replied Posie, gaining her composure. "I'll be fine."

"Posie," continued Laura, "We came here because we want to know what happened to your brother too. You see, he worked for a company that did some bad things. We don't think Zane was involved; because he left some notes in his file, indicating his anger over the situation. But we have reason to believe Zane may have held the key to understanding exactly what went on at Matchless, you know, his company, before he left.

He may have told you something important. We may be able to use that information to figure out what happened to him. We want to meet Zane. We know how much you miss him. Help us and maybe we can figure out where he is or whether something terrible happened to him, God forbid."

"You're talking about the letter, aren't you, Laura?" said Posie, now decompensating again. Laura could see the tears welling up. Posie's eyes were bloodshot and her nose was stuffy.

"Can we see it?" asked Laura gently. "It may have the key."

"I am so ashamed. I haven't shown it to anybody before, not to the police, my pastor, no one." she replied. "It is sealed. I haven't opened it. I have been too afraid."

"There's nothing to be afraid of," continued Laura, authentically empathetic, feeling Posie's pain, but also trying to conceal her lawyerly mission.

Having an epiphany, Tristan weighed in. "Posie, maybe you're right. Since Zane didn't want you to open it if he returned, then you shouldn't, because, I agree, he'll return someday. Then you can give it back to him sealed and all. Then you'll never be the wiser about what was in it. You'll never know, because you had no reason to know. I agree. Let's forget it.

Posie, it's near dinner time. Would you like to join the three of us? We want to take you to dinner. I think Joseph wants Italian. Do you have a good Italian restaurant around here?"

Joseph looked at Tristan like he had lost his marbles.

"I hate Italian food," whispered Joseph under his breath.

"But what about the letter?" Posie uttered, in a broken, almost pathetic whimper. "What about the letter? We can eat later."

Tristan glanced at Joseph, picking up on his look of nausea at the thought of garlic bread. Then he saw Laura break a smile. Laura took over again.

"You're right, Posie," I think dinner can wait another half hour or so. "Why don't we go get the letter together? I will help you."

"OK, thanks, Laura," Posie said with the tone of relief one feels after they have heard the voice of a missing child. "It's in my bedroom, in a shoebox up in my closet."

Laura and Posie stood up together. Laura took Posie's hand, and they disappeared into the hallway next to the living room entrance. They were gone only five minutes; an eternity to Tristan who wasn't certain how he was going to handle the letter's contents and another Posie relapse. He wasn't licensed in Kentucky. He thought he may need some medical reinforcements. Depending upon the content of the letter, he was already thinking about his law enforcement assets too, especially the ones who could cross state lines.

—   —   —

Posie and Laura reappeared. Laura was holding Posie's right hand, and Posie was holding a standard white business envelope in her left. They paused in the entryway to the living room. Both Joseph and Tristan stood up, almost involuntarily. Posie took the lead. She was obviously shaking and needed to sit down. She shuffled past the living room, toward a formal table in the adjacent dining room and started to sit down, taking one of the guest chairs along the side of the table.

Laura, still holding Posie's hand redirected her to an arm chair at the head of the left side of the table, as they entered the room. Tristan took a chair to Posie's left and Joseph sat to Tristan's left, keeping a sharp eye on the front door that he could see about thirty feet away across the furniture in the living room.

As she was seating Posie, planning to sit to Posie's right, Laura could not help glancing up at the dining room wall facing her, eerily basking in the fading afternoon light through a dusty double hung window. There she saw a color portrait of a man and a woman, painted when they were probably in their mid thirties. Both were obviously tall and thin. The woman was seated in a blue, high back upholstered velvet chair, wearing a bright yellow sun dress. The man, standing with his left arm over the back of the chair, wore a light blue sport coat, dark blue trousers and a white shirt, adorned with a bright yellow tie that matched the woman's dress. Both were also wearing very slight, obviously dignified smiles. Laura knew immediately who they were. The resemblance was remarkable, even for fraternal twins. On the wall to the right of the window, there must have been twenty framed photographs of all shapes and sizes.

Suddenly, Laura heard, "Oh my God; now look what I have done!" The exclamation came from Posie. Laura had lost track of Posie for just an instant. She looked to her left to find Posie leaning over the left arm of her chair, looking at the carpet below. Nothing was in Posie's left hand and nothing was on the floor.

What ensued would have won a first prize on "America's Funniest Home Video." While Posie sat still slightly shaking, now with both hands on the white dining room table cloth, all three of the "Goldman Trio" literally burst from their chairs and nearly collided heads under the table, looking for the white envelope that had fallen from Posie's hand. There it was, near the middle of the underside of the table, laying face up on the floor, having simply obeyed some gravitationally induced, envelope aerodynamics as it sailed to the carpet, like a poorly designed paper airplane. It was just as if the last will and testament of a recently deceased, billionaire rich uncle had disappeared from the hands of the family attorney, in front of two salivating nephews and one really salivating niece.

Still under the table, all three delayed for a moment and then stared at the cursive writing on the front of the envelope, facing them.

"To My Sister Posie - Do Not Open Unless I Do Not Come Back to Get This Envelope When We Agreed - Your Loving Brother, Zane"

Tristan picked up the envelope and trying to regain some degree of dignity handed the envelope to Posie as he took his seat, still to her left. Once Joseph and Laura had re-seated, Tristan could see that this drama was not going too well. Posie started shaking as she read her brother's instruction on the front of the envelope. She had obviously read it many times before.

Tristan began," Posie, let me help you. Do you have a letter opener nearby?"

"Yes, Dr. Baines," Posie answered. "There is one in the top drawer of the credenza directly behind you. I know where it is. I use it to open my bills and personal letters. It was the same one Zane and I shared when we lived together years ago. It is the right one for this moment."

Tristan found the simple 8" steel letter opener and placed it on the table in front of Posie. She pickled it up, with some steadying of her hands, skillfully inserted the opener blade into the upper fold of the envelope and slit it open without tearing it. She performed the overdue surgery with the confidence of one who was removing a skin lesion that had grown too big for too long.

She pulled out six sheets of yellow lined paper, each folded in thirds. There before her, she knew may be a voice from the grave or simply a message from her errant loving brother, who, in her mind, may now be fishing off the coast of Alaska.

She read the first line on the first page; then lost her nerve. In a instant, just a fast as Laura, Tristan and Joseph had dived under the table, Posie got up, burst into tears and fled to the living room, sitting down on the couch. She sat there on the edge of a cushion weeping and sniffling again, both hands over her eyes.

Joseph suddenly rose and said in very calm voice, "Let me see to her." He left the table and went into the next room, sitting down next to Posie and offering some inaudible reassurances. Within moments he was off to the kitchen again to fetch a glass of water.

Laura assumed Posie's seat, and both she and Tristan looked down at the folded letter. Tristan spread out all six sheets side by side and they silently read it together.

11/22/05

"My Dearest Sister:

If you are reading this I may be dead or held some-where against my will. I have been involved in some bad things that I have tried to stop. If I go back to work, I will continue to try to stop them.

As you know, I have tried real hard at my job at Matchless. Now I have been there for over 21 years. I have been treated well; but since the older, Mr. Olson, died in 2000, I have been cast adrift. I promised him I would look after his boys, Jimmy and Eddie. Jimmy is OK; but

Eddie is evil and greedy. We have just got a big order from the government to build more trailers than we can. They are headed to folks who lost their homes after Hurricane Katrina this past summer. We can't do it. I am being forced to operate my assembly line, which is the main one, in a way that hurts some workers and even killed one, just a short time ago. The workers are poisoned by formaldehyde from the glue in the wood used in the trailer.

Now for another one of the bad parts. Eddie Olson is a crook. He has been giving a lot of kick-back money to a government man named Cyrus Cooper. I don't think Cooper's boss, Frank Osborne, knows about it. Even worse, four days ago I overheard a terrible phone call outside of Eddie Olson's office while I was in the next room waiting to talk to his brother. Eddie has a big mouth and was yelling. He should have made the walls thicker. Later, I slipped into Eddie's office (I know I done wrong) and saw some papers on his desk.

Eddie is mixed up with some group out of Illinois called CADIXX. I think they are the mob or even worse. I overheard him talking with some guy about picking up hundreds of tons of toxic waste from the making of our trailers. He promised this guy; I think his name was Orton, Morton, or maybe, Gordon, something like that. Eddie promised CADIXX over one and a half million dollars to haul away the waste.

Dearest Posie - Eddie was supposed to pay half the money real soon. He says he can't and he had another fight with the guy at CADIXX and now, worst of all, he told this guy that it was all my fault. On top of that, I had a fight with Eddie on the day one of the workers was killed. I'd rather skip the details for now. It was then that Eddie told me I had to take a leave of absence. So I am going on this trip.

Before I left, I learned from Jimmy's secretary at Matchless, a gal named Missy, that Eddie intends to stiff this guy at CADIXX. Missy told me that she also heard a big screaming match when Eddie talked to CADIXX again about the payment. She heard Eddie yell "Don't threaten me!" and then he used the "F" word.

Eddie told her he was going to build a big steel building on our site and put the waste in there for the time being. Posie, this is all so crazy. I must tell you dear sister, I AM SCARED. I thought I would get away and do something I love to do; go deer hunting. I am going alone which is safer. I will be near Anniston, Alabama in Calhoun County. I will be out of cell range. I will be taking my Jeep, you know the one.

If you read this letter and I am still gone after thirty days, please call the police in Anniston or the sheriff in Calhoun County. _Take them this letter_. It has all the details they need

More importantly, call Kentucky OSH, that's OSHA for Kentucky. Tell them that I have many files with documentation of how Eddie and his brother are poisoning their workers.

Worse yet and _this is the most important part_ - the trailers they are delivering to the Katrina victims are loaded with way too much formaldehyde. Missy said that Eddie is lying about the readings he makes in the trailers before they are delivered. He and his brother have known about this formaldehyde problem for years. They have done it before when building trailers after 9/11. Last June they cleaned up their act for a while. To make trailers for the current order fast enough they have to dirty up the air in the new ones with formaldehyde again. The levels of this poison in the trailers Eddie and

Jimmy have blessed will cause people to get very sick and even cause cancer. They need to be stopped.

Finally, this latest thing about the toxic waste. Eddie plans to store on site. It is illegal. I guess you should call the EPA and also show them this letter. I don't have no documents on this part. I just heard it.

I love you dearest sister. I think about you all of the time and know we will meet again, here on earth or in paradise. Momma and Daddy will feast at our table again.

Your Loving Brother,
Zane

Laura and Tristan finished reading Zane's letter. They just stared at each other, watching each others wheels turn. Tristan felt like he was going to be sick.

It wasn't "Orton" or "Morton" - Shit it was "Gordon!" - that is, Gordon A. Gasher (GAG) who had been yanking on Eddie's "short hairs" for the $1.6 million. GAG, nurse by training, fraudulent plant RN for the CADIXX, Alton, Illinois incinerator; degenerate fiend who oversaw the abuse of his daughter and the disfigurement of his wife, Heather, nothing less than the amputation of her ring finger, wedding ring and all.

He had been looking for this madman for over four years, even harder since last summer before the FEMA trial. Tristan was still planning an exciting retribution party for his good friend, GAG, who would be his guest of honor to enjoy a demonstration of the latest advances in Pain Medicine; not control or mitigation; instead control and intensification, of course, while, avoiding any form of sedation. Waterboarding would feel like genital caresses compared to what Tristan had in store for good old GAG.

Now it was likely that The Resistance was also involved in this deadly scheme to silence, Zane Adamson, the wanna be whistle-blower who didn't get a chance to blow his whistle, except possibly post-humously, after his letter jumped from his sister's shoebox. About 11 months after the failed litigation against Matchless and over 13 months since Asher had first told him about The Resistance, Tristan clearly realized now the extent to which the spider's web was taking on greater definition.

Laura realized it too. Tristan could see it in her eyes. But this was neither the time nor the place - not in Posie Adamson's dining room while she sat in the next room weeping over her brother's disappearance.

Tristan knew Zane's letter was a powder keg, containing multidimensional information coming from a dozen directions, all of which needed to be correlated and understood. It was going to be an extreme challenge for him, and he was an old hand at this sort of thing. Laura was a youngster; but she waded into the swamp rapidly and without hesitation. Tristan looked at Laura with admiration, like a proud father. He knew, watching her eyes, facial expression and the way she moved her hair away from her face that she was just a kid - but a kid who was becoming or was already his peer.

Although she didn't have Asher's experience, Tristan knew she was smarter than Asher by far. Working so closely together over the past year and a half with her, Tristan was occasionally uncomfortable, overwhelmed by feelings of admiration that he had occasionally confused with infatuation. He was over that. He knew how much he missed Heather and Tess. He had not seen them for over two months, and it had been over a week since they talked last. Tristan sensed the attraction nevertheless. Now it was coming from Laura. He wasn't sure how she felt; he only knew that at some point, he may have to throw some cold water where it didn't belong.

Laura spoke first. "Well, you know what we have here. What do you want to do? I know the entire document and especially the third from the last paragraph have got to go to our federal appeals team in Atlanta, pronto. Of course, we need to call Asher first."

Hearing Laura's crisp, definitive comment, question and

directives, Tristan refocused on the matter at hand. He did know what they had in front of them. It may be enough to resurrect a case worth hundreds of millions of dollars, if they could prove the authenticity of the letter, and it was corroborated with other documentation in Zane's files.

In addition to the direct mention of CADIXX and GAG's involvement with Eddie Olson, there was also a major criminal dimension to the case on the part of Matchless by itself. Willful negligence to harm workers was a charge that could circumvent any worker compensation remedy and could lead to punitive damages. Then there were the criminal charges of conspiracy, bribery, money laundering, illegal dumping of hazardous materials, and worst of all, murder.

Question was simply whether murder was left to Eddie alone or had he needed his pals at CADIXX to help matters along?

Actually, Tristan didn't know much about the investigation into Zane's disappearance. He assumed it was a missing person's case that had long gone cold and was probably closed.

At the moment, his thoughts turned back to Posie. He hoped she would let him keep the letter. He could not share its contents with her, at least right now. She needed support and attention right away. He looked into the living room where Joseph was still making his best efforts to comfort her. Tristan got up and went into the living room, leaving Laura at the table, re-reading Zane's letter. It was nearing 6 PM.

"Posie, do you have a friend we could call for you? You need to be with someone now and maybe through the night. And I could call your doctor, if you like," said Tristan kneeling in front of Posie to make eye contact.

"Dr. Baines, that is very thoughtful of you." responded Posie. "I can call my friend Mary, from the bank; she is a widow and lives alone. We spend time together because we both like gardening. I think she will come over, and we can eat together. I apologize that I haven't made any dinner for the three of you. I know you asked me out; but I'd rather stay home. Mary will bring over some food; a light dinner is all I can take at the moment.

I know you will want to keep Zane's letter. You can have it; just send me a copy, well sealed in an envelope. I don't want to know what's in it right now. We can talk later."

With that remark, Posie reached up and took both Tristan and Joseph's hands. She squeezed them gently, bowed her head and prayed.

"Thank you God, for sending me your three wonderful servants, Oh, Lord. They have turned a page in my book of life that I have not been able to turn myself. Bless my brother, Zane, wherever he is and bless these three friends who I know will find him and bring him back to me. In Jesus name, Amen."

With a dignified countenance, not seen since they met, Posie rose and hugged all three of the "Goldman Trio." She kissed Laura gently on the cheek and whispered in her ear. "Laura; Dear; you work hard to help Dr. Baines and Joseph solve this dreadful mystery. You will won't you?"

Respecting her generational demotion, Laura kissed Posie back and whispered in return, "Of course, I will Posie. I will do my level best to support Tristan and Joseph, who without me, could never crack this case."

Posie looked at Laura awkwardly; then offered a weak smile, thinking how times have changed.

Overhearing the interaction, Tristan actually yawned. After they left Posie's home, as they were walking to their rental car, Tristan poked Joseph on the shoulder, and then began checking the contacts list on his cell phone. Alphabetically, he started with "EPA", then went to "FBI" and finally to "G" for "Goldman."

As he approached the car, Tristan said, "Say, Joseph, let's let Laura drive. I'll get in the back seat." As he opened the rear door behind the driver's seat, Tristan's eye missed Laura's middle finger by less than an inch.

CHAPTER 31 - CALLIE AND THE FBI

DATE: Friday 9/11/10 - about five years and two weeks after Katrina.
LOCATION: Ashland, Kentucky

—   —   —

It was barely light outside Tristan's suite in the fine old Ashland Palace Hotel. It was nearly 6 am on the ninth anniversary of 9/11, the morning after meeting Posie Adamson and choking on the content of her brother, Zane's, letter.

As often was the case, Tristan couldn't sleep - especially after acquiring unexpected and disturbing information close to bedtime. And to make matters worse, he couldn't do a damn thing about it until morning. He didn't go to bed until nearly 4 am anyway. But he still had to wait until 9 am to be certain to reach those who could raise some hell on his behalf.

"Oh how, sometimes, it is such a small stinking, rotten world," he thought to himself. There it was in front of his face, in Zane's letter to Posie. There was the evidence that CADIXX had had its hand in the pocket of Eddie Olson and Matchless Enterprises to the tune of $1.6 million. No doubt those bastards had also pulled some strings in the disappearance of Zane on his so-called hunting trip, where he probably had been the quarry, not the hunter. In someone's mind, Zane's danger as a whistleblower obviously outweighed his value as a Matchless Enterprises line foreman. So he just had to go.

Then he remembered the e-mails that Laura had uncovered back in Dallas, especially the one involving some guy named Lance Whitmore, maybe a relative of federal Judge Henrietta, herself.

"When greed is planted in the soil of corruption and watered with filthy money, expect anything," pondered Tristan. He knew there were no limits to the spread. Now, he was face to face with the overgrowth of the lethal jungle it had created.

Tristan lay there semi-somnolent, continuing his painful analysis of everything. It was now over a year ago, in July 2009, when Asher revealed his brother Saul's mix-up with The Resistance - along with the involvement of CADIXX and "nurse," Gordon A. Gasher (GAG) in its nefarious operations. This was the same GAG whom, he was certain, mutilated his wife and brutalized his daughter in 2006.

After figuring these connections back in '09, Tristan had become strangely withdrawn, seemingly powerless, depressed and ineffectual. Was it self-pity? That would be a new one. For once in his life, he hadn't been sure what to do. At the time, he felt the feds and, especially, the local cops were useless. He wanted to act boldly, on his own, skip the trial and his obligation to Asher. But he knew he couldn't.

Tristan lay there watching the brightening of the faint pink, now yellowish glow on the wall next to his bed. But the collision of thoughts wouldn't let up - he was mentally perseverating, stuck on the unbearable truth. His head was spinning, as he began to combine what he had known before the trial with what he had just learned from Zane's letter, last night. It was fulminating, unstoppable, like an erupting geyser. His anger rose from the depths of his inner being. It was volcanic and surged from his gut and his brain at the same time, forging, in him, a new sense of purpose.

With this new sense of empowerment, pleasantly emerged an overdue feeling of self-esteem, of pride in his abilities to act. If he incurred risk, he would handle it as he always had done in the past - effectively, thoroughly and completely, until it simply went away or became so vanishingly small that it just didn't matter anymore.

Tristan pondered the grim reality that the information revealed in Zane's letter was current in 2005. It was now 2010. The trail was probably ice cold. He intended to thaw it with a blow torch.

More than anything, he wanted to kidnap GAG and skin him alive, using some very special techniques Joseph had taught him a few years back. He knew where he was. The bastard was still working at CADIXX in Alton in his protected, fraudulent bubble of deception. GAG had resumed his position at CADIXX as the nurse in charge of their small medical department right after Tristan's devastating testimony had cost his company $60 million. There, he was still in a position of respectability, after Tristan was certain he had orchestrated the hideous payback on Tristan's wife and child.

It was true that the local cops from Alton and St. Louis had grilled GAG and many others about Heather and Tess' disappearance in '06. GAG was a person of interest, based upon Tristan's complaint to the police. But GAG denied everything. He said he didn't even know Tristan, except that he was the expert who testified against his company. And GAG said he disagreed with Tristan's claims that families living just outside the fence line of the incinerator's operations had been chronically ill for years, from emissions of arsenic, lead, mercury and a brutal assortment of chlorinated and aromatic hydrocarbons.

GAG denied he had had any conversation with Tristan before he testified. He denied lying to Tristan, claiming that the Madison County Epidemiologist, Carla Hastings, in charge of the Alton, Illinois area, had submitted phony data to exaggerate the neighbors' health problems. He denied asking, then demanding that Tristan change his testimony, the crime of witness tampering. Lastly, he denied threatening Tristan, warning that his obstinacy would play badly, very badly, for those closest to him.

And it did go badly, most diabolically, while his wife and daughter were trying to enjoy a late September afternoon at the St. Louis Zoo back in '06.

And while they suffered, Tristan rendered scientifically probable, financially devastating testimony against GAG's employer, CADIXX, that morally bankrupt corporation that for years had poisoned hundreds of its neighbors - men, women, children and even their family pets without remorse or compensation.

GAG denied it all, and the cops believed him.

Tristan had been certain he was going to deal with GAG

immediately after he had hurt Heather and Tess. But he knew if GAG's body was found dissected on some abandoned factory floor in East St. Louis, he, himself, would suddenly become a primary person of interest. "Revenge is a dish best served cold," he reminded himself. I need to wait. Back in '06, Tristan reassured himself that he would deal with GAG, at the time and place of his own choosing.

Now, as he thought it through on 9/11/10, literally four years later, Tristan realized he had let it go for too long, and it had become stale. Heather and Tess were OK; he had seen to that. He had set them up in rural Vermont. They had hunkered down without incident for three and a half years with Heather's sister and her husband.

Alone, isolated and miserable, in Wyoming, Tristan was recruited to go back to work for Asher in May of '09. Now nearly another year and a half had slipped by. It was a year and a half filled with enormous successes and equally depressing failures. And now he found himself in a gorgeous hotel suite in, of all places, Ashland, Kentucky.

Tristan's whirlwind of thought could not be stopped. He knew he had decided, naively, to have the law handle the matter of his family's violation. He thought something would surface back in '06 or '07 to put the local cops back on GAG's case; but nothing happened. Nothing.

Then in '09, a month or so before the FEMA trial, Tristan heard Asher reveal his brother Saul's lamentations about The Resistance; and he saw GAG show up on The Resistance organization chart, for God sakes, as none other than the Chief Enforcer, or better said, "Chief Thug and Avenger." Tristan wasn't entirely certain what was in GAG's job description; but he thought he had a good idea. Whatever it was, it meant pain and suffering for others; not just any pain; but the poison that could only come from a man who would cut off a woman's finger as punishment for her husband's supposed crime.

Tristan knew he had to resume the goal of destroying this low-life by whatever means. But Tristan still worried. He knew he still had to be careful about becoming a suspect if any harm were to befall GAG. On the other hand, Tristan fantasized he could make it look like suicide, a badly orchestrated, preferably slow hanging, maybe by a necktie, or even piano wire.

Tristan had his hands full with the FEMA trial in 2009. He had no time for anything, except checking on Heather and Tess in Vermont, at least once a week, by phone. Thank God they were fine; not too scared anymore; but longing for him, in person.

After he testified in late September, 2009, he and Joseph left New Orleans. Both briefly returned to their families, Tristan to Vermont and Joseph to Colorado.

Tristan's hoped his reunion with Heather and Tess would save his sanity; but it didn't work out that way. The farce with his drunken brother-in-law that led to the paranoid, nighttime brandishing of his gun at a pair of truck headlights was the last straw.

Heather's insistence that he depart early and leave Tess behind had crushed him. But Tristan still promised they would be together soon. He meant it; Back in Wyoming, at the compound, GAG had struck again; this time by leaving an ominous note, another fiendish poem, revealing that he knew Heather and Tess' whereabouts. Moving them both back to Wyoming and hiding them there was the only option.

But now Tristan was himself again. He was determined to resume his natural identity. He was morphing into a capable, hardened, even dangerous defender, focused on the serious, unfinished business of GAG first, then CADIXX and The Resistance a distant second and third. But Tristan knew that mismanagement of the tasks at hand could seal his fate and spell doom for everyone in the Baines clan.

After he and Joseph returned to Wyoming, following the FEMA trial in '09, involving Simon and Sethie Williams, they tried unsuccessfully, for over five months, in late '09 and early '10, to track down damaging information on GAG. Then, about two months later, after they came up empty-handed, Tristan was called back by Asher, a second time, in the spring of 2010, to look at some new cases, unrelated to Simon's claims, in hopes for a big settlement. In these new claims, the target of the trailer formaldehyde damage was not the lungs, but the skin, causing devastating rashes, allergies and daily torture for the victims.

The skin cases settlement was big, over $148 million from dozens of new defendants, thanks in large part to Tristan's reports and testimony. As for Simon's case that went to trial, it was a bust, for all kinds of reasons. The judge's rulings were called into question, so the case was appealed within the federal system. And Simon's family was still going after Coastal General and the good Doctor McKenna, for millions, for nearly killing Simon during his "routine" diagnostic work-up at the hospital in the summer of '09.

If Tristan's "meddling" in Simon's case, unsuccessful as it was, put him again in the telescopic sights of The Resistance, the new $148 million dollar settlement landed him directly in the cross-hairs.

This time, unlike before with Heather and Tess, they were not going to shoot non-lethal bullets or engage in beatings or mutilation. Now, it was going to be a .30-06 (thirty ought six), one of the U.S Army's historically favorite sniper rounds. No need to decapitate with a dull butter knife; a head-shot with a .30-06 would simply make Tristan's head disappear.

—   —   —

With less than two hours sleep, he swung himself out of bed, and with the help of Zane's letter, he was determined to blow the lid off GAG and, maybe, CADIXX, before the day was over. He showered, shaved, dressed and made some coffee. Then, he sat at the computer desk next to his bed.

He pulled a yellow pad from his briefcase, next to the plastic pocket sleeve containing Zane's six page letter, the original. The plastic sleeve was the same one a car repair shop uses to hold a customer's ticket. They were virtually indestructible, and Tristan trusted them to protect everything from his case materials to photographs.

Tristan looked at the clock. It was time. His first call was to the Anniston, Alabama district attorney. After two attempts, he managed to contact her. He explained the situation. She actually recalled the case; apparently for whatever reason (it was before her time on the job). She heard that the feds had stuck their nose into the search, very early on; but she wasn't sure why. In any case, this was good news because Tristan was disappointed after his experience with disinterested local law enforcement. The worst were the departments in Alton, Illinois and St. Louis over the past few months, when he and Joseph had searched for dirt on GAG. This DA's attitude was refreshing.

Tristan went to a local copy store, scanned Zane's letter and sent it to her via secure e-mail as a .pdf file. She said she would get back to him in a week or so after she had time to review the document and to perform appropriate research.

Tristan's next call went to his old friend, Ray Fuller, who was now the Special Agent in Charge (SAC) of the Criminal Investigation Division (CID) at the EPA field office in Louisville. Fuller told him there was already an ongoing investigation involving CADIXX. Their waste transport division was very suspicious. And their permits were not in order. He was not even certain the toxic materials they transported were dumped where CADIXX claimed they were. He asked Tristan to send over a copy of Zane's letter for him to examine.

Next, Tristan decided to contact the FBI field office in St. Louis. He would wait on contacting the FBI in Birmingham, Alabama even though they would probably be one of the leads in the investigation into Zane's disappearance or possible kidnapping. Tristan decided to act on a hunch. Even though things had not gone too well for him in his previous contacts with the St. Louis FBI, he knew this new information in Zane's letter had to interest them.

If he could find Special Agent, Jessie Wheaton, who had been his contact earlier in 2010, he knew he would save a great deal of time and might make some headway. Special Agent Wheaton had been a sympathetic listener when he first spoke with him. He already had Tristan's statements about CADIXX and Gasher, the GAG. But he had not heard from Wheaton for months. Tristan had held back, at least for the time being, on bringing up The Resistance, much less

GAG's relationship with them. He sensed the need for caution and didn't want to be labeled a nutcase quite so soon, especially when he had more solid information to share with the feds.

Tristan knew the explosive information from Zane should close the loop and circle the wagons around CADIXX, GAG, and Matchless Enterprises in one beautiful arc of forensic logic. After this, the feds had to launch a full blown investigation.

He still had Agent Wheaton's direct number; so he called. He went directly to voice mail.

"This is Special Agent Jessie Wheaton of the St. Louis FBI. I am not at my desk right now. Please leave you name, number, the time and reason you for your call; and I will get back to you as soon as possible. Thank you for calling,"

"Oh, shit," said Tristan. "I am sitting on enough information to choke a horse, and I have to wait. A possible murder or maybe kidnapping, illegal dumping of toxic waste and new information on the existence of a criminal conspiracy that risked the lives and health of over 60,000 Hurricane Katrina survivors."

Six minutes later, Tristan's cell phone rang. He looked down at his caller ID and saw no number; just US Government. "There is a God," he thought. "And She is kind," he smiled, thinking of Heather and Tess.

"Hello, Dr. Baines; this is Special Agent Jessie Wheaton on a recorded line," said the caller in as plain a manner as his charcoal suit, white shirt and light gray tie. "Sorry. I was on the other line. What can I do for you?"

"Thank you for calling back so soon, Agent Wheaton," answered Tristan. "Please call me Tristan. We have a lot more to talk about; much more than we discussed a few months ago."

"OK, Tristan. Now what do you want?" responded Wheaton, sounding a little colder than Tristan had expected. Tristan had never met the 44 year old veteran, who was now the Assistant Special Agent in Charge of the FBI field office in St. Louis. Tristan could sense that Wheaton had taken scalps-a-plenty to get promoted to this important position.

"Agent Wheaton, I don't know exactly where to begin." exclaimed Tristan shoring up his voice with an authority to match Wheaton's. Tristan knew he only had 30 seconds to capture the interest of this man; otherwise it was back to square one.

"Well, Dr. Baines, take a deep breath and begin at the beginning," interrupted Wheaton, almost sympathetic, but frozen as ever.

Tristan decided to jump directly to Zane's letter. He would leave his concerns about Heather's calamity and five or six other issues until later.

"Agent Wheaton, do you recall, when I spoke to you several months ago, I was trying to locate a man named Gordon A. Gasher, GAG, for short?" offered Tristan.

When he heard Tristan's question, there was a silent pause. Without answering Tristan's question, but seeming to have anticipated it, Wheaton, said, with a thaw in his voice. "Dr. Baines, uh, Tristan; would you mind holding for a minute? I would like to bring one of our Intelligence Analysts on the line, a young lady, named Callie McGavin. I think she needs to be a part of this conversation."

"Of course," said Tristan, noticing his heart rate increase and seeing a glimmer of light and hope at the end of the tunnel.

Three minutes of dead silence began to dampen Tristan's expectations.

"Yes, Jessie. I am here; Hello, Dr. Baines. It is a pleasure to meet you." said a very formal, alto voice that sounded much more youthful than her 36 years. Tristan immediately conjured that the voice was probably uniformed in female attire just as boring as her boss's formalwear.

An invitation to join this type of conversation was almost routine for Callie McGavin, a 12 year veteran of intelligence gathering, whose career was rocketing into orbit. Straight out of graduate school, she worked for two years as an analyst for the CIA at Langley. After gaining a reputation as a calculating, unrelenting man-hunter, she decided to accept an offer to go on board with the FBI full time. First in the New Orleans field office, then New York City, and finally St. Louis, two years ago - almost 50 major cases, now literally indispensable.

"Tristan, I have a surprise for you," said Wheaton, who had conferenced the three of them. "I have transferred us to a more secure line. Is anyone listening at your end?"

"No," said Tristan. "I am alone in my hotel suite at the Ashland Palace Hotel, in Ashland, Kentucky. And, by the way, I have a big surprise for you too." retorted Tristan, wondering what the hell was going on. His reception with law enforcement of any kind had gone from ice cold, to simmer - and he was hoping for a comfortable boil.

"Who wants to go first?" quipped Tristan, feeling somewhat light-hearted and confident.

"After our last conversation, several months ago, I clearly recall your concerns about nurse Gasher, or GAG, as you call him." said Wheaton, plowing forward.

"I took extensive notes; and of course, our conversation, as is this one, is recorded for posterity," said Wheaton, now clearly in a thawed mode. "Miss, uh, Analyst McGavin can explain further. Callie, go for it."

Tristan prepared to listen, thinking this analyst was probably staring at a 42" monitor with his face and shoe size, on it, along with a hundred other pieces of Tristan-specific information.

Sounding more like a college professor than an analyst, Callie began:

"Dr. Baines, we have been tracking this Gordon Gasher for the past three months. He remains a mystery, frankly; he seems to have about three or four past identities and maybe more. He went on our watch list after the EPA reported a possible criminal conspiracy, involving twelve individuals, eight men and four women. All of them currently work or have worked for CADIXX, an organization that operates an incinerator, along the Mississippi due north of here in Alton, Illinois. We are aware of your civil litigation case back in 2006, against CADIXX and the investigation into your wife and daughter's brutal injuries and abduction. I am sorry.

Back in '06, we actually had two agents working with local law enforcement on your family's case because of the abduction. The investigation is still open; but is approaching cold case status. St. Louis Police told us that the forensic artist's sketches created with your help and that of your wife and daughter have yielded no serious suspects.

We have a sketch of GAG, as you call him, but he does not match any of the suspect photos we have on file. Nor does the sketch match the face of the man we interviewed. As you know; this nurse denies any of the allegations you made against him. You may not be aware that he passed two polygraph tests. If he is lying, he must be superhuman.

But, I digress," continued Callie.

"Callie, let's go back to the EPA," said Wheaton, resuming a tone of authority.

"OK," continued Callie, sounding now anxious to lower the boom. "The EPA has been tracking the waste management and hauling activities of CADIXX for almost three years, since the fall of 2007. Their criminal division asked us to perform a detailed investigation of your man and the 11 others, whom they think are involved in very serious environmental violations, including the illegal dumping of toxic waste. Their trucks are unsafe, ill-equipped and do not meet a dozen DOT standards and regulations. They appear to be charging customers to haul waste, not to permitted and licensed landfills; but to a swampy, nearly inaccessible, area in southern Alabama, believe it or not on federal land.

Now for the interesting part. Some of the waste hauled and dumped by CADIXX came from a trailer manufacturing company in Warburg, Kentucky. You guessed it - the name is Matchless Enterprises, the company you testified against in the FEMA trailer litigation. Too bad you lost."

The last comment stung. Tristan knew the case was being appealed; and he knew his latest efforts brought $148 million to a bunch of other plaintiffs. But Sethie and Simon Williams had come up with zilch. He decided to upgrade Miss McGavin's intelligence on this issue later. No need to interrupt.

Callie kept talking without a pause, "So, Dr. Baines; that is all I am authorized to tell you at this time about the specifics of the EPA and, now, our investigation. We are preparing a subpoena to obtain records from CADIXX sometime soon - and they already know about it. We expect we may have to make a site visit in the near future, likely, unannounced, if they do not appear to be cooperating."

Silence. Tristan started to fill the void but waited.

"Jessie, can I continue?" asked Callie, softening her tone. Her voice suddenly took on the tenor of a 16 year old, asking her father, if she could have the Jeep to go four wheeling in the Ozarks.

"Go for it Callie, just toe the line and don't drive off any cliffs," replied Wheaton, in a tone sounding just like the Dad who stupidly relented on his daughter's reckless request.

"I am working with Special Agent Wheaton on several different cases right now." Callie continued, almost with a sense of relief in her voice. "When he told me your story, I intensified my search to come up with more information on this man, GAG. My counterpart over at the EPA is an investigator who has handled dozens of criminal dumping cases before. As I said earlier, this man, GAG, seems like he has no past. We're not entirely certain about his real name. He has no criminal record that we can find. Not even a DUI. We have a copy of his nursing license. He went to the nursing school at Washington University in St. Louis, before it closed. His name on the certificate is Gordon Alten Gasher. Initials GAG. What an inspiring last name for a nurse."

Tristan interrupted, "I haven't revealed my surprise yet - but I want you to know I actually called the EPA, Criminal Investigation Division, just before I spoke with you. I have a friend, in Louisville. His name is Ray Fuller, way up in the organization; actually, at a level where he can put some guns in the field, if it becomes necessary. I met him when he was a rookie, out taking water samples in glacial ponds in Montana twenty years ago. We have worked on at least a dozen major cases since then.

I sent him a .pdf copy of my surprise about two hours ago."

Wheaton, chimed in. "Why Louisville?"

"I'll tell you in a minute, and it will all make sense," Tristan replied.

Wheaton continued, "OK. But, Tristan, please send me what you sent Fuller at the secure e-mail address I gave you when we last talked. I should receive it in about twenty minutes, after it is checked for viruses. In the meantime, give us a verbal update about what you told the EPA."

"OK," began Tristan, realizing he had piqued the interest of the FBI. They wanted to know what he knew, and when and how he came to know it. He seriously doubted they intended to play fair and reciprocate in the process. Tristan's most immediate objective was to make them an ally to his overall causes, like taking down GAG, nailing CADIXX, and exposing Matchless, while helping Asher's appeal. Now, he had to add to the list his latest adopted cause of unraveling the mystery of Zane's disappearance. For the moment, he needed the feds. The alternatives, acting as a vigilante, were not appealing at all; at least, not for the moment.

Feeling a bit high on the opportunity, Tristan tried levity. "There is a lot to say. Gotta pencil and yellow tablet? You may want to take notes on something that doesn't require batteries."

"I have nothing of the sort," laughed Callie.

"Alright Dr. Baines; I get the point," snapped Wheaton. "We're waiting!"

Ignoring, Wheaton's slight and liking Callie even more, Tristan confidently proceeded, trying not to discount the talents of the professionals with whom he was dealing.

"Are you ready? This man, GAG, showed up again, this time in a nearly five year old letter held by a woman named Posie Adamson, in Ashland, Kentucky, sister to a line foreman and insider at Matchless by the name of Zane Adamson. He has been a missing person going on five years, after he went hunting near Anniston, Alabama in the fall of 2005. This, by the way, was a couple of months after Hurricane Katrina, when Matchless received an $80 million dollar order from FEMA."

Almost in unison, Wheaton and McGavin said, "We already know about the case."

Wheaton continued, "I've known since 2005; I, I ... mean since 2007."

McGavin continued, "Uh, Special Agent Wheaton means.... not us personally; but the Bureau field office in Birmingham has been involved since the fall of 2005, a few days after Adamson disappeared. I was in New York at the time."

It almost slipped by Tristan. "Why the mention of Birmingham FBI involvement, so soon after Zane went missing?" he asked himself. "Forge ahead, anyway. Be careful," he cautioned his tongue.

"Well, now I will provide you with the missing link." crowed Tristan, looking forward to bringing down some justice on the head of GAG.

"Anyway, I have sent you a scanned copy of Zane's letter. His sister, believe it or not, has held the letter, sealed, since the time of his disappearance. She just couldn't bring herself to open it. Two colleagues and I just spent several hours with Posie yesterday, frankly, to see if she could offer any information that might help our federal appeal of the FEMA trial loss, the one Callie has obviously researched so thoroughly,"

"Sorry, Dr. Baines," quickly offered Callie. "I didn't mean to..."

"It's OK. It's OK," consoled Tristan. "Later, if I talk to you again, I'll fill you in on all the gruesome details."

"Oh, I am quite certain we will be talking again, more than once," replied Callie, moving up an octave. "You'll have your chance."

"The letter, back to Zane's letter," struggled Tristan, trying to keep in focus. He sipped his coffee and quietly rejoiced that he had skipped breakfast as usual. If he had had a cheese omelet, fried potatoes, toast and orange juice, he would be left with the cognitive skills of a pencil eraser, unable to string together two consecutive syllables.

"Based on this letter, I think we can conclude the following," continued Tristan, looking down at his copy. First, I think this man, Zane Adamson, insider and dear friend to the founder, Monty Olson, may be dead, his body long ago the food for worms.

Alternatively, he may have been kidnapped or is in hiding to avoid assassination. Had he returned to Kentucky from his hunting trip in Alabama, I think he planned to blow the lid off the illegal dumping operations, the mistreatment of Matchless workers by overexposure to formaldehyde during trailer manufacture, and, worse yet, the intentional sale and delivery of contaminated trailers to FEMA that passed them on to Katrina victims. The latter resulted in unnecessary suffering among trailer occupants and increased risk of cancer. In addition..."

"You don't need to re-try your case, Dr. Baines." interrupted Analyst McGavin. "We get the picture and know the whole story. I have read your deposition twice and the trial transcript in its entirety once and even a bit more; sorry for the interruption."

Callie tried to sound apologetic; but didn't really mean it. She had heard old goats like him flame on during her investigations many a time in the past. "Please, do continue." she nearly whispered.

Getting the joust and pledging to be briefer, an effort no different from asking a toad to "Meow," like a cat, Tristan continued. "The letter reveals bribery and corruption involving at least one employee at FEMA; and here comes the best part.

Zane also wrote about a man named '...Orton, Morton, or maybe, Gordon,' who was on the other end of a discussion, he overheard, with Eddie Olson, the older brother of the current president, Jimmy Olson. The father, Monty, has been dead for years. I am confident the man mentioned in Zane's letter is GAG; that is Gordon...Gordon A. Gasher.

So GAG rears his head again, this time probably trying to negotiate the illegal transportation and dumping of Matchless' toxic waste with the help of CADIXX.

It must be him. After all, how many men with first name, Gordon, do you think work at CADIXX?

The letter is problematic, however, and just offers clues to GAG's direct involvement. Based upon Zane's letter, it looks like Olson welched on the deal, deciding not to pay CADIXX 1.6 million big ones. So GAG and CADIXX may not have received the bulk of the money owed to them to transport and dump. Instead, Eddie Olson, perhaps with his brother, Jimmy's involvement, has dumped the toxic waste somewhere on their manufacturing site in Warburg, Kentucky.

In answer to your question about 'Why Louisville?' Agent Wheaton, it is the closest field office to Warburg; but then, you already knew that."

Waiting for his remark to sink in, Tristan continued, "If you want my opinion, Zane Adamson was preparing to blow the cover off these illegal operations. Someone, probably, at Matchless or CADIXX decided he had to disappear - and bingo, he did. If it involved CADIXX, then GAG will have had his hand in it; just like he had his hand in ruining my life. Is Zane dead? Without a body, we may never be certain."

Silence.

Tristan wasn't certain whether he had talked too much again; so he decided not to mention the bribery activities of Lance Whitmore. Tristan still didn't know for sure whether Lance was a relative of federal Judge Henrietta Whitmore, aka "Henny" and "The Harpy", perhaps, even "Momma," in The Resistance. Above all, he knew one thing for sure - she was the destroyer of the hopes of 60,000 displaced Katrina victims who were given gas chambers for lodging, after that terrible storm.

"Callie, Jessie; are either of you there?" petitioned Tristan, deciding to drop titles.

"Yes, yes, we're both here, Tristan," said Jessie, seemingly distracted and obviously deep in thought. "We're just reading the letter you sent us, allegedly from Zane Adamson."

"What do you mean, allegedly?" countered Tristan, slightly miffed, but trying to keep things copasetic. "I told you Posie Adamson gave me this letter just yesterday. I doubt she wrote it herself. If she did, then, why? I have the feeling you know more about this letter than you're saying. Have you seen it before?"

Something was up, and Tristan wanted to know what it was; but doubted he could get it out of them.

"Well, Dr. Baines," Callie continued, deflecting Tristan's question. "He didn't tell... I, I, mean we didn't expect it. I told you; our colleagues in the Birmingham field office have been on this case, starting in 2006, a few months after Adamson went missing. Local law enforcement had exhausted all of their leads and come up with nothing; so they called our counterparts in Birmingham. They recently told us there wasn't any letter; uh, let me rephrase that.... I mean, nothing was said about any letter"

"Really?" thought Tristan, confused but still focused. "Why would the authorities in Birmingham say anything "recently" about a letter from Adamson, one way or the other, since we just learned about its existence two weeks ago and saw it only yesterday..... unless, unless..... they had seen the letter years ago, along with the man who wrote it? Good God, Callie is deliberately trying to tell me something!"

"Careful, Careful," Tristan warned his tongue, also noting another deliberate McGavin slip. "She just said Birmingham jumped in a few months after Zane disappeared. Earlier she said a few days. Which is it? I think I know. Good God, they must have...."

Tristan remained silent. He paused, thinking what to say next.

Wheaton broke the ice, trying to support Callie, who didn't need anyone's help.

"Well, as you said, Tristan, it might have been a kidnapping, down there in Alabama, involving this Adamson, fellow." forced Wheaton.

"So the Birmingham field office was called in after a few months back in '06 to help local police in Anniston. I reiterate - that office has recently been assisting us in the CADIXX dumping probe too."

"What's that got to do with anything?" jousted Tristan, unable to resist poking Wheaton. "You said the dumping probe didn't begin until the fall of 2007; almost two years after the Birmingham FBI weighed in on the Adamson case."

"Did I say that?" blurted Wheaton.

"No, Jessie, I said it!" said Callie, pretending regret; but certifying another element on Tristan's timeline.

Then, out of the blue. "Say, Dr. Baines, this isn't an inquisition, is it?" Callie asked, trying to cover her tracks and thinking about her next performance review.

"Oh, no, no, of course not. I apologize. It's just like me to ask one question too many," answered Tristan, realizing that self-deprecation got you something in return, most of the time.

It was time. Tristan needed an exit strategy that kept him on good terms with his federal resources.

While planning his next move, Tristan put it all together. True, in 2007, St. Louis probably called Birmingham to coordinate the investigation of CADIXX illegal dumping in Alabama. But, in 2005, days after Zane's supposed disappearance, it must have been the other way around. Birmingham probably called St. Louis, because they needed to comprehend an incredible story, involving illegal interstate activities within the St. Louis FBI jurisdictional area. A story they had heard firsthand, from a live "dead man," or had read in his letter to his sister.

Thank you, Analyst McGavin!

Before, Tristan spoke next, Wheaton beat him to it. "Dr. Baines, thank you for sharing this letter with us. It does tie together some loose ends. Why don't you give us a day or two to authenticate and absorb this content, and we will get back to you. I have your cell number and promise that you will hear from either me or Analyst McGavin by the middle of next week."

"Fair enough," said Tristan, with a genuine inflection of gratitude in his voice. "I'll look forward to it."

"Goodbye, Dr. Baines." offered Callie, "Talk to you next week."

They hung up.

At St. Louis FBI headquarters, Intelligent Analyst McGavin turned to Special Agent Wheaton. "Jessie, do you think he knows?"

"Yes, Callie, he knows." quipped Wheaton.

"Thanks to you, the old fart figured it out ten minutes ago," chuckled Wheaton. "You think I'm stupid and in a coma? You're such a soft-hearted soul; now I know why you washed out as a water-boarder at the CIA!"

Wheaton continued, in a more serious tone, "It really doesn't matter. Let's look at the big picture.

Give me two more months; and we will have enough evidence to persuade any federal judge in this region to issue warrants, allowing us to pay a visit to CADIXX up there in Alton, where we can carry out everything, including the petty cash receipts for the vending machines."

"Sounds like a plan," responded Callie.

Wheaton expounded more, "It doesn't matter if Dr. Baines knows about our man in Birmingham or not. The Baines family has suffered enough. Our raid at CADIXX may likely 'Snag the GAG.' That should help Baines find closure, if that bastard is really the one who nearly wrecked his family."

Callie gave him the look he deserved with his stupid rhyme. "Jessie, I think the good Dr. Baines is holding back something, something big - much bigger than CADIXX, Matchless, GAG or the fate of Zane Adamson. I can just feel it. I will try to tease some of it out of him next week. Gently. I think this guy likes to answer questions. I think he has a lot to say. Why did I feel like I was talking to my Dad during this conversation?"

"Beats me, Callie. Is your Dad a doctor, an engineer, a survivalist and ex-army Ranger?" asked Wheaton.

"OK, two out of four," said Callie, as she picked up her hard copy of Tristan's FBI file and left for lunch.

CHAPTER 32 -
EDDIE AND GAG

DATE: Wednesday 10/20/10 - About five
years and seven weeks after Katrina
LOCATION: St. Louis, Missouri

—   —   —

The filth was on the floor and was also present in the form of two, so-called, human beings, seated across the table from each other in Room 214 of the motel dive off St. Clair Avenue in East St. Louis, Illinois. Both men had agreed upon the location of their face to face meeting, commensurate with the depravity of their intentions and the darkness in their hearts.

The first man walked over to the window and pulled the dingy translucent curtain across it in an effort to block out the nerve wracking flashing of the sign across the street. How classic - just the word 'Bar,' stared at him every three seconds in a red-orange, obnoxiously bright neon. It was driving him crazy, as the twisted light illuminated the lime green walls of the $29 a night motel room. The other man didn't seem to care.

Turning his back to the window, Eddie Olson, fallen brother of Jimmy and son of Monty, began: "OK, Gordon, we've been beating around the bush for the past twenty minutes. Why are we here?"

"Why are we here? Why are we here?" hissed Gordon A. Gasher, GAG for short. "You are so pitifully challenged, if you don't get it. You are lucky to have the two legs that carried you through the doorway of this shithole. If I had had my way, you would have already decomposed months ago in some quicksand about a mile from where you live."

"Jesus, Gordon, I have paid you almost 50% of what you have

asked. I know its been a few years; but you only picked up and dumped 5% of the waste, anyway. I have disposed of the rest myself. You know you don't need to deal with another ounce of the shit.

I don't have the money; but I will get you the other $800K plus interest over time." Eddie pleaded, carefully scrutinizing the bulge in the North Face jacket, GAG had not taken off when he came into the motel room from the cool fall night outside. Eddie paused and carefully reached behind his back to check the Charter Arms .38 he had in his waist band.

"I thought we were here to discuss this arrogant gadfly, Tristan, uh, excuse me, Dr. Tristan Baines. "You were the one who told me that he and two others had gotten to Posey Adamson. I won't ask how you found out. I don't care."

"Listen, Olson." demanded GAG. "We'll talk about Baines first; and then we'll visit about the remaining $800K and the $1.2 million in interest that has accumulated on your tab since '05. That will be as lethal a discussion as the one we're now going to have about Baines."

GAG leaned forward and a mild "clunk" could be heard, as his coat swung forward and hit the table's edge. GAG continued, "Your precious Matchless was sued by this law firm Goldman and McDonald out of Dallas. The lead counsel was Asher Goldman, another one, along with his brother, Saul, whose day will come. You won dipshit. Had Iris McDonald gone after you, the outcome might have been different.

Don't think your defense boys in Louisville and New York were so great. Consider you owe us, and I don't mean CADIXX, for saving your asses. We have only called in favors like this one on two previous occasions; and they were in different federal court jurisdictions.

The reason you're here is that short of just killing Baines, we want to ruin him first; make an example. He has cost defense firms all over the country and abroad over $900 million in losses during the past 20 years; and now that he is back at work, he may do as much damage in three. I want your entire file on him so my people can make his life a dreaded nightmare."

Then GAG thought a violently recurring thought to himself, "We will put him in a living casket, while we destroy his career, his reputation and his life. And then we'll kill him, his bitch and his stinking kid. I still have the scar on my left hand where the little brat bit me five years ago. And the balls of my colleague have never been the same since Baine's wife kicked him while I was tying her down before surgery.

We will find them both, sweet Heather and now, Tess, almost grown. I know where they are anyway."

Gasher's meds were wearing off. He started singing to himself. "Come out. Come out wherever you are, my two ladies. Don't you want to spend some more time with Uncle Gasher? You left so soon. If I had had my way, I would have kept you forever. But five years ago, we let you go. Today you would never see poor Tristan again."

Gasher suddenly twisted his head, like he was trying to crack his neck. An easily audible "knuckle crack" sound could be heard in the room. He released an "Ah-h-h," like the purring of a cat. Then came back to stare at Eddie Olson. Gasher knew that Olson knew nothing about The Resistance at all. He knew that Matchless just paid $100K per year to some "Legal Defense Fund (LDF)" that was structured to do research on plaintiff's whores, like Baines. He had no idea where that money went; but he did know if he didn't pay his dues, some bad things would happen. It could be a misdirected or stolen load of raw materials; maybe a suspicious fire at the plant, or even an electrical disaster. So Eddie, along with at least 200 other supporters of the LDF paid without complaint. The trouble was that the money had to be paid in cash, in dribs and drabs, so the funds could be buried in this account or that. LDF told them how to do it.

Gasher looked at the pitiful slug across the table. If Eddie only knew that seated in front of him was the Chief Enforcer for The Resistance. "LDF" was nothing but the "legitimate" front-end of "The Accountant" division of The Resistance." You pay your dues to LDF and you fund The Resistance. It was as simple as that. This moron knew nothing about his involvement in the torture, abduction, and mutilation of Heather and Tess Baines. Some in The Resistance had wanted to add rape to the list; but GAG gagged on that option. He just couldn't perform.

GAG knew he had to make this a short meeting. He had already said what he had come to say about Baines. He still had to threaten Olson's life if he didn't pay CADIXX the money he had promised for hauling away the tons of formaldehyde and other chemically contaminated waste that had accumulated a few months after Katrina, while Matchless was filling the FEMA order. So what if CADIXX never had to perform? They wanted their money anyway. This idiot Olson thought he could eliminate his obligation to pay the original $1.6 million for the job, by burying the waste on his own plant site. He did pay half. But so what?

GAG knew that CADIXX wasn't interested in Baines anymore. The Resistance now had Baines in their crosshairs, not CADIXX. And they had given the job to GAG.

GAG had the best of both worlds. He could continue to practice nursing as the head of CADIXX's small medical department at the incinerator operations in Alton by day; and could spill blood by night. It was just the way he liked it. GAG snapped to as Eddie squealed.

"I want this guy gone, just as much as you do, Gordon," said Eddie, up an octave. He might as well have asked Gordon, if he could kiss his ass. "Five other of our competitors and some of their subs kicked in almost $50 million to Goldman, in that settlement, just a couple of months ago. Their defense firms drove us crazy asking for information on Baines and his buddy Joseph True... something. He's some wise ass Indian that is Baines' right hand man. The other one at Goldman's office who was such a pain was a gal named Laura Swain, uh, attorney Laura Swain. She's..."

GAG interrupted, "Olson, we know about both of them. Enough! I am here to tell you if you have some dirt on Baines, that we can use, we'll cut you a break on your, should I say, obligations. Maybe 50 or 60 grand."

Eddie felt like he wanted to throw up. 50 or 60 grand on a debt of over $2 million. He knew it had to come to this someday. He had a plan and it was in his waistband.

"Say, I'll have Missy Malark, our secretary, gather everything we have on Baines. I'll even quietly call our lawyers and ask for more. Our lawyers in New York will have the most information. The local fools in Louisville should be writing wills and real estate contracts. They are useless.

Look, Gordon. This guy Baines is despised. He's hated. I am surprised he's still walking the earth. I remember some comment from Michael Attington, one of the partners in our New York defense firm that Baines had disappeared for a few years after some tragedy befell his family. Wasn't he the one who soaked you, at CADIXX, for millions? When was it, '07?"

"No," jerked GAG, "It was '06.

"What is this?" asked Eddie, sensing that he may be prying too much. "Some vendetta against Baines because of that shellacking, whenever it was? Don't you think that if anything happened to Baines, CADIXX will be the first place the law visits?"

GAG didn't care. Let him think what he wants. "Yeah, Eddie. It's all about CADIXX." lied GAG, clearly voicing his disgust at the man sitting in front of him. "We don't want to harm Dr. Baines. We just want to see to it that he retires to his retreat in the Snowy Mountains of Wyoming. We want to see him spend time with his wife, raise his lovely daughter and see her grow like a weed. The man should be teaching at a university or something.

It is true that we resented his participation in the incinerator case a few years ago. But, what the hell; I don't want him as a friend or anything like that - I just want him not to matter anymore. You know that the LDF has an interest in this issue. Your dues are going to a good cause. I expect they will come up with some dirt we can sprinkle on Baines' head."

"OK, I get it," answered Eddie, sensing the meeting was going on too long. Why did he feel like he was a turd headed to a septic tank? He looked at the man in front of him. He saw him space out, crack his neck and then tune in. He saw him take something from his pocket and swallow it dry. Eddie was worried.

"Please excuse me, Gordon." whined Eddie. "I have to use the bathroom." Eddie got up and disappeared into the water closet, barely big enough to turn around in. He pulled the five shot undercover .38 from his waistband and put the revolver in his right pocket. After a few minutes, he exited the toilet. As he opened the door into the foul sleeping area, he felt the cold steel against his temple.

"Drop it, you asshole. I should kill you now!" belched GAG. "Put the gun on the table, then drop to your knees and put both hands behind your back."

"What the hell is this?" screamed Eddie, thinking he may want to raise the attention of others in the motel. What was he thinking? Screams in an East St. Louis flop house were like the chirping of birds on a spring day in St. Louis' Forest Park. He decided to keep quiet. "Gordon..."

"Look, I've had enough of your bullshit, Olson." said GAG, as he picked up Eddie's gun, put his own back in his pocket and then quickly zip tied Eddie's hands. "You will provide the information I have requested and you will direct deposit all of the funds you owe us within five days. You greedy pig; you took a two million dollar bonus after you screwed FEMA, your employees and the poor slobs who had to endure your trailers. Now you are going to give it back to us."

Eddie started to tremble. He knew GAG was not going to kill him; but he didn't know what was coming next. GAG went behind Eddie, who was still on his knees. He reached into his pocket and pulled out a long sharpened needle nosed pliers. The ends had been ground to a razor sharp edge.

"I think you are right handed, aren't you Eddie?" asked GAG as he put a reassuring hand on Eddie's shoulder.

"Yeah, I am right handed, Gordon. Remember, I need it to write your bank transfer, you asshole." said Eddie, trying to conceal the tremor in his voice.

"Well, whatever," whispered GAG, starting to feel the stiffness in his pants. It came up every time; just before the fun began, as long as it didn't involve sex. "I think I'll visit both limbs anyway. If you scream, I will put a bullet in your head. Someone will think another drug deal in the parking lot went bad and they won't find your body until the stench alerts the weekly cleaning lady."

"Gordon, No!" cried Eddie. "I wasn't going to pull my gun on you. I'll pay....I'll pay"

Eddie's mouth opened and was suddenly blocked by a stuffed rag that came out of GAG's coat. Like lightning, using all of his medical training to grab the target, GAG took the pliers and plunged the sharp end into Eddie's right elbow right at the funny bone. He aimed with surgical precision. In a millisecond, he pulled out a piece of Eddie's ulnar nerve and left the tissue dangling like a piece of overlooked toilet paper. There was very little blood, at first. He grabbed Eddie's neck and kept the rag stuffed tight as Eddie slipped forward into unconsciousness. GAG dropped him to the floor.

He figured, "What the hell?" No need to get the left one too. This asshole has got the picture.

GAG studied the piece of tissue on the end of his pliers. There was skin, blood, and some reddish white connective tissue surrounding a pure white core that looked like a small piece of string cheese. He reached in his pocket and took out a small pharmacy bottle, filled with his favorite, liquid formaldehyde. Very carefully, while Eddie lay on the floor in front of him, he opened the lid and dropped his souvenir into the bottle, watching it swirl back and forth as it hit the bottom of the container. Then he put it back in his pocket to secure its safety, excited to add it to his collection in the basement of his home.

Eddie started to whimper. GAG noticed the tears in his eyes. He checked to see if Eddie could still breathe with his mouth stuffed so full. Convinced that he would not suffocate, GAG took his gun and smacked Eddie across the back of his head. Eddie lay there and didn't move; but continued to breathe through his nose. Next GAG cut the zip tie binding Eddie's hands. As GAG wiped off the blood and small amounts of hair from his gun barrel, he opened the motel room door and walked out into the chilly, humid autumn night.

CHAPTER 33 - EDDIE GAGS

DATE: 10/31/10 (Sunday Halloween Evening)
About five years and two months after Katrina
LOCATION: Warburg, Kentucky

— — —

"I should have shot the asshole when I had the chance," Eddie Olson lamented to himself as he sat in his office on a Sunday Halloween evening, October 31.

Nine days after the mutilation of his right elbow at the hands of nurse Gordon A. Gasher (GAG), Eddie Olson returned to Warburg after his third appointment with his neurologist at the University of Kentucky Medical Center in Lexington. He had also seen an orthopedic and neurosurgeon at UKMC to look at the mess. All this took place the week after he barely made it to the emergency room at Barnes Hospital in St. Louis on that drizzly Wednesday night - namely, the night when GAG made his mark on him in that filthy flop house in East St. Louis.

How a man could have accidentally stuck himself in the right elbow with an ice pick was a story that pressed the imagination of the intern who first evaluated him when he came into the emergency room. The young physician thought about calling one of the St. Louis city cops who was assigned to the ER to investigate Eddie's story, but then figured Eddie had suffered enough.

There really wasn't much that could be done, immediately for Eddie except to clean and bandage the wound, give him a tetanus shot, some pain medication and place him on a 10 day course of antibiotics. Eddie told the intern he was from out of town, so the doc printed the medical record and told him to make an appointment as soon as possible with a neurologist and/or a surgeon. The damage to his ulnar nerve at the elbow was severe. The nerve was almost cut in half and Eddie suffered movement impairment and sensation loss involving half of his ring finger and the entire little finger in his right hand. Part of his palm was also numb, below the impaired fingers. Left untreated, the injury could cause muscle wasting and some serious disability in his grip, among other things.

Eddie pondered the horrible encounter with GAG. He had been put on notice, almost a week ago, to gather the entire Matchless legal file on Tristan Baines from the recent federal court formaldehyde trial. CADIXX, with GAG's help, wanted these files to dig up dirt on Baines to try to ruin his reputation and paint him as a loser. Eddie knew the demand was just a precursor to GAG's intention to eliminate Baines altogether. GAG never admitted it; but Eddie knew better. He knew GAG's sadistic credentials. He had a ruined right arm and hand to prove it.

Eddie told Missy Malark to assemble the files, the one at Matchless and the others at their two law firms in New York and Louisville. They were still working on it.

In that filthy East St. Louis dump, Eddie had also been put on notice to wire the $2 million GAG demanded. He gave him five days to comply. That impossible sum accounted for Matchless Enterprises', hence, Eddie's five year old obligation for CADIXX to pick-up, transport and dispose of 400 tons of toxic waste, derived from manufacturing the trailers FEMA had ordered right after Katrina.

Matchless only manufactured enough trailers to account for about 192 tons of waste and CADIXX had moved only about 10 tons. But that didn't matter to GAG; he wanted all of the money anyway. The original amount owed was $1.6 million for the whole job and Eddie had coughed up half; but didn't have the funds to cover the rest. Now over the last five years, Eddie's remaining $800,000 debt had mushroomed into $2 million with interest. So he panicked, failing to return call after call and e-mail after e-mail from CADIXX. Instead of allowing CADIXX to pick up what waste there was, Eddie buried it in the far south east corner of the Matchless property. It was placed in an unlined "S" shaped ditch system, almost the length of two football fields. So the groundwater, just twenty feet below the bottom of the ditch was at risk - who cared?

Eddie gave some serious thought to stalling, using the Baines files, as the carrot to buy him some more time. He was already six days past the deadline for the wire transfer. He came into work on Sunday night to be alone and try to figure out a new plan. Day after day, he became more worried. He carried a new gun, this time a .40 caliber Berretta. GAG, the bastard, had taken his sweet little Charter Arms .38 revolver. His Berretta was a semi-auto that held 12 rounds and one in the chamber. It wasn't nearly as concealable as his five shot .38; but he didn't care. He figured he needed the extra firepower. Eddie's two year stint in Vietnam had hooked him on the Model 1911A1 Colt .45; but trying to conceal that weapon would be like a camel trying to conceal its hump.

Eddie knew it was Halloween eve. He thought back to better days; when his Dad, Monty, took Jimmy and him trick or treating. Monty was a great father; but he used to eat half the candy left in Jimmy's and his bags after they went to bed. Eddie never had any kids during his two marriages, so he never had the pleasure of sharing that wonderful autumn holiday with any children of his own.

Eddie looked at the new order for 300 trailers sitting on his desk from an oil and gas outfit up in North Dakota. He had marketed hard for that order. The state was booming and housing was difficult to obtain. He knew the trailers would fill the needs of workers until more permanent apartments and condominiums could be constructed.

Eddie had long ago filled Zane Adamson's position with Mavis Franklin, a malleable woman, whom he could intimidate and boss around. Over the past two years, Mavis had become a bit more problematic. She was less overtly defiant to Eddie than had been Zane; but in many ways she was much stronger. Mavis had been among the workers on the FEMA project who had ended up in the hospital with bronchitis from formaldehyde overexposure on the assembly line 1.

Mavis made her quotas; but insisted that raw materials that made it to the line were "baked out" long enough to keep any chemical over-exposures during assembly at less than half those allowed by OSHA.

She told Eddie she wasn't screwing around; she was not going to take any chances with her workers and run the risk of their suffering the way she did five years ago. Mavis still had reactive airway problems. She wheezed heavily anytime she stepped from her house out into the cold or was around any kind of smoke or even perfumes.

Eddie stared at the new order. Just like he had since well before Katrina when Zane was around, Eddie had been lying to Mavis for at least the past four years about any and all formaldehyde levels associated with Matchless products. He especially lied about formaldehyde levels in the outrageously expensive "bake-out" oven room Jimmy Olson and OSHA had "forced" Eddie to construct to handle trailer raw materials like plywood and prefabricated cabinets.

Even worse, Eddie lied about the levels in the indoor atmosphere of delivered products. After all, Eddie had a chemistry degree and knew how to fudge the data; and he did in any way possible to save a nickel, even at the expense of workers and customers. Nothing had changed and no lessons were learned.

There had been some complaints from customers; but Eddie had overseen the design of the new post-Katrina warning labels that came with all Matchless trailer models. Formaldehyde was explicitly mentioned, and basically the label told the customer to open the doors and windows, if the smell inside was unacceptable. As for the workers, he managed to fire the ones who were the most chemically sensitive, even though Mavis occasionally complained. Before he was through, he had a crew of mutants who loved the smell of formaldehyde like it was their lover's musk.

Eddie relaxed and looked at the new $12 million order from the suckers up in North Dakota. It was a rush job - so he could surcharge them another $1.2 million. He had already bought the raw materials. The "bake-out" room was full to the brim and the first batch of cabinets and plywood was cooking. For the past three years, they had been buying formaldehyde free insulation, so none of it was in there to take up room. Eddie knew he had to meet payroll and other overhead; but there was still a million in bonus money for him and his pathetic brother to split. Someday he would figure out a way to split zilch with Jimmy. He knew he had enough to get CADIXX off his back; but he wasn't going to budge. "Those bastards are trying to extort something for nothing. I'll see them in hell, first," he thought.

He looked at his watch. It was nearly 9:30 pm. Eddie knew that tomorrow morning, on Monday, they would need to move the first batch of raw materials and cabinets to the assembly lines. Mavis would want the chemical measurement data to accept the stuff, so that manufacturing could begin. Eddie kept a little secret to himself. Before and even after the FEMA trailer formaldehyde disaster, he had depended upon a supplier in San Francisco who could obtain Chinese plywood at 30% less cost than American made. This plywood had double the formaldehyde content in its urea-formaldehyde glue; but so what? Eddie figured, he would get rid of it in his bake-out room or just let it ride to final product where he could cover his ass with his warning labels. The bake out room was stuffed with the Asian affliction, ready to poison again.

Eddie suddenly remembered he had an aggravating problem. On Friday, two days before, the stationary, probe system that monitored the formaldehyde measurements in the bake out oven room had failed. It looked like it had been vandalized. No one had made the time to trouble shoot and correct the problem.

Eddie had no other choice. To obtain his measurements for Monday, he would have to enter the oven room himself to make the measurements. He would be in a poisonous environment. He had done it before, to cheat on several occasions; so he was prepared.

Eddie thought aloud, "Damn those criminals who wrecked my equipment. Probably disgruntled workers who couldn't handle a little eye burning. When I catch them, I'm.... Aw... Screw it. I am tired; but I might as well head over to make some measurements to shut up Mavis tomorrow and get the show on the road."

Eddie glanced at the computer screen in front of him. Suddenly, he noticed an e-mail in his inbox. He looked at the e-mail address of the sender and did not recognize it at all.

"Why didn't it go to my junk mail? God I hate this. No privacy anymore," he thought. He decided to open it.

Without warning, there was a burst of red on his screen that rapidly turned to a white background. Next emerged the caricature of a head with a sad smile, the opposite of a happy face, with red paint dripping from a bald scalp, just like Eddie's. It was a dynamic portrayal. The features on the face became contorted and suddenly, the face began to scream and scream like the first wail of a hound caught in a steel leg trap, not knowing it was doomed to linger for days without food and water. But then, the screams became louder as the hound eventually realized he was finally to die; to become the meal of those who were watching and waiting, patiently, unfazed by his agony.

Eddie reached for the mouse and tried to turn off the sound. He failed; the scream and agony of the face became even worse as he pulled the charger plug from his laptop. Without AC power, the laptop went to battery back-up and the screaming continued. Eddie was terrified. Finally he turned the computer over and pulled out its battery. Only then did the horrific screech disappear in an instant.

Eddie spoke aloud, "Some bullshit Halloween prank. Probably those vandalous pricks. Good God! How did they get to my computer? I probably have a virus on this machine. I'll deal with it tomorrow. In the meantime, to the dungeon, I shall go to make those formaldehyde measurements whatever I will them to be."

Still shaken more that he cared to admit by the screaming e-mail, Eddie rose and started to walk to the door. He decided to take his Beretta out of his waist holster and leave it on his desk. He thought "I'll only be gone for a short time. Anyway, I'm going to put on my protective equipment and the gun won't be accessible. I don't want it exposed to those dammed chemical fumes. It's not a stainless steel model and the finish may corrode."

After a short walk that took him outside into the chilly autumn air, Eddie crossed a treed area to the north side of a free-standing building, about 80 by 100 feet in size. It was a metal building painted light gray. The perimeter lighting shadowed the vacant branches of nearby oak trees as they eerily danced across the side of the building. "How well suited for Halloween eve," he thought.

Eddie approached a well-lighted entrance to the bake-out building that he knew led to an inside staging area. He unlocked the outside door and turned on some lights, as he went in. Eddie had done this dozens of times before. From this room, he planned to enter an airlock that led to the bake-out, oven area inside. When he entered the staging room, he could feel the warmth of the air. At 130 degrees Fahrenheit in the bake-out oven room, even with R-30 insulation on the walls and R-60 on the ceiling, the staging room stood at an uncomfortable 85.

Eddie knew the drill. He planned to go into the oven chamber from the airlock, fully gowned wearing a white Tyvek "bunny suit" covering his entire body and shoes. He would wear gloves and a full face-mask respirator that was supplied air by a hose from an oil-less compressor. This pump would bring outside air into Eddie's mask while he stepped into the oven chamber to make his measurements. As usual, he planned to take in a direct reading instrument using PPT (Photoelectric Photometry Technology) to grab instantaneous formaldehyde measurements in the air. Eddie knew that the duration and temperature of bake-out, ventilation rates in the chamber and an assortment of other variables would determine when the product was ready to move on to Mavis and her crew.

All the calculations had been completed. He knew how to alter the instrument to make certain the "Mavis-ready" measurements were all under 10 ppm (parts per million) before the product would be released in the morning. So what if the levels were really 500, 1000 or even 5000, levels high enough to destroy and even pickle human tissue? Eddie didn't care. He would be safe making the measurements. He figured that a few more overexposures on the assembly line were acceptable causalities to make the deadline and keep the margins high.

Eddie entered the airlock through a large metal door fitted with a two foot by two foot, one inch thick, tempered glass window. He liked that window because, once inside, he could see out into the staging room. Others, who were in the staging room, could also look into the airlock to make certain the worker planning to enter the oven was OK.

There was an identical window in the door separating the air-lock from the oven room, where all the out-gassing plywood was located. When workers entered a "live" bake-out oven, Eddie knew that the SOP (Standard Operating Procedure) required two "buddies," with bunny suits, masks and air-paks, in the in the airlock, to watch over anyone entering the oven and to rescue them, if necessary.

Even if he could pay them to play the part, Eddie didn't need any buddies. He had entered a live oven before, alone, usually at night or on weekends on several previous occasions when he had special data needs. He wanted it that way, so he could fudge the measurements in peace.

Once inside the airlock, Eddie closed the windowed metal door to the staging area, discerning that mechanical ratchet sound that locked it. The door was air tight and impossible to open since the airlock was under negative pressure or a slight vacuum relative to the staging room. Only by pushing the red emergency plunger on the airlock side of the door or by moving the large red lever on the staging room side could someone reverse the process and allow entry or exit from the airlock.

Eddie was in. The airlock door was secure; so he donned all of his PPE (Personal Protective Equipment), turned on the airline supply compressor and opened the latched door to the oven area. He stepped into the oven.

Suddenly, Eddie heard the screaming e-mail. The sound was un-mistakable and the volume unbearable.

"E-e-e-e-e-a-h-h-h-h-h-h!.... e-e-e-e-e-a-h-h-h-h-h-h!.... e-e-e-e-e-a-h-h-h-h-h!

It was piecing his brain like an ice-pick.

Suddenly it stopped.

"It was coming over the emergency loudspeakers in all three

areas," he thought. He looked up at the speaker in the oven area where he was standing. Nothing. Well, maybe something, just a crackle.

"No; it's just my imagination," he agonized. "It can't be.

Eddie decided to abort. He reopened the door separating the oven from the airlock and stepped back into the airlock to take a look into the staging room. He could hear the hiss as the airlock atmosphere rushed into the oven. He closed the door and approached the staging room window. He looked through. Nothing; but an empty room basked in a sterile, blue-white fluorescent glow. While looking around the staging room, he heard the pumps kick on to bring fresh air back into the airlock. After the prescribed five minutes, he took off his protective hood. He glanced down at his direct reading formaldehyde meter that had grabbed a sample in the oven in the moment he had been inside. It's flashing red LED display immediately caught his attention.

"God, 10,420 ppm; that's high, even by my standards," he mused. "That Chinese stuff is really a killer. I'll have to figure out how to fudge my way out of this one before tomorrow."

Eddie looked through the window again into the staging area. Then he heard the pumps kick on again. The air was warmer than expected. It had a disturbing, slightly sweet smell to it, and it burned his nostrils and eyes, but just a little bit.

"I've done enough for tonight," he thought. "I'm going home."

Eddie looked around in the well-lighted airlock. Nothing was awry. Overhead he thought he heard the emergency loudspeaker crackle, again. Then nothing. The overhead fluorescent light flickered but maintained its brilliance. "Screw this; I better get out of this room. Those vandals may have messed with more than the instruments. Shit!"

He could feel an upchuck of panic come from within, slowly at first, then headed like a projectile into orbit.

Eddie spoke aloud, "God, man, get a hold of yourself. Nothing is wrong."

As he started to strip off his PPE, he heard the loudspeaker come abruptly to life. It could not have been more clear; the tenor-alto voice resonated in the room:

"A tisket, a tasket, a green and yellow basket; went to bed, then suddenly bled, through orifice and casket."

The macabre rhyme was followed by a loud "knuckle cracking" sound. The voice continued - like the cawing of a crow:

"Pay! Pay!
So not today... then when?
Too late! Too late!
Accept your fate... with no whining, much less debate.

Whiff! Whiff!
Inhale your gift... like fragrance to thousands, you forced to sniff.
Cry! Cry!
It is no lie... the aroma like lye, will burn and fry.
Die! Die!
Do not sigh... I will feed the need..... to report the scene that ends your greed."

The insane rhyme repeated and repeated and repeated ever louder.

Eddie began to perspire as he lunged for the red emergency plunger on the airlock side of the door. It collapsed as designed; but the door remained closed and locked.

The air was becoming warmer and thicker. He started to choke and cough, just a little at first. As sweat poured into his eyes, he could feel his tongue begin to swell. He grabbed his shirt and put it over his mouth and nose. No use.

He lifted his respirator and put it over his face. No use. The offending smell was coming through his mask.

Eddie pressed his face to the window, only inches from the smile on the other side of the glass.

The smile was worn by a tall, lanky figure, dressed entirely in black. The visage stepped back, but Eddie couldn't make out the figure's face hidden behind a darkened veil.

Eddie saw the creature lift what appeared to be a remote control with an LED display. The numbers and letters on the display were illuminated in bright red; Funny, he thought, it flashes just like mine.

Through his tears, Eddie could see "250 ppm"

With black gloves, inches from the window, Eddie watched ghastly fingers push, a "5" followed by three zeros.

Eddie heard the pumps kick on abruptly again and heard a hiss of air entering the airlock through his respirator. He tried to bend the hose to stop the flow; then realized the foul air was also emerging into the airlock through the vents in the wall.

Three minutes elapsed.

Eddie began to bang on the glass, feeling around for anything he could use to break it. Now blinded, groping, he managed to find a small brass valve assembly left behind on a changing bench set against the far wall.

He hoisted it above his head and brought it down on the door, missing the glass entirely. He kept banging and banging, now with real tears mixed into those formed by the blistering effects of formaldehyde on his corneas.

Eddie realized his miss. He felt for the glass with his burning fingertips and aimed again. This time a direct hit; completely without effect on the one inch tempered glass.

Eddie now realized he was going to die.....horribly.

His lungs began to scream with pain and fill with fluid. He closed his eyes and held his breath as he felt the skin on his face begin to peel away.

The time for panic had passed. He was like a fish out of water, frying in a skillet.

Five minutes passed.

The figure decided it was time to reprogram the remote control for the coup de grâce.

Poor Eddie missed it. He was on the floor, when the fiend, punched in a "1" followed by a "0," a "4," a "2," and another "0."

Two minutes later, the ghoul peered through the glass at Eddie's lifeless body on the floor of the airlock, his eyes, nose, mouth and skin awash in his blood, not unlike death by Ebola.

Within seconds, a delicate little bell on the remote sounded; and the LED display flashed the final equilibrium reading of 10,420 ppm.

What precision...it matched the reading on Eddie's meter that had fallen a few inches from his left knee.

The figure smiled as he watched both meters flash in perfect unison. Looks just like the beating of a heart, he thought. Maybe next time; yes, definitely, next time.

CHAPTER 34 -
CANINE CRISIS AND
REDEMPTION

DATE: Friday 12/17/10 - About five years
three and one half months after Katrina
LOCATION: Baton Rouge, Louisiana

—   —   —

"He's dead; my God he's dead!" she wept inconsolably. It had been
three days; and she still couldn't stop weeping, coughing and whimpering. No sleep, no food, no rest. She knew she had to get control of
herself. She was utterly dysfunctional. He was just a dog - not a human,
loved one or friend. But she couldn't help it at all. A wave of emotion and
guilt came over her - especially under the current circumstances. The
next several years were completely mapped out. He wouldn't have been
alone anymore. He would have long awaited company - but not now,
not ever - not since he bounced off the right front bumper of some car
going 25 miles per hour. The driver probably never even saw him. He
probably just heard a thud - never even stopped. One witness called the
police; but without a license number, they couldn't do very much; and
besides, they were too busy with real crime and other violations of civil
order. He died after about 10 minutes. Fortunately, he lost consciousness, probably from the loss of blood.

"It almost all worked out. Now what are we going to do?" she sobbed.

—   —   —

Almost four and a half years, she thought. Four and a half years since
that summer day in 2006. Now it was mid-December, 2010. She still

had the crumpled piece of paper with two clearly marked names and telephone numbers, written directly below that photograph, the one that had caused her to spill her coffee and almost throw up - almost four and a half years ago. It was safely put away in the top drawer of her bedroom dresser. She had never told George about it. She never told anyone about it. It was her secret. She always worried though, whether anyone had seen her take the photo off that SPCA bulletin board in the municipal water building in New Orleans and stick it in her left breast pocket, right over her heart.

Back then, Sgt. Melanie Hatfield knew at once, from the moment she glanced at the familiar markings on the pooch in the photo. The dog in the picture was the stray she had adopted or actually, appropriated. It was a picture of her dog - but not really her dog.

Instead, this dog was someone else's lost pet that she claimed for her own, a treasure she had found lying half dead by that soaked parish canal road. But she rationalized, Dumbo <u>was</u> hers. When she had first seen the bulletin board picture, over 10 grueling months had already elapsed since she had saved him, since she had begun to love and nurture him. Over 10 months has slipped by since he had gone lost, the night after a living hell, named Katrina, had visited the earth.

Only three times in the past four and a half years had she pulled the picture of Dumbo out of her dresser drawer and looked at it to be sure. The last time was over a year ago and now she was about to do it again - but for a different reason, one that was way overdue.

The last time she looked at the photo, she had stood there, standing above the dresser drawer, continuing to think - there was no doubt about it; her Dumbo was someone else's dog. Marked on the photo, she knew his real name was "Rambo." When Melanie had found him, she had been unable to read the first two worn letters on his name tag, the "R" and "a." She could clearly see the last three were "..mbo." So in honor of the dog's large floppy ears and her favorite childhood cartoon character, she decided to add a "Du..." to the "...mbo" and name him, Dumbo. Kind of a silly name she thought; even sillier when one considered that it was the name of a dog owned by a tough Louisiana

National Guard Sergeant - but it made her smile, the only thing that mattered at the time.

For four and a half years, Melanie kept rationalizing why she never called those phone numbers on the paper, below the photograph. One was written below the name of some doctor and the other below someone named, Simon Williams (age 11), as it was printed in ink. On those three occasions since 2006, when she had looked, Melanie became riddled with guilt for hours, sometimes, days; but she did nothing. She could have called that doctor. Her name, printed as, Dr. Patricia (Dr. Pat) Simms, was right there, right there in clear English, above her cell number.

Melanie puzzled about the relationship between Simon and this Dr. Pat. Was Dr. Pat Simon's mother or what? She had no idea. None of this mattered. Both might have moved away, anyway, and forgotten about Rambo/Dumbo or whatever you want to call him.

Then, like a dunked tennis ball, it surfaced again. She forced her nose into the reality of the situation; bottom line - she had kept Simon's pet and had not even tried to call him.

Now over 30 years old, in mid-December 2010, Melanie stood above her dresser still thinking, preparing to look at the picture once again. This time she had a plan - born from the tragedy that just occurred. But first, she felt the need to rehash what had transpired over the past four and one half years.

The Thanksgiving holiday was over. In early November, she had taken her middle school students on a field trip to the Audubon Butterfly Garden and Insectarium in New Orleans. Everything went as planned. The buses picked up the kids one morning early and took them on the approximately two hour drive south from Baton Rouge to the Big Easy. The kids in her 8th grade science class had been ecstatic about a chance to cut their other classes and go see a bunch of termites, butterflies and giant spiders. Of course, living in Louisiana afforded them the opportunity to see bugs that were bigger and scarier than any housed in the museum. The joke was that the critters in the museum were trying to break out to roam the bayou because the food was better.

Since the summer of 2006, when Melanie was Sgt. Melanie Hatfield, she had led a quiet, fairly inconspicuous, very happy life. After returning from her Katrina duty, she remained active in the guard until the summer of 2009 when she broke her ankle during an Advanced Individual Training session with the army at Fort Benning, Georgia. It was a bad break that occurred when she jumped from an obstacle wall and landed on a rock, hitting her heel and rolling her ankle at the same time. This type of injury wasn't supposed to happen - so she thought. Next time, although there was never to be a next time, she vowed to lace her boots more tightly.

Melanie's career as a science teacher had rocketed upward in every way. Her students at Lookout Middle School in Prairieville knew that she had been a soldier who had served during Katrina with dignity and honor. Her classroom lectures and lesson plans had been audited and reviewed several times; and on each occasion, she earned the highest marks. She loved teaching astronomy to her students; but found that the not infrequent cloudy evenings in Louisiana, coupled with the humidity and increasing amounts of light pollution near town, stifled her efforts to see anything but the moon, Jupiter, Mars, Venus and Saturn.

Other celestial objects were harder to see, especially the fainter nebulae that under better conditions could be normally picked up with the school's one and only Celestron 8" Schmidt-Cassegrain telescope. Keeping astronomy an important part of her curriculum; but as less of a hands-on subject, she turned her attention to the natural sciences, where outdoor Louisiana was a paradise on earth.

Bear, deer, cougar, alligators, frogs, lizards and many other creatures God decided to make were there in abundance. Plant after plant - too many to name, much less to learn - but Melanie's students did learn all they could absorb; and she soon gained a reputation as one of the best middle school science teachers in the entire state of Louisiana.

She became a teaching superstar. Often Melanie took a few students outside on the school grounds during lunch break for a walk along the small creek next to the parking lot. Like magic, her classroom was recreated in green, brown, red, yellow and blue splendor. The kids loved it.

On some of those occasions, while exploring nature on the school grounds, she brought Dumbo. He made a much bigger hit than the flora and fauna. He ran from kid to kid, seeking pats, scratches and belly rubs. His energy spread joy to the learning process, especially when he would try to catch a frog and fall into the creek. Melanie and Dumbo formed a tightly knit pair, and the students sensed it. No one had any idea that Dumbo, perhaps, could have been reunited with his real owner, someone named, Simon or even another person named, Dr. Pat, early on, if Melanie had only tried to find either of them.

For about a year after Katrina, during her tour in New Orleans, Melanie was courted by fellow guardsman, Corporal George Michaels. She had known George before Katrina. He was a veterinarian's assistant at Best Pets near Baton Rouge and had treated Melanie's dog, Sammy, before the storm hit. While on duty in the first few days after Katrina, Melanie fortunately located George in her unit, when she had radioed that she was bringing in a badly injured canine she had found by the roadside with her partner, Cpl. Troy Ashton.

Melanie and Ashton had been on patrol for looters, right after the storm had hit. Had Ashton had his way, he would have put a bullet into the poor pooch, already a canine victim of violence, suffering from a gunshot wound to his right hind leg when they found him, next to the sewer infested flood waters. Luckily, Melanie pulled rank, had Ashton stand down and got him to help her bring the dog back to their base - against regulations.

Once there, George examined the nearly lifeless animal and then persuaded their medical officer, Dr. David Lowe, to lend him wound cleaning solution and a suture kit. Lowe pushed the envelope even further; so George gave the dog some IV fluids for several hours on the first day. Melanie cared for the dog like he was a fellow soldier. Within seven days, the dog was up and about, frolicking and eating as if nothing had even happened.

Dumbo, as she named him, lived, prospered and grew to be loved by all whom he entertained with his antics, fetching, running and licking every hand in sight. Everybody in her entire unit, with exception of only one or two devoted cat lovers, liked having Dumbo around. When he played, he broke the monotony and reminded many of their own dogs at home. Everyone knew, however, that their mascot, Dumbo, belonged to Sgt. Melanie Hatfield, with George Michaels, a distant back-up.

Over the 10 months she served in New Orleans, Melanie's parents took care of Sammy, the dog, she left behind, at their house in Baton Rouge. When Melanie brought Dumbo "back from the hurricane," he got along with Sammy, right from the start. Dogless at the time, George offered nothing to the trio except himself. Melanie, Sammy and Dumbo let George into their closely guarded circle. In no time at all, George concluded he had better propose to Melanie, or lose three good friends - so he did, in June; and they were married in August of 2007. In many ways, Dumbo and Sammy were the glue that kept Melanie's bond with George so pure and so tight.

When Melanie returned from Katrina duty in 2006, Sammy was already ten years old. He was in good health at the time, and her parents had taken good care of him while she was gone. One evening in the latter part of October 2007, about two months after she and George were married, Melanie was cleaning off Sammy's muddy feet when she noticed an almond shaped lump on his right foreleg. She showed it to George. He told her to sit down for a second while he examined the lesion and the rest of Sammy's leg. When he finished, he looked a bit ashen. He told Melanie he wanted to take Sammy into the veterinarian's office to have him examined by Dr. Fox and have an x-ray taken. At the time, he didn't tell Melanie his educated diagnosis was that Sammy had a small osteosarcoma on his leg. An osteosarcoma is an aggressively malignant, sometimes painful, bone cancer that is seen not uncommonly in older dogs. Unfortunately, George was correct. Closer examination by Dr. Fox revealed two other bone lesions and several metastases to Sammy's lungs. The poor dog was doomed. There was no good treatment, much less a cost-effective one. Melanie agonized over Sammy's condition. She had had Sammy since she was 17 and now she was going to lose him.

For the next two months, Melanie and George cogitated and calculated. They contacted no fewer that four professors of veterinary oncology and had Sammy seen by two specialists at about $800 per consultation. The conclusion was unanimous; enjoy him while you have him; keep him well nourished, hydrated, out of pain and prepare for the worst. Just after the New Year, while Melanie and George held Sammy tight, Dr. Fox administered the deadly intravenous cocktail. Looking directly at his friends, Sammy's eyes glazed over; then he went to sleep forever.

When Melanie first brought Dumbo in for an exam in the fall of 2006, Dr. Fox estimated Dumbo's age to be about three. He was a virile, blue healer mixed breed. Dr. Fox said that she had rarely seen such a characteristic marking on the head and snout of a dog before - a pure white diamond. After Sammy's demise, Dumbo appeared depressed, or, at least, what humans would project his behavior to be. He moped around the house and actually soiled the carpet a couple of times when he wasn't let outside fast enough. He kept sniffing around Sammy's now empty dog bed, over and over again, probably wondering when his pal was going to return home. This behavior continued for weeks. Melanie threw out all the toys and bedding both dogs had shared; and after another couple of months, matters started to improve. Within six months, Dumbo's behavior normalized to one at least three octaves below what it had been when both dogs had enjoyed life together. Melanie and George talked about getting a puppy to replace Sammy; but decided that "Sammy reborn" was a bad idea for the foreseeable future.

— — —

The next four years were good to Melanie and George. Melanie's career continued to blossom. She was now over 30 and George was 31.

Before she got any older, Melanie thought she might consider beginning some coursework at LSU that would lead to her master's degree in a couple of years. George took continuing education courses every year to improve his skills in veterinary medicine. They just didn't get around to having a baby or another dog. Dumbo was all they needed or wanted - until the summer of 2010.

Late one Saturday evening, in early September, while Melanie and George were preparing to make some popcorn and watch a movie, George suddenly broke into a magnificent, enthusiastic smile and said quietly, "I've got some news that should cheer you up - but I won't bet on it yet."

"You've got what?" answered Melanie, trying to emulate her husband's enthusiasm, although she had no idea what he was so happy about.

"We're gonna have puppies!" he shouted.

"But we're not pregnant!" responded Melanie, trying to be funny."

"No, no, you silly lady," Dumbo's going to have puppies - he's going to be a Dad. I mean not yet - not for about seven weeks. He's still a stud you know."

Whadda you mean, George?" asked Melanie.

"I guess I'll have to remind you about the birds and the bees, although that doesn't seem to be our problem - so here goes," kidded George.

"Melanie, do you know the Hogans, about two blocks down on the right, this side of the street, you know, the ones who bring their kids by each year to "Trick or Treat?"

"I think so - oh, wait, I think her name is Audrey; I can't remember his or the kids," she responded.

"In any case, Mel, for the past eight months, the Hogans have had this two year old Blue Healer mixed breed female, looks just like Dumbo without the white diamond - except that this canine lady has ears that stand erect more like the characteristics of the breed. The dog was a gift, if you want to call her that, from Audrey's grandfather who lives out near Denham Springs. Well, they named her Alice. So

Miss Alice is kept in the Hogans' fenced backyard, not a big yard; but enough to give her a little exercise. Get the drift - Miss Alice is not spayed. Audrey's grandfather didn't think it was necessary and didn't want to spend the money; Audrey and her husband hadn't gotten around to it, yet."

"Roger, I seem to recall," added Melanie, "Go on; George, the dots are connecting before my eyes," as she raised her eyebrows. "Can they sue Dumbo for paternity benefits, in this parish, I wonder?"

"OK, OK - so I let him out of the house while you were gone. I didn't know there was a bitch in heat down the street - wait, that didn't sound very good, sorry," whined George. "I went looking around for Dumbo and heard some commotion over near the Hogan's house. Your dog - went roaming and was caught in the act with Alice; I might add, for over a half hour, because they couldn't get the two lovers apart."

"Oh - so now it's 'my dog!'" belted Melanie.

George continued, "I went to the side of the Hogan's house and could see the two lovers stuck together. By now, Audrey saw me. I quickly introduced myself and apologized. She was great about it; in fact she said that she had been thinking about having an "Alice" litter, that is, a more carefully planned one, so that she could give a puppy to her grandparents and a few other relatives. It's too bizarre an act of fate- don't get mad; but I told her, subject to your approval, of course, that I wanted pick of the litter as a stud fee!"

Melanie laughed - "Well, George, you're the one with the balls, OK! It's a good thing she didn't have Dumbo picked up for trespass."

"I've kept this quiet until we knew that Alice was pregnant. I found out today - no pregnancy test needed. The pups are due in about six weeks. If you want to, we can have a new Sammy or younger Dumbo or whatever, ready for adoption right around Christmas, when the pups are weaned."

Melanie looked at George for several seconds. With a thin smile on her lips; but looking like she was in physical pain, tears began to roll from both eyes onto her cheeks, then to the floor. George bent over to give her some tissue from a box on the table. While he stood there, Melanie quietly wept, turned and left the room.

George suddenly was overcome with guilt for this escapade. For the past two years, in addition to his vet assistant job, George had volunteered twice a month at the local parish humane society, where he helped run the adoption screening program. During this time, he had seen plenty of dogs he would have loved to have taken home to surprise Melanie - but the timing was just not right.

Now this mess happened. He usually kept Dumbo in their small, fenced backyard - so the gate latch was loose and he escaped to do what dogs are supposed to do. Big deal! It was careless - but he saw a way to make situation emerge as a "win-win" for everyone.

George worried as usual. Something about Dumbo was eating Melanie since Sammy's death; but he just couldn't put his finger on the problem. He knew what Dumbo meant to her, and he knew how much Sammy had meant to Dumbo. Dogs like most other pets love to have company. He knew it; Melanie knew it and Dumbo knew it - but every time he thought about adding that second pooch, he stopped, figuring that he had better not make such a decision without Melanie's full consent. Now the situation couldn't be better - they had a chance to adopt one of Dumbo's own offspring - preferably a male they could have neutered - then it would be father and son, as Dumbo moved into old age.

Melanie came back into the room - "I like the idea; it's about time we got some company for Dumbo," she said as she went over to give George a hug. "I like that Audrey Hogan; I'll make sure that Dumbo's gal stays in good shape. I guess Alice should have her litter in late October. I'm actually excited about this unplanned pregnancy - and we get the pick of the litter too. I want a Dumbo, Jr."

George replied, "Good choice - I agree; another stud in the family - but this one will unfortunately end up as a eunuch, so he won't roam the neighborhood knocking up other willing partners."

— — —

The next six weeks were a really busy time for Melanie and George. School was in full swing. Melanie had meetings after school, assignments to grade, and all the other time consuming activities for which teachers are not compensated, unless you're not counting the appreciation she steadily received from her students. George, who now functioned as capably as most veterinarians, remained hard at work at Best Pets. He and Melanie visited Dumbo's mate, Alice, over at the Hogan's house about twice a week. George made certain to bring over some special feed, especially formulated for bitches about to whelp. He helped the Hogans build a sort of birthing corral out of plywood, lined with plastic and filled with clean pine wood chips, ready to be put together quickly when Alice was ready to nest.

The day finally came, the third week of October. A couple of hours after dinner, Melanie and George received a call from Audrey - the birth was in progress. They put Dumbo in the backyard and trotted down the block to see the miracle in its full splendor. There it was. Before their very eyes, Alice gave birth to six puppies, one after the other over a two hour period. No problems. She bit the cord, ate the afterbirth and licked each puppy clean. The puppies started to nurse, all but two.

About eight inches from Alice's right hind leg, squirmed a tiny female. She was all black and looked like she was struggling to breathe. George examined the pup and moved her closer to one of Alice's teats. She barely made the suckling motions; she was obviously in some distress. Alice was busy with her other pups; but turned around without getting up and started to lick the little pup very vigorously. She also grabbed the other wayward pup, gently with her teeth and rolled him over to stimulate him like his sister. Both Melanie and George's jaws dropped simultaneously. When the other pup was rolled over, partially on its back, they could see that it was a male. They couldn't see for certain; but the ears were deformed. When Alice rolled the little guy over, Melanie burst into tears.

There before her; was one of Dumbo's sons; if she didn't know better, he was a clone of Dumbo. Unbelievable. The pup was gray/

black and had a large white diamond centered on his head - a stunning contrast, spotted in an instant. But what really blew their minds were the pup's ears - like two beagle ears - that didn't really belong - but there they were. Alice rolled the male and female stragglers over twice with her licking and watched as both finally became oriented. The need for nourishment prevailed. George still worried about the female - he knew she still wasn't breathing normally - but there wasn't much he could do about it at the moment.

Later that evening, Melanie and George went home and found Dumbo in the backyard trying to dig out under their chain link fence. He was covered in dirt, bad enough on his muzzle to cover half of the illustrious white diamond he had bestowed upon one of his pups. They brought him in, cleaned him up and gave him four of his favorite duck breast treats while they poured each other a little wine.

"Here's a toast to Dumbo, Jr. - that's the pup I want," cried Melanie.

"He's our pick of the litter," answered George, as he emptied half his glass. "Wait until I tell Dr. Fox. She cared for Sammy in his last weeks; now we'll have her take a look at Dumbo, Jr. in a few weeks. She'll spend hours trying to figure out the genetics of the ears and the diamond marking - she'll think we really cloned our dog."

—   —   —

Now it was mid-December - three days after Dumbo was struck by a car in front of the Hogan's house. Earlier on the evening of the tragedy, after escaping from Melanie's yard, Dumbo had made it to the Hogan's where he dug into their enclosure to visit his mate, Alice, and their puppies. When he saw Mr. Hogan, he skedaddled out of the pen, headed for home; but veered into the street and was struck by a car head on - struck by a driver who never stopped, was never apprehended nor held accountable, or exonerated, for that matter. After all, it was just a stupid dog that paid the price for stupidity.

Dumbo never had a chance. Hogan saw him lying there bleeding to death - shattered like a dropped light bulb. Besides himself, he called Melanie and George to give them the bad news. They both sprinted to the scene, Melanie hobbling along on her bad ankle. Everyone decompensated, especially, Melanie. They took Dumbo's broken and bloody body to Dr. Fox's office. They decided to have him cremated; and Dr. Fox said that she would take care of everything. They suffered and cried; but the pain would not go away.

Her mind was racing. How could this be? It was only a week and a half before they were scheduled to bring home Dumbo, Jr. - "the clone" they called him, who had grown like a weed over the past eight weeks. She still wanted him with all of her heart; but without Dumbo there to help raise him, their home would never glow with the brightness she anticipated and expected.

Melanie stood in front of her dresser, fingering the knob on the small drawer containing the manila envelope that protected the piece of paper on which was attached a photo of Dumbo and the names and contact phone numbers of his original family. The paper was really a very simple plea for help from a little boy and a doctor, asking "Have you seen my dog?" - the plea she ignored for four and a half years. Now she knew why she had saved this message - but it didn't make it any easier. She had a chance here; but more ashamed and ambivalent than ever, she choked on her thoughts - not because she lacked the resolve to redeem herself; but because she was afraid to face the music, the correct but dreaded decision that was the prerequisite to mental salvation, restful sleep, and the hopeful elimination of her burden of guilt.

Suddenly, the magic that defined much of her life jolted her and set her course straight like a child replacing a derailed toy train car back on its track.

For the first time in over a year; but now with an entirely different intention, Melanie opened the top drawer and took out the box - the box containing the old faded picture of the lost dog, named Rambo, the dog she was now certain had been Dumbo - the picture mounted on crumpled paper with the name and phone numbers of Simon Williams (age 11) and Dr. Patricia (Dr. Pat) Simms.

Now, without the slightest hesitation, with conviction and without fear that she would be ridiculed, berated or called insane, she reached for the phone and dialed Dr. Pat's cell number, reasoning there was a better chance that her number remained unchanged compared to Simon's. She was exactly right.

—　　—　　—

She dialed.

It was after business hours. It rang three times

"Hello, this is Dr. Patricia Simms. To whom am I speaking, please; and how may I help you?" the voice at the other end answered.

"Doctor, you don't know me. My name is Melanie Hatfield-Michaels. I live in Baton Rouge, where I am a middle school science teacher. You will not believe what I have to say. Please do not be angry with me - but I obtained your phone number from a lost pet bulletin board put up by the SPCA in Orleans Parish, in the summer of 2006. I was a guardsman working in the building, at the food bank. Your number was below the photo."

Immediately losing her professional air of sincerity, responding somewhat sarcastically, and acting like she was expecting the call, Dr. Pat snapped, "OK - so why are you calling me now, over four years later?"

"Doctor.....I....I....am so-o-o sorry," pleaded Melanie, as she completely lost it and broke down into uncontrollable sobs. "You don't understand."

Dr. Pat cut her off immediately, balancing her physician born compassion for someone who was obviously hurting so badly, with her righteously indignant desire to smack her face. "You have him; don't you....don't you?"

"Yes - I-I mean, no. I don't. He's dead, killed three days ago by a hit and run driver here in Baton Rouge."

"Dead! Dead! So why are you calling me now - to make matters worse? Are you certain it's the same dog?" screamed Dr. Pat.

"I am sure....I am sure." wept Melanie.

"I knew this would happen," said Pat, displaying even greater exasperation. "I went back to the bulletin board and found the picture missing about two weeks after it was posted. I assumed that someone had taken it and planned to call. No call. No nothing."

Pat continued her roar, "Do you have any idea how badly Simon Williams, the little boy who lost Rambo, has suffered? He still believes in his heart that his dog is alive somewhere and will come home one day."

Melanie responded, "I can't even imagine the pain I have caused him. I am so very sorry."

Melanie was about to continue - but stopped short of the thought nearly falling off the tip of her tongue. Instead, she proceeded to tell Dr. Pat the whole story of her finding Rambo, caring for him, his "sort of" adoption by her National Guard unit and her taking him back with her to Baton Rouge, where he had been living a very good life with her, George and Sammy, before he died. She started to go on but stopped again.

"Doctor, really I'm calling because...because I...I want to see Simon and you to try to make things better. I know I should have called. I fell in love with Dumbo...er...Rambo after I saved his life. He would not have made it without my help and determination to keep him alive and the medical assistance of my husband, who is a very skillful vet assistant."

Dr. Pat, rebuked her. "I don't see how. It's too little too late. I appreciate your call. I've got your name and number. But, I don't think we should talk again. I don't want you to contact Simon under any circumstances. I would prefer to keep things as they are, rather than break his heart completely in two. To know that someone like you had it within your power to call, at least to see if it was Simon's dog. It's so shameful. It's so downright cruel. We need to say goodbye."

"Dr. Simms, I will respect your request that I don't contact Simon. I want to make things right, even though I know that it's probably too late. I'm just up here in Baton Rouge. Maybe you might reconsider. Please let me know." Melanie pleaded even harder.

"I doubt it, Ms. Hatfield - Micha..., um....whatever." Simon's 14 now; he's still very vulnerable. There is no telling how he will take this story of yours. It's a good thing - he's such a gentle soul."

"Look, Dr. Simms; please." Melanie persisted, still not certain what to do; but noting ever so slightly a hint of softening in Dr. Pat's voice. She jumped at the chance. "Christmas is next week. I thought something good could come of it."

Realizing suddenly that she sounded like a wishful fool, Melanie felt the impulse to say more, much more - but stopped. She was still paralyzed by ambivalence - not because she had called and reached out; but because she did not quite have the commitment to fully repair the situation.

Dr. Pat responded, calmly, "OK, Melanie, what do you propose?"

"I don't quite know," lamented Melanie, now controlling her tears a bit better. "There is really no way to make this up to Simon and you, except to see you both in person and tell you how sorry I am. It's my fault entirely."

There was a long, silent, painful pause.

"I'll tell you what, Ms. Hatfield-Michaels, said Dr. Pat, checking Melanie's name in her notes, "A few of us are getting together at "Pegleg's Barrelhead" a restaurant in New Orleans at 6 PM on Christmas Eve. You are invited - only you. Simon, his brother and his Mom and Dad will be there, along with their lawyer, a young lady.

Also coming is a close doctor friend of mine, from Wyoming, named Tristan Baines. I think Tristan is also bringing a friend. Come to think about it, your sincere contrition could be an important Christmas present for Simon. He is growing up fast and sees so much that is negative in his life. Your stepping to the plate with accountability and apology may help him to see the brighter side of your darker self that allowed you to be so cruel and inconsiderate."

Melanie hesitated, still ambivalent, not about her gratitude for the invitation, but, instead, about exactly what to say next. "Dr. Simms. Thank you so very much. My husband will drive me down to New

Orleans, and I will be there. I promise to make Simon's Christmas the best one he has had since he lost Rambo. I hope both of you will find it in your hearts to forgive me."

"You have my number; see you then," replied Dr. Pat, flatly. Then, she added, more softly, "Melanie, I am trying to understand. It did take guts to finally make the call. I appreciate it - somehow, I have always known it was coming. I look forward to seeing you on Christmas Eve. Feel free to bring your husband in. Goodbye."

Melanie hung up, coughed, and then broke down again, with an outpouring of tears. The elephant was off her chest; but the monkey was still on her back.

Minutes later, Pat called Tristan and explained what had just happened.

"So, she finally called," exclaimed Tristan. "We've had suspicions about our good ex-Guardsman for about three months, now. After I promised Simon, I would look into finding Rambo, if he was still alive, I came up with very little for months. The trail had gone cold until just recently. Joseph ended up costing me plenty to track this lady down. He was going to confirm that she had the dog and confront her very soon. We were hoping we could buy Rambo from her and return him to Simon as an overdue Christmas present."

"God, Tristan, you could have told me. I was so shocked by her, uh, Melanie's phone call."

"We didn't know for sure, Pat. I am really sorry. I really didn't expect her to call you. I didn't think she still had your phone number."

"Tristan, did you say you planned to try to buy Rambo from her?"

"If possible," Tristan responded.

"You can't!" continued Dr. Pat. "She told me that Rambo was killed three days ago by a hit and run driver."

"What?" cried Tristan. "God, I've got to call Joseph now. What happened? A hit and run? Is that all you know?"

"She is grief stricken herself, Tristan," returned Pat. "Despite what she did, I feel sorry for her. She wants to meet Simon and tell him the whole story. I don't see how she has the guts to face him.

You know, on second thought, Simon's meeting her might be a very bad idea. I shouldn't have made the offer. Oh God, I told her where we'd be having a Christmas Eve party."

"Wait, Pat; I have an idea," said Tristan. "Look, I'm heading to New Orleans a couple of days before the dinner. I'll need to check with Sethie to see if it's OK; but I propose that Joseph and I scour the shelters for a few days and try to find good looking mutt to give to Simon at the party, whether this, Melanie shows or not.

Now that I think about it; I agree, completely. I think we should call her off. We shouldn't even tell Sethie about this; and I can't let Simon's heart break twice. I'm not sure he can take it."

"I'll call Melanie back and explain. We don't want her to come, period. The rest sounds like a plan, Tristan; a good, warm hearted plan. And I forgive you for blindsiding me. I guess you didn't mean it. And anyway, you're a good man, Tristan Baines," ended Pat.

"I'll let you know what happens. Now I've got to get a hold of Sethie and Joseph," said Tristan, feeling her compliment flow warmly into his ears. "I don't deserve it," he thought. "I should have called her weeks ago."

Tristan called Joseph and gave him the heads up. He told him that Pat was going to cancel Melanie's visit to meet the family. God, what a bad idea to begin with. Getting Simon a pup for Christmas; now that was a different story. He hoped Sethie would agree.

Well, it didn't work out at all. Tristan contacted Sethie, and she stood firm. No dog! The whole matter was in the past, she reasoned; and besides, she said, Simon would probably not settle for any dog but Rambo. End of story.

Tristan was really crushed. He had made a promise to Simon; one that he would not be able to keep. He decided that telling Sethie the entire Sgt. Melanie story would be better saved for another time; telling Simon was out of the question, probably ever.

He had another week to think about a plan to make Simon smile. Tristan unexpectedly felt some tears well up in his eyes.

He didn't like to break promises.

CHAPTER 35 - MURDER AND STING

DATE: Friday 12/24/10, Christmas Eve - About five years four months after Katrina
LOCATION: Alton, Illinois; Louisville, Kentucky; St. Louis, Missouri; Warburg, Kentucky;

— — —

8:30 am (CADIXX Operations Annex, off state highway 100, north of Alton, Illinois):

Gordon A. Gasher (GAG) twitched his neck as he sat uncomfortably close to Leon Marbury, Senior Vice President at CADIXX in charge of the Alton incinerator operations. Leon also had discretionary authority over CADIXX waste transportation and disposal activities when trucking originated at the incinerator.

"Gordon, we've known about this investigation for over four months," rasped Leon, getting over a two week long cold, struggling to find some comfort in spite of the tie around his neck. Somehow the tie seemed to be getting tighter, either in his imagination or based upon the reality of the FBI investigation, he and his cronies had been facing.

"I've been out for four of the past five days, and our people tell me we've got to move fast to turn over what we have about our Alabama dumping destinations or else. You know how these people can operate, Gordon. They show no mercy. They will eventually get what they want. Frankly, I don't want to be a casualty of this investigation and go to jail for what those idiot drivers have been dumping down on some redneck's farm.

I've got three lawyers working on this and to a person, they warn me to give the feds a lot of useless material, tons of it to slow them down and to turn over the incriminating crap to their law firm. They will call it privileged, or it will end up as vapor and ashes flying over the St. Louis arch. One of the newly minted lawyers was corrupted so fast she already sounded like the big shots. She suggested sending the feds our petty cash records if it could delay them by five minutes. God, Gordon, I'm scared. I'm not a good liar.... I think....."

GAG interrupted with a vicious snarl, "Leon, you sack of shit; are you through? I'm not going to sit here and hold your hand, analyzing, when to cooperate and when not to cooperate with some dickheads at the FBI."

Taken aback, appearing uneasy at the abrupt interruption, Marbury suddenly noticed GAG's clothing. GAG was dressed in tan 5.11 outdoor tactical pants, a green L.L. Bean hunting shirt and some Bean hiking boots. It was the black concealed carry vest that caught Leon's attention. He looked like he was going camping or hunting; but Leon uncomfortably contemplated it was too cold to camp and too late to hunt. GAG sat at the head of a large conference table with his back to the PowerPoint screen and the gray fabric wall around it. Marbury stood to his left about four feet away.

"The bottom line, Leon. Uh – will you sit your ass in a chair already?" GAG continued, with anger still in his voice. Marbury complied, sitting two chairs away.

"There is much more to this than just dumping some toxic shit in a swamp in Dixie. You understand, don't you – even if we try to control what the feds get their hands on, there may still be enough there to get all of us slowly and tortuously murdered, not just sent to jail. And it won't be government that does us in.

It's like this Leon - Momma and the General have already vetted each one of us, and they feel comfortable none of us will talk - all except you, Leon. Your thoughts, old friend?"

Silence.

"What's the matter, cat's got your tongue?" GAG continued, now with a smirk on his face. Without warning GAG turned his neck left and then back to the right, using his left hand to hyper-rotate his head. Marbury ignored the loud crunch of cartilage popping.

"Gordon, what in the hell are you talking about?" gasped Leon, as he now reached up to loosen his tie and collar, now soaked with perspiration, not from any lingering fever.

"I'm reliable, Gordon I know what it means to shut-up. But you know the deal - We charge customers full boat to pick up, transport and dump the waste. We save 80% by dumping some of it on a cracker's back 40. The stupid hillbilly kicks back 5% to the driver. We know about it. We let the driver keep it - it'll go to good use for more booze, pills and truck stop girls. Our drivers have been ripping us off for years, and we don't care as long as they get the job done. Anyway, we adjust what we pay the damned fools. We pay in cash; but the feds might still get us on money laundering or racketeering; I don't know which. Frankly, I'm more worried about the state authorities and the EPA.

By the way, I thought we paid off some of those assholes. Weren't your buddies in The Resistance taking care of..."

"Shut-up, Leon! I've warned you before. Never and I repeat NEVER ever let those words fall from your stupid lips," bellowed GAG. "If you ever come close, again, I will cut out your tongue, dice it into tiny pieces and feed it back to you mixed in macaroni and cheese, through a stomach tube."

"Gordon, you just brought it up," Leon whined. "What's with all this bullshit, anyway? Whoever they are, Momma, the General - this is idiotic - what are you, some secret fraternal order like the Freemasons or the Rosicrucians, playing like children? What is this bullshit, Gordon? 'Momma, don't let yur babies grow up to be cowboys...' What is it I heard from one of the higher ups in 'Da Resistance,' Gordon? You're the head 'Enforcer!' Jesus, it sounds like a 70's TV show!"

GAG leaned forward and gently pushed his chair away from the table.

Leon was on a roll. "And you know; Gordon, I never did want to give any money to that Legal Defense Fund, LDF, whatever, you call it. Even though they supposedly keep, the…the, sorry, the "R" word, going. Shit, I'm not sure how effective that fund is, anyway.

We've still been nailed several times, including back in '06 when that asshole, Baines cost us a bundle. You were supposed to get him to retract his testimony. Didn't you tell him you would pay him 25 grand to "re-do" his numbers? And look what happens; he goes in there, testifies we have been poisoning 600 neighboring families for the past two decades; and we get creamed for $100 million, including punitive damages!

Where is that guy anyway? I heard he crawled back to his mountain hideaway after his wife and daughter were kidnapped. It was all over the newspapers for weeks. He got them back, I understand, Ha! 'A little worn for the wear,' I believe.

Now, Gordon, I have a hunch you played some role in the whole affair. You didn't get a little something on the side, did you?"

GAG looked sick to his stomach. "You'll talk like a mina bird, Leon. I know you will. Momma was right." GAG slowly rose from his chair.

Leon was paralyzed by the apparition, emerging before him. Silhouetted against the white board, like a penguin's tux against its feathers, GAG stepped twice in Leon's direction, simultaneously pulling out the gun he had with him in St. Louis, to kill Eddie, if he had needed killing then. It wasn't Eddie's puny .38 taken from him after GAG relieved him of his ulnar nerve... with a needle nosed pliers. This time, GAG had added a silencer to his Beretta Px4 sub-compact, chambered for .40 caliber.

Leon saw the gun. He started to get up and scream; but before the screech could exit his lips, GAG stepped forward and put a bullet through his right temple at point blank range. Leon fell forward, the left side of his head hitting the table with a dull thud, while a widening puddle of blood and brains spread out under his scalp.

GAG re-concealed his handgun and left, as he had planned, leaving a blabbermouth silenced before the coming storm.

— — —

9:00 am (EPA Field Office Headquarters, Louisville, Kentucky)

There were six official vehicles and 16 investigative and law enforcement personnel gathered in front of the four story government building. Of the eight carrying guns, there were six EPA armed agents (leading the raid) and two FBI Special Agents, Louisville Division. The rest of the group included four federal crime scene (Evidence Response Team [ERT]) investigators, three technicians to do all the heavy lifting and one high level EPA supervisor. Seated in the supervisor's van was a civilian.

The entourage was embarking upon the normally three hour journey to Warburg and the offices of Matchless Enterprises, Inc. Enroute they planned to meet two Lewis County deputies and two from Carter County just in case someone decided to flee across county lines. They knew they had to get going because there was a light snow falling. Everyone in the outside world was praying for a White Christmas.

All of the warrants were in hand. The "no-knock" raid was planned for noon; but it looked like it was going to go down around one pm, given the weather slow-down. The calculus that defined the "go-no-go" decision to raid the plant on Christmas Eve predicted little resistance and a high probability of catching two big fish, Jimmy Olson and his crooked lawyer, Percy Loeb, the senior partner of Marcus, Greene and Loeb out of Louisville. FBI surveillance put both Olson and Loeb at the scene.

Eddie Olson was dead, found trapped in the plant's chemical bake-out room on Halloween night about seven weeks before. A coroner's investigation was underway; and the preliminary verdict was "death by toxic inhalation, primarily formaldehyde and other unknown agents, complicated by asphyxiation from aspiration of vomit and blood." It was a brutal death scene. Suicide or even murder had not been ruled out because it appeared that Eddie Olson or someone else had taken the fresh air supply hose upstream of his air compressor and routed it into the formaldehyde chamber. This fatal modification caused the compressor to feed contaminated air into Eddie's respirator. The coroner's notes compared it to a similar set-up when someone commits suicide with carbon monoxide and deliberately routes a hose from the tail pipe of his car into the passenger's compartment.

The entourage made the trip from Louisville in four hours, rendezvousing with the sheriff's deputies on time. They crossed the plant perimeter and took the single security guard into protective custody. One EPA agent disarmed him and relieved him of his radio, just as he was about to do his job. All clear, they drove up to the administrative office entrance at 1:27 pm.

Ray Fuller turned to his passenger and said quietly, as if to avoid being overheard, "Keep your head down and do not exit this vehicle. I may have to enter with my boys and girls, and we don't know what to expect. There will be plenty of time to look around outside. I don't want anyone to get hurt, especially you; and I don't want anyone to recognize you. Remember, you are here as our guest; not as part of your job description."

"OK," answered his passenger, speaking just as quietly as Fuller and wondering why. It appeared unnecessary to talk softly, when they were alone, sitting in an idling, unmarked van forty feet from the Matchless office front door. His passenger reached over and raised the heat. "You know, it's been a while and nothing much has changed; but we better get moving to beat the snow cover outside, before some landmarks get obscured."

—   —   —

10:30 am (FBI Field Office Headquarters, St. Louis, Missouri)

"You want to go on this one?" said Jesse Wheaton. "It could get interesting. We'll have eight SWAT on standby and eight other agents, including me, going in first. You're on ERT (Evidence Response Team), aren't you?"

"You know I am, Wise Guy." responded Callie McGavin rolling her eyes at her squad leader. "If I don't hold your hand, you jerks won't know what to do, what to ask or where to go."

"Touché, you're probably correct," toyed Wheaton, knowing he could never get Callie's goat. She was too serious, too smart and too effective. Wheaton rethought that recurring thought to avoid getting on Callie's shit list at all costs. He knew she held grudges for a very long time, sometimes forever.

"OK, seriously," Wheaton continued. "We'll take five more from ERT in first and have several more in back-up that can come later. If all goes well, we won't need SWAT; but one way or another, we'll be clear for your crew to go in and set up your crime scene perimeter, no more than 30 minutes after arrival."

"Fine with me, Jesse." said Callie, putting on her coat and hoisting her "go' bag on her shoulder.

I'll tell the rest of the team to assemble now. But Oh, Jesse, by the way, I got a call from Dr. Baines, yesterday. He's either clairvoyant or he's got us wire-tapped. The old goat called to wish me good luck. I said why and he said I knew 'darn tootin' why. Those were his words, exactly.

The guy is an anachronism, who likes to appear stuck before 1900. He wished me a Merry Christmas and ended with 'Wish I could be there, but I have to make a party in New Orleans.' before he hung up.

"That worries me, just a tiny bit," responded Wheaton. "I'll have to look into it later. In the meantime, that bastard gets to spend Christmas Eve in New Orleans. Maybe I'll try to find some Crawfish Etouffee at that local pizza joint in Alton after the raid. You never know!"

"Legend has it, Baines won't be eating shellfish. I think he keeps 'sort of Kosher,'" laughed Callie.

"I see you've been studying his file, Analyst McGavin," quipped Wheaton, returning the smile.

"OK, enough putzing around. Let's do it!" barked Wheaton, getting pumped as always when heading for some fun.

The FBI convoy consisted of eight vehicles, including one Iraq hand-me-down, APC to carry the SWAT team. The rest were the five typical unmarked black Suburbans, the chariots of the Bureau and two vans for the ERT. Leaving at about 1:00 pm, they covered the 24 miles to their destination in just about 40 minutes. All of the warrants were in order. CADIXX and its corrupted surrogates never knew what hit them.

— — —

1:27 pm (Administrative Offices of Matchless Enterprises, Outside of Warburg, Kentucky)

"What's this all about?" screamed Missy Malark. "Who are you people? I'm calling the police!"

"We are the police, Ma'am." barked Ray Fuller, showing his EPA badge and throwing the search warrants on her desk. "Now tell me, where is Mr. Olson and Mr. Loeb? We know they are both here."

The door to Olson's office suddenly opened, and a giant of a man blocked the doorway. "We'll be right with you," yelled a voice standing about ten feet behind the human barricade. "No need for a ruckus, now," the voice continued; now partly obscured by the distinct background noise of a large document shredder.

"Get the hell out of my way," yelled Fuller, pulling his sidearm.

Before he could take a step forward the goon in the doorway started to step back and close the door. In less than a second, an even larger EPA agent stepped forward and swung his right elbow into the barricade's jaw. The guy went down like a ton of bricks. Four agents, including Fuller stepped into Olson's office. It was all there in plain sight. There must have been a small mountain of shredded paper, all over the room. There stood Jimmy Olson and his lawyer, Percy Loeb, jackets off and sleeves rolled up.

"20 more minutes and we would have finished," laughed Loeb. "Just doing a little spring cleaning in December. Have fun, my friends. I hope you have plenty of Scotch tape!"

"Get on your knees, assholes, and put your hands behind your heads now, both of you," bellowed Fuller, dodging two other agents who were dragging the body of the barricade out the doorway. "You're both under arrest."

While one agent zip tied their hands behind their backs, another agent read them their rights. Fuller went back into the outer office and spoke to Missy. "Ma'am; you'll have to come with us for questioning. Sorry to ruin your Christmas Eve."

"God, it's over now. It's over now, finally," whispered Missy, now openly weeping. "It was bound to happen. It's such a relief. First the worker injuries, the terrible suffering; the poor, poor souls living in those trailers, meant for good; then Zane's disappearance; then Eddie; even he didn't deserve that fate."

"I'm ready. I'm ready for salvation," she wailed as she dramatically raised her hands over her head. "Dear God, I'm ready to cleanse my soul and my heart."

Incredulous, Fuller was actually touched by the scene. This woman was weeping harder and harder. He feared hysteria; so he went over and touched his hand lightly to her shoulder. In a second, she threw her arms around his burly frame and continued weeping, her head buried against his windbreaker. "God, she would turn state's evidence right here, if I asked her," he thought. "We are gonna need to look after this lady," he smiled to himself.

Carefully, helping Missy to sit down in a chair next to her desk, Fuller left the office scene behind him to go back to his van.

"It's OK, now we can get out and have a look around," said Fuller to his passenger. The snow was falling lightly and had accumulated on the windshield.

His passenger complied, exiting the van and pulling up his hood against the weather. He walked around to the driver's side and said, "Let's start in this direction. I'm guessing it's about 200 feet from here," he said in a dull monotone. He sounded depressed and tired at the same time. Fuller and his passenger crossed the sidewalk to the entrance of the building they had just raided. At that moment, two agents came through the doorway, escorting, Olson and Loeb. Olson looked up, briefly catching the passenger's face.

"It can't be! It can't be! It can't be! You bastard! You're dead! Dear God, you're supposed to be dead," bellowed Jimmy, as he broke free from the agent escorting him. In a comical run with his hands tied behind his back, Jimmy head butted the passenger from behind. They both went down and the melee began. Four agents rushed to retrieve Olson. As they grabbed his arms from behind and lifted them upward, an audible crack could be heard as Olson's right shoulder blade fractured.

The passenger had rolled onto his back, face up, lying in the snow dusted grass. He looked at Jimmy, full on.

Jimmy lunged again and broke free falling on top of the man. Inches from his face, a froth of spittle on his mouth, wincing in pain, Jimmy, uttered, "You're not real. It can't be!"

"Oh, but it is," said the passenger. "It is real, you degenerate cur. After over 20 years, I know exactly where you dumped it. And you'll have 20 years in prison to lament your failure to get rid of me."

"Oh, they would have found it eventually anyway; but I wanted to save them some time. And, the bonus to boot has been to see you suffer. Oh, I cry for Monty. I cry for Monty," he said as he rolled over and stood up, leaving the whimpering Olson on the ground.

"Let's go, Ray. Let's get it over with," he continued. "I want to see Posie again, as soon as possible."

"OK, Zane," slipped Fuller. "What the hell, take me to the mother lode. Olson just cost us 100 grand to redo your witness protection profile. Oh, shit, are they gonna scream at headquarters!"

—   —   —

1:42 pm (CADIXX Operations Annex, off state highway 100, north of Alton, Illinois):

The FBI convoy pulled up to the entrance of the CADIXX Operations Annex in Alton, Illinois.

CADIXX senior vice-president, Leon Marbury had been dead for about five hours. His body lay slumped over the large table in the second floor conference room, with a bullet hole in his right temple and a congealed mess puddled beneath his scalp.

Gordon A. Gasher, (GAG), the perpetrator of Marbury's final exit had disappeared, skillfully and permanently, or, at least, for as long as he desired to evade the law and others who may have him in their cross hairs. GAG had given up a lot. His decision to murder Marbury to keep him from singing like a canary had been an easy one, because he hated the bastard and enjoyed the kill. And it had been a strategic one to prevent Marbury from telling the feds what they would need to know to close in on CADIXX's illegal dumping activities.

But more importantly, GAG put that bullet in Marbury's head to shield the sacred activities of The Resistance. It was a calculated risk for GAG. He knew he could murder, disappear and then reappear when he saw fit, under a new name with the anonymity to carry on his work the Chief Enforcer for The Resistance. Going underground would give him some sorely needed free time to think, scheme and plan ways to make his enemies miserable.

The time off from his, now, extinguished position as nurse medical director at CADIXX would allow him to catch up on some "get-even" projects he had to admit he loved the best. GAG decided to finish the job when it came to the continuing menace of the gadfly, Tristan P. Baines, MD.

After he killed Baines in the slow and certain manner he intended and Baines, correctly deserved, he would then re-locate, capture and torture Baines' wife, Heather and their brat, Tess, now 17 years old by GAG's calculations.

It was time to cuddle more than Heather's amputated ring finger and Tess' bruises and tears. Time had passed and GAG's remedies had become more terrifying and permanent. He pledged he would do whatever it took to eliminate the entire Baines clan as a factor in bleeding The Resistance of its precious resources.

Special Agent Jessie Wheaton didn't like the looks of the entrance to the CADIXX annex. It was simply too quiet. There were no security guards present, and no one could be seen in the ground floor reception area. No clerks, secretaries or executive types were visible through the large tempered glass windows.

"Have the SWAT, all eight, clear the reception area and the entire first floor now!" blurted Agent Wheaton into his lapel microphone.

"Roger, will do," responded the SWAT commander.

All eight SWAT team members proceeded through the unlocked front door into the reception area, each carrying a HK MP5A3 9mm submachine gun with a retractable stock. Fully clothed with body armor and helmet, they were not taking any chances. The front door was open. No one was around. The first floor was empty, all 12 offices and the large conference room. Scattered in several offices, were piles of shredded paper and boxes filled with official looking papers, memoranda, e-mails and commercial documents.

"Subjects absent on this floor; no one is around anywhere we can see. We are continuing the sweep," called in the SWAT commander.

"Shit, they have been tipped," yelled Wheaton into the microphone. "After your sweep, proceed up stairwell to second floor. Do not, I repeat, do not use elevator! But post a man at elevator doors on the first floor in case anyone decides to try to exit. Stairwell should be at far east end of building on north side according to our map."

"Roger, will do. After remaining first floor sweep, will proceed up stairwell to second floor and post man on first floor to prevent exit," responded the commander. Wheaton liked this guy – especially when he repeated orders to confirm his communications.

Three minutes passed.

"No subjects, anywhere to be seen on the second floor either, Jesse," called in the commander. "All clear. Wait! Negative on my last remark. Just notified, there is a body in the east side conference room slumped across the table.

Please call for ambulance now. But it appears subject is dead from gunshot wound to head. The remainder of the second floor is clear. But give us some more time to sweep for ordinance or any other hazards on both floors before calling in ERT."

"Roger, will call ambulance now," replied Wheaton.

"Well, Callie get your crew ready to go in as soon as SWAT gives the word," asserted Wheaton.

"This is a cluster…!" blurted Wheaton, slapping his hand against his holstered compact, .40 caliber Glock 23. "Who tipped these guys? We'll begin to collect whatever paperwork we can. You and your crew set up your perimeter and begin to do your investigation. This whole damned building is a crime scene and will be treated accordingly. We're going to be here for a while."

"Got it!" snapped Callie, as she turned to the analyst next to her. "First, Bernie, you and Matt, begin to yellow flag the building perimeter. The rest of us will head inside, as soon as SWAT gives the all clear. I will go with Josie to the second floor. Mary, you and Albert check the first floor area, especially where the boxes are clustered. Anything unusual – hands off. Get it re-cleared with SWAT – and I mean it. I don't want someone to lose an arm, an eye or worse from some booby trapped letter bomb."

Callie and her group began to go to work. Eight minutes later, the EMT's arrived, along with one of the emergency room physicians who decided to come along to help. The doc on the scene pronounced the man in the second floor conference room dead and estimated that he had been a corpse for several hours, since rigor mortis had already set in.

The coroner was coming over within the hour.

They took the liberty of removing the man's wallet from his right back pocket. His driver's license identified him as Leon S. Marbury of St. Louis, Missouri.

Callie called down to Wheaton to check out Marbury.

"This guy is on our CADIXX list as a big shot – VP in charge of Incinerator Operations and coordinator of CADIXX waste hauling activities. He would have been an important source to interrogate," shouted Wheaton into his microphone, still trying to keep calm after finding the coop mostly empty and all except one dead chicken gone.

"Too bad this guy has been murdered; I wonder just what he was planning to say," thought Callie.

68 boxes of records and other assorted items were removed from the building, along with nine computers and five external hard drives. Wheaton was not optimistic. Many of the CADIXX business materials had already been placed in banker's boxes, seemingly prepared ahead of time, deliberately, as bait for the game ahead.

Two hours after the raid had gone down, Callie McGavin brought a bagged item stained with blood to the attention of Special Agent Wheaton. It was a business card. On it was written:

"Gordon A. Gasher, RN, Director of Medical Services, CADIXX Incinerator, Alton, Illinois."

"Where did you find it?" inquired Wheaton.

"On the table, beneath the corpse's head," responded Callie. "I didn't move the body; but I saw it stuck to the scalp when the coroner lifted the body to take it away. He agreed I could take it for more detailed examination."

"It might not mean much," said Wheaton. "It was probably just present on the conference table; left there by someone, maybe this nurse, Gasher. I doubt if anyone would be dumb enough to leave his business card at the scene of a murder, if he had anything to do with it."

"Maybe you're right," said Callie, trying to humor her ERT leader. "On the other hand, Dr. Baines warned us..."

"Wait a damn second, Gasher, yeah, Gasher," said Wheaton. "Isn't he the same guy Baines warned us about? Yeah, I am certain of it."

"Well," continued Callie in a calm voice with her usual smile and eye roll, "I am happy to have jogged your memory, Jessie."

"Callie, let's get on this, now. First, call Dr. Baines to see if we can fly him up here from New Orleans. I want him front and center with us in St. Louis. I think he can be of great help in this investigation."

"Roger," Agent Wheaton, kidded Jessie. "I have no doubt Dr. Baines will enthusiastically participate in our investigation; if he has not already hunted down Gasher and inflicted his personal revenge; in which case, I will just ask to see a body part.

Let me see what I can do."

CHAPTER 36 - SIMON'S PARTY - PART I

DATE: 12/24/10, Friday, 5:00PM
LOCATION: Home of Melanie Hatfield-Michaels and husband George, Baton Rouge, Louisiana

— — —

Over the previous four days, Melanie Hatfield-Michaels had received three voice messages from Dr. Patricia Simms regrettably but clearly disinviting her to Simon's Christmas Eve party. Melanie erased them all. She didn't care. She was going anyway.

"You've got to be kidding me, Melanie," argued George Michaels, raising his voice to an unaccustomed level, especially when arguing with his wife. "You're going to ruin Christmas Eve and expect me to join you to crash some stranger's party down in New Orleans?

We don't even know these people. We're going to look like fools. I thought we were going out to a quiet dinner together. Anyway, you are never going to make it on time, if it starts at 6."

His wife of almost four years, Melanie Hatfield-Michaels stood at the light tan counter island in their kitchen and looked back at her husband, standing in the living room of their small but cozy home in the remote suburbs of Baton Rouge. They wanted it that way. They needed room outside, a reasonably sized yard for pets and George's favorite hobby, gardening.

Melanie wasn't sure what to say next. She had procrastinated yet again, paralyzed by ambivalence with regard to Dumbo. Now, when she had a chance to cleanse her guilt on the issue, she was running well over an hour late.

While George was talking she started for the door, off the kitchen, which led to the laundry room and their new puppy. but she stopped not wanting to get George upset any further.

"Look, Mel, I get the picture – we had Dumbo for over five years and the dog brought us joy and happiness. We can't help it if we lost him last week. OK, he was killed by a car. These things happen. We didn't do anything wrong. Fortunately, we still have one of Dumbo's pups to fill his place, thanks to the Hogans.

If you hadn't rescued Dumbo after Katrina, he would have died over five years ago, for sure. You stopped that idiot Troy (Cpl.) Ashton from shooting the poor dog, when you were on patrol. Remember, I was there when you called in. It's lucky I was and still am a vet assistant; so I sympathized. I was the first one you called after you found him. I waved you in and got Dr. (Captain) Lowe to take care of him.

Jesus, Melanie, the dog was treated, for all intensive purposes, by a board-certified human cardiologist, who just happened to remember how to treat a gunshot wound, in a dog, no less. We hid that dog for weeks; and eventually everyone loved him, even Col. Masters. Anybody else in command, and Dumbo would have been sent to a kill shelter after five days.

What were you supposed to do? – So you kept him. You are one of many who rescued animals and kept them. You had no idea who the owner was for years, until you looked at that crumpled photo and scrap of paper buried along with everything else from your duty during Katrina. Hell, I don't know why you kept those stupid things; much less looked at them after all these years.

Melanie, Melanie, look – are you even listening? Oh shit, let me get you some Kleenex – for God's sakes."

Pleading his case at even higher intensity, George continued, "So you found a photo of a dog on a bulletin board, Rambo, or whatever, his name is that fit the description of our Dumbo and out of some guilt you want to go visit the kid who lost his dog.

God, Melanie, clear your head. First, you may have the wrong kid. Second, how do you think you will be treated when you tell him you kept his dog for over five years?

You just want to show up at a Christmas Eve party at some fancy restaurant and offer your condolences when the kid's dog is dead? You can't even give him his dog back. I agree that would be a 'Hallmark' bittersweet ending, but you have nothing to give him but your regrets and reassurance that his dog was loved and well cared for since you essentially took the dog from him. They will probably throw us out – or worse."

Melanie finally got a grip and came back with her usual vigor, fluency and determination.

Her work as a high school science teacher, outside of the military, prepared her for more than this squabble with her husband. To lighten up the bantering, she decided to pull rank, a practice she had even tried in the bedroom on several previous occasions, much to George's delight. "Listen, Corporal Michaels, this is Sergeant Hatfield speaking, you are acting like the unfeeling, non-empathetic bastard that you can be when you want to be."

Thinking her paraphrasing the Army's recruiting slogan would begin the process of winning over George, she continued, "George, please have a little understanding here. I called that number on the old bulletin board notice and spoke to a delightful lady, a Doctor Patricia Simms, who told me she is still the pediatrician for this young – now, teenage boy, Simon Williams, who lost his dog during Katrina. His dog was named, Rambo, interestingly and maybe prophetically close to our Dumbo.

Dr. Pat, as she likes to be called, told me the toll that loosing Rambo had on Simon. The kid was a basket case for months. She was apparently treating him for some kind of chronic problem, because each time he came back to see her, he brought up the loss of his dog. Simon finally gave her a photograph of Rambo; and it was she who posted it.

I saw the photo. I took it off the bulletin board. The picture was a dead ringer for Dumbo because of the ears and that giant white diamond on his..."

"Melanie. I've heard the story 10 times and twice since Dumbo was killed." George interrupted, actually tuning into Melanie's pain; but still determined to cancel the trip to New Orleans on Christmas Eve.

"George, for God's sakes, Dr. Pat invited us both to go to have a nice dinner and meet Simon and his family." Melanie persisted. "They're having a party or something, at this place called Pegleg's Barrelhead; and there are going to be some other friends there. Some other doctor, she said, named, Reins, Baines, or something like that, who helped Simon a few years back. I know I'm running really late; but at least I'll get there for dessert.

Look, George, I want to meet Simon. That's final. I am certain he will want to know what happened to his dog; and as you said, be reassured that Rambo/Dumbo was loved and loved, until this recent accident."

George thought he was tipping toward giving in. But Melanie was hard-headed and had won her way in too many of these encounters, throughout their marriage. George decided to throw down the gauntlet, even though it rarely worked.

"Mel, I am not going with you to New Orleans, period." George asserted. "It is a bad idea. If you are going, then go. But I'm going down to O'Brien's for a beer and some brats. I would love for you to come with me."

It was a gamble and George lost. Melanie started to sob again.

"Where's the Kleenex?" she asked, boiling inside at the insensitivity of her husband and wallowing in the guilt she felt by never trying to contact Simon in the early months after Katrina.

George turned and headed for the front door, still hoping that Melanie would change her mind and come with him. As he was walking out, George said, "Mel, you know where I'll be. I'm taking the F150." He left and all of a sudden the house seemed horribly empty and lonely. Christmas Eve; what a mess.

She heard the truck leave the driveway. It was now 5:45 pm. If she wanted to get to New Orleans by 7 or even 7:30, she knew she had better get moving. It was going to take at least an hour and a half to travel the 80 miles between Baton Rouge and New Orleans and she had to leave extra time to get lost.

She went upstairs, showered and changed, putting on a simple but adequately fancy, dark blue dress and some black pumps with only one inch heels. She added a small string of white pearls that George had given her for her birthday. As she headed downstairs, she glanced at the clock in the kitchen. It was now 6:15 pm. The party and dinner had already started. She put on her coat and opened the front door. Suddenly, she relapsed; the ambivalence that had plagued her since she had spoken to Dr. Pat set in. She wanted to purge the guilt; and yet she didn't really know how.

"Dumbo, Jr. I can't leave him here," she thought. "The pup is only nine weeks old, for God's sakes. I'll crate him; give him some water and a blanket and just prepare myself to clean up the mess when I get back late tonight."

Then she reversed herself again. "No! No!" she suddenly thought. "I'm not going to take him. He'll be fine in the laundry room. We've got a gate. The dog will have plenty of food and water. If I'm lucky, he might even hit the newspaper spread all over the floor, at least when he goes #2."

Melanie might just as well have walked in circles. She was totally confused. She exited the front door and jumped into their 1997 Jeep Cherokee, George's contribution to their marriage and a vehicle that George prided himself in keeping in perfect running condition. She pulled out of the driveway and headed on the shortest route to Highway 12 that would then take her to Interstate 10, the direct shot to New Orleans. She turned on the radio. It didn't work. "Great, she thought – so much for George."

Five miles down the road, she pulled over; put her head on the steering wheel, banged it with both hands, and started to bawl like a baby. After a few minutes, she lifted her head, wiped her nose and eyes.

"God, that asshole should be here with me." she cried aloud as she pulled a U-turn from the shoulder and headed back to the house. "The pup will be better company than George, anyway," she reasoned. She figured she would get to Pegleg's about an hour and a half to two hours late, if she didn't get lost or break down on the highway in George's Jeep. It was already 6:30 pm. One part of her hoped she would arrive before the party was over. The other didn't.

—   —   —

6:00 pm (Pegleg's Barrelhead Restaurant, New Orleans, Louisiana)

Laura Swain was having a great time spending money and telling people what to do. Thanks to Asher Goldman's generosity after the $148 million settlement with over a dozen defendants in the second round of the FEMA trailer, formaldehyde litigation, Laura was given $10,000 to throw a Christmas party for some very special people.

After the loss of the Simon Williams' case before federal judge Henrietta Whitmore, Asher and Laura had worked hard to reinvent the claims against the assortment of remaining defendants. Thanks to the work of Tristan and others, they were successful in reaching a settlement; but people like Simon and his mom, Sethie, and their family were, more or less, shit out of luck.

Actually, Laura had made the suggestion to honor the unsuccessful struggle of the trial by throwing a goodwill party for the losers. Since the time of the trial, Tristan ruminated, more often than he would have liked, about his role as the unsuccessful expert who had testified on behalf of Simon. Even though there were several legalistic reasons for the loss, consensus was that there were no major technical or scientific ones. By this time it was simply sour grapes to continue to agonize over the events as they had occurred.

To ease the pain of the loss, Laura suggested that Asher funnel a few thousand dollars to Simon's family. Laura understood that Asher had made a fortune from the $148 million settlement. To her astonishment, Asher agreed to provide $25,000 toward Simon's future education in addition to funding one hell of a Christmas Eve party. Apologizing that he couldn't be present for the festivities, he had given Laura a check to present to Simon and his family after dinner.

With such a large budget, Laura began working in late November to set up the Christmas Eve party at Pegleg's. She knew a certain amount of travel would be involved; and she never declined a chance to visit New Orleans, especially to stay at the Ritz again. She arranged for the two other "out of towners," Tristan and his side-kick, Joseph Trueblood to stay at the same hotel.

The special in-town guest was Dr Patricia Simms, Simon's pediatrician. She also testified at trial; but had taken a beating on her qualifications to render an opinion on causation. Laura knew that the disrespectful treatment of Dr. Pat by the defense was outrageous. The lady was a board-certified pediatrician who wrote a report, with good scientific documentation, concluding it was the formaldehyde in the Matchless trailers that had aggravated Simon's asthma.

Another expert, supposedly on Simon's side was deliberately not invited. Hailing from the "Ivory Tower" at Hautair, Dr. Chris McKenna stuck a knife in Simon's claims, Tristan's testimony and that of several other experts at the FEMA trial. She declined to correlate the obvious, for whatever reason.

More inexplicably, McKenna ignored the fact that Simon nearly died under her care in Boston when he underwent the inhalation challenge with formaldehyde she had ordered as part of his work-up. The poor kid suffered a cardiac arrest and had to be resuscitated in the vapor chamber. Luckily, he recovered without any residual problems. No one knew exactly what had gone wrong; but the technician who worked for McKenna's lab was found murdered shortly after the event.

Tristan thought the shocking demise of McKenna's technician had very ominous ramifications. He reasoned that the events in the chamber could have been an unsuccessful attempt by someone in The Resistance to murder Simon. Tristan couldn't prove a thing. He wasn't even certain that McKenna had any knowledge or involvement in what could have been a fatal disaster. On the other hand, McKenna's testimony that hurt Simon's case certainly made her a suspect for having possible ties to The Resistance. Tristan simply did not know.

Notwithstanding the indigestion of McKenna and Simon's ordeal, Tristan wanted to maintain a good relationship and not burn bridges with Coastal General and the Hautair system of hospitals. He made this commitment, primarily out of respect for his relationship with Dr. Lila Gruber his very old friend and colleague. Tristan also wanted to be able to refer future patients for evaluation. If Tristan played his cards right, he would ensure McKenna became irrelevant; undoubtedly a humiliation to which she would not take kindly.

Needless to say, McKenna wouldn't be coming to the party. But Sethie, Simon and the rest of the Williams' family would be hearing McKenna's name frequently over the next few months during the family's malpractice trial, against Coastal General Hospital, Hautair University and McKenna personally. Asher wasn't handling the case. The family had retained local counsel in Boston that had successfully sued both the hospital and the university on previous occasions.

Including the entire Williams' family, (Simon, Sethie, Reggie and Reggie, Jr.), a total of eight people planned to attend Asher's Christmas Eve bash.

"Please, Sir. Put the table over there, under the fishnet and leave the white tablecloth on," directed Laura Swain to the Maitre'D. "We're going to need seven, make that eight chairs."

The guests had already arrived and were waiting to be seated in the private dining room at the upscale restaurant affectionately known as "Pegleg's" to those who could afford the menu and could spell the names of at least eight out of the sixteen vineyards on the wine list.

Tristan, standing with Joseph, was about to speak to Laura, when he spotted Simon, standing alone, but not far from his family. First things first. With a warm smile on his face, Tristan walked over to Simon.

"Simon, so how are you feeling?" effused Tristan. "I haven't seen you in such a long time."

"Issa fine, Dr. Baines, all considered. Issa in school and havin' a good time," responded Simon as he matched Tristan's grin and reached forward to shake his hand. Tristan was pleasantly surprised by how much Simon had matured in just a little over the year since he had seen him at the FEMA trial. He displayed a dignity and personality well beyond his 14 years.

"Tell me, Simon....Oh, Hello, Sethie, how are you?" exclaimed Tristan, suddenly surrounded by the entire Williams clan. "I was just about to ask Simon to tell me his favorite subject in school." While watching Simon for a response, Tristan shook Reggie Sr.'s hand, patted Reggie, Jr. on the shoulder and gave Sethie a hug.

"Well, Simon. Tell Dr. Baines what's yous like the best," encouraged Sethie, also with a smile.

"Dr. Baines, Issa want to be an animal doctor or a veti'narian. I love animals and would like to help people too," said Simon looking straight at Tristan's eyes.

"Eye contact," thought Tristan. "Most unusual for a 14 year old. This boy has some real potential."

"You mean, a "ve-ter-i-nar-i-an," don't yous Simon?" corrected Sethie, glancing at Tristan, then carefully, at Reggie, Sr. and then back to Simon. Sethie tightened her lips, as she looked to her son for a response. A moment elapsed.

"Yes, Momma, I means 'veterinarian,'" responded Simon, correctly pronouncing the tongue twisting word. His smile disappeared, and he looked at his brother.

Tristan thought, "Well the long struggle has begun and not a moment too soon. Simon probably has the brains to endure four more years of high school, four years of college and four years of veterinary training, not to mention a year or two of fellowship. But the equally important questions were did he have his family's support; and simply put, did he have the grit to become a doctor of veterinarian medicine?" Tristan knew a thousand and one things could arise to derail the boy's ambition.

"I hope you can make your dream come true," said Tristan, aloud. "It's hard work; but I think you can make it. I would like to stay in touch with you, as you progress through school. Simon, keep that smile; it will take you a long way as a doctor."

"Did I hear somebody say they wanted to be a doctor?" asked Dr. Pat, as she headed over to give Simon a hug and shake Tristan's hand. "I knew you would reach that decision. It's a bit early; but I think you're on the right track."

"Pat, great to see you again!" exclaimed Tristan as he gave Dr. Pat a polite handshake, then a hug. "Simon wants to be a doctor alright – the kind of doctor I have often thought I might have wanted to be, myself – an animal doctor!" As Tristan looked at his trim, nicely dressed colleague, he thought about the autumn before last, when he and Dr. Pat sat outside the federal courthouse in New Orleans, just after she had testified. Tristan had been on-deck, about to be batter-up and McKenna was in the dugout preparing to launch her testimony, supposedly to help Simon, but destined to play an important role in sinking his case.

Tristan glanced at Laura, who glanced at her watch. Tristan stepped toward the table, when Dr. Pat gently touched his sleeve and said quietly, "Tristan, do you have a second? It's about that phone call I told you about."

"Sure," said Tristan, as he looked back at Laura, who again, checked her watch.

The two physicians stepped to the corner, next to the entrance and conferred for several minutes. When it was over, Tristan, said, "Thanks, for the 'heads-up' Pat. I'm happy you called her off. I am sorry to say' but Sethie nixed the puppy idea. I didn't tell her about Melanie. No point in ruining her dinner. I'll tell her later; but I won't tell Simon. Maybe you should wait until he's 18 and tell him, yourself when it's all behind him and you're ready to graduate him from pediatrics to adult internal medicine."

The private room at Pegleg's was brightly lit. The walls of the room were adorned with a large variety of seafaring icons, from fish netting, an anchor, and large seashells to a ship's spoked wheel or helm. Everything was mounted on faded gray-brown, wooden planked paneling. At the far end of the rectangular room was a beautiful 100 gallon salt water aquarium, filled with 14 breathtaking fish in colors ranging from yellow and blue to orange and indigo. Two five foot wooden dining tables were placed end to end and covered with a single large, spotless white linen tablecloth. Everything was in order. The two waiters had taken beverage requests and everyone was milling around getting re-acquainted.

Joseph, Reggie, Sr. and his son were over in one corner by the aquarium, talking about fishing in the delta. Joseph was being polite; but felt compelled to ask, "Tell me, Reggie; how's the deer hunting?"

"Well, we live in 'Loosiana;' it's not whut Issa like to do; but from whut I hear, it about the best you could ask fo,'" answered Reggie, politely studying Joseph's lean and sturdy frame, one earned by someone who was accustomed to hard, punishing outdoor work.

Laura stood at the head of table and began with a loud, "Excuse me, everyone. But we're going to have to sit down in just a minute or two. It is now 6:25; and we have the room until 9 pm when a late night party has it reserved.

On behalf of Asher Goldman, I would like to wish you all a Merry Christmas Eve and thank you for coming. As you know, things at trial did not work out the way we had hoped; but we want to remind you we have appealed the case. These things take time; we are somewhat optimistic; but it will be an uphill battle. It is clear Judge Whitmore was not on our side. She acted unfairly on several issues; hence we have hope that a higher court will give us some justice; especially when provided with the new case details we recently acquired quite by accident.

A few months ago, we uncovered shocking information about the illegal activities that took place at Matchless Enterprises after they received that big order from FEMA right after Katrina. We have some information from the letter of a whistleblower, unfortunately who has apparently disappeared. We're working through the legal morass to see if the federal appeals court will consider the content of his letter as testimony and order a new trial."

Suddenly, as if out of nowhere, Reggie, Sr. blurted, "Mah God!

I's hate t'hear dat whut fur. We's suffered as a family in dem trailers, supposed ta keep us safe after dat storm. We's believed in da good will of da government an dem trailer makers tuh reach out an give us a hand. Well, I'm one whose says I's vote to bite that damned hand, next time and go it alone. We's be better off. Sorry to interrupt, Ma'am."

"Bite the Hand that Feeds You!" exclaimed Laura. "I like that Reggie. I think it's gonna stick." An uneasy silence ensued. No one said a word. Then Laura began again.

"Now let's put all that aside. After all, it is Christmas Eve; and I hope you have brought your appetites with you!"

Following her last remark, Laura motioned to the two waiters, discretely positioned outside the room, to enter and begin taking orders. Everyone took their seats. Sethie and Reggie, Sr. sat at the opposite heads of the table. Simon sat to the left of his mother and Reggie, Jr. to the left of his father. Tristan sat to Sethie's right with Laura on his right. Dr. Pat sat to Simon's left with Joseph on her left.

Laura specified the seating at the table for a reason. She wanted Tristan and her to be seated directly across from Simon with Sethie close by to make the tribute to Simon easier after dinner. Laura also wanted a better view of the doorway to the private room to keep the waiters on their toes. Joseph didn't like to sit with his back to the entrance to the room. He relented, figuring Tristan could cover the entrance if anything were to go wrong.

Laura looked at the group quietly sitting at the table beginning to get comfortable with each other. She began. "Sethie, would like to say a prayer before we begin?"

"Issa a little sad after those true words said by Reggie. Maybe, Dr. Pat?" responded Sethie.

"Dr. Pat. Would you like to offer a prayer?" followed Laura.

"I'd be happy to," said Pat, as she rose from her chair.

"Now, everyone bow your heads, please." began Dr. Pat. "We are blessed to be together here on the eve of the birth of our Savior, Jesus of Nazareth. May we remain humble before God and appreciate all of those things in life that mean so much. I especially refer to our families, our health, our neighbors and this wonderful country in which we live.

May we always show mercy and compassion to those less fortunate and spread our bounty to all who need it the most. Thank you again, dear God, for this gathering of friends on this most joyous occasion. Miracles do occur. We must believe in them. In Jesus name, Amen."

Everyone at the table was temporarily a little stunned by the beauty of the extemporaneous prayer offered by Dr. Pat. Pat looked around and smiled. Then she continued, "I hope I covered everybody's spiritual beliefs," turning her head to Joseph, who nodded and smiled. Then she turned to Simon, sitting next to her; put her arm around his shoulder and whispered in his ear, loud enough for all to hear, "OK, now let's eat!"

Hors d'oeuvres were ordered and served. It was evident that everyone was hungry and eager to eat up Laura's budget. Joseph was developing a stronger relationship with Reggie, Sr. as they commiserated about their life joys and struggles. Dr. Pat focused her attention on Simon and some brief interchanges with Tristan on the several other children she had treated after Katrina for a wide variety of ailments.

"You know, Tristan," said Dr. Pat between a couple of forkfuls of her broiled tilapia, smothered with capers and a creamy lemon sauce, "There were many other children in my practice who became ill from those trailers. It was not just the formaldehyde and other chemicals that made them sick. Forgive my mentioning this over a meal; but a lot of those trailers were contaminated with black mold."

"I am not surprised," responded Tristan, as he dodged bites of his lasagna, one of only two Italian entrees on the menu. He wasn't a great fan of seafood. "You know there can be some severe allergic reactions to that mold that will cause mucous…"

"OK, you two," abruptly interrupted Laura with a little bit of food left in her mouth, feeling slightly queasy at the direction of the conversation. "I am certain the rest of us at the table are on pins and needles to hear more about those disgusting effects AFTER dinner – say, even, never!"

"Sorry," responded Tristan, knowing fully well he had crossed that line for effect while he winked at Dr. Pat. Out of deference to Simon and Sethie, he had no intention of grossing out anyone, not too much, anyway. Doctors love to misbehave in this manner; often with poor results.

Reggie, Jr., now 18, sat quietly throughout the meal, only occasionally exchanging a word or two with his father. Joseph, sitting across from him, broke the ice and said, "Say, Reggie; have you ever wanted to go out west?"

"Never, give it much thought," responded Reggie, Jr. as he looked up from his bowl of chicken and pork gumbo. "Issa workin' full time and don't git no vacation, anyway."

"Where are you working?" asked Joseph, sizing up the young man, carefully not wanting to cause him any embarrassment.

"Got a job doin' construction," answered Reggie, putting down his spoon and reaching for some pepper. He wasn't used to being a part of the conversation; but seemed to enjoy the attention, knowing that everyone's focus was more on Simon. "Issa learn'in framin' and some other carpentry. Keeps me busy; but a little less in the winter."

"When I was your age, I worked construction for over five years, too" rejoiced Joseph, delighted to have struck some connection or so he hoped. "It was tough work' didn't pay too well and was hard on the body, although it helped to keep me in shape."

"Yous right about that!" echoed Reggie. "Issa already got some problems with my left knee once in a while." Reggie, Jr. let on a quiet smile and got back to his gumbo, while Joseph realized he had exhausted the extent of their conversation, at least for now.

After they had all finished eating; but before any dessert orders had been taken, Laura lifted her spoon and gently tapped it against her water glass.

"I hope everyone has been enjoying their dinners. I have an announcement to make," exclaimed Laura, rising from her chair; leaving behind her meal, only half eaten. Joseph looked across the table with a devilish smirk as he saw Tristan ignoring Laura's remaining trout;

but sizing up her six remaining, small boiled potatoes, all covered with parsley and butter. Tristan never did have a cholesterol problem.

"Simon, you have been the focus of a lot of hard work that still might pay off," continued Laura. "We all know how difficult this ordeal has been for you, your parents and your brother, not to mention the rest of your family. Katrina cost you, like so many others more than anyone should have to endure. You lost your grandfather and your uncle, not to mention your precious dog Rambo, who wasn't much more that a puppy when he fell off the roof while you and your family barely clung to life in the first few nights after the storm.

Simon, you and your brother are the future. We are confident you will succeed. I overheard Reggie, Jr. say he is working construction. What a great start in the trades. I predict he will work his way up to supervisor within a few years. You, Simon have a very long way to go. ..."

Tristan listened intently to Laura's remarks, carefully wondering how he was going to make his move. He had worked very hard on Simon's behalf; but had failed. It was as simple as that. His subsequent effort to help dozens of others, injured while living in FEMA trailers, was financially successful. But nothing could change the fact that the first case, tried on Simon's behalf had gone badly.

Tristan had no intention of letting the matter rest. The case was on appeal; but there were no guarantees that justice would be served for Simon and his family.

In Tristan's mind, Judge Henrietta Whitmore was a crook and may even have ties with The Resistance. Tristan knew it; based on his instincts and from the bottom of his soul. For all he knew, Whitmore might be "Momma" or even the "The General," on Saul Goldman's organizational chart of The Resistance, Tristan had seen in Asher Goldman's office a year and a half ago. So what could he do about it? "Absolutely nothing; at least for now," he thought. The whole stink about beginning the statute of limitations when Sethie stepped foot into the trailer and a dozen other issues ate as much at Tristan as they did Asher and Laura.

"I earned a lot of money from both of these cases." Tristan internalized, while Laura continued her tribute to Simon. "Now I want to give something back; I don't know what; but something."

"Simon, it is not too early for you to plan for your formal college education," Laura continued. "So on behalf of Asher Goldman and everyone associated with his firm, I am proud to present you with a little something to kick off your educational efforts."

Opening her purse, Laura withdrew a plain white envelope. She started to hand it to Sethie; then abruptly changed her mind. Instead, she placed in front of Simon.

Simon stared at the envelope for a moment, and then looked over at his mother. "Itsa OK, Momma" said Simon, phrasing the remark more as a declaration than a question.

"Sethie looked across the table at Reggie, Sr. smiled and said, "Go ahead, Simon; open the envelope from Mr. Goldman."

Simon opened the envelope and saw immediately it was a check. He studied it for a minute, a little confused by so many zeroes. He paused and as he handed the check to Sethie, he offered, "I think, this issa check for twenty five thousand dollars."

"That's right, Simon, twenty five thousand dollars to go towards your college fund," crowed Laura. "Asher, um, Mr. Goldman figures you've earned it. After all, you had to put up with all those medical evaluations, and you had quite a time of it in Boston. Thank God you're OK."

Without another second passing, Tristan rose from his chair and stood next to Laura. He looked at Sethie, then Simon. Gripped by the moment, processing the entire events of the past year and a half, Tristan exclaimed, "And Simon, I am going to match that amount right now."

"Oh, sweet Jesus!" blurted Sethie, "Thank yous both so, so much!"

Laura looked first at Sethie and then at Tristan. Blindsided by Tristan's gesture, she smiled, not feeling upstaged in any manner whatsoever. In fact, Laura was absolutely delighted. She had tried to get $50,000 out of Asher anyway.

There was silence for several seconds, then:

"Reeeally?" blurted Simon. "Yur not pullin' ma leg is you, Dr. Baines?"

"No, I'm proud to help," said Tristan as he reached into his wallet for some folded checks, he kept handy. The reality of his gesture hit him. He paused for a second and quickly concluded that his course of action was appropriate. It also made him feel very good. Tristan took out his pen and wrote the check, made out to Mr. Simon Williams for twenty five thousand dollars. In the memo line, Tristan wrote; "Gift for Your Future – Use it Wisely!"

A happy commotion broke out at the table with applause from everyone.

As he handed the check to Simon, the proceedings were suddenly interrupted by the hostess who seated guests as they entered the restaurant. She looked around and found Laura, still standing next to Tristan. It was a little after 8 pm.

"Excuse me, Ms. Swain; there is a woman to see Dr. Patricia Simms. Her name is Melanie Hatfield-Michaels," said the hostess. Laura started to walk around behind Sethie to approach the hostess and the visitor; but Tristan gently tugged at her wrist and said, "Hang on; wait a second." Laura sensed Tristan's concern and stood still.

Dr. Pat shot a shocked and horrified look at Tristan.

She stood up, turned around and pretended, "Who is it? I wasn't expecting anyone." Pat feigned a vague recollection of something she couldn't pinpoint. Like an actress on cue, her face reflected her "miraculous" recollection of the conversation with someone named Melanie about Simon's lost dog, Rambo.

Pat clearly remembered the purpose of Melanie's visit and immediately regretted the offer she had extended to Ms. Hatfield-Michaels. She had canceled. She left three voice messages telling her not to come. Now she was worried and so were Tristan and Joseph. Maybe they could help control the collateral damage.

Dr. Pat started toward the entrance to the private dining room where Melanie and the hostess were standing. Before she could join them, Melanie whispered to Dr. Pat; but loud enough for Laura, Tristan and Sethie to overhear.

"Dr. Simms," expressed Melanie in a somewhat pleading tone. "Remember me? I'm Melanie Hatfield. I came to meet Simon. Is that him sitting at the table, with his back to me?"

Pat whispered back, "Are you insane? I left you three messages, asking you not to come. I changed my mind."

"Too late; here I am," smiled Melanie.

When Melanie whispered her greeting, Simon was busy studying his checks; oblivious of the intrusion. Everyone else was distracted, except Joseph, who turned to confront the disturbance he thought could escalate at any moment. He couldn't hear what was said. But while he looked over at Tristan, he reached inside his coat and reassuringly checked the butt of his sub-compact 9mm Beretta, the same one that had saved Laura, Tristan and him a year and a half ago during their attempted abduction back in New Orleans.

He remembered his shock and surprise in the evening of the day Tristan had first evaluated Simon. A simple limo ride out to dinner had almost led to Tristan, Laura and him becoming the main course for critters in a Louisiana swamp. Besides the three of them, no one else at the table knew about what had happened. Joseph wasn't taking any chances.

Now, he thought, he may have an ex-military psycho to deal with.

Laura turned to Tristan and whispered, "What the hell is going on here? I think we should escort this lady to the street."

Joseph now started to get up from his chair. Tristan waved him down.

"Look, Laura; Pat told me all about this; things haven't gone quite as planned," replied Tristan, trying to avoid Simon's attention. "It's going to go away, very soon."

Tristan nodded to Joseph, who then engaged Simon to make certain he wasn't distracted by the visitor behind him.

Before Dr. Pat could return Melanie's greeting, now Sethie rose from her chair and approached the group in the doorway. Looking at the disturbing array of faces, the hostess excused herself and promptly left.

"I heard my son's name mentioned," uttered Sethie quietly, quickly glancing back to see if Simon had caught on. He had not. He was now talking to Joseph. He showed no interest in the two women and his mother, now standing in the doorway to the private room.

"Well, what do you want with Simon?" persisted Sethie, this time in a louder tone. Dr. Pat, who could see the unpleasant potential of what was about to come down urged the three of them to move out of the doorway and around the corner toward the entrance to the restaurant. Melanie rehashed the entire story to Sethie. Dr. Pat knew it already, having heard it about a week ago when Melanie called. Pat knew she had to act quickly to initiate her own form of damage control.

"Look; it's all my fault. I miscalculated here. My intentions were noble; but my judgment was terrible. I never should have invited her here. I called her three times to rescind the invitation. Now she's here and only God knows why," pleaded Dr Pat to Sethie. By this time, Sethie was virtually speechless; but that did not conceal her being roaringly pissed off.

"Do you mean to tell me that yous had Simon's dog or think yous had Simon's dog for over four years, had our phone number, didn't call and now yous show up on Christmas Eve to try to meet Simon, make friends with him and tell him his dog, Rambo, supposedly under your care, wuz kilt by a car a week ago? Yous insane! Yous a lunatic!" exclaimed Sethie, raising her voice enough to be heard by both Tristan and Laura still standing around the corner in the private dining room. From their perspective, they couldn't make out Sethie's precise words; but knew there was one hell of a commotion in progress.

Melanie was without words. As she had, several times that day, began again to burst into tears. Ignoring Sethie, she pleaded and lied over intermittent sniffles, "Dr. Simms, I don't understand. I thought we had an agreement. I have no ill intention. I just wanted to meet Simon, uh, your son, Mrs. Williams; really to tell him how sorry I am; to tell him that I cared and loved his dog for the past several years with all of my heart.

Please understand; I didn't even see the picture of Dumbo until almost 10 months after my unit and I at the National Guard had more or less adopted him."

"First off, his name wuz 'Rambo'. Mah boy can't know bout this! It'll break him. Just will break him," whimpered Sethie to Dr. Pat, not ignoring what Melanie had said; but just demoting it to insignificance. Her maternal instincts kicked in. She had to protect her son.

"I's still don't understand; if yous had the number and had a picture that matched the dog yous found, then why didn't yous JUST MAKE THE CALL!" bellowed Sethie, knees beginning to buckle. Pat grabbed her elbow.

They were starting to make a scene at the entrance of the restaurant. People were looking. The hostess didn't know what to do. She couldn't ask them to step outside into the chilly air, although she was going to consider it the next step. She left to consult with the restaurant general manager.

Sethie continued to let loose. "Ms. Hatfield...Melanie, or whatever yous name is, if yous only knew what a hurt yous have caused by not sending back Rambo. That boy in there has grown up without his pal, his friend, his companion. He cried for a month and off and on for over a year. Dr. Pat will tell you. He drove himself and all of us to a grief that almost overshadowed the loss of my Pappy and the murder of my brother, Samuel. He still isn't over it. He carries a picture of Rambo in his billfold. He refuses to own another pet. We's tried to buy him a new puppy. He'll have none of it."

Melanie was speechless. Anything she could have said to keep matters from fracturing further would have been like trying to drive a truck over a bag of potato chips and expect a positive outcome.

Sethie turned to Dr. Pat. She said nothing. Her anger and frustration had also turned to tears.

Pat took a deep breath, still bewildered by her poor judgment in inviting Melanie to meet Simon. "Look, Sergeant," said Pat, now feeling a bit of physician empathy for National Guardsman Melanie, especially after being reminded of the 10 months Melanie had owned the dog before having a crack at making things right, "I need to take Sethie back into the other room to sit down."

As Pat looked in the direction of the private dining room, she turned her back on Melanie and saw Tristan walking toward the three of them. "God, here he comes, Dr. Damage Control" she hopefully thought to herself. Joseph wasn't far behind, his right hand still moving in and out of his coat.

As Dr. Pat was trying to figure out a graceful exit, she decided to make the best of Tristan's arrival. "Melanie, this is Dr. Tristan Baines. He was a doctor who evaluated Simon for a number of medical problems after the hurricane. Say, Tristan, Melanie was just leaving. Tristan, would you be so noble as to help Melanie out to her car?"

Demoralized, Melanie, now sobbing even harder, replied. "That's OK; I don't need any help."

Wanting to make certain, this woman engaged her car's transmission and got the hell out of their lives, Pat looked at Tristan, who discerned her objective, and said, "Oh, I insist. It's been a long drive for you. I'm sure Dr. Baines can say our 'good-byes.' I hope you can appreciate we must keep this entire matter from Simon for his own benefit."

Without saying another word, Dr. Pat escorted Sethie back into the private dining room. The hostess and the general manager were coming around the corner. Tristan stood there, looking at Melanie, unable to speak for a second; then he offered. "Please, Ms. Hatfield, uh, Melanie, where are you parked?"

"Not far from the entrance," said Melanie, as she looked up at Tristan, showing anger, disappointment, embarrassment, and frustration on her tear-soaked face all at once. "It's OK; come with me."

Two minutes elapsed. Melanie took out her key and unlocked the front door to her electronically boring 1997 Jeep. Tristan politely opened the door for her. She got in; rolled down the window, and looked up at Tristan. "Thank you, Dr. Baines. I'm sorry it didn't work out." She began to roll up the window. Before she started the motor, from the back of the Jeep, there emitted the cleanest, clearest, screeching "puppy yelp" ever uttered by a member of the canine race.

"What's that?" exclaimed Tristan, having a hunch his trip to the parking lot was not in vain.

Again, this time louder. Then a third time.

"Melanie, put her head on the steering wheel, just like she had done when she pulled the U-turn to head back to pick up Dumbo, Jr. before heading the 80 miles to the Big Easy.

A fourth time. Melanie, paralyzed by ambivalence, the same self-ish emotion that had gotten her into the mess she was now in, looked up at Tristan and emoted, "Well, it looks like the little guy wants to come with you."

With that, Melanie got out the car; went to the rear of the Jeep and opened the tailgate. She reached into her pocket and took out a crumpled, worn photograph of a dog with two phone numbers written below the image and several tack holes in the top. She handed it to Tristan and then slid back the small kennel onto the tailgate.

"Look at this picture, Dr. Baines; Now tell me I'm not finally doin' right," she wept, barely getting out the last words in a coherent manner. Next, Melanie opened the kennel door and lifted its precious occupant up into the dim light, for Tristan to get a clearer look. Tristan meticulously compared the pooch in front of him to the worn image in Melanie's picture. Suddenly, a warm and cozy feeling came over him that made his toes tingle. There before him was a clone of Simon's lost dog, Rambo. Tristan's comfort made him feel like a child, taking his first look at that canine visage that has been eternally credited as a human miracle cure for everything from depression and loneliness to stomach cramps and cancer, since the invention of fire.

Melanie held the pup for a moment longer while Tristan kissed its nose. Without warning, amidst the excitement, the little pup suddenly let loose and peed on them both. Well, that really broke the ice.

"By the way, Dr. Baines, said Melanie quietly, wiping a tear from her left eye. "Can you guess who's the father of this pup?

Tristan's eyes looked like saucers. Astonishingly, he was speechless when he heard the question. Before he could utter a syllable...

"Here," said Melanie. "Take him and make Simon happy again. I need to go...now!"

Suddenly, Melanie threw her arms around Tristan and gave him kiss on the cheek. Then she handed him a towel from inside the kennel to clean up the pup pee; and finally, she put the kennel on the ground. While Tristan brought the puppy to his chest and cuddled it tightly, the little fellow let out a tiny squeak of approval in recognition of the new destiny he perceived awaited him.

Tristan tucked the pup under his arm, picked up the kennel and headed for the front door of Pegleg's. Awaiting him at the top of the steps was the general manager and another guy about twice Tristan's size. Behind both of them, Tristan spotted Joseph, walking in his direction with a quiet smile of self assurance spread across his face.

CHAPTER 37 - SIMON'S PARTY - PART II AND THE GAG GIFT

DATE: 12/24/10, Friday 8:45 pm
LOCATION: Pegleg's Barrelhead
Restaurant, New Orleans, Louisiana

— — —

Tristan stood in the parking lot looking up at the general manager and his oversized associate, standing on the steps above him at the entrance to the restaurant. The brute was probably a bouncer or just the manager's good friend, assigned, on special occasions to keep the peace. It was starting to drizzle, an uncomfortable condition that was contributing to the escalating tension in the air.

"Sir, I hope you don't intend to bring that dog into our establishment," said the manager, with a bit of a bark in his voice. The brute standing next to him glared at Tristan and looked like he might take the puppy back into the kitchen for a slow parboil and then serve him as a delicacy, billed as a canine veal cutlet.

"No, of course not," answered Tristan, looking up at the two of them, blinking to move the mist from his eyes. By this time, Joseph, who had headed to the restaurant exit to check on Tristan, appeared behind the two men. Sizing up the situation, Joseph "accidently" pushed past the brute, knocking him off the first step and nearly causing him to tumble down, the other four, an event that would have topped at least 6.0 on the Richter scale.

Suddenly Joseph sarcastically emoted, "Oh, I am so terribly sorry, Sir. Are you OK?"

The brute swung around and looked at the tall, wiry, extremely fit, full blooded Arapahoe Indian. With fury in his eyes; the brute regained his balance and started back up the steps in Joseph's direction. Then he noticed Joseph's right hand reach into his coat, his arm assuming a position that disclosed his intent, if things headed south. Compiling all factors in less than two seconds, the brute cooled on the spot and then warbled, almost like a bird, "OK, OK, no problem."

Tristan studied Joseph's crisis management methods with admiration. Then, looking past the brute and nodding in Joseph's direction, Tristan cheered, "Oh, by the way, I'm with him!"

Joseph smiled and said, "Hang tight, Tristan. I think I know someone who should come visit you in the parking lot. And I'll bring you your raincoat."

Three minutes later, the manager and the brute had withdrawn inside. Tristan ascended the steps and sat down under an awning on one of two small benches situated outside the entrance of the restaurant. He held the puppy on his lap and rubbed it behind the ears.

Five minutes went by. It was now after 9 pm the "witching hour," for the Goldman party's use of their private dining room. Pegleg's entrance now became its exit as the doorway filled with the other seven attendees of the Christmas Eve bash.

What ensued next was as reminiscent as the delightfully dramatic scene one would expect to see when attending a baby shower for your first grandchild.

The "Oohs" and the "Ahhs" were countless. Everyone wanted to hold the pup. The poor dog shifted hands more in the next five minutes than he had for his entire eight weeks of life, until then. After the puppy-fest quieted, Tristan stood up and asked Simon to sit down on the bench. The rain had let up; but still commanded the attention of the eight friends and one mutt huddled under the restaurant awning. First, Tristan asked Simon to take out his picture of Rambo that he kept in his billfold. Next he deposited the puppy onto Simon's lap.

"Go ahead, Simon," said Tristan. "Look at the pup. Now who does he look like?"

"Golly, Dr. Baines; he looks just like Rambo; but he ain't him; that's fur sure," responded Simon.

"Well, do you like him?" asked Tristan, deciding to squelch his desire to tell the whole story of this pup.

Sethie looked on, shocked by the entire matter; actually a little disoriented, not immediately concluding that Melanie Hatfield-Michaels was the source of this puppy that was about to enter their lives. Dr. Pat wasn't far behind; also, not expecting Melanie to have delivered such a surprise. Simon had no idea where the puppy came from, except it seemed to maybe be a gift from Tristan. Joseph stood by, surveying the parking lot and glancing periodically back into the restaurant to see if anyone was coming.

Simon hesitated. "Well, I's think so; but he really ain't Rambo."

"But lemme look a bit closer," he said as he leaned down to get a better view of the puppy's face. There were all the markings; the floppy ears, the bright eyes and most importantly, the large white diamond fur contrasted against the pup's dark brown muzzle.

The puppy looked back up at Simon and within seconds started to lick his cheek; slowly at first; then like he was determined to wash his entire face. Everyone saw the magic come over Simon. A smile emerged from deep within, and tears unmistakably filled his eyes. Simon sat there transformed like someone who finally had caught his breath after four years of trying.

"I think I like 'em; I do like 'em," cried Simon now visibly shaking and crying. Afraid again of facing loss, he turned to Sethie, Reggie, Sr. and his brother, who were standing nearby. Looking, this time more at his father, he continued, "Can I have 'em? Can I, please, Poppa? He's not Rambo; but he looks just like him. Dr. Baines brought him to me for Christmas!"

Minutes elapsed on the fairly chilly, misted porch in front of Pegleg's Barrelhead. Sethie and Reggie, Sr. saw the emerging joy; and more importantly, the signs of normality that were showing on Simon's face - the miraculous results that only the love of a pet, that instant tonic, can bring to the human soul. Reggie and Sethie had their son back.

Seven words rolled off Sethie's tongue, as she reached over and hugged Simon and his new puppy.

"Yes, yous can have him, my son," said Sethie quietly.

Tristan watched the proceedings and drifted a bit, reminiscing about a time long ago when he was in medical school when he had brought his own dog, among two others, to the hospital as part of a newly experimental "pet therapy" program. He remembered the reaction of his patient, that little girl, Dorothy, dying of leukemia, when she saw Tristan's white lab mix, a little female, named Riah.

Even in those days, it had been quite an ordeal to clear any animal to be around kids whose immune systems were compromised while on chemotherapy; but it was worth it. No patient developed an infection. The program was transformative in bringing joy twice a week to over a dozen needy children.

Every story was different; but the introduction of those pets into the lives of dying boys and girls was better than any man-made palliative offering. Just as importantly, Riah and her two canine pals in the program loved it. It was almost as if they could sense the disease in the children, and they tried their best to fill the void in the hearts of those kids who had suffered so much.

The pup had the same effect on Simon. Nothing less than a puppy poultice over a broken heart. The effect was miraculous and instantaneous.

Melanie told Dr. Pat, Sethie and Tristan about the puppy's lineage - all of them decided that the story would be too much for Simon to bear at the fragile age of 14.

Give him another seven years, then, maybe, if ever. It really didn't matter. Simon was whole again.

— — —

The party broke up. The Williams family took the puppy home. A new name would come later. Dr. Pat and Tristan agreed they had a lot in common and promised to stay in touch; both as friends and colleagues.

The late night group scheduled to take over the Goldman party's dining room had canceled at the last minute forfeiting the $300 for the room reservation. Laura, Tristan and Joseph returned to the restaurant to pay the tab. Not too bad; only $1265 plus a 20% tip. Laura paid, and the three of them, all staying at the Ritz, headed for the door.

The rain had stopped completely; and the parking lot glistened under the faint street lamps, almost like it was coated with a frosty thin layer of snowflakes. For some reason, Laura was emotionally high as a kite and was acting like she had finally completed a full semester project in law school. She was bubbly, happy that the party had gone well and extremely happy for Simon. She confessed to Tristan she was on the verge of buying a pup herself; but figured the temptation would pass in a day or two. She would have to settle for her two gerbils and one canary for a while longer.

"Say, Dr. Baines and brother, Joseph, how about a nightcap?" asked Laura with an authentic grin on her face. "Where would you two like to go? I'll drive and have a diet Coke when we get there."

Tristan and Joseph had driven to Pegleg's together. They looked at each other. Joseph spoke first. "Say, Tristan. I'm beat. Why don't you take out this young Perry Mason for a diet Coke and be back to the hotel by eleven. You don't need chaperoning; but we have a plane to catch late tomorrow afternoon."

Tristan laughed. "Yes, Mommy. I think I can have Ms. Swain tucked in by eleven and prepare for our on-time departure tomorrow."

"Well, then, I'll see you back at the hotel." said Joseph.

"Thank you, Laura. for a great meal, great company and a wonderful evening. Merry Christmas! Now don't you and Tristan get into any chauffeured limousines, Ya hear!" he joked, in clear reference to their near death by chauffeur a year and a half before.

Joseph departed. Ten minutes later, Laura and Tristan got into Laura's rental car.

"Well, where to, Dr. Baines?" said Laura. "If you weren't so old and everything was closed, I'd ask you to take me dancing," she kidded with a bright smile on her face.

"You know, you're right," said Tristan. It's after 9 pm on Christmas Eve and everything is already closed or closing very soon. Why don't we just head back to the hotel? We can always have a toast to your success; and we won't need a designated driver."

"Great idea. Diet Coke, isn't what I had in mind," said Laura as bubbly as ever. "I need some refreshments after the stress of planning and executing that party. I think I'll ask Asher, if I can keep what's left in the budget. I think it will be close to $800. I need a new flat screen," she joked.

"I'll second that. I'll put in a good word with Asher. You deserve it," said Tristan, trying to keep the small talk going."

Fifteen minutes later, they pulled up into the parking garage of their hotel and then headed for the lobby of the Ritz. Everything was subdued at the front desk. Very quiet Christmas music played in the background. The decorations in the lobby were spectacular, from the glistening lights of the snowflakes suspended from the ceiling to the twelve foot artificial Christmas tree placed in front of the sixteen foot window. The bar was closed.

Laura looked at the tired figure in front of her, twenty years her senior. She knew he was trying to be polite; but probably wanted to hit the sack ASAP, alone. But she also sensed he wanted to show appreciation for the hard work she had put into the evening, the party and controlling what could have been a very unpleasant outcome with Melanie, Simon and the puppy.

Laura understood the story of Tristan's personal ordeal; after all she had been the one who had been the most instrumental in locating him those 19 months ago. She knew about his wife and daughter; about their kidnapping, the trauma to his daughter, Tess, the mutilation of his wife, Heather and the general details of the necessity for them to go into hiding. More importantly, Laura knew that the astounding events of the past few months justified fear and caution, even terror.

"The world is not such a great and safe place," she thought. "Especially when there were ghouls around like those in The Resistance, like that fiend, Gordon A. Gasher (GAG)."

The list was too long to be coincidental, beginning with the strange death of Dr. DUI, Asher's first expert and Tristan's predecessor.

Next came Laura's abduction with Tristan and Joseph and then Simon's strange, near death experience.

"Oh, yes," she continued thinking, "Let's not forget the murder of McKenna's lab tech, Zane's disappearance, and the probable corruption of the federal judge overseeing their first trial - the list was just too long to be coincidental.

Unknown to her at the time; but also prominent on the list of disasters orbiting her life was the justifiable and poetic end of trailer magnate, Eddie Olson.

Everything on the list, of course, was accentuated by the life and times of Gordon A. Gasher (GAG), that degenerate excuse for a human life form, pitifully disguised as a medical professional in the form of a nurse, ordinarily the noblest of all human caretakers. In the finale, before the FBI bust at CADIXX earlier that Christmas Eve day, Laura was also unaware of GAG's latest murder and his sudden disappearance.

What a burden. She and Tristan had worked very closely throughout this nightmare scenario for the past 19 months. She loved working with him; but it was far from over. They still faced several indeterminates, all with the potential to end badly.

The fate of Asher's brother Saul, who took such risks to reveal the existence and basic structure for The Resistance. She knew Saul's time on earth may be narrowed to the snuffing out of a candle. Then the whereabouts of Raymond Somersville, the rogue helicopter pilot, who was a dead ringer for the chauffer who led Tristan, Joseph and her to their abductions and near deaths on the day that Tristan first examined Simon before the FEMA trial. She knew the asshole worked for GAG, but could prove nothing.

A great mystery still revolved around the good Dr. Chris McKenna. Laura despised the bitch. Her possible ties to anyone but her own ego were just unknown at the time. Laura knew she would not submerge like the bottom feeding creature she was. But for McKenna, the case against Matchless would have prevailed.

And, of course, the other variable was the to be determined outcome of Asher's federal court appeal of the Henrietta, the "Harpy" decision, against his client, Simon Williams.

Laura wanted, with all her heart and mind, to salvage what she could from these past several years. Yes, the $148 million settlement made Asher and his law firm whole; but nothing could palliate the lack of closure facing her and, for that matter, Tristan Baines in the near term. Tristan still had to go back and piece his life together. Reunite with his family and live happily ever after. She didn't give him an encouraging prognosis.

Laura respected him; and she found herself in the uncomfortable position of wanting to be closer to him - not romantically - but just to comfort him, as she perceived his unrest.

"Why don't I escort you to your room, Dr. Baines?" joked Laura, reversing protocol; but within the comfort range of one in her generation; no different than initiating a call to a boy asking for a first date. "I won't exactly tuck you in; but I'll have that glass of wine with you in honor of the importance of this evening."

Tristan looked at Laura. He was tired. A bit uncomfortable, he heard himself respond, "I accept, young lady. I accept your offer to be escorted 'home from the prom.'"

They went to the 8th floor where Tristan was staying. Laura was on the 11th. Laura put her arm through Tristan's as they slowly walked down the hallway to his room 847. Almost reflexively, Laura reached up and put her left hand on Tristan's left cheek and without asking, kissed him gently. Like a father about to hug his daughter before she left for her first date, Tristan responded with a firm, warm hug. Then he slid his room key through the card reader on the door. He pushed on the latch and the door seemed to open by itself. All of the lights were off in the room, except that emanating from what appeared to be a strikingly bright lamp set upon the eating bar that separated the kitchen from the living room.

Tristan did not recall such a light. He moved a step or two into the room and Laura followed, not certain she had made the right decision.

Tristan was transfixed on the lamp. He couldn't make it out. It did not belong in his room. He moved three steps closer, reaching for the light switch on the wall but missing the toggle.

Laura then saw the lamp and became transfixed herself. There it was, a bright orange-red lamp, shaped like two large beverage tumblers, joined at their wider bases. The tumbler bodies appeared to be made of glass and were transparent, filled with some highly viscous globs that were moving up and down, slowly, up and down.

The viscous, plasticized material inside was moving under the heat of the lamp. It was separating and rejoining, rhythmically, over and over again. Inside, within, the goo, however was something else. Something separate; something that did not play together with the thermal blobs. It caught Tristan's eye. It was tumbling over and over again. It was long, slender and white. A peculiar, intermittent, shockingly bright glare came from its center as it tumbled and caught the light of the lamp. It was eerily periodic, almost like it was suspended inside an orbiting spacecraft, tumbling, weightless; the light like an intermittent pulsar.

Tristan finally moved forward and stood over the lamp for a closer look. It was a lava lamp, from days of old; but it was not empty of something Tristan perceived to be of unimaginable horror.

There, in from of his eyes, tumbling, tumbling, cart wheeling were two conjoined objects, the identity of one, certified the identity of the other.

Laura stepped forward and saw Tristan reach for his handkerchief, put it to his mouth, while making the most pathetic, whimpering noise.

She looked at the object that should have been but was not misplaced in the lamp. She gasped aloud.

There, before both of them was a severed human finger, the forth finger, of which hand was indeterminate. But around the finger was a beautiful ring, a ring of unique design that Tristan recognized at once.

There before him was a severed, now mummified finger, graced by the wedding ring he had designed for his wife, Heather, almost 20 years ago.

No more needed to be said.

He was staring at the severed finger of his wife, Heather, floating like debris within this hideous lamp.

Tristan slumped on the barstool and put his hands over his face with his elbows on the counter, less than a foot from horror before him.

He could feel the heat.

Laura approached him and put her hand on his shoulder for comfort.

Tristan took his palms from his face and stared, transfixed; he felt the maelstrom rising.

But he couldn't bring himself to unplug the lamp.

He was sickeningly fascinated by the scene, now distorted by the tears in his eyes.

Breaking the spell, Tristan noticed the corner of the small white business card protruding from the round base of the lamp. Using the end of a pen he pulled from his pocket, he carefully slid it from beneath the lamp. It was calling card of death itself:

CADIXX
Gordon A. Gasher, RN,
Director of Medical Services
CADIXX Incinerator, Alton Illinois

Signed below the name was simply, "Merry Christmas, Doc!" and nothing more.

Tristan looked at Laura. A sense of serenity and calmness now reigned as he seethed,

"Give me just three more months, and I will kill them all."

He turned to Laura, who was speechless and devoid of expression.

"Wanna help?" he asked.

He looked into her eyes, as she nodded her head in the affirmative.

"OK, then. Now, I wonder, if Joseph has turned in?

Let's go see."

ABOUT THE AUTHOR

James P. Kornberg, MD, ScD a.k.a. JP TruDoc is a MIT, Harvard, and Dartmouth trained clinical physician-engineer, author, and medical-legal expert who has treated and/or evaluated tens of thousands of persons afflicted with every conceivable type of hazardous substance exposure. He has consulted on over nine hundred important toxic tort litigation cases since 1980. He lives with his wife, Sally, on their remote ranch in the mountains of Southwestern Colorado.